About the author

JOHN HUNTER is a compulsive entrepreneur and the author of thirty-six technical publications and two screenplays. He was born in England in 1945. After Technical High School he spent nine years in the military travelling the globe; some of which was on active service in Northern Ireland and in the deserts of Saudi Arabia. This was followed by two years as a Sales Director for a 'Wooden Boat' building company. Working in wood inspired him to start his first business designing and manufacturing educational toys and equipment for handicapped children.

After this business was taken over he became involved in marketing for an international publishing group producing DIY car repair manuals. This experience enhanced his love of books and he went on to Managing Direct a small publishing company marketing specialist books for the construction industry. This further honed his publishing experience to the point that he founded his own business; the first electronic publishing company in the UK, where he authored numerous market leading technical titles. The business expanded into world leading construction estimating software where they became market leaders and in 1991 he was awarded the British Design Award for his estimating software. After thirteen years the business had survived a major recession and grown into a successful group at which point he decided to sell it, to have more time for personal development.

He quickly realised that retirement was not for him and as a private pilot started another business chartering high performance aircraft to other pilots. His lifelong passion for the environment guided him into a further business 'alternative fuels'. He designed a system for converting petrol powerboat engines to run on LPG. This was demonstrated on national television when he established the first British Offshore Powerboat Speed Record for a 'Green Powered' boat, at nearly 100 mph. Finally, after four years running a Film Production company as Managing Director and Producer, he decided to leave main stream business to concentrate on writing.

Why Parallel Worlds?

Since the seventies when the 'Gaia Theory' originated, John Hunter became fascinated with the environment; with this awareness he researched everything that he could find on the subject including ancient civilisations and the causes of the damage being inflicted on the Earth by man. There were many discoveries and military funded experiments that bothered him and lingered in his mind. The concept of 'Parallel Worlds' became an obsession and the medium for sharing some of his thoughts and concerns with other people, in a manner that combined interesting facts with a fast pace action story.

PARALLEL WORLDS

John Hunter

Published by: Parallel Worlds Publishing May 2011
First Edition

Email: parallelworlds@btconnect.com
www.parallelworldspublishing.com

Copyright © 2011 John Hunter
ISBN: 9781461103332

Contents

Chapter - 1

Iraq 2009

It's extremely hot and difficult to breathe as desert dust from the operation fills the air. Five large armoured Caterpillar bulldozers driven by a corporal and four young mechanical engineers, on their first overseas posting are stirring up a dust storm. They are working inside the perimeter fence of a new US military supply base, levelling the undulating sand dunes to create a flat area for helicopter landings. The base is in Iraq near the border with Saudi Arabia, just south of Baghdad. In the protection of the air conditioned cab of one of the bulldozers is Hudson, a twenty year old private. He confidently manoeuvres the massive machine, adding power as he drives its blade deep into the next dune resembling a nine foot wave. As the blade cuts into the dune, sand slips away revealing a black, two foot diameter pillar rising vertically out of the sand, in that split second the bulldozer strikes the object. A brilliant white flash is followed by silence.

The radio in one of the other bulldozers is answered by 'Pete' another young mechanical engineer who acknowledges the call from his corporal,

"Pete did you see that flash?"

"Yeah incredible, what was it?"

"No idea, possibly ordnance, Hudson was in that sector I'm going over to check it out, you keep working."

In the distance Pete sees the corporal's bulldozer change direction, heading towards the area where the flash was seen. After fifteen minutes driving through the dust cloud the corporal cautiously stops behind Hudson's bulldozer. Leaving his engine running, he dismounts and walks round the side of Hudson's silent machine, opening the cabin door he finds it empty. He stands on the door frame, looking round for Hudson he shouts at the top of his voice.

"Hudson", "Hudson", "Hudson" there's no response.

He pulls himself into the seat then sees the black post in front of the bulldozer noticing immediately that the huge blade has a large chunk missing where it's touching the post. Now concerned that it could be some sort of unexploded bomb or missile he decides to call his team. Picking up the radio handset in Hudson's cab he finds it has no power, after checking all the switches he discovers that the bulldozer is electrically dead.

He returns to his machine, climbing into the cabin he reaches for his radio which is now picking up background static. He orders the rest of the team to return to base until they find out what's happened to Hudson. Moving off, he slowly searches around the immediate area for any sign of Hudson, finding none, he heads back to base to report the incident to his superior who can authorise a detailed search of the area.

In a temporary portacabin used as the briefing room the corporal makes his report to the gathered group, Major John Schick his superior, Captain Mike Henderson head of bomb disposal and Lieutenant Mark Johnson the Marines head of security. The corporal describes the bright flash, the fact that there was no sign of Private Hudson, the damage to the blade of the bulldozer and its total lack of electrical power. Captain Henderson asked him to describe the metallic object.

"There was about six feet sticking out of the sand, a large black metallic post with a domed top approximately two feet in diameter."

At this point Major Schick takes control, he orders the bomb disposal team to immediately investigate the object then seal off the sector, whilst the security team make a full search of the area to discover the whereabouts of Hudson.

Several hours later the corporal and heads of department return to Major Schick's office.

"Did you find Hudson?"

Johnson explains that his squad searched the area thoroughly with helicopter support,

"There's no sign of him, no footprints from his machine, nothing, he seems to have vanished without trace."

Schick turns to Henderson,

"Could the explosion have killed him?"

"There was no sign of any explosion nor any remains of Hudson."

Schick is rattled,

"No explosion, then what caused the flash?"

"We don't know yet, strangely the only damage to Hudson's machine was where the blade touched the post, draining all the electricity from the bulldozer. We've excavated four metres down into the dune the post seems solid and just continues into the sand, it's not like anything we've come across before. It certainly doesn't appear to be any kind of bomb or missile and it's not emitting any radiation, so far we can't identify the metal it's made of, except that it's extremely hard."

Schick cuts him off,

"Then what do we know?"

Henderson explains,

"We are continuing to excavate the object which is fixed to something deep below the sand, its slow work as we have to shore up the hole to keep the sand back and are working by hand.

Schick asks,

"Why can't you use a machine?"

Henderson is getting annoyed,

"With respect sir, we're disposal specialists until we've a better idea of what we're dealing with we need to treat the object as potentially dangerous, that's why we're digging by hand."

Schick apologises,

"I've got the commanding officer breathing down by neck, demanding an explanation and nothing to tell him about this incident, others on the camp saw the flash too. Let me know as soon as you find something."

Johnson cuts in,

"What about the search for Hudson, we've covered the whole camp area, there's no way he could have got past the perimeter fences."

"Search again, he must be found, I want some answers before the CO calls me back."

Two hours later Schick is sat at his desk studying maps of the camp area when his field phone rings, it's Henderson,

"Major, I think you should come out and have a look at this."

Schick is impatient,

"What is it, what have you found?"

He waits in silence as Henderson explains,

"The post is thirty foot tall, it's embedded in the top of a stone structure that seems to be pyramid shaped, the deeper we dig the larger it gets. We've cleared an area around it to a depth of ninety feet and it goes further, whatever it is, it's looking to be a very, very large structure."

"Is there anything else?"

Schick asks pointedly,

"Yes sir, the stones round the top have strange hieroglyphics on them and our radios are picking up loads of static, we checked this out, there's a weak electromagnetic field emanating from around the structure and it's getting stronger the deeper we go."

There's a short silence,

"Henderson, do you think this is an antiquity or something to do with Saddam Hussein's military?"

"From what we've seen it looks like an antiquity, the markings remind me of some very old script I've seen in Baghdad. I've a feeling when it's fully excavated it will look like one of the Egyptian pyramids, it's just the electromagnetic field that doesn't make sense."

"I want you to carefully excavate the whole structure, seal the whole area off and personally make sure it's not damaged in the process. This could be an important find, I'm going to report to the Commanding Officer, it's his decision what to do next."

"Sir, Is there any news about Hudson?"

"No, the second search has failed to find him but they're still looking, I'll let you know if we hear anything, in the meantime get back to the site I'll come over after my meeting with the CO."

A dust covered Humvee arrives outside the camp headquarters. Schick gets out entering the main building which is another block of temporary portacabin's stacked onto several floors. Passing through the reception area the administration sergeant announces his arrival to the Commanding Officer, Colonel Jack Thomas,

"Major Schick please go right in, the Colonel's expecting you."

Schick knocks on the door and enters, saluting smartly to his superior officer. Jack Thomas is sat at his desk smoking a cigar.

"At ease John, it's good to see you, take a seat, coffee?" Schick sits down and relaxes.

"Thanks Jack, a coffee would go down well."

Thomas picks up his phone, a few minutes later the sergeant arrives with two mugs,

"Well now let's get down to this strange business of yours."

Schick explains to Thomas all that's happened, placing a written report with photographs on the desk in front of him. Thomas leans back in his chair silently puffing on his cigar, after some time he leans forward confirming he understands what's been said and explains what he's going to do.

"John if this pyramid is important we need to have archaeologists with cryptologists working on it. If, as your team has suggested, it's emitting some form of electromagnetic field this needs to be reported to the EMF specialists at the National Security Agency, which I'll do immediately. Until we know more about what this is, it will be classified as Secret, please make your men aware of this."

Thomas leans back puffing on his cigar,

"As you well know it's now our responsibility to protect any important archaeological sites, a task the United States has so far failed to do successfully around Baghdad, where the museums have been plundered and ransacked, I don't intend to let this happen on my patch, is that clear?"

"Yes Jack, I've already given explicit instructions for the team not to cause any damage during excavation. They've sealed off the entire sector."

"John until further notice I want a 24 hour marine guard around the site, no one gets in without my specific authorisation, OK."

"It's done already."

Thomas continues,

"And what's happened to the driver, Hudson?"

Schick pushes the report towards him,

"Jack, it's in the report, we've no idea. There's no sign of Hudson, no explosion, no tracks, he's vanished. We've searched thoroughly without success, if he'd been injured he could have collapsed in the sand perhaps been buried by the wind, but in that case the infra red on the helicopters would have picked him up. It's a complete mystery."

Thomas stands up to his full six foot three and ends the meeting, Schick salutes as he turns to leave,

"John thanks for the SITREP (Situation Report), keep me up to date with everything that happens I've a strange feeling in my gut that this is only just the beginning."

Schick leaves the headquarters building creating a cloud of dust as he accelerates the Humvee into the desert towards the site. As he gets closer he is surprised by the amount of work that the bulldozers have done in moving a small mountain of sand, creating an enormous crater, in the centre of which sits the top of a large pyramid with a black pillar rising out of its top. As he gets out of the Humvee Henderson comes across to greet him.

"Hi John, welcome to the excavation, so far we've dug out over five hundred tons of sand and there's more to go, it just gets bigger as we uncover more layers of stone blocks. Interestingly the stone is highly polished and cut very precisely, the joints are difficult to find fitting perfectly, whoever built this were master craftsman."

Schick is mesmerised by the sight before him,

"It already looks as tall as the Giza Pyramid in Egypt."

Henderson shakes his head,

"We've checked on that, I think it's going to be taller. The Giza Pyramid was originally 485 feet tall with each side of its base 755.5 feet long covering an area of 13 acres, we're getting close to that already, so you can imagine how much sand we've shifted and there's more to come. Strangely the disturbance affecting our communications gets worse the more we uncover, at this depth our radios won't work for up to half a mile from the structure. How was the meeting with Jack Thomas?"

Schick brings him up to speed with their discussion explaining that the CO is passing it up the line,

"Our orders are to dig the pyramid out completely documenting and photographing as much as possible, then to clear and secure the site until the experts get here."

Chapter - 2

Timbuktu, Mali, West Africa

An unmarked, modified desert Sikorsky H60-60G Pave Hawk US Special Forces helicopter stirs up a cloud of sand as it lands on the outskirts of the fabled Malian city of Timbuktu, which is located 15 kilometres north of the River Niger by the edge of the Sahara desert in Mali, West Africa. The door slides open, four armed US marines take up station around the helicopter. A well built man in his late thirties steps down, dressed in jeans and desert combat jacket without badges or markings. He carries a black holster containing a Smith and Wesson Compact automatic on his belt and a document pouch under his arm. Putting on his Rayban sunglasses and desert cap to shield his eyes from the bright sunlight he unzips his document pouch that is stamped with the badge of the NSA. He takes out a map, using it to orientate himself with the single storey buildings facing him.

His name is Rick Taylor. He's a good looking man apart from an old scar on his forehead where a bullet ricocheted off his skull nearly killing him during a covert operation on the Russian border. Rick is a veteran Special Agent of the National Security Agency/Central Security Service. After he left the Navy Seal Teams he studied cryptology at MIT University where he became one of MIT's top cryptology students. It was his later work with Electromagnetic Fields that attracted the attention of the NSA who recruited him to join their specialist unit. Rick is single but married to his work. His female relationships tend to be very short lived a few weeks at the most, almost as if he's afraid to make a long term commitment.

He looks across at the impoverished old city with its collection of small plain houses built from local handmade, tan coloured mud bricks that blends them perfectly into the desert. The noise of the helicopter's arrival has attracted a group of dusty, curious local children. As the helicopters engines shut down the desert silence is deafening. The silence is broken by the sound of a diesel engine as a very dusty white Toyota Land Cruiser appears from one of the narrow streets, heading toward the helicopter. Rick is expecting it and walks over to meet the vehicle. Before the Toyota comes to a complete stop he has the door open. Clambering in he greets the driver, Mohamed, who is a desert Tuareg in traditional loose fitting robes with a blue turban wound round his head veiling part of his face. Rick speaks to him fluently in French instructing him to go to the Ahmed Baba Institute on the Rue de Chemnitz, the Toyota moves off bumping its way across the uneven ground as they skirt round the city. Timbuktu is currently home to around 32,000 inhabitants, a mix of desert people; Songhay, Tuareg, Fulani and Mandé, most of whom coexist in conditions of simplicity and degrees of poverty. This is in complete contrast to the golden period between the 11th and the 14th Century when the ancient City of Timbuktu had a population of 100,000. Its status originated because of its important strategic position between the Sahara Desert and Niger River. Timbuktu was a wealthy trading post attracting Berber, Arab and Jewish merchants, becoming a great centre of learning for travellers wishing to break their journeys at the intersection of the east-west and north-south Trans Saharan trade routes. The merchants brought gold from the south which they traded for valuable salt from the north.

The Toyota passes several sand coloured domed Nomad tents set up on the outskirts just as they had done for centuries before, with their camels tethered alongside.

Mohamed turns into the city, heading down a narrow street towards the centre. On each side of the street most of the ancient brick buildings have single storeys surrounded by low walls, some in better upkeep than others reflecting the level of poverty of their owners. Every now and again they pass a white, taller more modern villa with a predominant parabolic satellite aerial on the roof; these are the homes of the few wealthy people working for non-governmental organisations. The vehicle slows to a walking pace as they come to a crowded street market. The shoppers are more intent on the stalls than traffic. The Toyota is brought to walking pace by a very tall Tuareg sitting astride a tiny donkey that's ambling slowly along the centre of the street. The rider has his feet stretched out in front of him to keep them from scraping the ground, a comical sight.

The manuscript library of the Ahmed Baba Historic Research Centre is housed in an inconspicuous, traditionally constructed building made from the same mud bricks as the houses, the ancient wooden entrance door looks none too secure. Inside the research centre the walls are lined with shelves, stacked with dusty leather bound manuscripts. In the centre of the main room is a large wooden table, behind it sits Samuel (Sam) Amos an American Doctor, who at thirty five is a highly acclaimed Archaeologist and renowned expert in ancient languages. Since university Sam has been an active member of the gay community. He has worked for various government agencies when they have required expert translations from ancient documents. Sam is sitting with the curator of the research centre, an old friend from University, Ishmael Haidara who is responsible for cataloguing and documenting the 30,000 manuscripts so far discovered which form an important part of the relatively unknown advanced history of West Africa. Usually the manuscripts have been written in ancient Arabic on fragile yellow parchment imported originally from Europe.

Some of the oldest of these cultural treasures are manuscripts dating back to 1198 most were found buried in the desert or hidden in caves or odd places by local families over the centuries, as they were revered as heirlooms of their ancestry. The manuscripts prove that a comprehensive knowledge of Astronomy, Mathematics, Science, Medicine, Poetry, Music and Law existed in Africa over a thousand years ago. Sam is in Timbuktu at the personal request of his friend Ishmael. He is studying a particularly old and unusual manuscript as unlike the others that Ishmael has studied, it's not written in Arabic. Ishmael interrupts the silence in the room, which apart from the heat, dust and very basic furniture, is reminiscent of an English reference library,

"Have you any idea what this strange language is?"

Sam stops working, looks across at Ishmael from over his glasses, smiles then slowly lights a Marlboro cigarette. The smoke drifts lazily up to the ceiling, highlighting the dust in the atmosphere.

"Well you're right it's certainly not any form of Arabic I've ever seen"

Ishmael sighs in disappointment,

"Then you can't help me?"

Sam draws on his cigarette, smiles again,

"I only said it wasn't Arabic, not that I didn't know"

He pauses for a second to make his friend suffer a little longer.

"This manuscript is fascinating, it's written in very ancient Sanskrit, a language I've only seen once before, in the Vedus Scriptures dating from 4000 BC. Sanskrit was the Classical Language of India and Hinduism, where on earth did you find it?"

Ishmael is shocked.

"It came from a find on the outskirts of the city along with other Arabic manuscripts, can you translate it?"

Sam looks at the frail manuscript in front of him.

"It will take more time than I have available this trip, unless it's possible for me to take it back for a few weeks. Providing you've something to pack it in that'll protect the pages, they are very delicate. I'd also be able to accurately date it for you."

In the Toyota Rick and Mohamed take a diversion to avoid the throngs of people around the market, now they're able to progress a little faster down the narrow streets, passing numerous ancient domed bread-baking ovens that are omnipresent and essential in this city. The bread is baked on the street as it has been for centuries. Their diversion takes them past the Sankore Mosque built in the 15th century which now double's up as the university complex.

Driving along its walls they pass tall tapering towers built of mud bricks, which because of their height are reinforced with numerous old timbers protruding a few feet out of all the walls.

They arrive at their destination in the centre of the city stopping outside the Ahmed Baba Research Centre. Rick tells Mohamed to stay with the vehicle then enters the building. As his eyes adjust to the dim light he discovers he's in a small entrance hall, hearing a cough followed by a voice he recognises in the next room, he steps through to see Sam and Ishmael, who being engrossed in their work have not heard him arrive.

"Sam Amos, I thought you'd given up smoking."

Sam and Ishmael look up surprised,

"Rick, I wasn't expecting you yet?"

Rick introduces himself to Ishmael,

"Sam you did get my message?"

Sam nods, apologising to Ishmael,

"It looks as if my time is up I'm needed elsewhere, may I take the manuscript with me? Ishmael hands him a flat cardboard box which is tied round with string.

"It's wrapped in protective paper let me know when we can have it back."
Rick checks his watch,

"We have to go now."
Sam shakes Ishmael's hand then kisses him on both cheeks,

"Good bye old friend I'll return the manuscript personally, it would be good to spend more time together."
Rick and Sam leave the Research Centre.

"Rick where to now, the airport?"
Rick explains he has a Pave Hawk nearby. Sam, is surprised,

"How did you get permission for that?"

"Well I guess one of our clandestine organisations lined the Mali Presidents' palm with gold, lots of gold."
They get into the hot Toyota, Mohamed starts the engine and moves off, speeding through the streets as quickly as the local traffic allows. Sam lights another cigarette offering one to Rick who refuses.

"Rick, tell me why you've dragged me away from my work, and exactly where we're going?"
Sam has worked with Rick and the NSA before on specific translation projects that require expert knowledge of archaeology or obscure ancient languages.
Rick tells Sam he'll brief him once they're airborne. Twenty minutes later, Rick looks at his watch then calls the Pave Hawk pilot on his radio.

"We'll arrive in five, warm her up, ready to go immediately we're on board."
The pilot acknowledges,

"Affirmative"

Five minutes later they're airborne, Rick starts to relax as the helicopter banks away from the city. Despite there being no smoking on military helicopters Sam lights another cigarette. Looking directly at Rick,

"Now how about telling me where we're going and what this is all about?"

Rick explains they're on their way to Iraq, a location 1,150 miles away as the crow flies, they'll be refuelled in the air with two stops depending on time. They're to be part of an expert team called in at the highest level of the NSA to examine an unusual pyramid structure that has been discovered under the desert at a new supply base south of Baghdad.

"Why is it unusual and why me?"

Rick explains everything he knows about the events leading to the discovery. The unusual electromagnetic fields emitting from the Pyramid, the fact that it was buried completely prevented it ever being picked up by satellites.

"Sam we needed you, because apart from the Pyramid, they've discovered strange symbols and markings which may give us some clue to its origin or purpose. You for your sins are one of the best experts on ancient languages that the NSA has ever worked with, that's all I know to date. We're going to be in this helicopter for at least twenty four hours so I would try and get some sleep, if you can."

Although Sam is used to being called upon at short notice he asks,

"Why, if this is so urgent aren't they flying us by jet?"

Rick laughs,

"It's a covert operation they don't want us too comfortable. This aircraft can get us to our destination without attracting too much attention."

Twenty four hours later the Pave Hawk is arriving at its destination, the Supply Camp. Rick asks the pilot to hover close to the excavation site so that they can see the pyramid from the air, the pilot commences his descent.

As they approach the site Rick and Sam get their first view of the pyramid sitting at the bottom of a very large crater surrounded by sloping walls of desert sand, the engineers have cut a long sloping access road down to what seems to be an entrance. Rick and Sam are glued to the windows.

"Rick, it's massive, much larger than other pyramids I've seen, it looks to be of a different construction the stone looks like glass, that mast at the top is weird too, I can't wait to get down there."

Rick is equally awed by the sight before them, but is suddenly distracted as his headphones crackle, the pilot's urgent voice instructs them.

"Strap in, emergency positions we're going down."

The helicopter seems to hesitate for a moment then banks away from the pyramid obviously in trouble. It commences an emergency decent, auto gyrating onto the desert floor without engine power. The pilot flares the aircraft just before they hit the ground, landing harder than usual. Rick and Sam are more than a little shaken. After taking off their headsets they go up to the cabin to find out what happened. The pilot is busy checking his instruments.

"We just lost all electrical power, here look at this."

He points to his weather instruments,

"Somehow we just passed through a large electromagnetic disturbance, but from where?"

A Humvee skids to a halt beside the helicopter which has force landed some distance from the site. Henderson races over to the helicopter as the door opens with Rick and Sam at the top of the step.

"You guys all OK, we thought you were goners."

Henderson introduces himself,

"Captain Mike Henderson, we tried to warn you to stay further away but our radios are not working at close proximity since we completed the excavation, the signal from the pyramid has become so strong that none of our communications function for up to a mile."

Rick and Sam are coming to terms with the intense heat it's like stepping into an oven.

They introduce themselves to Henderson who offers to take them over to the pyramid. A recovery team is organised to collect the helicopter. Rick explains he has orders to take command of the project asking Mike if anyone else has arrived.

"Yeah an English lady, Professor Joanne Simons arrived yesterday, since then she's been taking measurements around the pyramid, strange women, doesn't seem to like men around her but very professional certainly knows what she's doing. We've set up an office and accommodation for you on site, we thought you'd prefer to be nearby, it's only portacabin's but they do have aircon."

Rick thanks him and is curious to know how the aircon was possible with the electrical interference.

Mike smiles,

"That was the easy job, we located the generator outside the zone of disturbance then ran shielded cables into the site we'll supply you with anything else you need. I'll also be nearby for any assistance you may require. My priority at the moment is finding a way of getting our comms working."

Rick thanks Mike for the phenomenal excavation task his team has accomplished and setting up their facilities. The four marines from the helicopter transfer Rick and Sam's bags into the back of the Humvee then Henderson drives them to the site. The pilot and crew head off in another vehicle towards the supply camp.

Chapter - 3

The Pyramid

It's now late afternoon as they drive down the long ramp into the crater stopping outside the portacabin's which are in the shadow of the great pyramid. Getting out of the vehicle they are intimidated by the majesty and sheer size of the structure towering above them, its polished blocks reflect the sunlight like mirrors. Sam is entranced by a strange feeling that has overcome him as he walks over to examine the base blocks. In almost disbelief he runs his hand over the smooth surface which is more like glass than rock. A woman's voice calls to him breaking his concentration.

"Dr Amos, it is magnificent isn't it."
He turns to see a tall blonde striding towards him from the portacabin,

"Sam it's good to see you. Welcome to the great discovery,"
She shakes his hand,

"Jo, it's great to see you again it must've been seven years ago, in Cairo if I remember correctly."
Joanne smiles as she recalls then looks serious,

"You were preoccupied with pyramids I'm surprised you remembered me."

"Jo, once met you are never forgotten, I heard on the grapevine something happened to you in Cairo after I left, you seemed to disappear for a couple of years, what was it?"
Jo looks down at the sand,

"Sam, it's not something I can talk about yet, not even to you,"
Sam respects Jo's privacy and returns to studying the base blocks.

Professor Joanne Simons (Jo to her friends) is forty years old and a leading Egyptologist, her particular speciality is her extensive knowledge of pyramids, her work over many years has taken her to some of the most inhospitable places in the world, including Egypt, Mexico, South America, Europe, and to almost everywhere pyramids have been found. She has a natural authority combined with a practical, independent and confident manner. With many years spent in hot climates Jo has developed a deep natural tan which highlights her blonde hair, her good looks are emphasised by the loose fitting safari style jacket and trousers which hang over her physically fit body.

Rick comes over. Sam introduces him to Jo who is fascinated to hear that his speciality is electromagnetic fields in addition to cryptology, as she too has encountered EMF's in Egyptian Tombs.

Jo invites them to have coffee and a snack so that she can brief them on what she has discovered in the last 24 hours. Rick and Sam are starving.

"Jo food first, we've not eaten for some time and the coffee in the helicopter was crap."

They follow her into the first sand coloured portacabin which is the office area and are hit by the most wonderful smell of fresh percolated coffee. Jo places a coffee pot on the table in front of them.

"This is the priority, I'll show you round once your caffeine levels are higher, that was a remarkable entrance you made. We saw you go down, I was about to call Washington for some new assistants."

Laughing, they sit down at the table which is covered with sketches of the pyramid and photographs of various aspects of it. Whilst drinking their coffee Sam offers round his cigarettes they all take one. Sam is surprised glancing at Rick,

"It's a relief to know I'm at last in good smoking company, as I'm sure we're going to end up in some pretty confined spaces together, apart from this cabin."

The portacabin's office area is already well organised with three desks, a large board table around which they are sitting, powerful laptop computers, scanners, printers and a large array of more specialised equipment, including an oscilloscope. Jo suggests she shows them round their accommodation so that they can freshen up before discussing the pyramid. They follow her to their small individual rooms which have just enough space for a single bed, tiny sink and a grey metal wardrobe for clothes. Then to the rest area, which is a small kitchen with basic equipment, a large fridge and dining table with four chairs. The toilets and shower are through a door into the adjoining portacabin. After dumping their gear and taking a quick shower Rick and Sam make their way back into the office, on the table there are three plates loaded with sandwiches and three cold beers. Rick and Sam snap open a beer each and sit down.

"Jo this is just what we needed."
Once they have devoured everything edible on the table they clear away the plates as Jo sits down.

"OK guys it's time for work, let's get started."
Rick grins at Sam.

"I was under the false impression I was in command here?"

"Rick, not any more, you'll find she's a very determined and capable lady."
Jo lays out the drawing of the pyramid, placing round it the photographs she has taken. She then explains what she's been doing.

"This is the largest pyramid discovered anywhere in the world, its height is 630.5 feet, each side of the square base is 982.15 feet long and the angle of the pyramid is 66 degrees. The base covers an area of 20.8 acres which, if you know your pyramids makes it 30% larger overall than Giza. I've carried out some preliminary calculations and if they're also in scale with Giza's construction then there are likely to be 3.2 million blocks weighing from 2.6 tons to 91 tons each. What's more, its corners are aligned with the four points of the compass exactly following the alignment of Giza, if you draw a line from the North Pole to Giza it passes dead centre through this pyramid."

Rick asks,

"How could they have managed to transport that amount of stone here then create such a perfect structure?"

"Well that's the big mystery with pyramids we've yet to solve."

Sam compliment's her on what she has achieved in 24 hours, and asks.

"How old do you think it is?"

Jo estimates a minimum of 5000 years old. He asks about the area on the drawing showing what seems to be an entrance jutting out horizontally from one side.

"This is where this pyramid is really different from others I've seen, there seems to be an entrance on this side which looks as if it opened to allow access, unlike Giza where there were small narrow passage ways leading from other hidden entrance structures located away from the pyramid. This one has what you could call a front door built into it, which if it were open would create an entrance 20 feet by 20 feet."

Taking one of the photographs she hands it to Sam,

"The entrance is surrounded by symbols that I would guess are in a form of Sanskrit. If so, I hope you two are going to be able to translate them."

She hands another photograph to Rick,

"This one was taken at the top of the pyramid, around the base of the post, as you can see it has a circle of words and symbols, which again I think are Sanskrit. This will interest you Rick, she takes him across to the oscilloscope showing him the waving green line. This is reading the electromagnetic signal causing the communication problems which I understand were responsible for your emergency landing."

Rick is absorbed,

"This is quite an unusual wave form. Luckily I've brought more sophisticated equipment with me that will provide us a more detailed analysis. I'll set it up in the morning; after I've looked over the bulldozer that started all of this."

As it's now dusk they decide to have one more beer and turn in early so that they can catch up on sleep. Rick is also suffering from jet lag after his race across the globe to collect Sam. Jo suggests that they take their beers outside, sitting on the steps of the portacabin the stars are bright in the wide expanse of the dark blue desert sky, looking across at the pyramid Rick notices something odd,

"Jo is it my imagination or is the pyramid glowing slightly?"

"Yes it is, remember the Giza pyramid was once covered in polished limestone which they believe would have caused it to reflect florescent light from the stars and sun."

"You mean like a marker beacon?"

Jo explains that from the air or any distance it would be exactly that.

"Jo, are you suggesting that 4000 year old Egyptian aircraft would have used it for navigation?"

Sam chips in,

"It's maybe not far from the truth. The ancient Vedas scriptures of India clearly describe aircraft being used 5000 years BC."

Rick finishes his beer,

"That's enough for me, on that note I'm going to bed to dream of flying Pharaoh's."

Rick wishes them good night then goes into the portacabin.

Sam and Jo are also suffering from their journeys and decide to do the same,

"OK let's get some sleep, see you in the morning bright and early."

"Jo before we go in, if there is anything you want to talk to me about Cairo you know it will only be between us,"

"Sam, thanks but it's still an open wound I'm not ready to talk about it,"

They follow Rick to bed.

They are woken at 08:00 by the mouth watering smell of bacon cooking and coffee, an army chef is in the kitchen preparing their breakfast. The three enter the small dining area to find breakfast served in true military style, Rick asks the chef who organised this.

"Mr Henderson's orders sir, I've been attached to you personally to make sure you have everything you need."

Jo asks.

"What's your name? We only use first names in our unit, no Sir's." The chef replies,

"Lance Corporal Jones, I mean Charlie, Sir."

Jo smiles introducing Sam and Rick.

"And I'm Joanne, Jo to my friends."

Charlie reluctantly agrees and relaxes, serving them a very full breakfast. Over breakfast they discuss their individual tasks for the day, Rick is going over to the damaged Bulldozer while Sam and Jo decide to take a closer look at the pyramid door. Rick will join them later. His vehicle arrives then as he leaves Sam and Jo make their way round to the door on the eastern side of the pyramid. They examine the polished stone work in great detail, exasperated as there doesn't seem to be any visible joints in the large stone that they believe is the entrance door. Two hours later it's getting very hot, the sun is now high in the sky, the stones of the pyramid are adding to the temperature by reflecting the heat at them. They're baffled.

"Jo this is certainly the entrance but the massive stone is one piece inside the two feet border which has the symbols and characters around it, they must be significant."

Sam uses his digital camera to take close up images of the entrance, then sitting on a folding chair he starts to copy the images before him onto a large pad. Jo comes over to him almost speaking to herself,

"Depending on its thickness this centre block of stone, at 20 foot square, must be the largest and heaviest in the pyramid which is strange as if this is an entrance it would be impossible to open it."

"Perhaps it's not meant to be used that frequently, personally I think these symbols are the key, if we can work out what they mean. Once we've finished here I want to go back, print the photographs and see if I can translate these symbols. I think they're based on a very ancient version of Sanskrit and need my laptop at hand to confirm what I suspect."

Jo is curious,

"And that is?"

"I think these are sequences of numbers, but I don't know if I'm correct, I'm going back."

Jo follows him.

"There's nothing more I can do here at the moment, we really need to get inside."

In the office several hours later Sam is sat at his computer studying the enlarged photographs and making notes around the symbols.

Sam is working on the translation. He is lost in a sequence of numbers with a list of words which he has underlined and trying to make sense of:

Sanskrit	English
Pari sád	surrounding thing, coil
Vájrabâhu	weapon-armed
Ená	in this way
Ghus	sound
Ínvati	set in motion
Svadhâvant	possessing inherent power
Sácâ	at the same time
Muc muňcáte	make free

Vrnîté	accept
Vis vivesti	be active
Ketŭ	appearance, shining out, ray
Viçáte	enter
Susaraná	good passage
Cá kaçîti	pay attention to
Supráníti	safe guidance

The sound of a vehicle disturbs Sam's concentration, followed quickly by Rick noisily entering the office he's covered in desert dust his clothes patched with sweat.

"Hi Rick."

Without a word Rick makes a beeline for the water machine drinking cup after cup of cooled water, after a few minutes he turns to Sam.

"Sorry about that, you wouldn't believe how hot it was where they'd left the bulldozer."

"Did you find anything interesting?"

Rick wipes the sweat off his face with a dirt covered cloth,

"Yes, several things, give me five minutes I need to clean up, my brain needs to cool down in the shower then I'll tell you all about it, how about you and Jo, what did you find?"

"Lots of strange and interesting things; take a shower we'll talk later."

Jo and Sam are studying the notes that Sam has put together when a refreshed Rick returns. As he sits down Jo asks him what he discovered.

"The bulldozer was as Henderson described it, no visual sign of an explosion, marks or damage other than the blade which got most of my attention. Where it touched the metal post the blade seems to have dissolved around where it made contact, there were no metal pieces found in the sand. My instruments did pick up unusual electromagnetic particles around the area where the steel had disappeared.

"What do you mean particles?"

"I've not been able to identify them yet, but my theory is, that when the blade touched the post it received some sort of electromagnetic pulse which caused the flash, disturbing the electrical frequencies in the steel atoms, causing them to dissipate, this would also account for the draining of all electrical current from the bulldozer."

"Wow!" is Jo's response,

"It sounds fascinating but I don't really understand a word you have said, can you please simplify it for me."

"Sorry, I got carried away, as you know everything is made up from atoms, you, me, this building, our bulldozer, your pyramid. The atoms all have a nucleus, with protons and electrons swirling around the nucleus, almost like a planet with lots of satellites spinning round it, minute voltages of electricity maintain the atoms and hold the atoms together, OK so far?"

Jo nods her head.

"Go on."

"The atoms have a natural resonance that maintains them. For example the human body and brain, being a collection of atoms, resonate at around 7.8 hertz. This happens to be in tune with the Earth's fundamental resonant frequency of 7.8 hertz. Deep in our cells we are basically electrical machines which is why, when there's an electrical storm in the vicinity some people feel heavy, depressed or have headaches. This is caused by the electrical storm disturbing the electromagnetic fields overhead and therefore changing the resonant frequency that our bodies are accustomed to until the storm passes. What I think happened and need to confirm is, when the digger impacted the post it received an exceptionally large shock of electromagnetic energy causing a large change in the resonant frequencies of the atoms in the steel which made them dissipate into the atmosphere. Hence no missing pieces were found, this could also account for the missing driver and the unusual electromagnetic particles."

"If that was the case why didn't the rest of the digger disappear?"

"Good point Jo, it was possibly because there may have only been a small amount of residual energy in the post rather than a continuous current, but enough to affect the blade and driver, this I need to check out."

Sam lights another Marlboro which he always does when thinking or under stress and looks up at Rick.

"Some time ago I was reading an article on various aircraft that disappeared in the Bermuda Triangle. One, a military cargo aircraft had apparently vanished close to the coast, all the search and rescue found was the nose wheel in shallow water, which when examined showed traces of unidentified electromagnetic particles, is this similar to what you think happened here?"

"Exactly right, if the aircraft had entered an area where for some reason there was an anomaly in the earth's magnetic field it could have disrupted the atoms causing them to separate hence no wreckage other than in that instance one wheel."

"Rick is this why your people have hushed up finding this pyramid?"

"Yes, unlike other archaeological finds, until we know what it was built to do, we must treat the pyramid as potentially dangerous. Anything that has the capability and power to alter or cause electromagnetic fields could have serious consequences in the wrong hands. Now tell me what you've been doing?"

Sam pulls his notes to the centre of the table,

"I've managed to translate some of the symbols around what is undoubtedly the entrance door, there are words with nine sets of numbers, as of yet, I've not been able to establish their significance to each other, although I'm fairly confident that the numbers are correct. The door is one large piece stone with miniscule joints around it so tight that a sheet of paper wouldn't fit into the crack. I have a feeling that these words and numbers are the key but how such a heavy block could be moved is beyond me."

Rick takes a copy of the phrases with the set of nine numbers,

"This reminds me of the riddles of my childhood and code breaking later in life."

He lights one of Sam's cigarettes, Rick stopped smoking six months ago but since being with Sam has started again in earnest, Sam notices and laughs.

"The trouble with reformed smokers is that you always smoke someone else's."

"Sam, don't be so tight if it wasn't for me you wouldn't be here, anyway your cigarettes help me think"

Jo steps in she wants to get started,

"Come on boys we have a problem to solve, let's get on with it."

Rick teases her.

"I carry the rank of full Colonel, not boy."

Jo sits back.

"Ok Colonel, then act as if you are one."

Smiling, Rick now turns his full attention to the page in front of him. Sam and Jo leave him alone with his thoughts and go into the dining area each with a copy of the notes. A couple of hours later Rick picks up the field telephone and calls Henderson, he asks if he can bring over his frequency modulator from the helicopter, Henderson arranges to deliver it that afternoon. Rick walks into the dining area confronting Sam and Jo who have been going round in circles.

"Hi, you two any ideas what it means?"

Sam sighs,

"Nope, and having overheard the telephone conversation why do you want a frequency modulator?"

Rick has had an idea and explains,

"If we assume that the translation may not be completely literal and they're instructions for gaining access, then there are several phrases that I've underlined that might be relevant to our task, I think that with a little poetic licence the words that apply to the door could be as follows; 'Using sound in this way will set in motion and make free to enter a good passage with safe guidance'."

Jo looks at him strangely,

"You think that sound will open the door, what sound?"

"Jo, I think that the numbers are frequencies, which is why I wanted my frequency modulator as this would enable us to try different frequencies on the door."

Sam is sceptical.

"And you think the door would open just like that?"

"Whoever built this pyramid is certain to have been a very advanced civilisation, if they understood electromagnetism, why not secure their treasures with a frequency lock; the principle is not dissimilar to the remote control on a modern car or a bank vault."

Jo claps her hands,

"Well done, that to me seems plausible, it's a lot better than the zilch we've come up with, perhaps you are some sort of Colonel after all. So what do we do now?"

Rick asks Sam if he thinks it's worth trying,

"Yes, certainly it's worth a try, I must say I didn't think about the numbers being frequencies, I was convinced they were a code."

"So was I and they may still be a code, but I've a feeling we're on the right track, as soon as the modulator arrives we'll find out."

An hour later a Humvee pulls up outside, Charlie comes in carrying a 2 feet square carton which he places on the office table.

"Colonel"

He corrects himself,

"Rick, this is the equipment you asked for, it's portable and rechargeable, if you need anything else let me know."

Charlie leaves. Rick immediately opens the carton taking out a black box the size of a brief case, opening it they see it is fitted with a miniaturised state of the art frequency modulator with various lights, keypad and switches.

"Rick, how come they happened to have one of these here?"

"I brought it with me, thought it might be useful."

Sam stares at him,

"Are you sure there's not something you know that you're not telling us?"

Rick quickly changes the subject taking various items out of the box.

"Give me a hand."

They plug the unit into the mains current to check that it's fully charged. In the box there are several halogen torches, he hands one to each of them putting the others in his rucksack.

"The batteries in these waterproof torches are good for 100,000 hours, very bright and virtually indestructible."

Sam switches on his torch and is surprised at the strength of the light coming from the array of tiny bulbs under the protective glass. Rick hands them a small radio each.

"These are shielded transceivers they may work if we do get inside, they're preset to our personal frequency so all you have to do is press the transmit button and speak."

He suggests they each take water in their rucksacks. Jo is surprised,

"Rick you seem very confident that we're going to open the door."

"You just never know, we should be prepared just in case, there's an hour to sunset so we could give it a try whilst there's a little daylight left."

Sam and Jo are anxious to start immediately and leave the office with their rucksacks. Rick follows with the modulator under his arm. They arrive at the portal Rick sets up the modulator on a small folding chair then unfolds the small umbrella shaped antenna which he points towards the door area. Taking Sam's notes he switches on the device, an array of lights appears, using the small numeric keypad he keys in the nine frequency numbers. After a few minutes Rick's ready,

"OK here we go."

He transmits the first frequency, an almost inaudible hum sounds from the door area. Sam and Jo exclaim in unison,

"Did you hear that noise?"

Then silence, Rick works slowly through each of the remaining numbers transmitting each frequency into the door, with the transmission of each frequency there's a slight hum for several seconds followed by silence. After trying all the frequencies over and over again with the same reaction, nothing else has happened. Sam goes over to Rick,

"You know that was very close, something definitely reacted to what you did, there's something missing, what've we missed?"

Sam picks up his notes, scanning them again and comparing them with Rick's notes. Fifteen minutes passes.

"Rick there's something, one phrase that you didn't highlight that might be relevant."

"What is it?"

Rick and Jo are despondent that the frequencies have not worked. Sam points to one of the words on his notes.

"Sâcá means 'at the same time', perhaps the frequencies have to be sent together."

"Sam, you're a genius that could be it, why not, it wouldn't make sense for anyone to try that, it's a perfect defence."

He makes an adjustment to the modulator.

"Well here goes."

He presses the transmit key, they wait with bated breath. Nothing happens for several seconds then the hum starts again but instead of stopping, it increases in volume for two minutes then stops followed by silence. They wait but nothing happens, after a few minutes Rick, despondent switches off the modulator and closes the lid.

"It was worth a try, its back to the drawing board."

At that moment, an escape of air like an opening airlock hisses from the cracks around the door blowing out a film of fine dust, followed by the louder sound of large bolts smoothly sliding back, then silence. They stand mesmerised hardly daring to breathe the sun is now quite low and casting its long shadows. As they watch the giant six foot thick stone door silently moves out of its surround towards them then slowly swings, hinged on the right hand side, like a heavy bank vault door. The enormous door opens a full ninety degrees then stops. The twenty foot by twenty foot square opening is ink black inside, with the limited light available they can see three, three foot diameter metal bolts recessed into the edge of the door facing them.

Sam apprehensively lights a cigarette.

"I wonder why the entrance opening is so big."

Rick ignoring his comment opens up the modulator.

"Before we go in there, I want to try something, stand away from the entrance."

He presses transmit, the door closes as silently as it opened, followed by the smooth sliding of the massive bolts.

Jo shouts,

"Rick what are you doing?"

"It's OK, I wanted to make sure it worked both ways, if we were inside and it closed how would we get out?"

Jo and Sam look at each other.

"Good point, we hadn't thought of that."

As it's now quickly getting darker, Rick asks if they want to go in tonight or wait till tomorrow morning. The archaeologists in them want to go in immediately but all agreed it would be best to think through what they had learnt and start first light tomorrow morning when it would be cooler. As they leave, Sam says,

"One thing's for certain, at least it'll still be there in the morning, let's get an early night although I don't expect any of us will get any sleep tonight."

Chapter - 4
Inside the Pyramid

By six o'clock next morning, they've had breakfast and packed their rucksacks with everything they think will be useful for their exploration. Rick takes the modulator and radios off charge, then sending a last email from his laptop he closes it and puts it in his bag. He calls Henderson giving him a verbal report of their progress and their intentions, Henderson said he'll drop by later that afternoon. At last they're ready, saying good bye to Charlie they make their way back to the portal of the pyramid in bright morning sunlight. There's a positive nervous tension in the air as they set up their equipment for entry, Jo has a small digital movie camera and is creating a record of everything they do. Rick switches on the modulator, after pressing transmit the hum within the pyramid starts as before, followed by the smooth sliding sound as the bolts are released. The massive door swings slowly open. After Rick packs the modulator into its case they slowly walk towards the entrance where the sunlight penetrates the inky black of the inside. They cautiously step into a large cold rectangular room fifty feet wide by eighty feet long, its high ceiling is supported by walls sloping up at the same angle as the pyramid, it's thirty feet high at its lowest point. All the walls including the inside of the door are made from a highly polished black marble like material with gold markings.

In the centre of the room is an enormous black slab table made from the same marble like material as the walls, twenty feet long by five feet wide and five feet tall, down each side of the table are four very large black throne style seats, the backs of which are ten feet tall. Sam and Jo are silently wandering around the room with their torches reflecting off the floor which appears to be one single slab of polished black marble.

Rick takes a more powerful lamp from his bag placing it in the centre of the table, as the room is now completely illuminated they are able to get a better view of the gold illustrations on the walls. Jo is first to break the silence she is sitting on one of the high thrones with her feet some distance off the floor.

"This is certainly no burial chamber, it makes me feel like Alice in Wonderland with the size of this furniture, it must have been made for people at least ten feet tall."

Rick has been studying the inside of the door.

"The technology and workmanship used here is remarkable, it's airtight similar to the anti blast doors at the NSA's underground facilities, yet its thousands of years old. But where does the electrical power come from?"

Sam is at the furthest end of the room examining the plain black wall which has markings around it similar to the door they have just entered, he slowly walks back studying the gold illustrations of different shaped pyramids etched into the walls, as he does he calls over to the others.

"What's very strange is that there's no dust anywhere, the place looks completely sterile." Rick runs his hands over the table.

"You're right it looks as if they had cleaners in here this morning, how come?"

He climbs up onto the throne next to Jo to get a better view of the wall in front of them, Sam joins them.

"The reason there's no accumulation of dust could be that it was pressurised, remember when we first opened the door there was a hiss of escaping air."

Jo asks Sam what he thinks about the gold illustrations on the black walls.

"I think they're elongated maps of the locations of pyramids, it seems to be a world map, if you look here on the wall behind us these are countries north of the equator, on the opposite wall are countries south of the equator, if I'm right we should be just about there."

He points to the largest of the pyramid shapes,

"These symbols underneath each pyramid I believe could be some sort of map reference."

Jo jumps down walking slowly round the room filming with her camera,

"Sam, I thought I'd visited most of the pyramids in the known world, but there are dozens shown here that no one knows exist."

"Perhaps they exist but have been buried like this one was, either accidentally or deliberately to hide them. I don't believe these were originally constructed as burial pyramids either, nor those in Egypt, they were ancient structures that emitted some sort of positive energy so the kings decided to use them as burial places."

Rick suggests,

"If this is the largest perhaps it's the control centre for the rest, but to control what?"

Sam has been trying to make sense of what the room they are in is used for,

"To me, this is a meeting room, there's nothing here other than a boardroom table, chairs and charts of pyramids, in relationship to the size of the pyramid this is a very tiny space. I think it's time to explore further, there seems to be another door at the end of this room, where those markings are, I suggest we try the same frequencies again."

Jo completes her measurements of the room then finishes filming everything around them.

"Yes, I'm ready."

Rick sets up the modulator and antenna on the end of the table nearest the wall,

"Ok let's try it."

He presses transmit they wait in silence watching the wall. A noise behind them makes them turn. The main door closes with a thump then the bolts slide into place.

Jo whispers,

"Oh shit, I hope we'll be able to get out, if not this'll be our burial chamber."

As they stand looking at the main door they hear the familiar hiss of air then the sliding of bolts behind them, turning to face the back wall they see a fine line where the air blasted out a small amount of dust, slowly a door the same size as the main door silently opens towards them, the inside of this door is lined with the same shiny black material. It's absolutely pitch black inside. They go back to the table to collect their things. Rick packs the modulator, puts it over his shoulder and picks up the lamp. As they turn on their torches, Sam stops, lighting another cigarette.

Jo comments,

"Rick these people were obviously technologically very advanced so how come we're carrying torches, you don't suppose they use frequencies to switch everything on and off?"

"Perhaps they don't need light, they see in the dark or something."

Rick agrees with Sam,

"When we get into the next chamber or whatever it is I'll try some experiments, it's a good point, unless Jo's right."

They enter a twenty feet by twenty feet square passage which is completely lined with black polished stone, the surface's reflect their lights, there's nothing ahead of them, only the black corridor heading into the distance. Stopping just inside Rick places his hand on the wall,

"This smooth marble or whatever it is, is strange, why line the walls, floor and ceiling with it?"

Jo runs her hands over it too.

"There are no joints it just seems one piece that goes on forever."

She shines her torch onto a grid pad on which she has sketched their entry point into the pyramid.

"If this tunnel continues straight ahead I reckon it leads to the centre of the pyramid." She looks up, "Could this black lining be some form of screening, like Henderson had to do to the wires from the generator?"

"Screening from what?"

Sam joins them,

"Jo, I agree I think it's screening to keeping something in or maybe out, but what I wonder?"

Rick shines the lamp down the corridor the inky blackness seems to absorb the beam of light.

"Shall we continue?"

Jo smiles back at Rick,

"You just try and keep me here, I'm going on."

They move forward cautiously as they do, the door behind them closes.

"Rick what have you done?"

"Nothing, it's closed itself, unless we've tripped something."

He passes the lamp close to the wall then does the same thing on the opposite wall.

"There it is."

Sam asks,

"What is it?"

Rick shows them both a small circle in the wall,

"It's a sensor. We've tripped something like our infra red sensors at the NSA which must have closed the door."

Jo nervously asks,

"But what else might we have we tripped?"

Rick tells them to stand absolutely still as he walks back through the sensor towards the door, silently the door opens again, he then steps back towards them and it closes again.

"Jo you happy now, it's only an automatic door closer."

They laugh nervously not completely convinced, slowly moving forward checking each side of the wall in front of them, after about 100 feet Sam stops.

"Shush" then listening hard,

"Can you hear that noise?"

A soft hum had started somewhere in the distance. They could all hear it. Rick puts his ear to the wall.

"Nothing, this place must have a remarkable power source if it's remained active for 5000 years or however old it is."

He takes a small box out of his rucksack which is a portable device for measuring electromagnetic fields,

"It's not reading anything, I bet that's what the shielding is for, to screen from electromagnetic fields." Glancing at his watch he asks,

"Jo, how long have we been in here?"

"Must be over an hour why?"

"My watch shows we've only been here for 5 minutes."

Jo and Sam look at their watches they show the same time as Ricks. Sam nervously lights another cigarette.

"Something's happened to time it's affecting our watches, slowing them down there's nothing else it could be as they're all working. Look how slowly the second hand is moving."

The hum is now a little louder as Rick and Sam move forward again, Jo stands still staring ahead.

"Is it my imagination or is it getting lighter in here?"

They stop, staring into the darkness which is no longer inky black but is getting lighter by the second, a florescent glow is getting brighter as they realise the whole ceiling is lighting up. They are now able to switch off their torches and lamp. Rick believes the sensor that closed the door must have also switched on the lighting.

"This place is full of surprises and we've barely started"

The corridor is now completely bright with what seems to be natural daylight. Now more confident they make faster progress down the passage, they continue for another half hour until in the distance they see the passage ending at a black wall. Jo takes a small palm like computer device from her breast pocket Rick asks

"What are you doing?"

"As we can't use our GPS in here I've brought a type of pedometer, it records how many steps I've taken so we can try and work out where we are in the pyramid, it also records if we change heading so assuming its compass has been working, we can download the data onto my laptop to see where we've been. So far we seem to have been going in a straight line from the entrance towards the centre."

While they've been talking Sam has gone ahead, stopping ten feet before the wall.

"Hey guys I've found more sensors in the wall, let's hope the end of the tunnel has another door that'll open when I break the beam."

"Wait for us." Shouts Jo,

They hurry towards Sam and together slowly pass through the two sensors. They stand waiting and watching, the familiar sound of the hiss of air followed by the sliding bolts greets them, followed a few seconds later by the whole end of the corridor opening towards them. Rick comments,

" Looking at the size of the these doors I get the impression that no one was supposed to get in here, I wonder what's in store for us next?"

Sam looks into the new opening which is totally pitch black,

"Hopefully we'll find something to help us work out exactly how old this place is and why it was built. It's a contradiction, it's got to be many thousands of years old, yet, the small amount of technology we've seen is more advanced than exists today."

Jo switches on her torch moving forward very slowly into the space ahead of them. Their torches reveal only smooth walls, together the move ahead focusing their lights on the floor which is black. After about ten feet of shuffling along, they hear the door behind them closing. Jo sighs,

"Not again."

As the door closes they see the lights in the passageway behind them fading back to black. At the same time a faint glow starts to lighten the darkness pressing down on them, within seconds they are brightly illuminated then shocked into silence by where they are.

Chapter - 5

The centre of the Pyramid

They are overwhelmed by the sheer size of an enormous pyramid shaped room packed with futuristic technology before them. Rick's the first to break the silence.

"This can't be possible it's got to be something Saddam's people constructed."

In the centre of the room is a large black column fifty feet in diameter at its base, the column is fifteen feet tall. Sitting on top of the column is a very large opaque, oval glass globe, one hundred feet in diameter, above which, the fifty feet black column continues upward into the apex of the room rising at least four hundred feet above them. Below the globe, an opaque glass strip is set into the side of the column facing them it connects the globe to the floor with symbols on both sides similar to a thermometer. Jo is filming.

"I can't believe this either Rick. There's no doubt the stonework was constructed a minimum of 5000 years ago, don't forget I had a sample dated."

The feint hum omnipresent since they entered the pyramid, changes note increasing slightly, several large opaque crystal like objects inside the globe start to glow, then the glass strip in the column facing them illuminates with a green light slowly rising from the floor which stops at the first symbol. They sit down together on the black floor trying to take in what's around them. Sam rummages in his rucksack taking out a bottle of water and pack of cigarettes he offers them round, this time Jo and Rick both take one. From where they are, they can see set around the walls are what seem to be work stations consisting of large black tables with throne sized seats similar to the ones found in the entrance. Sam is trying to take in the dimensions of the area,

"This space must be at least six hundred feet long by six hundred feet wide and I would guess about four hundred feet to the top, this has to be the centre of the pyramid."

His words are interrupted by a further increase in volume of the hum, the green light in the tube on the column rises to the next mark. Around them panels in the tall black walls flicker above each of the large tables, the flickering stabilises into blank display screens with symbols down each side, the screens are twenty feet wide by ten feet tall. Rick gets up slowly walking over to the nearest screen, as he gets closer to the table below the first screen, he calls the others over.

"Look at this."

Sam and Jo come over.

"This just gets more and more incredible."

The top of the first table has 10 small display screens glowing from its surface, each similar to the large ones with symbols around them, Rick touches the black surface of the table.

"These screens are part of the marble or whatever it is, the same as the walls, I wonder how they did this?"

Sam considers what they are looking at,

"Rick you remember when we were talking about the bulldozer, you said that magnetic fields could change the way atoms held together, perhaps whoever built this could manipulate electromagnetic energy to alter the resonance of the atoms in the walls and tables to create lighting or these displays."

Rick looks closely at one of the smaller screens on the table,

"You could be right, but if they can do that, what else could they have done?"

Jo looks at them both,

"You said 'could have done', if this technology is so advanced and still functioning after over 5000 years, what makes you think that they're in the past and not still present on the earth?"

"Jo you're an archaeologist, an expert on the past like me, that concept is too much for me to consider at the moment, we need to have a good look round to see what else we can find, remember this place has been buried and could not have been accessed for thousands of years. If they were able to manipulate gravity it would account for how they managed to move such large stones and create such large structures in the first place."

"Rick where do you think the energy comes from to power this place?"
Rick is taking three chocolate bars and drink cans out of his rucksack,

"I've no idea at present but those fluctuating Crystal things in the glass globe seem to be some sort of energy source. Before we go any further, either of you hungry? I've brought some high energy drinks and bars to keep us going."
Jo and Sam pick up a can and chocolate bar, Rick sits Jo at the table he and Sam sit on the floor leaning back against the base. Sam looks at his watch again it's hardly moved during the time that they have spent in the pyramid.

"Are your watches still working?"
Rick and Jo look at theirs which are exactly the same as Sam's who remarks,

"We must have been inside for over two hours."
Rick reckons more like three hours.

"To me it looks as if the power source has slowed down our watches."
Sam corrects him,

"Rick, yours and Jo's are electronic, mine is automatic why should it be affected?"
Rick looks at Sam's watch,

"That's a very good question, unless something is happening to time itself."

At that moment Jo finishes her drink, still concentrating on her watch she places her aluminium drink can on the table. Immediately her can touches the table, a three dimensional rotating globe of the earth appears on the large display in front of them. Red points appear in different land masses with yellow lines radiating out from the points creating a grid around the world. Rick and Sam stand up.

"Jo what've you done?"

Rick looks at the table and notices the drink can which is placed on top of a symbol beside the small display screen nearest where Jo was sitting.

Jo is embarrassed,

"Sorry guys I just put the can on the table."

Rick tells them both,

"We must be very careful these must be touch sensitive surfaces, luckily all it seems to have done is switch on a display."

Sam is studying the rotating image,

"There's something wrong here, the land masses are not right."

Jo and Rick watch intently as the earth rotates,

"Rick, he's right those land masses are merged together into larger continents, just look at the central axis of the earth it's rotating vertically, the earth does not do that, it's actually tilted by 23.5 degrees."

Sam explains that sometime before 6000 years BC there was a catastrophe that separated the continents flooding much of the planet, this movement of land and water disturbed the balance of the earth tilting it off its axis to its current position. If that theory is correct then this pyramid and the technology around us could be more that 8000 years old. Jo is concentrating on the grid and the positions of the land masses some of which are recognisable.

"Sam you remember the myths of Atlantis?"

"Yeah, Plato described it as a continent in the Atlantic that was reached through the Pillars of Hercules, but no one's been able to prove it existed."

"Until now, just look at the continents, you can see the gap between what is now America and Europe, smack in the centre of the Atlantic is a large island land mass which has grid lines radiating out from it."

Rick cannot believe what he's hearing.

"Are you two telling me that this is what the earth looked like over 8000 years ago and that Atlantis really existed?"

"Rick, that's exactly what this is telling us, it's like looking at the planet from space, 8000 years ago."

Rick who is usually very open minded and scientific finds this revelation too much he sits down looking at the table, the small screen that Jo inadvertently opened with her drink can is a mirror image of the larger screen above them.

"Sam you got any cigarettes left?"

Sam hands his pack to Rick after taking one himself,

"I came prepared, no food or drink just cigarettes in my rucksack."

As they smoke Sam speaks about the implications of what they have found.

"This is potentially one of the most important discoveries in history, if, as we now have to accept is more than a hypothesis, a highly advanced civilisation existed on earth, then what happened to them? Who were they and where did they come from? This will create havoc with the religions that we've been forced to believe in, raising valid questions about our 2000 year old heritage bringing the whole Christianity story into question. This is very dangerous knowledge."

Jo agrees,

"Sam, this site and technology have to be protected from falling into the wrong hands, if it hasn't already."

"Rick as far as we know, we're the only people in the world that know about this, those outside just think it's an unusual pyramid. What we actually know, is very little at present, we have to examine every detail of this place before deciding unanimously what to do with the information."

Jo suggests that they carry on looking around as there must be clues that will help them find out who these people were.

"All we know for certain, is they existed a minimum of 8000 years ago, were possibly very tall, maybe 10 feet and technologically far ahead of us, even in today's terms."

Rick agrees, looking directly at Jo.

"We must be extremely careful not to touch anything else so far we've been very lucky. Who knows what touching the other symbols would have done?"

Jo retorts,

"We could easily find out, just leave it to me."

They start their examination from the door that they came through, Sam, being cautious, wants to find out where the sensors were, so that they could get out when they'd finished. They search around the door area without finding any sign of sensors, Jo is concerned,

"If there are no sensors how do we open the door?"

Rick suggests they try the frequency modulator. Just to be sure he quickly sets it up, presses transmit as they wait. Nothing happens he tries several times without success.

"What now, demands Jo?"

Rick packs away the modulator,

"There has to be a sensor or switch somewhere we'll just have to search until we find it."

Outside the pyramid Henderson and Charlie are surprised not to find any sign of their friends and the door closed. Henderson asks Charlie what time they left the office, Charlie checks his watch.

"About five hours ago Sir, perhaps they did what they wanted here and went somewhere else."
Henderson walks up to the door studying the tracks in the sand.

"They were definitely here, their footprints lead into the door which must have been open, there are none leading out."
Henderson looks closely at the door,

"Corporal, I reckon they're still inside, we'll give them another couple of hours then decide what to do."

"OK Sir, I'll be back in two hours."
Inside, Sam and Jo are at the far side of the room examining the table again.
Jo enquires,

"I wonder if any of these symbols opens the door."
Sam thinks so it would be too risky to experiment.

"Let's complete our look around first then concentrate on finding a way out. It has to be something simple such as another sensor placed in a different position we'll probably walk into it."
Rick is over by the base of the column looking at what he calls the power gauge, the clear glass strip between the floor and the globe. Its green level mark has stabilised at the third symbol. He walks round the perimeter of the base and discovers a large opening into a round room inside the column. He calls Jo and Sam over. Looking into the room they see a ring of nine seats in the centre, all back to back and facing the walls which have nine small displays, one of which has the rotating globe on it. Each seat is facing a lit display panel next to which are the familiar symbols, the walls are of the same black material.
Sam points out,

"These seats are a different size to the others we've seen, they're normal size. I wonder why they are different."

Jo points to the ceiling it's covered with small lights each one pulsating with a dull bluish light. Below each screen there's a sloping panel coming out toward each seat covered in what looks like a series of small round pads resembling a keyboard, each one has a small symbol in its centre. They stand in the entrance looking in, afraid to enter. Rick leans further in, studying each side of the entrance.

"It doesn't look as if there's any door or any sensors, shall we go in?"

Sam immediately agrees,

"This is definitely some sort of control centre I'd like to have a closer look at those symbols they may tell us something."

Jo says hopefully,

"Yeah, like how to open the door."

They walk round the seats in the centre of the room as Rick nervously reminds them,

"Don't touch anything."

Sam points out that beside each keyboard there are two light tubes in the surface of the panels with markings similar to the one on the outside, one of which is part lit in green, matching the level mark on the larger gauge outside the room. As the control area was obviously designed to be used from the seats it's much easier to see everything if they are seated so they each take a seat. Sam's trying to make sense of the symbols on the keyboard when there's a sudden hiss of compressed air from behind them. A thick opaque curved door appears from somewhere within the wall and closes, completing the outer wall of the room shutting them in. Rick and Sam try to force open the door,

"Sam it's no good, we have to find another way of opening it, maybe one of the symbols on the keyboard."

They sit down again. Jo is desperately examining each symbol searching for anything that may resemble 'door' or 'open'. The constant background hum that they have become familiar with grows in intensity.

Sam looks up,

"Hear that?"

At that moment, the level of the green gauge on each panel starts to slowly rise, steadily passing each mark changing colour through green to yellow as it approaches its maximum. Jo is getting rattled,

"Rick can't you do something?"

As she speaks the blue lights in the ceiling become brilliant white, flooding the chamber with such an intensive light that they have to close their eyes. The hum increases as they start to feel drowsy collapsing into the seats before passing out completely. They are unable to see the gauge go from yellow to red.

Chapter - 6

A different time and space dimension

They slowly regaining consciousness, Rick lift's his drowsy head first.

"Where are we?"

He slumps back down onto the bed. Sam starts to move, opening his eyes looking up at a white ceiling which seems a long way away, in the background he hears Jo groaning then turning, looks towards the sound.

"Jo, you OK can you hear me?"

She groans again then making an effort,

"Yes, I feel very strange."

She speaks as if she is still dreaming,

"We must have been rescued by Henderson. Is this a hospital?"

A natural question as they are all wearing long white robes. Rick has now regained a little more strength he's sitting up with his legs dangling over the side of the bed. He's surprised he can't touch the floor. He then realises they are in twelve feet long beds. Slowly as his eyes regain focus he is able to take in the large white room which is at least twenty feet high with a very large window at one end. Through the window he can see in the distance, trees and green hills.

"We must be in England, but how long have we been out?" no one answers.

They slowly recover their strength, delicately getting back on their feet they gently shuffle around the room feeling very stiff with aching pains throughout their bodies. There are eight beds in the room above each one is a flat display screen. The screens above their beds are active, covered in various coloured lights, wavy lines and graphs. As their senses are returning Rick is first to notice,

"There's no door in this room."

They look around the room the walls are all smooth, then appreciating the size of the beds. Jo asks,

"Sam does this remind you of anything?"
Sam slowly moves his head up and down.

"Yes, the Pyramid."
With considerable effort they walk barefoot to the window, Jo looks out and turn's to Rick.

"Rick, this must be somewhere in England."
Distracted she stares hard at Ricks face.

"You look different somehow."
She calls to Sam,

"Look at Rick's face."
Sam looks at Rick's face,

"My god I don't believe it."
Rick looks round for a mirror. There isn't one,

"What in hell's wrong with my face?"
Sam laughs,

"There's nothing wrong, your scar's gone."
Rick feels his forehead,

"How come, that's impossible?"
Part of the wall silently opens as a young, very good looking man with sun bleached blonde hair down to his shoulders, steps into the room. He speaks to them in perfect English.

"Then you've recovered a little from your trip?"
They turn away from the window to see standing in front of them an impressive eight foot tall, well built man looking about 28 years old. He has bronzed skin, his head is larger than theirs elongated and sloping back towards the rear like the old Egyptian images, adding to his appearance of height. He's dressed in a long white caftan style gown and holding a small tray with three silver beakers. As he moves closer they back away in unison.

"Don't be afraid, my name is Aacaarya, I've been assigned to look after you, we saved your lives by bringing you here, please drink this elixir it will help speed your recovery process. It will first make you drowsy, but after you've slept you will have more energy and less pain. Then I'll answer your many questions. When you are fully recovered I'll take you to our Elders who wish to meet you."

Jo asks,

"Where are we?"

Aacaarya smiles pleasantly, his perfect white teeth contrasting against his skin colour.

"Later. Now please drink."

They feel strangely comfortable around this man each taking a beaker, as they drink the contents they discover a sweet clear liquid which is not unpleasant. Aacaarya leaves, taking the empty beakers, with a parting,

"See you later we've much to talk about."

The door silently closes behind him. Jo looks at Sam and Rick, who are equally in shock,

"We're definitely not in England, unless we're having some sort of hallucination."

Rick shakes his head.

"Nope, he was for real; I for the first time in my life don't have a clue what's happened to me or where we are."

Sam is distracted, mulling something over in his mind.

"Got it, he said his name was Aacaarya, if it's spelt as it sounds 'double a, c, double a, r, y, a' that in ancient Sanskrit, if I remember correctly means something like 'a spiritual teacher'."

Rick yawns,

"That's very interesting but does nothing for me at the moment I have to lie down."

Jo and Sam are also suddenly feeling very sleepy and do likewise. Sometime later they awake feeling completely refreshed to discover another door is open in the room, inside which are three very neat piles of clothes, towels, shower and washing facilities. The clothes are white, consisting of high collared Indian style jackets with loose fitting trousers. Rick goes into the shower first.

"There're no taps or controls."

He steps in for a closer look as a stream of water pours down onto him from somewhere above, the water is strangely invigorating. After a few moments when he is ready to leave the shower, the water stops, followed by a warm blast of air from all round him that quickly dries him off. Stepping out of the shower he puts a towel round his waist telling the others.

"Try the shower it's the most invigorating experience, like being in a car wash but more subtle, just step in it does the rest."

When they are dressed they enter the main room, the door slides open as Aacaarya returns.

"How are you now, you should be feeling a lot better?"

Sam speaks for all of them,

"We feel much better than we have for some time, thank you. I don't even feel the need for a cigarette."

Aacaarya smiles,

"None of you will ever suffer that craving again."

"Why?"

Aacaarya explains,

"Part of bringing you here meant reassembling the particles, atoms and cells in your bodies which provided us an opportunity to fix anything that was in need of repair, like your lungs for example which showed the beginning of a disease that in time would have consumed you and was responsible for the continuous cough you have lived with for many years."

Sam is silent, Rick strokes his forehead,

"That's what happened to my scar?"

Aacaarya nods.

Rick prompts him forcefully,

"You promised to explain to us where we are, how we got here and why we're here?"

Jo adds.

"And when will you release us?"

"You're here because the Elders deemed it necessary, they'll decide when and if you're permitted to return."

He asks them to follow him. They walk down a short windowless corridor stopping as another door hisses open. They enter a large round room with a circular table in the centre surrounded by tall pointed high backed seats.

"Please sit down, the Elders have authorised me to explain as much as possible to you and answer some of your questions, before your audience with them."

Jo asks him to start with where they are,

"Geographically you've not left the pyramid, to answer your question more precisely, by trespassing in our pyramid you triggered a mechanism that alerted us and would have destroyed you. We allowed you to enter the chamber where we created an anomaly in the electromagnetic fields which made it possible for us to safely transport you to a different point in time and space, in essence, my world. Everything and every component of our bodies are composed of atoms which are made of particles of protons, electrons and in most cases neutrons. The protons and neutrons rotate within the nucleus which in turn has the electrons orbiting around it at vast speeds it's this energy that electrically binds our substance together. The powerful electromagnetic field in the pyramid caused the particles, atoms and cells in your bodies to separate, as you were not protected we had to reassemble them as you arrived, at that point of intervention we were able to correct some of the problems you had. We live on the same planet as your civilisation but in a different dimension of time and space, therefore currently our two worlds coexist on earth."

Jo is not convinced,

"That's impossible."

Aacaarya glances at the wall, immediately a large portion slides to one side revealing a large glazed window beyond which they can see a green panorama that contrasts with the white of the room they are in. The view consists of trees, green fields, a large lake beside which is a beautiful city. The buildings they can see in the distance are white, very tall with domed pointed towers. The city is dwarfed by a large white pyramid rising from the centre. Aacaarya smiles at their reaction to the spectacle before them.

"This wonderful city is the capital of our world. Its name is 'Atlantis', now if you would please let me tell you some of the history of our people it will help you understand. My people lived on the earth over 20,000 of years ago. We were a global, civilised and technologically advanced race that respected the forces of nature and lived in peace. Over time we learnt to harness the energies of the earth and its magnetic fields to provide clean energy for our cities and to power our transportation. This technology was and still is far more advanced than yours is today. We passed some of our skills and technology to help advance other civilisations, such as India, Egypt, South America, Africa, Babylonia, and Great Britain. Our grand capital at the time was located in the centre of the land mass of Atlantis between Africa and America, although you have not yet discovered Atlantis, you'll possibly know of ancient maps by Piri Reis in 1511 and Ptolemy's map recovered from Constantinople in 1400, then there was Kircher's map that was taken from Egypt by the Romans around the year 30 BC. They all showed the position of Atlantis, in the Atlantic Ocean. When the continent of Atlantis disappeared into the ocean its position changed considerably as the earth's tectonic plates shifted.

Recently an Italian, Professor, Marcello Cosci from the archaeology department of the University of Pisa an expert in satellite imaging and interpretation announced that he has discovered satellite images he believes shows the remains of our city of Atlantis on the island of Sherbo, just off the Sierra Leone coast in the Atlantic. For nearly 5000 years our world lived in relative peace, trade flourished between countries and the peoples we had interacted with lived in harmony with respect for the values of life and nature. It was a great period of intellectual and cultural development which we hoped would become a model for the future.

However this was not to be, there were elements within the civilisations we had assisted whose motivations were personal greed and power, they sought to disrupt the world we had created, for their own misguided personal gain. They transformed our technology from peaceful use, to weapons of mass destruction, to use a phrase that you are familiar with. They developed weapons not dissimilar to your missiles, nuclear bombs and weapons that focused the electromagnetic energies of the earth to create earthquakes and destructive weather patterns. They used them on each other to devastating effect, obliterating whole civilisations destroying everything in their paths.

It was only a matter of time before they attacked Atlantis. We prepared ourselves, as we knew that they had reached a point where the global catastrophe they were creating was irreversible, our Elders started relocating our population to a large city they had constructed on the far side of the moon, the ancient remains still exist and I understand your lunar probes and expeditions have taken images of them.

Before we had completed our task Atlantis was destroyed and this last violent event caused massive disturbances in the earth's magnetic fields creating movements in the plates of the earth. This movement separated continents sinking others including what was left of Atlantis, the melting of the ice caps flooded much of the Earth. The overall effect of this tremendous movement on the planet caused it to tilt on its axis as its balancing weights of land and water were redistributed, resulting in the earth rotating at its current angle of 23.5 degrees. Many of the people and animals that survived died later because the natural biorhythm resonance of the earth's magnetic fields had changed, altering their alpha brain waves dramatically, disturbing their minds until death followed insanity. It was a terrible global catastrophe caused by the greed, desire for power and the corruption of a small number of influential people; sadly nothing changes as your world demonstrates. When the Earth's environment and land masses finally stabilized, our elders created a new Atlantis on Earth but in a different time and space dimension, in fact a Parallel World, so that we could live on the mother planet without other civilisations ever being aware that we existed. Today our world consists of a sustainable 1 billion people who live in harmony, using our technology to provide all their needs and power, we've no crime, drugs, pollution, wars or illness as a result we have no need for police or military forces. We live long lives and manage our population growth so that our land resources are not overstretched."

Aacaarya changes his tone,

"Unlike your civilisation that allowed its population to grow in only 207 years, from 1 billion in 1800 to 7 billion in 2007, to sustain this growth your civilisation has ploughed up half the Earth converting it to agriculture in order to feed this unsustainable level of population, over fishing the oceans and driving many species to near extinction. In doing this you have been destroying the very elements of nature that help absorb the heavy pollution you are now creating."

Rick interrupts and is about to say,

"You seem very well informed about our world."

When Aacaarya curtly responds to his question first,

"We know absolutely everything your world does we monitor every single item of information that's produced."

Rick looks at him in disbelief,

"How did you know what I was going to say?"

"We're a telepathic people, I've specifically learnt to speak English since we knew you were coming, in fact your civilisation had telepathic skills but through lack of use lost the ability, apart from some of the aborigines in Australia who are still able to communicate through the use of their minds. Sam, I sensed that your mind is more open than your friends, you too have the capacity if only you have the confidence to develop the skill."

Jo asks,

"So your people can read our thoughts?"

"Only I and a select few are able to intercept your thoughts as our native language is not English but a very ancient language from which Sanskrit originated."

Jo feels threatened by this revelation,

"Do you hear every private thought?"

"No, I have the ability to block your thoughts which I have done on occasions to offer you some privacy."

Rick wants to know,

"How do you monitor our world?"

"Our systems monitor your world's communications including all public, commercial, industrial, space, military, classified, terrorist, television, scientific, political and private. These are all processed then categorised into files that are organised according to our priorities, by a team of what you would call communication specialists. We also have physical craft that can pass through time and space from one world to the other when we discover something that concerns or threatens us. In some cases we visit, like you are doing as archaeologists searching for something from our past.

"What do you mean by things that concern or threaten you?"

"For example when various countries have tested nuclear weapons or are carrying out experiments that could threaten our joint existence we would physically monitor those situations."

Rick is now curious to know more,

"And these are aircraft?

"Normally our visits are unseen as our craft use an anti gravity motor that allows us to travel at high velocity through the air or water with great manoeuvrability. We are able to manipulate the earth's magnetic fields around our craft. However there have been unavoidable occasions when our craft have been seen."

Rick stops him.

"UFO's"

"Yes, you refer to them as UFO's we encouraged the myth that our craft are from another planet in an effort to control the arrogance of your military, some of our craft could well be described as flying saucers and do travel easily in space. There have always been times when natural anomalies in the earth's magnetic field cause the parallel worlds to become temporarily entwined allowing one world to see images from the other."

Jo is curious,

"What do you mean, seeing images?"

Aacaarya is silent a moment then gives them an example.

"People in your world over many centuries had reported seeing fleeting images of strange cities which they thought were mirages, these images were only visible for brief moments caused by a passing fluctuation in the magnetic field, much of your paranormal activities are attributed to the same cause."

Jo is struggling, trying to make sense of this,

"Are you saying only cities; ghosts and Unidentified Flying Objects?"

"No, unfortunately some of these sightings have carried consequences that were beyond our control"

"What do you mean consequences?"

Aacaarya looks serious,

"If I answer this question it could compromise your religious beliefs, do you want me to continue?"

The three of them are curious to know more and ask him to continue.

"Then let me try to explain, I come from a long lineage of Elders, seven generations ago my ancestors were interested in having contact with various young idealists who wanted to improve your world, during some of the discussions an anomaly occurred for a short time and the young men were able to see the Elder who was speaking to them. The Elder was taller than I am and much older with a grey beard. One of the men was Jesus of Nazareth, he believed that what he saw was a being that he called God, as you know from your experience in translating ancient writings from different religions and beliefs, the Gods were tall and arrived from the sky in chariots of fire, unfortunately we were directly responsible for those embryonic beliefs, as whenever sightings and meetings took place we were revered as Gods, particularly in those countries that we helped.

The values and ideology that we developed with Jesus of Nazareth and others were adopted by many religions and over time the stories were retold, embellished and eventually distorted by their churches to suit their own designs and to instil fear in their followers, religious wars and persecutions followed. Currently the modern Catholic Church represents one of the worst examples of religious hypocrisy, misrepresentation, malpractice, power and intolerance and is now returning to its middle age roots with ancient services that no one understands."

Jo interrupts him,

"Are you saying that when the prophet Mohammad rose into the heavens from The Rock in Jerusalem that this was a vision of one of your Elders?"

"Yes, more or less, most of your religions are based in one way or another on visions from another time and space, nothing more."

He then surprises them and asks,

"I would expect that by now you are hungry, would you like something to eat before we leave for the city?"

The three of them are silent absorbing the revelations they have just heard.

Rick speaks first needing a distraction,

"That's a great idea I'm famished what about you two?"

Sam and Jo are also very hungry and ask,

"What do you have?"

Aacaarya asks them to relax and let him surprise them. Jo is getting a little tired of his surprises and wants to know what's going to happen to them.

"As I've already told you, it's a matter for the Elders to decide. After we have eaten I will show you round the city before meeting them."

Sam asks if that will include the pyramid as he would be most interested in seeing it,

"Yes of course."

The door hisses open as three beautiful young women about the same height as Aacaarya enter carrying three white covered trays which they place carefully in front of Sam, Rick and Jo. They simultaneously remove the covers. Rick has in front of him a very large 'medium rare' T bone steak, chips, onion rings and mushrooms all cooked exactly as he liked, Sam has a grilled sole filling his plate with a side dish of vegetables, his favourite dish, whilst Jo has in front of her roast lamb with Yorkshire puddings, roast potatoes and vegetables. Sam looks at both the other plates and asks.

"You obviously knew what our favourite dishes were."

Jo tastes hers,

"Wonderful, it's not so bad here after all, Aacaarya you're not eating?"

"No, I normally eat in the evening so I'll leave you to enjoy your meal together. I'll collect you later."

Three white jugs of water with opaque glasses are placed near each of them. The door closes as they start eating. Each meal is perfectly cooked with exquisite flavour, Rick looks up,

"Strange but this is the best steak I've ever tasted in my life."

Sam grunts in approval as does Jo but adds:

"Do you think he's listening in?"

Rick nods,

Sam says, putting his finger to his lips,

"Rick we have to find a way of communicating, you still fluent in your languages?"

Rick nods, turning to Jo he points at her, still with his finger on his lip she realises what he means and nods. They finish their meal in silence, Sam dips his finger into the glass of water drawing on the table the letters USSR Rick puts his first finger and thumb together making the divers sign for OK, Jo does the same. All three are fluent in Russian which is another reason why Sam and Rick were originally chosen by the NSA. Jo has an honours degree in Russian from her days at University before she decided to follow a career in archaeology. Sam suddenly gets up from the table,

"I want to try something."

He puts his finger to his lips for silence then goes over to the area where the door is located, he focuses his mind. After a few minutes of intense concentration and with considerable effort the door hisses open then immediately closes. Sam speaks in Russian.

"Now we can open and close the door."
Rick responds in Russian,

"How, No, tell me later we need to keep our powder dry."
Sam looking satisfied returns to the table,

"We must try to control our thoughts."
The door opens Aacaarya comes in, they're waiting to see if he mentions the door as Sam greets him,

"Thank you for a truly wonderful meal, how did they manage to prepare it so perfectly?"

"Remember I mentioned before that we are able to manipulate atoms therefore as everything is made up from atoms we can create almost anything we desire to perfection, providing of course we have a template, now if you are ready we shall commence our tour."

Chapter - 7

New Atlantis

They follow Aacaarya out of the building, into clear very fresh air and bright sunshine. For the first time they can see where they were being held, it's a large facility consisting of tall circular units connected to one another by long tall corridors; the pointed roofs seem to be made from a one piece circular solar voltaic panel. The buildings are surrounded by short green grass that stretches as far as they can see. Rick asks,

"What is this facility?"

"You could call it a medical facility or clinic."

Rick points to the roof,

"Are those solar panels?"

"Yes they're a type of solar converter much more advanced than your Solar Voltaic Panels we have created continuous sun here so it's logical to supplement our energy use."

As they turn away from the clinic an unusual hovering vehicle stops in front of them. It's oval in shape, a little larger than a Humvee with a glass canopy covering six seats; remarkably it does not have wheels and is completely silent. The canopy slides back as the door drops down toward them with steps allowing access. They feel dwarfed by Aacaarya as Sam and Jo climb into the rear whilst Rick chooses to sit up front with Aacaarya. There's no steering wheel or controls, just a dashboard with display panel and buttons illustrated with symbols not dissimilar to those they saw in the pyramid. Rick points ahead.

"There are no roads."

"No, our transportation doesn't need them we use anti gravity technology. I'm sure you're familiar with the concept Rick, your American Patent Office has many research patents filed for various antigravity drives. Before you ask, the grass you see has been genetically engineered to grow to a certain height and needs no cutting."

He touches one of the buttons, the vehicle moves smoothly towards the city in the distance. Rick enquires,

"You did not seem to start the engine?"

"No, the anti gravity motor is always running, all I've done is switched on the ion propulsion drive, it emits positive ions in front of the vehicle and negative ions at the rear, this provides the forward motion."

"That's fascinating we've experimented with ion technology but never perfected it. How do you steer?" Aacaarya touches his forehead,

"From here, I use my mind to control direction, the vehicles computer responds to thought patterns in the same way I opened the doors and windows at the clinic."

They pass through well ordered countryside with trees shrubs and groups of round white buildings there are many vehicles and people going about their business.

"These are dwellings?"

Turning to Jo,

"In England you would call them villages."

"Do you grow crops here? I don't see any fields."

Aacaarya seems pleased at her curiosity,

"Yes we grow everything, we keep our agriculture in separate zones adjusting the weather and climate in those areas to provide perfect conditions for growth, as this is a residential zone it's always sunny, there are many residential zones around the city."

The vehicle speeds past other round white buildings of different height, as they near the outskirts of the city the groups of buildings are becoming more numerous, similar to suburban estates with more people and traffic. They enter a long wide straight corridor with open fronted buildings down each side with printed signs above each one, in what they now know to be ancient Sanskrit, Aacaarya slows down.

"I want to show you something."

He stops in front of the next building, opens the door and asks them to follow him. They enter what is obviously a clothes shop with shelves and hanging garments. They're welcomed into the shop by a man with a long grey beard, obviously much older than Aacaarya. He greets Aacaarya in Sanskrit then smiles at Sam, Jo and Rick waving his hand around the things he has on display as if offering them. Aacaarya explains that if they see anything they would like then to please help themselves.

"Don't worry we don't use or need any form of money, our society is very different from yours, everyone is equal in terms of wealth and education."

Rick smiles at Sam,

"And no need for banks or bank robbers."

Aacaarya nods his head,

"That's why we have no crime, there's no greed or jealousy, we have everything we need, our civilisation is a very cultured and intellectual race, we have the best universities on the earth which are accessible to the whole of our population and more importantly no politicians."

They each take a new set of clothing, thanking the old man who waves them off as they depart.

The vehicle continues to the city walls, which are made from a magnificent, glistening white stone sloping up for hundreds of feet. The white expanse of the walls is broken up by numerous small black windows. A short distance from the city is a large expanse of water with vehicles gliding over it. Aacaarya explains that this is one of the largest lakes on the planet. They skirt around the city wall until they reach an entrance where the wall is open to its full height creating an enormous and impressive gate into the city. Jo is curious about the shopkeeper,

"How old was the shopkeeper?"
Aacaarya is concentrating on the increasing traffic,
"Jo, he's four hundred years old."
It takes a second or two for Jo to realise what he said,
"Did you say four hundred?"
"Yes, both you and Sam must have come across references in the ancient texts you've studied, that mentioned people of similar ages."
Sam has indeed read such references,
"That's true I've seen this in documents from several different countries but always assumed it to be a mistranslation"
Jo is intrigued,
"How old are you Aacaarya?"
"I'm only two hundred years old."
"That's impossible!" Jo exclaims,
"I'll try to keep this simple, biologically you and I are very much the same but our people have evolved differently in an altered time and space. We're able to control the chemicals and hormones that cause ageing. The ageing process is controlled by the pituitary and hypothalamus glands. The brain neurotransmitter indirectly produces hormones to stimulate the pituitary gland, which is very small and located deep in your brain behind the eyes. In your race as you reach puberty the pineal gland starts a process called calcification which starts the ageing process, as you get older this calcification around the gland increases. In conjunction with this calcification the secretion of the hormones that inhibit the ageing process decreases rapidly at highly reduced levels, hence you age.
However, the human body is a perfect electrical machine, if you halted the ageing process it would continue to function for a lot longer than your current life span, which depending on many factors can be between seventy five and one hundred and twenty years. In my case I've reached two hundred years, which for us is the point where I will gradually

commence the ageing process, this longevity also accounts for my people being taller."

Rick asks,

"How long is your normal life span?"

Aacaarya touches a symbol on the dashboard slowing the vehicle down to walking pace,

"Some of the elders you'll be meeting are six hundred years old; it's possible for them to live for another hundred years or more if they desire intervention to further inhibit their ageing process."

Sam taps Rick on the shoulder,

"This is incredible, it ties in with the references we've often talked about, Aelianus Claudius in the year 235 wrote of tall people that lived to extraordinary ages."

The vehicle is now entering the gate to the city. Rick asks Aacaarya where he's taking them.

"Well as you three seem to have an affinity for pyramids, I thought we should start there as it's the most important building in our city and the source of our energy in this world. You'll find it somewhat familiar as it's almost a mirror image of our pyramid in Iraq."

Sam asks,

"Is that where we arrived?"

"Yes, you arrived there and we transported you to the clinic for recuperation."

Rick has been studying how the vehicle is controlled whilst at the same time trying to conceal his real motivation behind his questions,

"How do you stop the vehicle once it's in motion?"

Aacaarya demonstrates by touching a symbol several times to speed the vehicle up and another symbol several times to slow it down. Rick has been attentive to the controls since they left and feels that if needed he could at least get it moving and stop, although steering would be a different problem best left to Sam. Jo and

Sam both have a great capacity for absorbing new facts and research but have found the information and revelations they have been exposed to in the last day overloading, they desperately need to discuss these facts privately. Aacaarya turns to them,

"Don't worry you'll have private time for discussion later, I realise that we've covered very profound topics that must be difficult to absorb, and all in a very short space of time."

Jo and Sam realise they must be constantly attentive to their thoughts.

They've passed through the entrance to the city, Aacaarya slows the vehicle down turning smoothly into an enormous square paved in white and surrounded by very tall white domed buildings. Between the buildings are small roads approximately three vehicles wide, which lead further into the city. The vehicle moves straight ahead into one of the wider roads. The road is perfectly straight and lined with magnificent green trees, similar to Cyprus, each the same height. The street is completely clean with everything well ordered rows of identical vehicles are neatly parked between the buildings and trees, leaving the main thoroughfare clear. The vehicles look a strange sight, hovering two feet above the ground. They continue for some time whilst Aacaarya provides a continuous commentary describing the various office style buildings they are passing,

"We are now in the centre of our world administration zone from here our Elders govern our global interests, similar to London or Washington. This great city is modelled on Atlantis which was a perfect circle."

In the near distance they can now see part of the great pyramid ahead of them. Rick asks,

"I am curious to know where your energy comes from. This city alone must consume a tremendous amount of electricity."

Aacaarya points ahead to the pyramid,

"This is one of the sources of our energy. We long ago mastered Zero Point Energy which your physicists refer to as the zero-point quantum fluctuations of vacuum space at zero degrees Kelvin. However we currently take a majority of our electrical power from the Magnetosphere which resembles a space current generator driving the Ionosphere and providing the flow of energy to the poles. This pyramid is both a receiver and transmitter to other parts of our world."

Through his work with the NSA and other government scientific research organisations Rick is well aware of the massive research being done in the USA into both of these potential energy sources. Rick asks,

"How long have your people been using these energy sources"?

"Over 10,000 years."

Aacaarya asks him to leave further questions about their power sources until they reach the pyramid as it will be easier to explain there.

"We are aware of your research programmes, one of which, our Elders are greatly concerned about as it threatens the survival of both our worlds. This is the reason you're here."

Sam wants to know,

"Which research programme is that?"

"The United States is involved in potentially the most dangerous ionospheric experiment called HAARP."

Sam asks Rick,

"What's HAARP, I've never heard of it."

"You won't have done it's the least publicised scientific programme we've undertaken its full name is High Frequency Active Aural Research Project."

Aacaarya interrupts, his face now severe his eyes seem to burn into Rick as he pulls over stopping the vehicle.

"Scientific Ionospheric research is your cover name for its real use, it's being developed as a global weapon by your Navy and the US Air Force, using scientists that do not understand the consequences of what they are doing and who are oblivious to the fact that they could destroy the world in the process."

Rick takes a deep breath turning to Sam and Jo,

"Since 1995 congress has funded the development of HAARP which was based on patents of a physicist, Doctor Bernard Eastland, this programme involved building large areas of phased array transmitters to create the largest ionospheric heater in the world in Gakona, Alaska. The purpose of these was to blast controllable super-charged high frequency radio waves into the ionosphere 200 miles above the earth, these radio waves are so powerful and electromagnetically charged that they interact with the ions which are electrons, protons or ionised parts of atoms like hydrogen, ozone or nitrogen. HAARP is able to distort the ionosphere whilst at the same time heating it."

Jo is concerned and asks,

"Rick, what exactly is the ionosphere?"

"The ionosphere or ozone layer as it is called is the electromagnetically charged shield that surrounds the earth's upper atmosphere, the lower ionosphere starts at 50 miles above the surface, the upper ionosphere goes from 62 miles to between 280 and 373 miles above the earth's surface, it protects the earth from lethal cosmic radiation from space and sun flares."

Jo demands to know,

"What exactly do they hope to achieve by interfering with that?"

"The purpose was to study the ionosphere to see if it could be possible to manipulate weather patterns."

Aacaarya raises his voice,

"What about telling the truth, HAARP is really about beaming high voltage electromagnetic signals deep into the Earth's crust, causing destructive weather patterns, to create earthquakes, typhoons, tsunamis, tornados, heat waves and storms, listening to and destroying communications worldwide, creating shields against Intercontinental Ballistic Missiles, mind control using Extremely Low Frequency radio waves that can manipulate the brains alpha waves, communicating with deep ocean nuclear submarines and changing the chemical nature of the atmosphere."

Rick is surprised and starts to defend what he has said. He is cut short by Aacaarya who angrily explains.

"These insane schemes started long before 1995. In 1945 Nikola Tesla announced a proposed death ray invention using high voltage electrical energy. In 1958 the US discovered the lower Van Allan Belt 2000 miles above the earth, rising to the outer Van Allan belt at 32000 miles above the earth which contains charged particles trapped in the Earth's Magnetic field. Later that same year the US Navy under project Pegasus exploded three nuclear weapons in the Van Allen belt to examine their potential for disrupting communications.

In the 1960's the US dumped 350,000 million 2cm - 4 cm long copper needles into the ionosphere to create a communications shield. In 1962 the USA and USSR started using Electro Magnetic Pulses in the atmosphere and over 300 megatons of nuclear devices were exploded depleting the ozone layer by at least 4%. In 1968 Moscow announced it had identified which pulsed electromagnetic field frequencies can damage the mental and physiological functions of man.

In 1972 Norway announced experiments with an ionospheric heater at Aricibo using a 100 megawatt heater. In 1973 it was observed that when the US launched Skylab that its exhaust gases halved the electron count in the ionosphere for over three hours.

In 1976 Russia started global experimentation with Extremely Low Frequency pulsed waves at frequencies of 10 Hertz, this project is called Woodpecker, and its effect caused their sudden collaboration with your US scientists who provided the Russians with the largest magnet available so that they could together generate a magnetic field that was 250,000 times stronger than the earth's. This 10 Hertz ELF signal passes through humans and as it corresponds closely to the brains 7.83 Hertz alpha wave resonance, as a result it can disrupt or manipulate human thought, changing emotions from aggressive to passive or vis-a-vis. In July 1976 the Tangshan earthquake in China which killed 650,000 people was coincidentally preceded by an airglow caused by the Russian ionospheric heater.

In 1979 the launch of NASA's High Energy Astrophysical Observatory caused large scale artificially induced depletion in the ionosphere over a horizontal distance of 300 km.

The plasma hole was caused by the rapid chemical processes between the rockets exhaust gases and the ozone layer. During the 1980's your world was launching on average 550 primitive rockets a year into the higher atmosphere, this number rose to 1500 in 1989. During this period when your space shuttle was introduced with its massive solid fuel booster rockets, each launch released 187 tons of chlorine and 7 tons of nitrogen, both of which destroy the ozone layer, added to the 387 tons of carbon dioxide all dumped into the atmosphere on each flight. One of the soviet aerospace experts at the time Valery Brudakov calculated that it would take only 300 space shuttle launches to completely eliminate the Earth's ozone layer and its protective capacity.

In 1985 we come back to HAARP when Doctor Bernard J. Eastlund obtained a series of patents, described as 'A Method and Apparatus for altering a region in the Earth's atmosphere, Ionosphere and or Magnetosphere. Today others have joined the race to have the biggest and most powerful ionospheric weapons and are simultaneously carrying out their experiments in the earth's most precious protective layers. These ionospheric research sites are located in

Alaska, Jicamarca Peru, Finland, Japan, Moscow, Nizhny Novgorod and Apatity, Kharkov in the Ukraine and Dushanbe in Tadzhikistan, in Norway near Tromso, Australia and Great Britain. As you'll know they have different names such as 'Eiscat' which are the European Incoherent SCATter Radar Sites and Super DARN sites. The current deep earth penetration tomography using extremely Low Frequency waves to find underground facilities has the capability to cause earthquakes and volcanic eruptions, your scientists have already discovered there is a connection between earthquakes and the ionosphere."

He looks directly at Sam.

"Can you begin to imagine the damage that these combined and continuous experiments are doing to the earth's vital protective layers?"

Sam who is not usually unnerved by anything utters,

"Christ Rick."

Rick looks back at Jo who he knows is a passionate environmentalist, she is fuming at him.

"What right do your people think they have to do these things?"

Ricks response is weak,

"We have to protect America and keep ahead of what the others are doing."

Jo fires right back.

"Protect America, how, by creating a competition against other countries, to destroy our planet. Now I know why we've been having so many unique weather related disasters this year tsunamis, earthquakes, freak weather, tornados, volcanic eruptions, birds falling dead from the skies and fish and whales dying in large numbers.

I bet the cause is not really Global Warming as all the papers have been telling us, this would creep up on us gradually year by year, not all happening at once. It's down to your lot."

Aacaarya moves the vehicle forward towards their destination and breaks the heavy silence,

"Once we've visited the pyramid we'll stop for something to eat, then we can explore this subject further."

Rick who has been disturbed by what Aacaarya has said, speaks quietly,

"So this is really the reason we're here?"

The vehicle swerves round a parked vehicle,

"Yes, as I said before, your responses to the Elders will determine whether you are to be returned or not."

Sam touches Aacaarya on the shoulder,

"What do the Elders expect us to do about this?"

Aacaarya turns,

"They've been considering direct action to stop this folly, before the earth's magnetic fields and protective layers are destroyed or a polar reversal occurs. What you say may influence their decision."

Jo asks,

"Exactly who are the Elders?"

Aacaarya was waiting for this question,

"They are a forum of ten of our oldest most powerful leaders. Five women and five men they are direct descendents of the Antlanteads who created our world and the protectors of its secrets. Their powers are beyond imagination. They will communicate directly through me I will translate for you."

At last the vehicle arrives in the centre of the city crossing a very large grassed square. The buildings facing the square are unusual, as instead of being white they have no windows and are faced in the same black polished stone they saw in the pyramid. In the centre of the square standing by itself is the magnificent pyramid, an exact replica of the one in Iraq. As they look up at its height the pyramid looks much more overwhelming than its twin in Iraq which sits in the desert.

It takes a little time to drive round the perimeter to the entrance door. Aacaarya's attitude to them seems colder as he stops the vehicle and opens the hatch. They disembark following Aacaarya, as they approach the door it immediately opens, to Rick's surprise.

"How did you do make the door open like that?"

Aacaarya smiles, it seems a long time since he smiled thought Jo.

"I opened it with my mind as I did in the clinic."

"How could you without using the frequency lock?"

"We don't have enemies here, therefore there's no need for the frequency lock which you cleverly managed to open."

Chapter - 8

The Pyramid of Atlantis

They enter the pyramid, which is identical inside to the one in Iraq. As they pass through the entrance area Aacaarya points to the gold charts on the walls.

"As you worked out, the images on the chart you discovered in Iraq were relay pyramids, most of which no longer exist, they were used to relay energy from one place to another. These charts are of our world today and the locations of our relay stations."

The next door opens they enter the long corridor which is lit from above,

"Do feel free to ask any questions I've been authorised to answer them for you."

Aacaarya leads them into the main pyramid shaped control room in the centre of the pyramid. The large screens are covered with pulsating lights and symbols which pass from one screen to the next around the room, on one screen there's a map of the world with a circle in the centre of each country these are all connected to one larger pyramid shaped symbol by connecting rows of pulsating lights. The glass dome high above them is glowing intensely with fluctuating florescent light from the Crystals. The place is a hive of activity yet there is no one else there,

Sam asks,

"Where are the people that manage this?"

Aacaarya explains that the pyramid operates automatically and is remotely controlled by the Elders. He points to the world map,

"This screen displays the current status of the energy being received and the stations around the world that we are transmitting to."

Sam is particularly interested.

"That seems similar to our power stations and national grid."

"Yes in principle, but unlike your primitive technology we transmit our electricity wirelessly, no cables or pylons, the pyramid in Iraq was the last of our receivers left in your world"

Rick asks,

"If it hadn't been used for many thousands of years how come it still had power?"

"That's easy, it held a residual electromagnetic charge, when your unprotected bulldozer touched the antenna it shorted a burst of energy to earth, that's why the drivers atoms were unfortunately dispersed into space. Around the top of the pyramid there's a warning to this effect written in the stone, which I understand you photographed. When the pyramid was constructed we never imagined that it would be possible for someone to be able to drive into the antenna."

Aacaarya takes them to the control room chamber under the brightly lit glass dome in the centre of the pyramid, the door is open and inside it's identical to the other pyramid, they stand outside.

"This is our control centre which enables us to move from a point in one time and space to a point in another. This is where you triggered your transportation to our world."

Jo wants to know,

"But how did we do it, we didn't touch anything?"

Aacaarya explains that the system is driven by sensors,

"When you entered the room and sat down you were immediately being prepared for travel."

Rick asks,

"So if we just went in and sat down, it would do the rest?"

"Yes exactly, just like that."

Jo and Sam back away from the entrance. Rick has something else on his mind.

"But how do you navigate to where you want to go?"

"What you really want to know is, if you were to go in, where it would take you. We only use navigation in our craft when travelling between worlds. This facility only allowed operators to travel from one pyramid to another when necessary, so the answer is, as there's only one other pyramid of this type left in the other world it would take you there."

Rick seeks a distraction for his thoughts, points to the glass chamber above their heads,

"What are the glowing objects in the glass dome?"

"They, my friend are very special power crystals of a type of barium titanate that we use to receive energy from near earth space, by focusing on them specific frequencies we modify their resonance, amplifying the power considerably before transmitting the enhanced beams of electromagnetic energy to the receivers."

Rick is genuinely fascinated and asks another question,

"Why did our atoms separate during our transfer, is that normal?"

"No, not at all, it was because the residual energy left in the Iraq pyramid was not powerful enough for a clean transfer, you were extremely lucky."

Having seen as much as they could take in Jo asks Aacaarya,

"Why didn't our wristwatches and other things arrive with us?"

"It was all down to the low power level, there was barely enough to transfer you, all your material things would have been left in the control room."

Jo smiles asking another question,

"Now how about that something to eat you mentioned?"

"If you're ready, let's go, I've another little surprise for you."

He leads them back to the vehicle driving them once again to the other side of the square then straight out between the buildings surrounding the square into a magnificent panorama. They're driving in open country beside the large lake they'd seen from the clinic. They head towards a group of low white buildings in the distance, when suddenly the vehicle turns abruptly right leaving the land heading directly towards the lake. The three of them shout in unison "look out" but the vehicle passes smoothly from the land to water then starts to submerge without slowing down. Jo utters "oh no" and grabs Sam's arm as the water rises up the side of the canopy.

Aacaarya's laugh breaks their moment of panic. Grinning at them, he explains that the vehicle is equally at home on land or under the water,

"Relax and enjoy the view."

The water is crystal clear as they descend into the depths trying to identify the many different types of fish. The ride is completely stable and smooth, Rick is first to recover from the surprise,

"This is an unbelievable craft, is it your personal vehicle?"

"No not really, we don't need personal transport, whenever we want a vehicle we just ask for one for the period we need it and it arrives, I do have this one fairly permanently though, because my specialised work involves travelling."

Aacaarya continues driving under water towards the far side of the lake. The vehicle surfaces breaking into a normal hover height as a pontoon type landing looms up in front of them. The pontoon continues to an open fronted building by the shore line. They reach the pontoon and moor alongside, stepping out onto the pontoon Rick and Sam look back at the vehicle with new admiration.

Aacaarya holds his arm out for Jo to take,

"We're going to a most fabulous fish restaurant."

They look a really odd couple arm in arm, his height towers above her. Jo calls to Sam and Rick,

"Come on boys leave the toy, I'm starving."

They sit down at a large outside table in the bright sunshine facing the lake; it's a most idyllic setting. The lake is flanked with willow trees and exotic shrubs covered in bright flowers everywhere. The front of the white restaurant is covered in highly perfumed Jasmine. Delicious smells of barbequed fish waft out from within the restaurant, inside there are many tall guests, men and women sitting at large tables chatting in their strange language.

Jo, Sam and Rick feel very small. The women seated near them are particularly attractive with high cheek bones and long blonde hair. Aacaarya explains that all the fish are fresh from the lake which by design is segregated into both salt and fresh water therefore they have every variety of fish available, including lobster which can be cooked any way they desire.

"So what would you like?"

An imposing waiter arrives looking about the same height and age as Aacaarya, Jo asks Aacaarya if she could have a Dover sole, grilled and served off the bone with a selection of vegetables. Sam decides to have a Sea Bass oven baked in coarse sea salt and Rick opts for a lobster grilled with garlic, herbs and butter. Aacaarya translates their order as Jo asks,

"Aacaarya what are you having?"

"I'm having the same as Rick I have a passion for grilled lobster."

The waiter brings white jugs of a sparkling water and four beakers, the jugs emit a very slight hum like a refrigerator. Curious Rick picks his up to pour into the beaker and notices that it is exceptionally cold to the touch, he hesitates. Aacaarya laughs at him,

"It's only a self cooling jug, nothing to be afraid of."

The water is particularly refreshing and stimulating. In short time the waiter arrives pushing a large table filled with their dishes, the table hovers just above the ground like their vehicle. The dishes are perfectly prepared and exquisitely cooked. After they have eaten they thank Aacaarya for an excellent lunch, they feel re energised by the wonderful food and sparkling water.

As they sit enjoying the sun and relaxed atmosphere Aacaarya returns them to reality,

"Are there any questions before we leave for our meeting?"

Sam asks,

"Yes, what do you think they want from us?"

"They'll be seeking your opinions they have studied everything about each of your backgrounds and consider that your advice could be helpful to them."

They have no more questions and return to the vehicle.

"It's not far from here."

Aacaarya closes the canopy, the vehicle moves forward leaving the lake. He takes them past the pyramid to the other side of the square into a smaller road between two large buildings which opens into another large square lined with trees and white buildings. Facing them is an enormous white palatial building with a central domed roof surrounded with smaller tall round towers topped with reflective domes.

Chapter - 9

The Forum

They stop outside enormous oak like wooden entrance doors which are twenty feet tall and covered in exquisite carvings with ancient symbols. The great doors silently open they are ushered into a grand very ornate reception area surrounded by large white sculptures of what must be past Elders.

Jo whispers,

"It's like being in the Vatican."

After a few moments an elderly man walks over to Aacaarya, he speaks to him quietly in Sanskrit. Aacaarya asks them to follow him, there's a very strange spiritual silence in the hall. Crossing the room they reach another pair of magnificently carved doors these also silently open, they follow Aacaarya into a large brilliantly white domed assembly room. It looks a little like a court room, on the far side is a high semicircular table behind which are sitting 5 men and 5 women, all of whom are dressed in long white robes. The bearded men have long grey hair the women are grey haired but have the characteristic high cheek bones giving them a natural beauty. Aacaarya ushers them to a lower table with three seats in front of the Elders. He asks them to sit as he remains standing facing the Elders. Then Aacaarya clenches his hands in front of him, lowers his head as a sign of respect then takes a separate seat near the lower table. The room is in silence as the lights dim. Turning to Rick, Sam and Jo, he speaks,

"The Elders have asked me to welcome you to Atlantis, they hope that you've been treated well and are finding our world at least interesting."

Rick responds,

"Please thank them for their kind hospitality and for transporting us here safely, we've been fascinated by what we've seen and learnt of your remarkable world."

Aacaarya closes his eyes a second then continues,

"We've been observing with great sadness the considerable destruction that your primitive civilisation and its leaders have caused our planet's environment over the years following your absurd industrial revolution and unnecessary attacks on each other. Despite the two world wars followed by Vietnam which your leaders stated, were the wars to end all wars, your latest invasions of Iraq, Afghanistan, the behind the scene disruption and influence in Palestine, Lebanon and Africa are crimes against humanity. Your military has killed millions of people displacing many millions of families leaving them without food, medicines, water, power or hope.

These insane misguided wars have no future and no end they will surely destroy all that are involved in them whilst damaging our precious environment. The arrogance of the United States of America, whose own economy is close to collapse, is now planning a suicidal attack on Iran. These are inexcusable crimes against humanity and the planet. We respect that it's not our right or responsibility to intervene if your races are intent on self destruction. However, we will not permit your civilisation to jeopardise the planets' survival by continuing to destroy the delicate balance of the magnetosphere. The ill-conceived HAARP project is very close to causing a catastrophic ignition of the ionosphere. If this happens it will cause the cremation of the planet, leaving the Earth dead, with an environment similar to Mars, where no form of life could survive, including our world. Unfortunately there is no country or organisation in your world that has the power to protect the Earth from this inevitable destruction. We have been left with no alternative but to assume and fulfil the role of protectors to ensure the future survival of our planet."

Rick, as the most senior, has accepted the role of spokesman he stands up looking directly at the Elders; Aacaarya closes his eyes as he communicates with the Elders, translating as Rick speaks.

"We cannot deny the global instability and the many grave errors that our administrations and leaders have been responsible for but it's not the populations of these countries that made the decisions to go to war or carry out this research. It would be hypocritical to punish the innocent. Admittedly we have many severe problems with limited solutions, is it possible that you could help us?"

"We've considered that possibility but had reached the conclusion, that although we have the ability to help you it would be of no use, your problems are in the minds of intolerant misguided military leaders and lobbyists in the Pentagon controlled by corporate America. The greed driven power seeking politicians will only try to take advantage of our goodwill for their own ends."

Sam looks toward Aacaarya and speaks,

"We are archaeologists not soldiers or politicians, we too have been shocked by what we have discovered about our world since being here, but I fear that there's little we can do personally. May I ask what options you have available to remove this threat to our world's survival?"

There is a minutes silence before Aacaarya responds,

"We have several options available, one of which we have considered, is that we could provide a demonstration of our power by removing all of the HAARP type research facilities that exist in different countries throughout the world. This would certainly set back and stop your current research programmes. Or we could remove other important global facilities that would have a more major impact.

The implication of doing this would be that your world would interpret our direct action as an act of war by an aggressor that they previously did not know existed. They would then turn their combined attentions to hopelessly trying to attack us. Your populations would be turned by your media to fear the unknown and like sheep would follow their leaders whose real agenda would be to win the race to acquire our advanced technology. We wish to continue living in peace but know that this option could lead to a war between our worlds on a scale your race could not imagine and equally could damage the planet we are trying to protect. Our strategy would only work if we could alter the hearts and minds of your world's leaders and politicians, a matter also within our technological capability."

Jo asks to speak,

"Is there not a compromise where we could be sent back as ambassadors, to at least try and convince them that they must shut down their atmospheric experiments, this could be supported by one irrefutable demonstration of your power that we could use to reinforce our arguments?"

Rick gives a disapproving glance at Jo as Aacaarya responds to her question,

"This was what we hoped might be a unanimous possibility but we sense one of you is not in agreement."

Jo and Sam look at Rick, who tells them,

"I need time to think about this."

There is a further silence until Aacaarya speaks.

"We will allow you this evening to consider the matter, you will return to the clinic where you can discuss this openly and privately, we'll reconvene early tomorrow. Colonel Taylor, if after discussions with your associates you still do not agree with their course of action, you will have to remain with us. The forum is closed."

Aacaarya bows his head asking them to follow him. They retrace their steps to the vehicle which is waiting outside in the bright sunlight. None of them speak as Aacaarya drives them back to the clinic, he parks the vehicle in a large garage type building beside two other identical vehicles, the garage is connected to the clinic complex. They follow Aacaarya down several passages and into their room. Jo is the first to break the heavy silence,

"Aacaarya thank you for today it's been a mind blowing and extraordinary experience."
Sam thanks him,

"And for a most memorable lunch"

"Sam it's been a great pleasure for me too, I've arranged for you to have access to our meeting room, the connecting door will be open. The ladies have organised what I think you call snacks.

"I'll collect you tomorrow morning."
He then moves to leave, glancing at Rick as he does, who responds,

"Aacaarya thank you, I just need time to go ever everything, there's an enormous amount to think about."

"I understand you need time, see you all tomorrow morning."
After Aacaarya leaves Sam turns to Rick,

"What the hell was all that about in the Forum, I can't believe that you don't agree with Jo's suggestion?"
Rick responds in Russian,

"Let's go next door, there's more to this than you think, for the moment let's stick to Russian."
They go through to the meeting room and sit around the table. Jo asks Rick,

"Is that all true about HAARP and what they're doing?"

"Yes, sadly but there's more, it's strictly classified even I'm not party to everything that HAARP is being used for. I was surprised today too. They obviously know a lot more than I do."

Sam cuts in,

"What's wrong with the idea of sending us all back as ambassadors to at least try to make our politicians see sense?"

"It's not that simple, there have been leading physicists who've raised serious concerns about HAARP's potential for causing atmospheric damage, most have been blocked or blacklisted, some have died under mysterious circumstances, you don't know the power of the organisations behind these experiments. They're ruthless they would not hesitate to eliminate us too if it protected their interests, there's too much at stake."

Jo angrily interrupts,

"TOO MUCH AT STAKE, if we don't do anything and the world ends, as seems likely, what will their 'stake' be worth then? You're thinking like one of them, you deserve to be left here. Perhaps the Elders are right we should just let them get on with eliminating all the sites themselves."

Rick gets up and paces back and forth,

"Don't you see it? They live here in sweet harmony in a perfect world controlled by the Elders who have the ability to manipulate their minds, that's brainwashing. They probably don't have such a thing as freedom of speech or freedom of thought, they don't know what taking a risk is they have everything provided for them, that's mind control of an entire world."

Sam points out,

"The only reason we're not yet subjected to mind control in the US is because the administration haven't perfected the technology yet."

Rick stops his pacing,

"That's not completely true, for some time they have been using very subtle mind control using specially programmed television commercials, for example during the build up to Presidential elections to influence voters. There's also a possibility that these people could be a threat to our way of life."

Jo protests,

"Not if we destroy the world first, they won't. I don't see any other way but to accept their offer then do our best to close down these crazy projects, particularly if we've proof of their power, people will listen to us, they'll have to."

Sam agrees with Jo but Rick is still not convinced,

"There's another way, if we worked together, we could escape tonight then do what you suggest but on our own terms without their control, I don't intend staying here."

Jo is surprised and angry,

"Escape, how, you must be completely out of your mind."

Rick asks them to hear him out,

"With Sam's help we can open doors, I reckon that I can control the vehicle, I've been watching carefully what Aacaarya was doing when he was driving, Sam would have to control steering and direction. We know the way to the pyramid which hopefully Sam could get us into and we know that it has the power to transport us safely back and how to do it, that's why I was asking so many questions."

Jo asks,

"And what happens if we get caught?"

Sam answers for Rick,

"We would just have to take that chance."

Jo turns on Sam,

"I am surprised at you I thought you were in agreement with their plan."

"I was, but Rick has a point, we could potentially get back, we'd also have the pyramid in Iraq as credible proof of what we know to date as, with a

tangible demonstration of their abilities and potential. We could do as Rick suggests, but on our own terms."
Jo sighs in defeat,

"You two are completely crazy."
Rick asks,

"Are you both in agreement?"
Sam and Jo look at each other as Sam tells Rick,

"Well we've come this far together, so let's try and get back together, OK now let's see if I can still open the door."
Sam leaves Jo and Rick, goes out of the room then down the corridor to the first door, a few minutes later he returns smiling,

"Well the first one opens and closes at my will let's hope the others do the same."
Jo has found the bag that the snacks were brought in and refills it from the table,

"This will keep us going, when do we leave"?
Sam looks puzzled,

"Do you two have any idea how long we've been here?"
Rick suggests,

"About two days or is it three?"
Jo has no idea,

"Rick, it's very strange but I've no feeling of how much time has passed."

"We'll leave as soon as the sun sets, we'll have just enough light to find our way."

Chapter - 10

The escape

Darkness begins to fall as they make their way along the corridor to the first door, Sam approaches ahead of the others. Stopping, he concentrates, the door obediently slides open. They pass through several corridors making their way through three other doors. Sam is already sweating with the mental effort needed to control the doors. At last they're in the garage area which is open fronted. The two vehicles they saw when they arrived with Aacaarya are still there hovering above the ground. Sam goes to the nearest one focusing on the canopy, this takes a little longer than the doors but eventually silently slides open, the steps dropping down in front of them. Sam whispers,

"Over to you Rick."

Rick gets into the driver's seat with Jo behind and Sam beside him. Rick touches the start symbol button, the panel lights come as the canopy closes, he gently touch's the throttle symbol the vehicle slowly edges out of the building.

"So far so good, now Sam, try to turn us right through 90 degrees."

Sam silently concentrates, the sweat dripping down his forehead as slowly the vehicle starts to turn to the right, but continues turning them in a complete circle through 360 degrees.

"Sam what are you doing?"

"OK Rick I didn't stop the turn, I'll try again."

This time the vehicle turns right stopping at 90 degrees. Rick gently touches the throttle again the vehicle responds instantly, moving in a straight line towards the distant lights of the city. The head lights of the vehicle have switched on automatically allowing them to see a good distance ahead. They follow the direction

Aacaarya had taken earlier then see the lights of other vehicles coming towards them. Jo lies down across the rear seats,

"I'll keep out of sight we must look terribly conspicuous given our lack of height."
Rick looks at her over his shoulder,

"Hopefully we won't have to stop."
The oncoming vehicles pass them without incident, they pass the shop they visited earlier and are now heading towards the city wall. Sam is mentally exhausted with the effort required in steering as Rick has to change direction again,

"Sam, turn right 45 degrees please,
They are getting closer to the city wall now looming up in front of them. Rick is getting anxious there are only a couple of minutes left before they crash into the wall.

"Sam, turn right now."
Sam raises his voice,

"Rick, shut up, I'm doing my best."
Nothing happens the vehicle is now rapidly closing on the wall,
Rick shouts,

"Look out, hold tight."
At one metre from the wall the vehicle turns abruptly sharp right following along the edge of the wall,

"Great, Sam that was just in time."
Rick looks across at Sam who seems to be asleep. Rick touches the symbol to slow the vehicle to a stop, leaning across he nudges Sam. Sam slowly opens his eyes, shaking his head he asks,

"What happened?"

"We nearly wrote the car off, but you saved the day."

"Rick, I didn't do anything I must have passed out."

"Unless the vehicle has some sort of proximity radar that takes control if you're going to hit something, cool eh."

Rick gently increases speed as the vehicle is now facing the right direction, towards the brightly lit gates of the city. They pass more vehicles coming towards them, as they get closer to the gate Rick asks Sam,

"Are you ready to do a 90 degree when I say?"
"OK."
Rick slows the vehicle down to a walking pace as they pass into the city entrance area,

"Turn now."
Sam concentrates hard, this time the vehicle responds perfectly, lining them up with the road at the other side of the large square. There are many people in the city with lots more traffic,

"Sam, I know it's hard but we're going to have to watch the traffic, the pyramid is in the distance straight ahead, if no one does anything stupid we should be OK, but stay alert."
Jo passes Sam a bottle of water from her bag,

"This is their rejuvenating water it'll help you."
Sam takes it drinking the lot,

"Thanks, that's much better I feel more awake."
Half an hour later they arrive at the square, the pyramid in the centre is emitting a florescent glow.

"Rick, we should try to park as close to the door as possible."
They manoeuvre the vehicle to a stop near the door,

"Sam you sure you're up for this?"
Sam looks over at Jo,

"Yeah thanks to Jo, the drink worked wonders, now let's see if we can open the door"
They stop and leave the vehicle, Rick pulls Jo back,

"Let Sam go ahead by himself so we don't distract him."
Sam is a few paces ahead of them standing facing the door, he concentrates focusing his mind. Suddenly there is a hiss as the big door slowly swings open towards them. Rick hurries them inside as the door thuds shut behind them. The lights in the entrance hall

increase in brilliance, Sam opens the next door without effort, they move quickly through the long corridor. Passing through the last door they arrive out of breath in the central area of the pyramid containing the control room. Cautiously they go over to the control room checking that it's empty. Before going in they decide to recap on what they are about to do. Sam is looking drained again after his mental effort with the doors. Rick asks them,

"Are you two sure you want to do this?"
Sam nods in approval as Jo asks,

"What do we do, assuming we arrive back in one piece?"
Rick has thought about this,

"Until we know what's been happening in Iraq I suggest that we keep everything that has occurred to ourselves. Then we can decide how best to proceed, in the meantime we create a legitimate cover story, that we were lost in the passages of the pyramid for two or three days, after all we did have emergency rations and water. No one else knows the frequencies to open the door so if we can get out and the door closes, no one will have access and the secret remains with us until we decide to make it public."

"Rick we agree, let's go."
They enter the control room entrance sitting down together. Sam has his head in his hands, Rick looks across concerned

"Sam, are you feeling alright?"
Sam slowly lifts his head up, looking at them both his face a picture of disbelief,

"Aacaarya has just spoken to me."
"Sam, how, what did he say?"
"Telepathy, he said good luck and we'll be OK."
Jo asks,

"Did he say anything else?"
"Yes, he said that my telepathic powers will get stronger each time I use them, he said they are now

strong enough for he and I to remain in contact with each other."

Rick asks,

"Is that all?"

"No, his last words were, do not under any circumstances return to the pyramid once we get out."

Rick is wondering,

"Perhaps Aacaarya allowed us to escape it almost seemed too easy."

At that moment the opaque door hissed shut closing them in the control room. The blue lights increase in intensity to a brilliant white, that's all they remembered. In Iraq there is great activity outside the pyramid door, Henderson with a group of engineers have been desperately trying to open the door, he's standing close to the door and calls the sergeant over,

"If we drill into the stone, here, here, here and here we could place charges to blow the door apart, it's been five wasted days since we started trying to open it using levers."

"Sir, we were told not to damage it."

"Sergeant, I know that, but we have no choice, they only had rations for two days and it may already be too late to get them out, assuming we can find them, it's sure to be a maze of passages in there."

The sergeant agrees sending a Humvee away to their stores for heavy duty drills. It's getting late in the day as they turn on the sodium flood lights illuminating the work area in a yellow glow. After half an hour the Humvee returns, they set up the drill to make the first hole, it takes four engineers to hold the enormous drill steady as a 2" drill bit touches the surface of the door and is switched on, after a few minutes they switch it off. The sergeant goes to the Humvee that Henderson is using as a control centre,

"Sir, come and look at this."

They walk over to the door looking closely at the spot where the drill was used Henderson can't believe his eyes,

"There's not a scratch."

"Sir, this drill bit would cut through almost anything including stone, this material looks like stone but it's harder than anything I've come across before."

"Sergeant, pop over to the demolition team explain the problem get them to bring some of the new plastic explosive tubes with remote fuses enough to go round the whole door."

The sergeant does as ordered returning half an hour later with two of the demolition experts. They start work immediately placing their plastic charge all round the door, after the fuses are in place, they're ready. They take cover a good distance away behind a Humvee, the senior demolition expert is next to Henderson with the fuse's remote control box in his hand,

"Are you ready sir?"

"Yes, OK."

He presses the button on the box,

There's a loud explosion followed by a cloud of dust and sand which takes time to clear, as it does they see the door exactly as it was before, undamaged except for a black mark round the frame where the explosive ignited. Henderson and the demolition team are by the door looking for any cracks, there's nothing only the black mark. Henderson asks,

"What next?"

The senior of the two suggests,

"The strength of that explosion would have opened most bank vaults; I suggest that we come back first light tomorrow with a much heavier penetration charge."

Henderson agrees dismissing the engineers and the demolition team,

"See you tomorrow morning at 0500 hours."

It's now almost dark as the convoy of five Humvee's leave, their headlights and sound of their engines fade into the distance, leaving the silence of the desert with the pyramid which is now getting more fluorescent the darker it gets.

Inside the centre of the pyramid, the crystals are glowing intensively above the control room a brilliant flash of light occurs within the room. Slowly the blue light returns to normal, Jo, Sam and Rick are slumped in the seats, after about 15 minutes Jo and Rick begin to move, there's still no movement from Sam. Very slowly Jo and Rick regain consciousness, they don't have the strength to move but just sit, as if in a trance. Another fifteen minutes passes Rick manages to speak,

"Jo, you OK?"

"Yes, I think so, I can now move my feet a little, how's Sam?"

With difficulty Rick moves his head to look across at Sam, whose eyes are now open,

"Sam, are you alright?"

Sam manages a slight nod and smile then closes his eyes again. It takes an hour before they are able to sit up and speak to each other. Jo is pleased to note,

"Have you noticed we're back in our own clothes and have our watches back?"

"Yes it's as if we've never left here, I think the feeling in my body has returned I'm going to try and get up."

Rick stands with great effort then as if gaining strength from the effort walks in a slow circle round the seats, he goes over to Sam who is now looking a lot better but hunched up trying to stand,

"Rick, can you give me a hand up?"

"Thanks Rick, I think everything's slowly beginning to function."

He grabs Rick's arm again for support taking a few tentative steps, each one better than the last. By the time he has circled the seats he is almost back to normal. They both help Jo to stand, walking her slowly round the room.

"Sam, I think we should get out of here, in case they take us back."

As they go to the door they see their backpacks exactly where they had left them, outside the door. Picking them up Jo says,

"Great we can have something to eat, I've no idea how long ago it was since we ate something."

The three of them slowly gather momentum walking to the first door Sam steps ahead and concentrates, almost immediately the door slides open without much mental effort. They slowly make their way along the corridor to the next door using Rick's frequency modulator to open it, they pass through the entrance area to the main door, Rick opens it easily they step out into the cold night air of Iraq. As they stand there the outer door closes behind them and locks shut.

They adjust to their new environment then notice the sodium lamps with tracks of vehicles with footprints around the door and the black marks. Rick goes over to the door running his finger through the black dust, sniffing it he says,

"Plastic explosive, I reckon Henderson's been trying to get us out."

As there's no one around and they're still feeling very weak they decide to go back to the portacabin to rest. Before they leave Rick stops them,

"Hang on I just want to try something."

He takes out the frequency modulator then tries to open the pyramid door. Nothing happens,

"I reckon they've changed the locks, let's get back I'm exhausted."

They arrive at the portacabin, dumping the bags they go straight to their beds without undressing dropping into a very deep sleep.

Chapter - 11

The disappearance

At 5.00 am they are woken abruptly by a pounding on the portacabin door, still half asleep they make their way to the door to hear raised voices outside. As they open the door, Henderson bursts in stopping dead when he sees them,

"Rick, when did you three get back?"

"Late last night, it's nice to see you too, what's up."

Henderson is almost unable to speak he orders them,

"Look outside."

Rick doesn't understand what's got into him,

"Christ Mike, what's the hurry we haven't woken up yet."

"You will in a second, just get outside."

Curious the three of them follow Mike outside. In front of the portacabin are five Humvee's surrounded by a group of engineers with the demolition team. To their absolute shock and disbelief there's no pyramid, a massive flat square imprint in the sand is all that remains.

Sam is behind Rick,

"It's gone, but how?"

Henderson cuts in,

"That's what we want to know and where've you been for the past five days."

Rick responds quickly before the others have a chance,

"We got lost inside the Pyramid thankfully we found the way out late last night."

The engineers are walking over the now empty site looking for anything that could help them understand what's happened. Rick invites Henderson in for a coffee,

"I need something stronger than coffee, how in hell are we going to explain this to anyone."
They go back into the portacabin as Henderson turns back,

"I'll be along minute."
He then goes over to his men instructing them to thoroughly comb the site for anything that could render a clue as to what's happened.
As they close the door Rick grabs the arms of Jo and Sam,

"Until we've time to work out what's happened, we'll stick to the cover story; we became lost in the maze of passages in the pyramid and couldn't find our way back."
He lets go of their arms, Jo makes the coffee.

"Do you both agree?"
Sam and Jo both agree that for the moment it would be best to keep things simple.

"Sam did you hear what Henderson said, we've been gone for five days."

"Jo that's five of their days, we know that time doesn't pass at the same pace on the other side."
Rick interrupts,

"Sam, what has happened to the pyramid it can't just disappear?"

"Why not, they said they'd provide a demonstration of their power, perhaps this is it. If they can accomplish that, they can do anything."
Jo brings a coffee over to Rick,

"He's right, and so are you, we keep quiet until we work out what we should do next."
The door opens as Henderson rushes in,

"Where's the coffee?"
He takes a mug and sits down with them,

"Now tell me what happened?"
Sam starts,

"It's been quite traumatic, we managed to get into the pyramid but the door closed behind us, like most pyramids it was a maze of passages, many that led nowhere, we kept exploring but none of our navigation or communication equipment worked so we tried to leave trails. We didn't find a tomb or anything just managed to completely lose our way. If Rick and Jo hadn't brought emergency rations we wouldn't have survived. We lost track of time, after what seemed several days of trying and then by absolute luck, we managed to find a passage that led to the entrance chamber with the door. Then after some time we discovered a lever that opened it from the inside. It was dark when we got out then the door closed itself behind us. We made our way back here exhausted and slept until you started banging on the door."

Henderson looks at them in disbelief,

"That's it?"

Rick nods,

"We tried to communicate with you but nothing worked inside."

At that moment there's a knock on the door the sergeant comes in looking for Henderson,

"Sir, I thought you might like to know, all our communications equipment is now functioning normally, there's no sign of any electromagnetic disturbances."

"Sergeant, there's nothing normal about this, thanks anyway."

The sergeant leaves as Henderson continues,

"We tried for five days to get the door open, we used levers and rams, couldn't scratch the surface with the most powerful drills we had then tried PE, the stone was unlike anything we'd seen before, even steel we could have got through but this was something else. After four days we thought you couldn't possibly be coming out alive, the CO reported this up the line. Rick, your lot, the National Security Agency have been monitoring the pyramid by satellite, when they heard that you'd disappeared they organised a specialist team to arrive tomorrow to take control. Now, when they arrive, all we'll have to show them is you three who supposedly disappeared, with photographs of the pyramid that has disappeared. No doubt by now, they'll have noticed that the thing they were monitoring through their satellites is no longer there and will want some answers."

Rick asks,

"Who are they?"

"No idea, apparently there are ten of them they intend debriefing everyone personally that has seen the pyramid. They want all documents and photographs handed over, now I suppose that will include you."

Henderson finishes his coffee then prepares to leave,

"See you all tomorrow you'll need time to get your things together for the meeting."

Rick asks,

"Mike, can you find out who these people are for me?"

"I'll try, call you later after I've seen the CO, the shit's going to really hit the fan when I tell him what's happened."

At last they are alone as they watch the last of the Humvee's move out. It's now 06:30 Sam makes three more coffees,

"We need to decide exactly what we're prepared to say tomorrow, we should make copies of everything we've done so far, our photographs, documentation and translations before they remove all the remaining evidence."

Jo agrees, she goes over to her rucksack, taking out her movie camera she switches it on searching for the film she took inside the pyramid,

"Rick, there's nothing here, it's been deleted."

"It was probably the electromagnetic field, similar to the old X Ray at airports, when we get back I'll get some specialists at NSA to see if they can recover anything."

Jo is annoyed,

"That's all the proof gone of what was inside the pyramid, all I've got left are the prints I took from outside when I first surveyed it."

Rick tells her not to worry then starts taking backups of everything on his laptop as does Sam who seems more tranquil about the loss of the camera data.

One hour later the field phone startles them Rick picks it up, its Henderson,

"Rick I've just come out from meeting with the CO, he's very sensitive about what's happened, he won't tell me much but he's been in touch with the head of the group that are on route, they know you're OK. They also saw the pyramid vanish from their satellite screens."

"Mike who are they?"

"Four of the top officials from the Pentagon reporting to the Director of the Defense Intelligence Agency the others are Feds, that's all I can tell you. The CO has asked me to transfer you to secure accommodation at the base I'll pick you up at 15.00 if that's enough time to get your gear together."

Rick acknowledges,

"15.00 we'll be ready."

Sam asks,

"Rick what's that all about."

"It looks as if matters are being taken out of our hands, the Director of the DIA has sent four agents the others are FBI. The CO wants us in secure accommodation this evening Mike's picking us up at 15:00."

Jo looks worried,

"Sam what does this mean?"

"I think we are in for some very serious questioning."

Rick interrupts,

"More like interrogation, that's why the Feds are with them that's their speciality, let's get our stuff together, get into some clean clothes, we have a few hours to discuss and plan our response."

One hour later they're refreshed and have packed all their equipment, taking care to hide their back up CD's amongst personal items. Sam suggests they get some fresh air and take a last look at the site in case it can tell them anything. They step out into the bright sunlight walking across to where the pyramid was. The sand under the footprint of the pyramid is compressed into an almost solid material Sam bends down to touch it,

"It's like concrete."

Jo and Rick are amazed as they look at the large flat area in front of them. Rick is feeling the heat as the sun is reflecting off the sand slab.

"It's unbelievable, there's nothing we can do here let's get back into the cool."

They return to the portacabin, Sam takes three cold beers from the fridge,

"Ok let's talk this out."

They sit round the table, Jo is the first to speak,

"We seem to have two options, either stick to the story we told Henderson to allow us time to decide the best course of action, or tell them we'll explain everything personally to the President or the Director of the DIA."

Rick's opinion is:

"It would be better to give them some information tomorrow, as if we use a cover story and then changed it later we'd lose credibility, we have to give them enough to ensure that we get the opportunity to tell the whole story to the Director or President, it's a matter of National Security we don't want junior staff knowing too much at this stage."

Sam doesn't agree,

"Why tell them anything tomorrow, just that it's a matter of National Security and that we need direct access to the top people to deliver the message personally, perhaps outline the possible consequences if they do not heed our warning."

Jo is an agreement with Sam,

"I think that's what we should do, you OK with that Rick?"

"Yes, I agree it's better to keep our powder dry until we have the right people in front of us, although they won't be too happy tomorrow."

Sam smiles,

"I don't give a fuck if they're happy or not, we've one chance to put our case and the Director of the DIA has more power than the President."

Jo has one condition,

"Rick, we only travel first class no more long haul helicopter rides."

"OK then that's settled, we'll have to be very careful how we handle this."

Sam has one more question,

"Rick, will this compromise your position with your NSA masters?"

"No, they all talk to each other, the NSA works alongside the DIA so I don't anticipate a problem."

They decide to go to their rooms for a rest before Henderson arrives. Sam lies back on his bunk with his hands under his head, he closes his eyes, immediately; he hears Aacaarya's voice in his mind,

"That was the right decision, you should start using your powers more, try to concentrate on what others are thinking tomorrow, focus on one person at a time."

Sam concentrates,

"Can you hear me?"

"Of course any time you wish to contact me, just concentrate on me as if we were facing each other, we'll be with you all the way."

Sam is already feeling a little tired with the effort,

"Sam the more you make use your ability the less tired you'll be, practice listening to people's thoughts, it will be of great help when you reach the Pentagon, but keep this capability to yourself do not make anyone, particularly Rick and Jo, aware of how advanced your skills are becoming, we have provided the demonstration you asked for, stay well."

Sam asks,

"How did you do it?"

"Not now, when you're stronger."

Sam drops into a shallow sleep, an hour later he is woken by further banging on the door of the portacabin. Henderson's driver has arrived, he helps them load their gear into the back of the Humvee they're driven quickly across the desert to the main buildings. They stop outside the mess block, in front of which are two armed marines who stand to attention as Rick approaches.

One of them addresses Rick,

"Sir, Major Henderson is waiting inside, go right in."

They go directly into an office area where the administration sergeant leads them through to a bar and lounge area. The lounge has a number of tables each surrounded by four worn leather armchairs, Henderson is sitting at one of the tables and waves them over, they sit down beside him,

"Would you like a drink"?

He calls the white jacketed waiter over ordering four beers that rapidly arrive on a silver tray. Henderson explains,

"This is what we use as the officers mess, its basic and the food's not too bad. We've provided three rooms for you as it's more comfortable and secure than the Portacabin's. The driver is putting your gear in your rooms, when you're ready to eat just call the waiter he'll organise it."

"We have a large reasonably well appointed meeting room in the mess that we'll be using tomorrow."

Rick asks,

"And why the security, what are you expecting?"

"You guys are celebrities now, can't risk misplacing you again, its orders from the top. So as I'm seeing them first I've got reports to prepare for early tomorrow morning, if you're OK I'll see you in the morning at 10.00 hours."

Henderson gets up to leave, his driver returns then offers to show them to their three single rooms which are conveniently close to the lounge area. Rick organises dinner,

"I'll call you at 19:00 we can plan our strategy in the bar."

They retire for another brief rest as they're still suffering low energy from their travel experience. At precisely 19:00 Rick knocks on their doors simultaneously both open immediately

"You two ready?"

As usual, Jo is famished,

"You bet, let's see if they have lobster."

Sam counters,

"More like hamburger and chips or field rations."

They amble through to the bar which is now getting crowded with off duty officers who're relaxing with drinks and conversation. As soon as the waiter sees them come in, he goes over to Rick,

"Sir, I've reserved your table over there, it's a little quieter, not that anywhere's quiet at this time of the evening."

They follow him to a table in the corner near a window and flop down in the comfortable old leather armchairs. They are looked at as oddities by the other officers as they are the only ones in civilian dress. The waiter brings their beers over with a handwritten sheet of paper,

"I'm sorry but that's all we have on the menu."

They order three large steaks and fries. Rick wants to make sure they're up to speed for tomorrow.

"When we arrive they'll already have seen Henderson's and your photographs of the pyramid, they'll speak with us as a group, but knowing the Feds they'll want to speak to us individually afterwards which we must deny them"

After dinner they decide to retire early to their rooms.

The next morning at 10.00 am they're waiting outside the meeting room. The door opens a young man comes out introducing himself.

"Good morning, I'm Steve Johnson"

He immediately recognises Rick,

"Rick, it's good to see you again, I'm surprised to find you involved with ancient pyramids, not your scene at all."

Rick shakes his hand,

"You know me, I can never say no, it must've been three years ago, still with the FBI?" Steve puts an arm round Ricks shoulder,

"Yes as always, you saved my arse then remember?"

Rick introduces him to Jo and Sam, Steve asks them to follow him. They enter a large room with folding tables set together to form a large open square, around the walls are white boards on trestles covered with photographs of the pyramid and satellite images. There are four men seated on the opposite side, they're all in the same desert fatigues as Steve with no rank indication. Steve offers them seats facing the men then sits down with them. Before anything is said the door opens and a waiter wheels in a trolley of coffees, serving a mug to all of them. Once he leaves, the man in the centre introduces himself,

"My name is Major George Dwyer I'm from the Defense Intelligence Agency and have been tasked with leading this investigation, you can call me George."

He reaches out in front of him opening three large folders,

"I've studied your interesting backgrounds in great detail and would conclude from what I have read that you are serious credible people that would present facts as you found them. The other people here are my associates you don't need to know their names at this stage. Could we start with you telling me exactly what happened from the moment you arrived? We have Henderson's detailed report and have reviewed the photographic data."

Sam remembering what Aacaarya told him is quietly concentrating on George trying to explore his thoughts, it takes him some time to focus and clear his mind of the other people in the room. Then almost as if something clicked inside his mind he was able to hear George's thinking behind his questions.

Rick explains,

"I was instructed by my director at the NSA to investigate this find because of the strange electromagnetic fields the Pyramid was generating and the ancient symbols. To do this, I needed an ancient language expert and a specialist in pyramids; Jo and Sam were top of my list."

Rick waits for a moment then continues to explain everything from the time they arrived to the moment that they opened the door to the pyramid. At that point George asks,

"How did you manage to open the door when Henderson failed?"

Rick explains that Sam had managed to translate the symbols around the door which he believed were numbers,

"I thought that they might be frequencies and used a frequency modulator to work through them, we struck lucky the door opened but closed automatically after we were inside."

George raises another question,

"How could a 4000 year old pyramid have a frequency lock? Henderson's report states that you were trapped inside and lost your way amongst the passages for five days with barely enough water and rations for twenty four hours. I want to know exactly what happened in that pyramid and what you found."

Rick takes a drink of water,

"With respect to your rank sir, what we've discovered and what happened to us is a highly classified matter that affects our national and global security, as a result we can only give our full report to the Director of the DIA personally."

George is surprised,

"What did you say?"

Rick repeats himself as George cuts in,

"All of us in this room have 'Top Secret' security clearances and I am the director's second in command, the Deputy Director."

"I'm sorry sir, but the message that we have, has to be given directly to the Director, you have read our files and know that we would not make this request unless we knew it was absolutely essential. My security clearances are 'Top Secret' too, which is why we must ask you to organise our transfer to the Pentagon."

George whispers to the two people either side of him then looks back at Rick.

"Are you speaking for your associates?"

"Yes."

Sam is relieved to discover that George seems genuinely concerned and understanding of their predicament.

George asks,

"Rick is there anything that you can tell me to justify this request."

Rick turns and whispers to Jo and Sam who nod, Rick continues,

"You now know that this pyramid had a frequency lock, which is remarkable enough for what we believe to be a more than 8000 year old structure and further, you've witnessed by satellite imaging, the fact that the Pyramid disappeared without trace after we escaped.

This clearly demonstrates that we are dealing with something completely out of the ordinary and behind it is a very advanced civilisation with power beyond anything that currently exists in our technological world today."

Sam for some reason is drawn away from George towards Steve he slowly regains his focus trying to explore what Steve is thinking. This time he finds it easier to clear his mind of the others and connecting with Steve finds that Steve is not thinking about their position but his own and how he can get prior access to the information. Sam is very disturbed by this, which causes him to lose concentration. He realises that he has broken into a slight sweat with the effort and returns his mind to the meeting before anyone notices.

George is making notes then looks up,

"That's very true."

I have one last question,

"Have you had direct contact with the advanced civilisation?"

Rick whispers again to Sam and Jo, who nod in agreement,

"Yes we all have."

George speaks quietly to his aides then addresses them,

"We appreciate that your report may appear to some, beyond comprehension and therefore your desire for secrecy. I look forward to hearing your detailed report and have just given authorisation for you to accompany us back to the United States; we'll be leaving this afternoon. In the meantime you are not to speak to anyone on or off the base and will remain together at all times. Steve and his team are assigned to you twenty four hours a day as your personal security.

We will inform him when the travel logistics are in place, any questions?"

"No sir and thank you for your trust."
Jo interrupts,

"One question sir, will we be flying by Jet?"
Sam smiles and George laughs,

"Of course, I heard about Sam and Ricks experience with the Pave Hawk, we'll only use a helicopter for the short trip to a nearby military airbase in Baghdad, then its military first class direct to KADW in Virginia."

"Thank you sir, but what's KADW?"
George smiles at her,

"It's the identity code for Andrews Air Force Base where the Presidential aircraft are kept including Air Force One."
They turn and leave the room. Once outside Steve tells them,

"We'll return to your rooms so that you can pack, then have lunch in the mess and be ready to leave."
The four of them go back to their rooms. Steve follows Rick into his room.

"Rick if there's anything you want me to look after, reports or backup information I can place it in the secure bag."
Rick turns with a slight concern on his face which passes instantly.

"No, no thanks Steve we don't have anything, we've not had time to commit anything to paper from a security point of view it is best left in our heads, thanks anyway."
Steve leaves,

"I'll be outside."
As he packs, Rick is wondering what the real motivation behind Steve's offer was. They finish packing their gear then head for the bar with Steve in tow behind them.

The bar is almost empty. After lunch they're having coffee when Steve touches his earpiece.

"The helicopter's on its way, we leave in half an hour, excuse me a moment I have to make a call."

Steve leaves them alone in the bar. As soon as he's out of sight Sam leans close to Rick,

"Rick how well do you know him?"

"Not well, we were involved in an operation together about three years ago, why?"

"I don't think we can trust him, we must be careful what we say around him."

"What makes you say that?"

"Call it a very strong instinct."

"Strange you should feel that, I had an odd feeling when he came into my room, he wanted to know if we had any documents or anything we needed him to place in the secure baggage, I told him we didn't have time to prepare anything it's all in our heads."

"I agree let's not write anything down, it's safer just us knowing until we make our verbal report to the Pentagon."

At that moment Steve returns,

"All finished, let's get our gear to the front door."

They gather in the entrance of the building watching as a Black Pave Hawk helicopter hovers close stirring up sand and dust as it lands, George with his four associates are waiting nearby in a parked Humvee. The door of the helicopter slides open, George and his associates walk across with their bags keeping their heads down as the rotors continue spinning.

Once they are aboard Steve ushers Rick, Sam and Jo across to the helicopter, they step up to the cabin to find that the Pave Hawk has been converted for personnel transportation with several rows of seats. Jo, Sam and Rick sit together in front of George's team with Steve and two other FBI agents sitting in front of them. They put on ear defenders to drown out the noise of the engines. Steve turns behind to Rick,

"Baghdad airport is 30 minutes away."

"Thanks."

Rick relays this information to Jo and Sam,

Chapter - 12

Attack above the Atlantic

Half an hour later the helicopter lands beside a Department of the Navy executive jet with American markings. As the door opens they are hit by the heat of the airport, they quickly disembark with their bags, crossing to the waiting aircraft, which Rick recognises as a Gulfstream V/550. They wait at the foot of the boarding ladder as their bags are stowed in the aircraft hold, Rick smiles at Jo and Sam,

"You'll both enjoy this flight, the Gulfstream is one of the finest business Jets in the world." Climbing the steps they enter the very sumptuous cabin then are ushered by the one crew member, a young efficient woman in a USAF uniform, through the first cabin which has four luxurious leather seats, two each side with a window and small table between them, then along into the second cabin which is the same layout as the first, they are told this is their area. As the doors between the cabins are open they can see George and his men sitting further back in the rear cabin. Sam, Jo and Rick are sitting together leaving a spare seat in their cabin, as they hoped Steve decided to locate himself with his two associates in the forward cabin. Once they're strapped in the young woman comes back and explains,

"As soon as we're airborne I'll bring some drinks, the galley is forward the two toilets and washrooms are in the rear of the aircraft, any questions for now?"

Jo asks,

"How long will the flight take?"

"We usually cruise at about 51,000 feet, it's a nonstop flight of 6211 miles, and at our cruising speed of 530 miles per hour will take approximately 12 hours depending on winds, plus we've a first class galley with everything you may require for a comfortable flight."

The engines whine to a start as the attendant turns,

"See you later I've got to go."

They relax as they sink back into the luxurious soft leather seats. The Gulfstream taxis to the runway, lines up on runway 33R and holds, the pilot carries out his engine checks, a few minutes later the whine from the twin Rolls Royce 710 engines increases in volume as the pilot releases the brakes sending the aircraft racing down the runway. The Gulfstream quickly climbs away from the desert, the undercarriage motors whir quietly under their feet as the wheels are locked away. The Gulfstream with its rear mounted engines is exceptionally quiet as it makes a banking turn to the left bringing them onto their new heading.

Jo is looking at a map she found in the seat pocket,

"Rick, where do we go from here?"

"This heading will take us across Syrian airspace then out over the Mediterranean, Spain into the Atlantic to Newfoundland with a short leg over to Andrews Air Force Base."

"Syrian airspace, is that allowed to military aircraft?"

"Don't worry, we have special clearances for such events, usually linked to something the Syrians want from us, it's a reciprocal arrangement."

The attendant arrives with a small trolley of drinks. Sam and Rick help themselves to large malt whiskies and pass one to Jo. The Gulfstream is now at its cruise altitude of 51,000 feet, they unbuckle their seat belts, reclining the seats for more comfort. George comes through carrying a glass and sits down in the empty seat,

"Hope you three are comfortable. There're blankets and pillows in the overhead lockers if you need them."

Sam is pleased to see George as he feels that he could be a useful ally,

"This is the way to travel, much better than my trip from West Africa to Iraq."

George sips his drink,

"Yeah, that must have been a horrific journey I heard that the landing was rather spectacular too."

Sam raises his glass,

"To the things we have to put up with for king and country."

George advises,

"With this being a 12 hour nonstop flight I'd try to get some sleep as soon as you can, it might ease the jet lag a little when we arrive."

"What's the plan when we arrive at Andrews Air Force Base?"

"We'll be met and driven the short distance to the Pentagon where the meeting with the Director and Commander, Lieutenant General Alexander Mitchell will take place. You can see we are taking your experience very seriously indeed."

Jo wants to know,

"What time should we arrive?"

George looks at his watch,

"Airborne at 16:38 hours Baghdad time which is 08:38 Washington DC time, add 12 hours flight time depending on head winds then say two hours to get from Andrews to the Pentagon that should mean we arrive at around 22.38 hours for supper, this aircraft has secure communications with the Pentagon so if anything changes I'll let you know."

"Thank you George."

George stands up,

"Thanks to you guys it's been a long few days, so if you don't mind I'm going to get some shut eye."

They watch him go, Sam tells Jo he's a good feeling about George she feels the same. Sam pours another round of drinks as Rick opens the overhead locker taking out three blankets and pillows which he deposits on the spare seat to put off further visitors from the forward cabin. They settle down for the long flight and are about to dim their cabin lights when Steve comes through, then noticing that they're ready for sleep, he sits down in front of Rick who is reading,

"Sorry to disturb you but just wanted to make sure you had everything you needed, I noticed George with you, everything OK with him?"
Rick puts his magazine aside,

"Yes thanks, very comfortable, George is fine, just talked about the flight time."
Steve starts to get up,

"I'll leave you to sleep; I expect it'll be good to have some quiet time together during the morning to get your report prepared."
Rick yawns,

"Yeah it will, good night."
Steve wanders back to his cabin to join his companions. They close their eyes falling into a drink induced shallow sleep. Four hours later they are disturbed by the sound of the military pilot's footsteps walking urgently through their cabin and into the rear cabin. He wakes George who then follows the pilot back through their cabin towards the cockpit, disturbing the three of them as he passes. After five minutes George returns,

"Sorry about that, I tried not to disturb you."
Rick asks,

"Do we have a problem?"
George sits down,

"It appears we have company, a small jet has been shadowing us since we left the coast he's staying a good distance behind us. It doesn't look as if he knows we're on to him so I've asked the NSA to obtain a satellite image to identify whose it is, we'll know soon."
Jo is now wide awake,

"But why would anyone want to do that?"
George smiles,

"You three with your knowledge are very hot property."

Sam joins in,

"But no one knows we are here or who we are."

George's face is more serious,

"True, no one should have known who or where you were, but there's no such thing as definitive security, once a message is sent, even in an encrypted state, who knows who else is listening. I've already organised an audit trail of exactly who knew about this mission and who they may have contacted, not that I expect any answers from doing so. Don't forget your vanishing pyramid would also have been picked up by satellites that don't belong to the USA."

Rick leans towards him,

"Presumably we'll shortly have someone shadowing him."

"That's in hand, a pair of F16's are on route to intercept in 20 minutes, it could just be coincidence, but I don't believe in coincidences, go back to sleep, there's nothing to worry about." Sam is now wide awake,

"Thanks George, please let us know when you hear more."

George promises to let them know immediately he hears anything and leaves. Jo has a slight look of concern,

"Rick I hadn't thought about other countries knowing about the pyramid."

"Every country has specialist personnel constantly scanning for anything odd happening in the rest of the world, it's a safe bet our pyramid's mysterious appearance and disappearance would certainly have raised eyebrows, its normal intelligence service practice, I wouldn't worry about it."

Sam has now poured them each another large whisky nightcap,

"Let's leave it to the professionals and get as much sleep as we can, I've a feeling we're going to need it."

They finish their drinks and crash out again,

One hour later they are disturbed again by the urgent rush of feet of the second pilot passing through their cabin. George is instantly awake and quickly follows the pilot to the cockpit.

There's a murmur of voices from the front cabin, something's happened. Rick gets up and goes forward to speak to Steve,

"What's up?"

Steve is looking anxious,

"They sent two F16's to intercept the aircraft that was following us."

Rick is impatient,

"We know that, what happened?"

"Rick, the aircraft destroyed both F16's and has resumed its position five miles astern of us."

"Did they manage to identify the aircraft?"

"Surprisingly no, all they said before they were hit was that it was an unmarked fighter possibly similar to our F-117 Nighthawk Stealth Attack Aircraft but different, that's all."

Rick asks,

"Could it have been one of ours?"

"No, George checked that, all 59 of our Nighthawks have been accounted for, although the Chinese are reputed to be working on their own version with the Russians, the J-XX it might be one of theirs although it's not supposed to be flying yet."

Rick thanks him and returns to the others, George is still in the cockpit with the pilots. As soon as he gets back to his seat Jo and Sam want to know what's going on, Rick tells them what Steve has told him. Jo is upset,

"Those F16 pilots are dead because of us."

"We don't know that for certain, they could equally be after George he's Deputy Head of DIA."

Sam asks,

"What next?"

Rick is about to answer when George comes in,

"You've heard the sad news about the F16's."

Jo buts in,

"Was it because of us?"

George puts an arm round her shoulder,

"We have no idea why, it could be that being a military flight we're being tracked and when the F16's intercepted the aircraft the pilot panicked and fired off two missiles."

Sam wants to know,

"George what happens now, I understand the aircraft is still behind us."

"Yes, but at a safe distance, he seems to be content just tracking us, we've scrambled a flight of six F16's from a carrier task force, one is equipped with an anti stealth radar, they should be here in 40 minutes."

Sam just thought of something,

"If it's a stealth aircraft how can our radar see it?"

"Sam, this Gulfstream is equipped with the same equipment as Air Force One, although we can't see it, we're able to track its heat signature in real time relayed from one of our satellites, for your comfort we are also fitted with the latest missile countermeasure systems."

At that moment the pilot's urgent voice comes over the intercom,

"Fasten seat belts, seat backs upright, prepare for evasive action."

George rushes back to his seat and buckles in. Rick helps Jo with her seat belt,

"Don't worry but expect some extreme manoeuvres."

In the cockpit the captain and second pilot are at a state of high alert, the second pilot is studying a display screen showing the Gulfstream, behind them is a green light marking the jets trail that's following them. The second pilot is providing a running commentary,

"He's closed to missile range, trying a missile lock, he's fired two missiles inbound."

On the screen two thin red lines track rapidly towards them from the jet. The captain suddenly throws the Gulfstream into a tight turn to port, at the same time he puts the aircraft into a steep dive as the automatic missile countermeasures are deployed. The pod on the Gulfstream releases flares and chaff, at the same time starting infrared jamming to confuse the missile guidance systems. The Gulfstream is now descending at high speed as they feel the shock wave of two explosions above them. The second pilot is glued to the screen,

"Christ that was close, they exploded in the chaff cloud."

The captain eases the Gulfstream out of its dive and levels out,

"Where's the jet?"

The second pilot can't believe his eyes,

"It's vanished."

The captain orders,

"Check again that's impossible."

After a few moments the second pilot confirms

"Everything is working correctly, there's no heat signature he's completely gone, just vanished."

The captain climbs the Gulfstream back to their cruise altitude and resumes his heading. The second pilot confirms that the screen is clear. The captain announces on the intercom

"It's OK the threat has gone you can relax now."

In the cabin there is the sound of relief as seat belts are undone. George comes through to check on the three of them who are tidying up the mess of blankets and cushions that had been thrown round their cabin,

"You OK in here?"

Jo is the most shaken,

"Sam that was frightening."

Sam smiling turns to Rick,

"Not as bad as our Pave Hawk landing was it Rick."

The second pilot comes through. George greets him,

"That was a brilliantly executed manoeuvre, well done, but what happened to the fighter?"

The pilot explains the mysterious disappearance of the Jet. Rick looks at Sam and whispers,

"Just like the pyramid."

George excuses himself and goes forward to the cabin to thank the Captain for his remarkable evasion of the two heat seeking missiles.

The captain explains,

"It was really down to the missile countermeasure system, first time I've used them in a Gulfstream, it was a little hairy as you never know what they're firing at you."

George asks,

"Any theories about the fighter did one of its own missiles get it?"

"Not possible, we were watching the screen the whole time, the missiles exploded in the chaff cloud well away from the aircraft, it literally just disappeared, no explosion, nothing, it was being monitored by the satellite which confirmed it."

"Do you have any idea where it came from?"

The captain replies,

"No, there was no positive ID all we know is that it was an advanced stealth technology aircraft and not one of ours."

George turns to leave,

"Thanks again, we owe you our lives."

He heads back speaking to Steve's guys as he passes through their cabin,

As George comes into Ricks cabin he sees Sam opening a new bottle of Lagavoulin malt whisky, the last bottle although almost empty, became a victim of the Gulfstream's sudden turn, he smiles

"Pour me one too, I need it."

He takes his glass and takes a sip, closing his eyes in delight,

"That's good, very good."
Then he looks more seriously at the three of them,

"You must have a guardian angel somewhere, if that Jet had been able to continue his attack we would not have been so lucky a second time."
Jo asks,

"Were those bumps from the missiles?"
George nods,

"Yes, they were pressure waves the captain did a phenomenal job. Our navy pilots are some of the very best."

"Rick, when you said the Jet disappeared just like the pyramid what did you mean?"
Rick looks him in the eye,

"I was speaking metaphorically, both vanished suddenly and without trace, that's all." George is not quite convinced,

"We'll leave it for now, let's try and get some rest."
George returns to his cabin.
Sam leans across to Rick,

"He's got a point, I wonder if we do have someone keeping an eye on us, someone with a vested interest in the success of our mission."

"It's a reassuring thought."
They recline their seats, dim the cabin lights and settle down for the remainder of the flight.
Sam closes his eyes, but his mind is active and curious, he focuses on Aacaarya using all his concentration and asks,

"Aacaarya did you have anything to do with the Jet disappearing?"

"Of course, I told you we'd be with you all the way. The attack on your aircraft was an unprecedented attack on our mission we had to intervene."

"Then thank you for saving us, but do you know who sent it and why?"

"The aircraft was built in China but sold through Russia to an American Corporation. We transported it to an unused hangar at your destination 'Andrews Air Force Base', it's the hanger furthest North on the apron beside the western runway. At the appropriate time you can tell them where it is, your people should be able to investigate its origin and ownership. It will also help as a further demonstration of our abilities."

"But why Aacaarya, how did they know where to find us?"

"One of the new people is communicating with others outside his organisation, that's all I am able to tell you, you must work the rest out yourselves, use your skills, goodbye for now." Aacaarya's face fades from Sam's mind as he falls into a deep sleep. The rest of the trip is uneventful until they are awoken several hours later by the smell of fresh coffee drifting through the cabins. The first light of dawn breaks into the cabin as the attendant comes in with a large tray of fresh coffee and orange.

She smiles at Sam,

"That was quite an eventful night did you manage to get any sleep?"

"Yes, in between the odd missile attack, how about you?"

She pours three coffees,

"No, I'm used to not sleeping on flights its part of the job, there's a continental or cooked breakfast, which would you prefer?"

Rick and Sam order full cooked breakfasts, including Jo who normally does not eat breakfast attracting a look of disproval from Rick,

"Rick, we need all the energy we can get."

The attendant makes a note,

"OK, three specials in about 10 minutes."

She moves to the rear cabin.

The flight is smooth as they skirt across the Atlantic Ocean heading for Newfoundland. Jo glances out of the cabin window and starts as she sees three F16's flying alongside,

"For a moment I thought we had another problem."

Rick laughs,

"There's three more my side, they're our escort to Andrews, they're not taking any more chances."

They have a leisurely breakfast with lots of coffee, after the tables are cleared Jo heads to through the rear cabin to the washrooms.

Rick moves over next to Sam and speaks quietly,

"We need to find out who was behind that attack and who on board is setting us up."

"Yeah I've been thinking a lot about that too, you recall Steve has been very keen for us to produce a written report."

"Rick, I thought that was strange too. I've an idea, why don't we get my laptop down and be seen by everyone to be creating something, then back it up to CD with you and me having a copy each in our pockets, I could scribble a couple of meaningless pages in Sanskrit which they would have to get translated and would take time. We could use it as bait to see whose interested enough to steal it, we could easily watch each other and it might just take the heat off us, if they think they have got what they wanted."

Rick agrees,

"It's worth a try. OK that's agreed let's get on with it".

Sam makes a show of getting his laptop down out of the overhead locker, when he's certain that he has been seen from both the front and rear cabins, he sets it up on the table, then goes through to Steve,

"Steve, sorry to disturb you, but where're the power points for a laptop?"

"No problem report time eh?"

Sam nods Steve shows him where the point is situated under the tables. Sam returns plugging in his laptop.

He and Jo are concentrating on the screen as one of the guys from the rear cabin passes through,

"Working hard then?"

Sam looks up,

"After last night's events I thought we should get our report written."

"Good idea" and he moves on into the forward cabin.

It takes Sam an hour to finish what he was doing then he makes two CD backups. He places his laptop back into the overhead locker handing a CD to Rick,

"Look after this it's a backup."

Rick places it in his jacket pocket. Sam does the same then places his jacket on the back of his seat in full view of Rick. The intercom announces that they're now one hour from the Newfoundland Coast and are commencing their descent to 31000 feet. The sun is low in the sky as dinner is served. By the time they finish they're over the coast of Newfoundland heading for Andrews Air Base. The Gulfstream's six F16 escorts peel off to leave the Gulfstream to finish the journey through the relative safety of US airspace.

It's now dark as the Gulfstream commences its landing descent the captain announces that they'll be arriving in half an hour. George is on his way back from the communications area near the cockpit he sits down with Rick,

"How are you all feeling?"

Sam is first to respond,

"Not bad considering, a bit apprehensive about our meeting this evening."

George smiles,

"There's nothing to worry about, it'll be fairly informal Anthony Mitchell is a good man, I think you'll like him, I've known him for over 20 years as a friend and work colleague."

Jo asks,

"Tell me about the Pentagon?"

George looks affectionately at her,

"The Pentagon is the Headquarters of the United States Department of Defense and the nerve centre for command and control of all our forces. It was constructed in 1943 in the middle of World War II and believe it or not, is still regarded as one of the most efficient office complexes in the world, as well as being one of the largest. The Pentagon site covers 583 acres with the building occupying 34 acres including its courtyard. It's like a small city employing around 23,000 military and civilians plus another 3000 non defence support personnel, has its own restaurants including a McDonalds and Taco Bell, a shopping mall, subway, metro, railway station and various historical displays. There're over 17.5 miles of corridors on five floors each of which has close to 1000 offices and two basement floors."

Jo is very impressed.

"I had no idea it was so enormous, how on earth do you find your way around?"

"Everyone in the building is accounted for and has their purpose and place. The Pentagon has its own independent security force 'The Pentagon Force Protection Agency' they makes sure no one gets lost. On a lighter note, as you may know there is an open space in the centre of the Pentagon, this is informally known as 'ground zero', a nickname given to it during the cold war when it was assumed that the Soviet Union would target nuclear missiles at this central point. In the centre of the Plaza there's the Ground Zero Café and snack bar, during the cold war some of our people painted a target on the ground as a bit of gallows humour, although this was quickly painted over after the September 11th terrorist attacks."

They're interrupted by the pilot's intercom,

"Please take your seats and fasten seatbelts, arriving in 10 minutes. We'll be landing on the west runway, from the North, thank you for flying with the US Navy we hope you enjoyed your flight."

Sam asks Rick if he can have the window seat on his side of the aircraft for the landing, Rick switches seats without question. The Gulfstream is now on final approach, as it passes the runway boundary Sam is able to see the oval tops of the row of hangers alongside the apron. As they are arriving from the North it's the first hanger that interests him. The hanger doors are closed and there is no activity near it, unlike the other hangers on that side of the runway where there are considerable signs of activity. He wondered if the Jet is really inside and how it could have been possible. There's a squeal of rubber, the Gulfstream touches down manoeuvring to its taxi way, which takes it onto the western apron where a Black Hawk helicopter is parked. The Gulfstream comes to a halt in the bay beside the Black Hawk. The engines shut down, shortly after which the intercom announces that they can prepare to depart. There is activity around the aircraft as the steps are moved alongside then a blast of cold fresh air comes into the cabins as the main door is opened. After such a long flight they can't wait to get outside to stretch their legs, as they descend the steps they see their bags being quickly taken across to the helicopter. They gather at the base of the steps waiting for George and his people, as they arrive Rick asks,

"I thought we were driving to the Pentagon."
George grins,

"Change of plan, after what happened on the flight, I want to get you there in one piece, it'll only take us 15 minutes by air. It took longer than that to get the clearances to take a helicopter into Pentagon airspace."

Chapter - 13

The Pentagon

They take their seats in the Black Hawk as its engines start and warm up. Jo and Sam sit together Rick is in front of them alone, when one of Steve's guys sits down beside him. The helicopter takes off heading towards the Pentagon passing close to the Jefferson Memorial then over the Potomac River. Jo is glued to the window as the Pentagon comes into sight,

"Sam, look. It's massive."

Sam has been to the Pentagon before but never seen it from this perspective he is surprised too,

"It's a magnificent structure, make the most of this viewing opportunity it's very rare for them to allow aircraft this close."

The Black Hawk pilot banks the helicopter to the north, as he reaches the Pentagon from the south east he hovers over a grassed area near the northern tip of the Pentagon. The helicopter lands neatly on the grass as security guards from the Pentagon arrive to meet it. They disembark whilst the engine and rotors are turning, as the helicopter is only permitted to drop them off. Their bags are quickly taken by the security people who lead them up to the towering walls of the Pentagon. The Black Hawk departs heading back to Andrews Air Base. They are taken through a small door into a security area where they are all searched thoroughly, their bags X rayed and examined.

Visitor badges have been prepared for Rick Sam and Jo, George has his own pass along with his two associates. George gives orders to the head of security to escort Steve and his two FBI men to a rest room where they can be looked after until the meeting is over. Steve is obviously not too happy with this exclusion from the meeting but has no alternative and the three leave, escorted by two security guards. The senior security officer asks George and the others to follow him with another senior security officer bringing up the rear. They enter a large lift and are silently and rapidly taken up to the fifth floor, they step out into a large brightly lit corridor. Jo is taken aback as it seems endless in both directions with numerous numbered office doors on each side,

"It goes on for miles."

The security guard smiles,

"In fact it does Miss, on the five floors alone there are 17.5 miles of corridors, but it's not as bad as it looks, you can walk from any one point of the Pentagon to another point in only 7 minutes. This is zone E where the top brass have their offices, as it's the outer ring of offices they're the only ones with views to the outside world. We only have a short walk to the director's suite."

Jo always full of questions asks,

"How many offices are there on this floor?"

The security guard points to the nearest door numbered 5E475,

"Just under 1000, we're heading for suite number 5E500. It's just along here."

George interrupts,

"It's the office next to mine 5E501."

They follow the security guard along the highly polished corridors, which although it's late at night are a hive of activity with people coming and going to different offices, some in uniform others in civilian clothes. Sam has been deep in thought then drops back behind Rick and Jo. He touches George on the arm,

"George, excuse me could I have a private word?"

George slows his pace so that he and Sam are a slight distance behind the others,

"What's the problem?"

Sam looks around him,

"There's no problem, I know where the Stealth Fighter is and where it came from, we need to confirm this as soon as possible."

George is visibly shocked and suspicious,

"How in the hell, why didn't you tell me earlier?"

"I only found out as we were landing, to be honest I don't trust everyone that was with us." George recovers his composure,

"Explain everything you know to Anthony Mitchell he's 100% trustworthy, but why tell me now?"

"Without going into detail, I didn't want it to surprise you, in front of General Mitchell. Jo and Rick don't know either."

George smiles,

"Tony and me go back a long way, thank you for the thought, always remember I'm a great poker player, we'll talk later."

After a five minute walk they arrive outside suite number 5E500. George uses his pass to open the security lock they enter a reception area with comfortable seating from which there are three doors. The reception desk is manned by a female naval officer in uniform who greets George then asks them to take a seat. Picking up her telephone she announces their arrival. A few seconds later the door is hurriedly opened and an immaculately uniformed three star army General greets them with a smile.

He has very short cropped greying hair with piercing blue eyes. He stands very upright with broad shoulders and obviously very fit his 6' 3" bulky frame seems to fill the door space. He welcomes them with a firm hand shake as he introduces himself,

"My friends call me Tony don't they George?"

He slaps George on the back then shakes hands with his two aides,

"Well we've a lot to talk about, come on in we've constantly running coffee with a buffet." They follow him into a large suite, in the centre is a large highly polished meeting table he guides them to some luxurious chairs in front of his magnificent desk, behind which is a leather swivel chair. They each have a small table beside their chairs, coffee is brought in. All down one side of the office are large tinted glass windows through which they can see into the dark night, illuminated only by the lights of the Jefferson Memorial in the near distance, just across the Potomac River. It's obvious to them that Anthony Mitchell is an extremely professional and efficient man, someone who is used to successfully achieving his goals. The phrase 'Failure is not an option' springs into Sam's mind as he tries to weigh up the General.

"Right then, let's get down to business. I've studied each of your backgrounds, all of which are impressive I've noted that you've done good work for the NSA in the past which is why I respected your request to make your report to me personally. I understand you've a lot of interesting things to tell us about your very unusual trip. Before you start, I'm already aware of everything that happened up to the time you entered the pyramid and from when George met with you. I've seen all of the photographic evidence and studied Henderson's reports, so perhaps you can start with how you managed to get into the pyramid then what happened inside."

Sam explains he'd been working on translating the various symbols found on what they had identified as the entry portal, they proved to be sequences of numbers but there was no obvious way of entering them. Rick came up with the idea that they could be frequencies and used a modulator to convert the numbers into frequencies. Rick interrupts,

"It was only after Sam suggested that perhaps they should be used together that the door finally opened."

Rick goes on to explain the layout inside and the level of technology they discovered which contradicted the fact that the pyramid was constructed over 8000 years ago. Rick tells them how they found the central chamber describing it very accurately then how they entered the control room becoming trapped when the door automatically closed and they finally passed out.

Sam takes over from when they recovered consciousness, describing everything that happened during their time in the parallel world including the conversation with the Elders and their message.

Rick outlines his escape plan and how they got into the pyramid in the centre of Atlantis then using it to transport them back, culminating in Henderson's arrival telling them the pyramid had vanished, the rest they knew.

Sam asks Jo,

"Did we leave anything out?"

"No that's exactly what happened and to be honest I was shocked to discover the things we are doing to the Ionosphere."

George stops her continuing,

"There's something else, Sam explain to Tony what you told me about the Stealth fighter."

Sam takes a sip of coffee, Tony looks directly at him,

"Want something stronger?"

Sam nods,

"A whisky would be great."

Tony presses a button on his desk a few seconds later a bottle of malt arrives with four glasses,

"I think we all need one."

Sam takes a large swig from his glass then continues,

"As we were landing I was told by Aacaarya that they'd been responsible for saving us from the attack, as they had a vested interest in the success of our mission. He told me that the Stealth aircraft was built in China and sold through Russia to an American Corporation."

Rick and Jo look at Sam in shock,

"You didn't tell us that."

"No, I didn't have the opportunity with the Feds always so close."

Sam then explains,

"More remarkably Aacaarya told me that they had transported the Stealth Fighter to an unused hanger at Andrews for our examination and investigation, they did so to provide further tangible evidence of their capabilities. He said nothing about what had happened to the pilot."

The suite is in silence, no one speaks but the bottle is passed around again, Sam is trying to probe the mind of Tony finding that his motivation and thoughts appear to be genuine.

Tony comments first,

"It's almost an unbelievable story but I have to accept that everything you have told me is genuine and supported by tangible evidence, George I want you to get over to Andrews and see for yourself if the aircraft is there."

Sam interrupts,

"Sir, the condition is that we go along too, I know which hanger it's in, and we've a vested interest in finding out who's behind this."

Tony looks at George,

"OK after this meeting, you all go and take a look, but only the Commander of the Airbase will know why you are there, no one else."

George agrees,

"I'll organise it."

Jo is feeling very tired,

"I've had enough of aircraft for the time being, so if you boys want to look at your toys, that's OK with me but I need my bed so I'll pass on this one."

Tony has a question,

"Sam, how do you manage to communicate with them?"

Sam decides to explain a little,

"Aacaarya and I have a telepathic connection."

Tony asks,

"Can anyone else use it?"

"No it's something between us only."

"Then we're going to have to take very good care of you."

Jo would like to know his initial reaction,

"Tony, what about their message, their demands to stop the experiments, will this be done?"

"There's a lot more to this than just experiments, I don't doubt that your friends are aware of this and the powerful organisations behind this multifaceted research. Tomorrow morning I'll meet with the Secretaries of State and Defense and the President to discuss if the USA is able to accommodate their requests, and if we believe it's possible to convince the other countries to do the same."

Sam interrupts,

"Tony this is not something they have any choice over or time for negotiation, if they don't stop these experiments and start dismantling the sites, it'll be done for them. Sir, with respect, but do you realise they have the power to make the Pentagon, Whitehouse and the Russian Federations Ministry of Defense cease to exist, as they did with the millions of tonnes of stone in the pyramid and plucking the Stealth Fighter out of the air at a precise moment then delivering it half way across the globe in an instant."

"Sam I'm sorry, perhaps I didn't make myself clear, I'll personally do everything to accomplish the goals of this mission. The decisions are not mine we have to co-ordinate and convince other countries to do the same contemporaneously. More importantly we have to put in place arrangements to compensate for the loss of certain functions, for example if we closed a facility like HAARP tomorrow, one of the consequences would be that we would lose all communications with our deep water nuclear submarines. That has to be considered along with the fact that whoever is behind the attack on our Gulfstream has the resources and capability to attack any one of our other VIP aircraft including Air Force One."

Sam is not overly confident,

"Tony, that's the USA's problem not theirs, we have three weeks to demonstrate that we're serious in meeting their demands."

"Sam let me have two, three days at the maximum then I'll be able to give you a clearer answer we'll need you on standby, as you may be required to meet with the President and possibly the ministers from the other countries involved. I've recorded our discussion which will be transcribed into my report tonight and on their desks tomorrow morning. A copy will be sent to you at the Hotel by secure personal courier."

Rick asks'

"Sir is there anything else?"

"Not at the moment, in my 30 years in the army, this is the first time I've been presented with facts that are almost inconceivable that I must use to convince narrow minded politicians to agree with. You three have given me an enormous amount to think about."

Sam smiles,

"Tony, perhaps I can help there, I could ask the Elders to remove the Whitehouse and The Kremlin that should get their attention and would convince the sceptical politicians. I'm joking of course for the moment."

"Sam what a dangerous friend you can be, I'll certainly be very careful not to upset you. On a practical note, George can you arrange transport to take our friends here to Andrews then back to their hotel, we've booked you into the secure Presidential suite at the Mandarin Oriental Hotel it's just across the river, you three will be together and your FBI friends will provide security."

Jo asks,

"What about me?"

Tony laughs,

"George will arrange for you to go back immediately to the Hotel with Steve and his team."

Tony asks George to call him immediately he's confirmed the existence of the Stealth Fighter and to have Andrews put a permanent guard on the hanger, no one goes in without Tony's authority. Tomorrow we'll have our stealth specialists look it over; there may be something in it to indicate its current owners, who must at this moment be quite upset having lost a $45 million airplane."

Sam interrupts,

"Tony, we don't know if that was the only stealth aircraft they had, maybe they have others."

"I've already considered that worrying possibility. If you'd been travelling in a normal aircraft and not in our specially defended Gulfstream's we wouldn't be having this meeting."

"George on your way back you can drop Sam and Rick at the Hotel, as it's going to be almost dawn, we've given instructions for them not be disturbed during the day."

Tony sighs,

"Now I'll wish you a good night, some of us have work to do, thank you for a most extraordinary and fascinating briefing."

He shakes their hands,

"See you in 24 hours."

Jo leaves with one of the Security Guards who had been waiting outside, then is taken to the rest room where Steve and his men are waiting. Together they go to the main entrance, where there are two large black GMC four wheel drive vehicles with tinted windows. The driver of the first one takes Jo with her FBI team to the hotel which is 15 minutes away from the Pentagon.

George, Rick and Sam follow the other Security Guard to the main entrance and take the other vehicle, the driver informs them,

"It'll take about 90 minutes to Andrews at this time of night, maybe a little less."

George and Sam are sat together in the back with Rick up front. The driver hands Rick a Smith & Wesson M&P Compact Automatic then passes two others over to George and Sam with spare magazine clips.

Sam looks at George and the automatic in his hand,

"Why? Are you expecting trouble?"

George grins,

"Tony's orders trouble seems to follow you around so it seems sense to take a few low tech precautions."

They pocket their weapons then strap in as the driver races out of the Pentagons driveway Sam asks George,

"What did you think about the briefing?"

George considers the question,

"I think we've a good ally in Tony Mitchell, we'll know within two or three days the reaction of the Whitehouse and if he can deliver."

"I meant what do you personally think about this situation?"

George replies

"Well you've convinced me, I've known for a long time that we cannot continue abusing the protective layers around the earth without some payback, it's now time to exercise some control over our actions and this has to start at the top. You have a remarkable opportunity and may become the catalyst to accomplishing something I never believed would be possible in my lifetime."

Rick turns,

"George what do you know about the Chinese F-XX?"

"China announced they were developing an advanced stealth fighter as a joint project with the Russians who had managed to access our stealth technology. We know it was through the Serbians who somehow managed to shoot down a F117 Nighthawk during the conflict and kindly sold the remains of the aircraft to the Russians. Our intelligence tells us that the F-XX is still in the early design stage and not expected to be flying for another three years."

As there is little traffic the driver has made good time, arriving at the security gates of Andrews Air Base. They're expected, after showing a pass to the armed military police on the gate they are told to wait by the next building. After a few minutes the Camp Commander comes out of the building and gets into their vehicle. His United States Air Force uniform indicates that he's a Colonel.

He greets George,

"George, it's not often we see you out at this hour, nice of you to call."

George shakes his hand and introduces him,

"Rick, Sam this is another old friend Colonel Mark Hanson."

Mark tells George that they've secured the hanger,

"Tell me, what interests you enough to examine an empty hanger at this time of night?" George nods towards the driver,

"It's a surprise."

Mark gives the driver instructions as he heads along the western runway apron to the most northern hanger where USAF Special Forces soldiers are guarding the building. They park a short distance away then follow Mark to a small door set within the main hanger door. Mark opens it they step into darkness, he asks them to stand still as he instinctively reaches out for the switch panel. There is a clunk of power as the building lights come on, brightly illuminating the building with its clinically clean shiny floors reflecting the lights. In the centre of the building is the Stealth, a long futuristic aircraft, the fuselage is 60 feet long and 16 feet high, the aircraft surfaces seem to have a green sheen to them. They are astounded, Mark most of all, he turns to George,

"George, how could this be here without my knowledge, what's going on?"

"Mark, it's a long story, this is absolutely top secret we have specialists coming over later today and after their report we'll brief you, we were told only to confirm its existence this evening. What do you think it is?"

They all slowly walk round the aircraft which looks like something out of 'Starwars' it has an undulating streamlined fuselage with a single seat cockpit and all round glass canopy, under the cockpit there are strange shaped engine intakes resembling the open mouth of a shark. There are two small movable canard wings below each side of the cockpit. The main 45 feet wingspan is swept back and shaped with two small tail fins angled out from each side at the rear.

Mark is fascinated,

"Christ, George, this is some aircraft, it reminds me of intelligence mock ups of the new stealth fighter the Chinese are working on, but theirs is years off, what's more surprising are the similarities with some of the outer technology to our new F22A Raptor."

The aircraft is sitting on its undercarriage with the weapons bay doors open, Mark, George, Rick and Sam crouch under to take a look, they can see there are four AIM-120C radar-guided, medium-range air to air missiles remaining in their racks, with spaces where the other two were. Mark points out,

"Another strange thing these are American missiles not Chinese"

George turns to Rick and Sam,

"If it wasn't for your friends, we and the Gulfstream would've been finished. It could not possibly have survived a further attack with four of these"

Mark stops dead,

"This is the aircraft that attacked you? You were incredibly lucky to have survived an encounter with this, how come and how in the hell did it get into Andrews, it certainly didn't fly in?" George tells his friend,

"You'll have to wait a little longer for the answer to that question."

They walk round the tail and see that the aircraft has two shrouded exhaust outlets, Mark comments,

"Two engines just like the Raptor and a Mach 2 class aircraft."

Mark wheels a tall fixed step ladder over to the side of the aircraft,

"Let's see if there is any sign of the pilot."

He climbs up to the cockpit and looks in,

"No pilot the cockpit instruments seem to be in Chinese and Russian."

George steps away from the others to make a call using his secure satellite phone,

"Tony, hi, its verified, the aircraft is here and looks to be a very close copy of our F22A Raptor, another thing that's very odd, is it's fitted with American AIM-120C missiles, best get our specialists over ASAP, we should be able trace where they came from."

"Well done, take the guys to their hotel then get some sleep yourself I'll see you later today with an update."

As they would need a higher platform to actually get into the cockpit they decide to leave further examination to the specialists, George hurries them along.

"Come on let's get you to the Hotel. Mark, close up we'll see you tomorrow."

They leave the building and speed their way back towards the Pentagon the driver turns off into the outskirts of Washington just before they reach the Potomac River. George calls Steve to forewarn him that they are arriving in five minutes.

Chapter - 14

Mandarin Oriental Hotel - Washington

The driver stops outside the Mandarin Oriental Hotel the vehicle is immediately met by Steve who guides Sam and Rick through reception to the lifts, as they step into the lift Steve looks at Rick and Sam. noticing that they're both showing their tiredness,

"It's been a long couple of days, you can relax now, we won't disturb you, there'll be two of our agents outside the door, if there's anything you need I'll be in my room down the hall."

The lift stops at the top floor they step out and see facing them the door to the Presidential Suite which is usually reserved for visiting Heads of State. There are two agents sitting in comfortable lounge chairs each side of the door. As they reach the door Steve gives Rick and Sam a plastic door key.

They go into together, through a marble vestibule which features an exquisite exhibit of three Chinese compasses. The suite is 3500 square feet of absolute luxury, complete with grand piano, spa baths, chess table and a telescope to enjoy the panoramic views across the water and skyline of Washington. The windows are floor to ceiling with all round balconies that provide views of most of the city's historic landmarks. Walking through the luxurious study with its leather lined walls and 60 inch flat screen television, Steve points to the first room,

"Jo claimed that room, your rooms are here and here, they're all en-suite. Through there is the kitchenette with the bar and everything you should need."

Sam looks at his watch for the first time in many hours,

"Rick its five o'clock in the morning."

"Yeah, I wondered what was wrong with my body, its missing a lot of sleep."

Steve turns to leave,

"Rick anything you need buzz me, my room numbers by the phone, we'll catch up later today or when you resurface."

"Thanks Steve."

At last they are alone. Sam looks across at the dawn breaking across Washington

"It's beautiful, fancy a whisky before we turn in?"

"Why not, we deserve it. It's been one hell of a few days."

Sam throws his jacket down on a dining chair there's a thump as the Smith & Wesson in his pocket hit's the wood of the chair

"I've still got George's Smith and Wesson, I suppose it's a bit of insurance that hopefully we won't need."

Rick grins,

"After what we've been through to date, you just never know."

Sam brings a bottle and glasses from the bar, he pours two large shots of whisky, and they slump down in the sumptuous leather seats in the lounge looking out across the city.

"Heard anymore from Aacaarya?"

"No nothing since we discussed the fighter attack."

Rick leans back in the leather, kicking off his shoes he puts his feet up on the glass coffee table,

"I can't even begin to imagine how they accomplished taking out that fighter at a critical moment then transporting it to a closed hanger thousands of miles away."

Sam yawns and finishes his whisky. He carefully places his heavy crystal glass on the table, picks up his jacket and bag that had been brought up earlier, he points to the nearest door,

"That's my room. Good night see you later, much later."

Rick yawns,

"Yeah sleep well, see you later."

Sam seems to have struck lucky, as he closes his bedroom door he discovers a small suite, with a windowed infinity edge SOK tub that fills from ceiling height, it has an inbuilt television mounted above it. Although exhausted Sam is very impressed, he undresses then goes into the bathroom which is very large with a spa shower that has a multitude of body shower heads looking like something out of a science fiction film, the bathroom windows faces out over a balcony across to the marina. He takes one look at the shower controls it's too complicated for his exhausted mental state and decides to wash at the sink then crashes out in the most comfortable super king size bed he's ever slept in.

At midday Sam wakes, works out how use the shower and dresses, he finds four new shirts with two pairs of jeans have been left in his room, which is just as well as all of them had run out of fresh clothes. He opens the bedroom door to see Jo crouched over the suite's computer,

"Jo, good morning, how're you feeling?"

"I'm great thanks, slept like a log I've been working since eight; you look a lot better than last night."

"Do I smell coffee?"

Jo points through to the kitchenette,

"There's a fantastic breakfast buffet, help yourself."

Sam goes through calling back,

"Any sign of Rick?"

"You must be joking, he looked worse than you did."

"You said you were working, what have you been doing?"

Jo is rummaging through pages of printouts,

"I've been doing some research."

Sam is curious standing in the kitchen doorway with a mug of coffee

"What research?"

"Finish your breakfast, bring me another coffee then I'll show you, it's quite frightening."

A few minutes later Sam arrives with two mugs of fresh coffee and sits down across the table from Jo,

"Now tell me what's quite frightening?"

Jo looks at the pile of printed sheets in front of her,

"I thought it would be a good idea for me to understand a little more about HAARP after what Aacaarya told us, so, as I had some time whilst you babies slept in this morning I thought I'd do some research. What I've discovered in a few hours is worrying to say the very least and much worse than I ever imagined possible. The HAARP ionospheric research is fronted by various Universities across the United States and headed by the University of Alaska's geophysical department, their role is emphasised in press releases but states that the objective of their experiments is to develop the ability to control ionospheric processes that can be exploited by the Department of Defense, in fact HAARP is managed by a Doctor Malcolm Doyle of the Tactical Technology Office which is part of DARPA, the Defense Advanced Research Projects Agency. There are many acclaimed physicists that disagree with research that involves controlling the electro jet and creating the equivalent of nuclear explosions in the upper atmosphere but few are willing to jeopardise their reputations or government contracts by challenging the system. The funding and powerbase behind their organisation are large corporate defence contractors, lobbyists, the Office of United

States Naval Research, the Air Force research Laboratory and what's more concerning."

She glances across to Rick's door,

"The NSA and CIA are involved. There's a an old report amongst these printouts in which the CIA admitted that national governments already had the ability to manipulate the weather for military purposes. Sam, interestingly the original patents to these technologies were acquired by Arco Power Technologies in the early 90's then sold to E-Systems who sold them on in 1995 to Raytheon who is one of the largest defence contractors and continues to be involved."

Sam acknowledges,

"They're the size of organisation that would have the resources and finance to have access to a stealth fighter if they needed one, with enough influence over the intelligent services to keep it secret."

An hour later they're disturbed by Rick's door opening, he enters the lounge in his dressing gown with a lively,

"Good morning Jo, Sam you two look refreshed."

"I've been working since 08:00 and Sam's been drinking coffee since 12:00, it's now 14:30 and you've decided to honour us with your presence."

Rick says,

"OK, OK lead me to the coffee, I'll get dressed then join you in whatever you're doing, by the way what are you doing?"

"Research, coffees in the kitchen help yourself we'll tell you all about it when you're presentable."

Rick wanders into the kitchen, returns a few minutes later with a mug of coffee and disappears into his room with a,

"See you shortly."

Jo returns to the conversation with Sam,

"From what I've seen in the past few hours Aacaarya and the Elders were right to be concerned as any one of the ionospheric research programmes spread around the globe could cause a catastrophic change in the Earth's magnetic field or a polar shift, added to the environmental damage that is possibly attributable to these experiments over the past two decades."

Sam looks up from the page he was reading,

"It certainly looks that way, the fact they're now preparing to beam 100 billion watts of effective radiated power into the ionosphere, without knowing its consequences, is insane. 100 billion watts beamed for a one hour period is equal to ten times the quantity of energy generated by the Hiroshima Atomic Bomb. This reminds me of something I read some time ago,

"Did you know that many years after the testing of the first atomic bomb in the United States, Robert Oppenheimer its major physicist stated that they had no idea what would happen when it exploded.

Meaning, would the chain reaction stop or just keep going, the department of Defense knew full well that the scientists didn't know what the outcome of the experiment would be and pressed ahead anyway."

Jo is surprised,

"I didn't pick up on that, that's irresponsible."

"Yes but what's unbelievable is that there's no global organisation co-ordinating and controlling these experiments internationally."

He picks up another document that he's been studying,

"Look at this, the State Parliament of Russia produced a critical report in August 2002 on the subject of HAARP which was signed by 90 members of the international affairs and defence committee's before being passed to President Vladimir Putin. In the report they stated that they believed that:

'The U.S.A. is creating new integral geophysical weapons that may influence the near-Earth medium with high-frequency radio waves. The significance of this qualitative leap could be compared to the transition from cold steel to firearms, or from conventional weapons to nuclear weapons. This new type of weapon differs from previous types in that the near-Earth medium becomes at once an object of direct influence and its component.'

Jo is disturbed by what she's reading,

"Sam, do you realise how dangerous this mission is we've undertaken? We're hoping to convince the most powerful and invisible forces in the world to stop research that has cost billions to date, they're not going to let us do that, are they?"

Sam reassures her,

"I've thought a lot about that too but don't forget we're not alone, remember that the most powerful and invisible forces on this planet are supporting us and this mission, more importantly they have the power to enforce the closure of these global experimental facilities."

"They certainly saved us in the Gulfstream attack."

Rick's door opens he joins them flipping through their pile of papers,

"You two look as if you've have been having some serious fun."

Jo scowls at him,

"This is very serious stuff, not fun. It's scary, what's being allowed to be done in the name of research."

Jo angrily explains without stopping for breath what she has been doing all day. Rick sits silently then when she's finished responds,

"Through my work I've been aware for some time that HAARP is being used for military purposes but along with others we're not told everything, we've also been monitoring what other countries are doing in this field for the same reasons. The original motivations for this research were not for the military they were very much along the same lines as Aacaarya's people must have carried out a long time ago and now benefiting from, 'clean limitless energy and safe weather management'. The main HAARP facility near Gakona Alaska is just west of the Wrangell-Saint Elias National Park. They are transparent about their scientific work. They publish most of what they are doing with many results of their experiments available live on their website. They have regular open days when the public, interested parties including you could visit the site. However in principle, today I agree with you, with access to enormous amounts of military funding they are continuously able to increase the size of their antenna arrays and the power of their transmissions without knowing how far they have to go before irreversible damage is caused to the planet's outer layers and magnetic fields. There are many supporters of HAARP but not one of them can guarantee that what they're doing is harmless."

There's a knock at the door. Sam gets up and opens the door to Steve who comes in,

"Good day, it's nice to see you looking so well, I slept through until 12.00. I've just heard from George, Tony wants us all in his office in 90 minutes. If we can be ready to leave in an hour we'll have plenty of time, we'll collect you at 16:00 hours."

Sam points out,

"That's perfect just enough time for lunch."

Steve tells them,

"When you're ready just order from the restaurant it'll be brought up to the room, I have to go, another meeting."

He leaves them to organise themselves,

At precisely 16:00 they leave the hotel with Rick and the two other FBI agents, after a short drive to the Pentagon they're back in the reception area of Tony and George's offices. Tony arrives with George, both in pristine uniforms. After exchanging greetings they are escorted into the comfortable office taking seats around the meeting table. Tony immediately gets down to business and explains what's happened in the past twenty-four hours.

"For your ongoing safety we've decided to release a report that confirmed the loss of our Gulfstream in a collision with another aircraft over the Atlantic, with no survivors. We mentioned that in addition to the military personnel there were two civilian passengers on board. This was done on the basis that whoever sent the Stealth after you would not know whether they had been successful or not, as their pilot and aircraft disappeared."

Jo looks at Tony,

"You mean you killed us off?"

"There's only a very small possibility that they'll believe this story but it may just buy us a little more time before they try again, which they would certainly do if they thought you had survived. We've given you both new identities, in accordance with your expertise these are fully backed up, so in a sense Sam and Jo no longer exist, here are your new ID's, profiles, passports, credit cards and bank accounts. Your old ones will continue to remain unused for the time being until we feel it's safe to return you to your old lives."

Sam asks,

"Isn't there a flaw in this? Surely if you were able to track the Gulfstream by satellite before the attack so could others after the attack?"

Tony smiles at Rick,

"As you said Sam doesn't miss much."

"Sam, it's a valid observation but after the attack, the Gulfstream pilot activated the aircrafts own stealth mode disappearing completely from both our radars and everyone else's, that's highly classified information."

Jo is shocked when she opens her new passport,

"Doctor Diane Pemberton! That's not a name I like very much at all, I would have…."

Tony interrupts,

"Dr Pemberton exists she has a verifiable family and career history. Learn to live with her, study and remember the profiles, it may save your life in the future."

Sam is more familiar with the needs for this and does not bother to open his, he'll study it later. Jo asks,

"What about Rick's identity?"

"Don't worry about Rick he has many aliases, he'll tell you which one later."

Sam is concerned,

"Who else is aware of our new identities?"

"Only George you three and me, the people that created them do not know who they were for. In addition we'll have to inform your security team."

Sam asks,

"Why do we need a security team? If we're travelling incognito it makes more sense for the three of us to work alone, Rick and I have enough experience to be able to look after ourselves."

"There's no doubt about that, I've read your backgrounds, but why not have the backup?"

Sam is adamant and always to the point,

"We would draw less attention travelling alone and to be honest, I've reason to believe that one of the team has ulterior motives in staying close to us."

"What exactly do you mean?"

Sam has no proof,

"It's just a strong instinct."

Tony thinks for a moment,

"The only condition that I would release the security team is that you and Rick are armed at all times."

Jo interrupts,

"What about me? I can outshoot most men with a pistol."

Tony smiles,

"I was surprised when I came across that entry in your file. It mentioned you had unexpectedly taken a three year break from Archaeology after you left Cairo, this surprisingly included specialist arms training at a military base in Slovenia. The records do not mention what happened or why you felt it was necessary."

"There's probably a lot about me that's better left out of your files."

Tony smiles looking at her in a different light,

"That would not surprise me young lady, I'm sure there's a lot more to you than meets the eye. But I do like to know the people that I am working with and am therefore intrigued to know exactly what happened"

Jo responds firmly,

"Then I'm sorry, you will have to remain intrigued, it's not a subject I am willing to discuss,"

Tony shrugs,

"As long as it was nothing that will affect this mission we'll let it go at that, for the time being"

Rick and Sam look at each other in both wondering why Jo would leave her work for so long.

Turning to Rick Tony orders him,

"Take them down to our range tomorrow morning for an assessment then fit them out with whatever weapon they're most comfortable with, you know the drill."

"Yes sir."

Tony continues,

"I want them issued with secure satellite phones, they can be used to remain in contact at all times they're secure as they use our military satellites. All signals are encrypted and decoded on arrival, just use them like a normal cell phone, they'll work everywhere, and you will also have George and my private numbers."

Tony continues his briefing,

"Since our last meeting we've had our specialists crawling all over the stealth fighter, they have confirmed that it was built in China, we believe by the Shenyang Aircraft Industry for a Russian Agency that is involved with a Corporation that is closely connected with a major US defence contractor, we don't know yet which agency but they certainly collaborated in the design and construction, all the instrumentation is in Russian which would indicate a Russian pilot. Having identified its exhaust heat pattern we are trying to patch together from our satellite images its flight path to establish which airbase it took off from. We're not yet certain but our initial information seems to point to one of the secret Russian airbases, any questions so far?"

Jo asks,

"Yes, if Sam is right and that an FBI agent is working for both sides, surely they would not have tried to shoot the aircraft down with their own man on board?"

Tony looks at her sympathetically,

"I'm sorry, but for the high stakes involved these people would not hesitate to eliminate anyone if it achieved their goal, hence our need for absolute secrecy."

Sam asks,

"How secure is the report that you prepared?"

"Good question, its classification is 'Top Secret' it was prepared by me personally, the few people that have it, have it on a 'need to know' basis, all have Top Secret clearances and I hold a list of those people; perhaps I can continue with my report."

He continues,

"The investigation into the origins and ownership of the stealth is ongoing and will take some time. However the current mystery is trying to discover what the electromagnetic particles are, that are covering the aircraft. We believe they may have been caused by the aircraft's transportation to Andrews as they are not part of the stealth's construction materials. That's about all we have on the stealth for the moment."

At this point coffee is brought in, as the uniformed secretary leaves the room,

Tony continues,

"I've held secure high level discussions with the Secretaries for Defence of Russia and Norway who understand the urgency of this matter, they have promised to respond to me tomorrow with their initial reactions."

Sam is surprised,

"That was fast work."

"Despite what people think, we have regular dialogue with our counterparts in other countries. What's most surprising is the reaction from our own Secretary for Defence, they responded within four hours to explain that they've instructed the HAARP installation in Alaska to commence decommissioning on Monday next, that's in four days time. Apparently there's been growing resistance in congress over how much funding HAARP has been consuming."

Rick is very surprised by this statement,

"That's too much of a coincidence, what about the other sites, HIPAS near Fairbanks and the Aricibo Observatory in Puerto Rico?"

"Look Rick this is a good start, I'm waiting to receive a full report on the other sites then hopefully if we're seen to be setting an example other countries will realise that we regard this matter very seriously and will follow suit."

Rick does not look convinced, something is bothering him. Sam asks Tony,

"What about the Chinese?"

"They've refused to discuss their facilities but if we and the Russians decommission then they'll be prepared to reconsider their position."

Sam senses that Tony is telling the truth but cannot work out what's bothering Rick. Tony continues,

"You can visit Alaska under your new identities and confirm firsthand what's happening there. Rick can organise the trip, charging everything to the new cards you have, they're secure but don't fly direct from

Washington. Sorry Rick, for a moment I forgot that covert trips are your particular speciality."

Sam asks Rick directly,

"What's bothering you?"

"It's too easy, when you consider how much has been invested in HAARP then the organisations behind the money, they'd fight tooth and nail to prevent its closure unless."

Sam finishes Rick's sentence,

"They have something better, hidden away elsewhere."

Rick nods,

"Exactly, what I was thinking."

Tony turns to George, who has been silent throughout the briefing,

"You heard any rumours about other sites?"

"No, I'm sure we would've heard something if that was the case."

Sam senses that both Tony and George are not hiding anything.

Tony orders George,

"Use all our resources, have a good sniff around and see what you can find out."

Tony looks at his watch,

"Unless you have any further questions I've another meeting to deal with, thank you for coming, let me know what you find in Alaska, anything you need, use the cards."

Jo asks a final question,

"If we are supposed to carry weapons how do we get through airport security?"

Rick responds for Tony,

"Don't worry I'll organise that."

Jo says,

"Just one more question Sir, what's the limit on the cards?"

Tony is amused by Jo,

"There's no limit but if you went to buy a Ferrari or a Stealth Fighter it would be declined."

She laughs,

They leave the office the three of them are alone in reception. Rick pulls the two of them together,

"We'll only stay in the hotel for another two nights then we move into another hotel under our new names without the security team, from where we can plan our trip."

The door opens Steve asks them to follow him to the transport, as they walk along the corridor he asks Rick,

"How're things going with Tony, making progress?"

"Yeah, they're checking out a few things and you know how long that takes."

Steve enquires,

"What did they think of your report?"

Rick is careful,

"No idea, they're going to get back to us once they've assessed it."

Steve continues,

"We're being reassigned tomorrow to another project George has another security team taking over."

Rick acknowledges,

"Yes, so I hear, sorry to lose you but I'm sure there're higher priorities for your people than chauffeuring us back and forth."

They reach the vehicles and are driven back to their Hotel. As soon as they're in their suite Sam asks Rick

"What was that all about with Steve?"

Rick tells him not to worry, Steve had heard that they were being reassigned and believes that George has arranged an alternative security team.

"Tomorrow they'll be gone then we'll be able to relax and organise ourselves, I've arranged a secure vehicle to take us over to the range at 09:00."

Sam asks,

"Where's the range?"

"It's located on the outskirts of Washington about 45 minutes drive from here I think you'll be impressed."

Jo is quite excited by the prospect of showing that she's as good as the men,

"Is it on a military base?"

"No, it's a secret and very exclusive gun club used only by the top echelon of the likes of George, Tony and various specialists to keep them on target, perhaps we should have a small wager as to who will come out top."

Jo is immediately up for this,

"I wager a bottle of Lagavoulin for the top score."

Sam and Rick smile at each other confidently

"You're on, only after you tell us, what that was all about with Tony and your file."

Jo is embarrassed,

"Rick, I made it very clear to Tony, what happened to me in Cairo was my personal and private business. I am not prepared to discuss it further, other than to guarantee it will not jeopardise this mission. You both OK with that?"

Rick is not too happy,

"Jo, I'm asking because we're a small team and it's important to know our strengths and weaknesses"

Jo is silent, Sam cuts in,

"Rick let's leave it at that, I'm happy with what Jo has said, if she feels it's private then I respect her wishes".

Rick changes the subject,

"OK, OK I can't take you both on, particularly when I'm starving let's get something to eat."

After having dinner accompanied by an excellent Chablis Premier Cru they are relaxing after finishing their third bottle, when Rick tells them,

"Tonight, study your new identities we'll be using them tomorrow at the range, my new name is

Michael Knights, Mike to my friends it'll be good practice."

Jo's been thinking about what Rick said to George,

"You know Rick I agree with you about the sudden decommissioning of HAARP it doesn't sound right to me, too quick, unless they were forewarned somehow."

Sam says,

"Let's wait until we get there, we'll be able to get closer to the truth in Alaska away from the distorted influences of the Pentagon and Washington."

Sam opens his new passport,

"And from tomorrow I'm Professor Timothy Stevens; Tim to my friends."

They finish their wine and retire to study their profiles.

The next morning at 08:30 they're about to be briefed by Rick (Mike), he calls them over,

"Tim (Sam) and Diane (Jo) listen up. The transport is arriving at 08:55 we'll leave the room together and go to the lift area. I'll go down to reception alone to check that everything's in order. You'll come down together in the next lift then when you exit stay by the lift door until I call you over we'll go directly to the waiting vehicle."

Diane asks,

"Which is?"

"A black Range Rover Sports with black tinted armoured windows OK."

Diane grins,

"Why always Mafia black, it's a dead giveaway?"

Mike jokingly tells her,

"Not again woman, black is chic."

Mike reminds Tim to bring his Smith and Wesson and to stay alert. At 08:45 they leave the room then cross to the lift, the corridor outside the Presidential Suite is empty.

Mike enters the lift and goes down to the ground floor, as he exits he looks around the lobby, seeing nothing unusual he goes to the main door where the Range Rover is waiting, he introduces himself to the driver who checks his picture and starts the engine. Mike returns to the Hotel reception lobby as Tim and Diane step out of the lift, after checking round again he waves them over.

They leave the hotel and cross to the vehicle, which races away the second the doors close. The driver weaves through the traffic, along busy highways until they reach a much quieter suburb with long avenues of trees. The Range Rover slows down turning into the entrance of a large drive the driver stops at heavy duty security gates. A security guard comes out, speaks to the driver who shows him his ID, immediately the gates open, they enter a long gravel drive that passes through landscaped gardens, as they swing round a bend they see a very large country house, it looks like a country club or Country Hotel surrounded by trees. The Range Rover halts outside the magnificent pillared main entrance Diane turns to Mike,

"Why are we here? This can't be our new Hotel?"

"It's not a hotel, welcome to the most exclusive range in the United States."

They step out of the Range Rover then go to the main door which is opened for them by a doorman in livery, he ushers them into a large oak panelled entrance hall. On one side is a large mahogany desk behind which sits a tall and elegantly dressed woman. The woman greets them, pressing a button on her desk. A large green buttoned leather covered door opens and they are greeted by the arrival of a cheery, very well built man in his forties with close cropped hair, he is dressed in black overalls. He holds out his hand,

"Staff Sergeant Timms, I understand you want to use our facilities, please come this way."

The door leads into a lift, Sergeant Timms places a pass from round his neck into the lift control, they are taken down to the basement area. When the door opens they are greeted by the distinctive smell of cordite and gun oil.

"Please follow me."

He leads them down a long passage, passing a bank vault like door marked 'Armoury'. They enter the firing range which has separate cubicles for up to 10 people. Sergeant Timms explains that this is one of the most modern electronic ranges in the United States with mounted projectors to play out virtual scenarios,

"By the way call me Andy, Sergeant is just for upstairs, down here we're in my home territory where I am the absolute boss. Mike I've prepared everything you asked for in there." Pointing to the room behind the range with half glass walls,

"Shall we go in?"

He opens the door for Diane, Tim and Mike follow her; they stand round the table which has several polished mahogany boxes, each one containing a different type of automatic pistol.

"The satellite phones were delivered this morning."

He places another box on the table.

Andy asks Tim,

"What are you carrying?"

Tim takes the pistol out of his pocket,

"What no holster, we'll put that right later. Do you like the Smith & Wesson?"

Tim tells him,

"No other choice, I've not had the opportunity to find out, that's why we're here"

Andy turns to Diane,

"What about you, any experience?"

Diane's hackles rise, she picks up Tim's Smith & Wesson,

"This is the M&P Compact."

She easily slips the magazine out checking the ammunition,

"A 357Sig calibre, more stopping power than a 9 mm and most favoured by the Military and Police, its weight empty without mag is 22.2 oz its capacity is 10+1 rounds, the barrel is 3.5" long with a trigger pull of 6.5 lbs. But I prefer the new Beretta 90TWO which weighs 32.5 oz, its only 9 mm calibre but its mag holds 17 rounds; those extra 6 rounds could make a big difference in a fire fight."

She takes the new Beretta from its box checks that it's not loaded then strips it in a few seconds, just as quickly she confidently reassembles the weapon. Mike and Tim look on in amazement. Andy says,

"Ouch, I apologise."

Mike has recovered and laughs,

"We've got a bottle of Lagavoulin riding on beating her today."

Andy, now with greater respect for Diane, takes charge,

"I want you each to try both pistols to see which you prefer, my personal preference is the same as Diane's I like having 17 rounds at my disposal too, for the same reason."

They each take a weapon; Mike is only there for the practice as he prefers his old friend the Smith & Wesson Compact .375 which he's very familiar with. Andy explains that first they'll use standard targets and initially fire 5 shots each. They put on ear defenders and protective glasses. Tim is also using the Smith & Wesson whilst Diane uses the new Beretta, Andy watches from behind as they take up their positions,

"Fire, when ready"

There's a deafening sound as the three of them commence firing in the confined space, after each have fired five shots they check their weapons laying them on the table in front of them, Andy electronically brings their targets towards them to examine. Andy starts with

Mike's target which has all five shots within a one inch group in the centre,

"Not bad at all."

Mike and Andy go to Tim's cubicle his target has two in the bull with three shots in the second ring out. Andy is impressed,

"Not bad for a Professor, at least you would have killed the target."

The three of them then go to Diane's cubicle, immediately smiles appear on Tim and Mike's faces, Tim is quick to comment,

"Look at this, one in the dead centre with four complete misses."

Diane remains silent,

Andy looks more closely at the target,

"Wait a minute you two."

With a puzzled look on his face he brings her target closer, taking it off its clip he swears,

"That woman, is absolutely brilliant, it's a long time since I saw anyone that good."

Tim and Mike lean over as Andy points to the centre,

"All five shots through the same hole see how each one has plucked the edge in a different place; if I was you I would accept defeat and get the whisky."

They congratulate Diane, who is glowing with pride,

"Why gentlemen, I thought you were the best of the best, what a delusion."

Mike smiling says,

"Don't let it go to your head, let's swop weapons and try another five."

They repeat the exercise discharge a further five rounds after which Andy goes to Mike, whose grouping using the Beretta is slightly wider than with the Smith and Wesson, together they take a look at Tim's target his grouping is now consistently together in a one inch group but slightly off the centre. Andy is pleased,

"We can adjust that, it's how you squeezed the trigger on the Beretta you pulled it slightly to one side."

Then they're at Diane's cubicle, for appearance she blows the smoke off the end of the barrel, western style then puts the Smith and Wesson down, her target has a slightly larger hole in dead centre where all the 357 shells had passed through. This time they're very impressed and extremely respectful, Andy puts his arm round her shoulder,

"You are the first person I've ever seen do this with a 375 and using a Smith and Wesson, my heartiest congratulations."

"It's only a matter of standing position, technique, breathing and focus."

Andy offers them another challenge,

"If you want to do something a little more difficult and more fun, we'll use the virtual scenarios, we dim the light, one at a time you stand in the centre cubicle as various images appear, some armed and some not, you have to take out the armed threats before they get you, without hitting any innocent bystanders. The weapon that you will use is electronic, like an arcade game but its balanced and the same weight as the Smith and Wesson."

Andy clears the weapons putting them in the back room, then he removes the target frames as the rear wall slides open in each direction revealing a wide curved screen that sweeps right round the rear wall. He plugs in the pistol which looks an exact replica of the real thing passing it to Tim,

"You're up first, OK."

Tim stands waiting as suddenly the whole back wall of the range lights up as the projector starts and an almost three dimensional street scene is in front of him with people moving back and forth, suddenly the door of a bank bursts open an armed robber turns towards him, Tim aims, in a split second he fires, followed by confusion as several other people come rushing out of the bank, amongst them is another armed robber who raises his pistol in Tim's direction.

At the same time the door of a car parked near the bank opens another bandit aims at Tim who mutters "Oh shit!" and fires off two fast shots. Andy is watching a computer screen, that's one bad guy dead, one wounded and two civilians dead. Tim is surprised,

"How come, I only fired three rounds?"
Andy shows him,

"Two shots hit the two bad guys, the third passed through the first civilian into the second civilian behind him."
They spend an hour going through different scenarios and eventually their time is up. Diane is delighted she has wiped the floor with Tim and Mike, she says to Andy,

"That was the most fun I've had for years, absolutely fantastic. If we had this technology when I was younger I might have been an even better shot."

"Doctor, you are the best pistol shot I've ever seen in my 30 years service even without the technology, and a woman to boot."
Diane asks,

"Perhaps we can come back another time."

"With your skills, you're welcome any time and do remember, it's always going to be very different when it's a live target with someone trying to kill you for real, hopefully that won't happen."
He leads them back into the room, after cleaning the Smith and Wesson for Tim and the Beretta for Diane he puts each of their weapons in a box with cleaning kit, spare magazines and several boxes of ammunition, Mike keeps his own Smith and Wesson.

"All we need to do now is to fit you with discreet holsters, we have two types, belt or shoulder which do you prefer?"
Tim and Diane opt for the shoulder holster Andy brings out two beautifully crafted soft leather holsters which they try on adjusting to a perfect fit. Mike suggests they load a couple of magazines each and carry their

weapons ready in their holsters which they do, Diane says,

"This feels strange I'm going to have to get used to wearing it."

Andy brings over the box from George with three Satellite phones and chargers,

"There's something else too, George sent over three large black duffle bags, and he said that these will be useful for where ever it is you're going. This one's for the lady."

Laden with their new possessions they say good bye to Andy who has really taken to Diane,

"If there's anything you need or want to ask me, just call."

He hands her a card with his number, she kisses him on the cheek. They leave loading the Range Rover with their mysterious black bags. The driver returns them to the Hotel, just before they stop Mike tells them to make their way direct to the suite, as he has to take care of something in reception. Diane and Tim carefully make their way back to their suite and close the door. Diane can't wait to open her bag and unzips it pulling at the contents like a child unwrapping presents,

"Sam, I mean Tim look at this."

She takes out a heavy winter all weather jacket which is fashionable but is in a mixture of light and dark green colours not quite military camouflage but just as good, next come matching trousers and a pair of quality Gortex walking boots. She finds a matching baseball cap which she tries on immediately along with the jacket, there's a knock on the door followed by Mike coming in with a package.

"Diane, sadly, this is for you."

He hands her the package opening it she finds a green box, inside which is a bottle of Lagavoulin Whisky. She gives him a peck on the cheek,

"That's what I like in a man, honourable in defeat; Tim you bring the glasses I'll bring the bottle."

Mike looks at Diane's cap and jacket,

"You, off to Saint Moritz?" She laughs,

"Who knows where we'll end up, but Alaska's going to be pretty cold it was very nice of George to think about it."

Mike reminds her,

"George thinks of everything, that's his job."

Diane rummages further in her bag pulling out a black stiff waistcoat type garment

"What's this?" Mike grins,

"It's lightweight Kevlar body armour you wear it under your jacket when you think someone's going to shoot you. It stops most projectiles, leaving a nasty bruise, which is better than a hole in your skin."

Tim pours three large whisky's telling them,

"Leave the bag, this is a higher priority."

He hands them each a glass,

"Raise a glass to our markswoman who taught us not to be so arrogant as to assume anything about her."

Mike takes his glass over to the sideboard putting the three satellite phones on charge which look similar to a Blackberry mobile phone,

"These sat phones are also GPS's we'll need those when we get to Alaska, it's a tough unforgiving country, each of our jackets has a tracker built in so if we get separated we can always find each other using the GPS."

Tim points out,

"Presumably so can anyone else that has the code to the tracker."

"True, but I believe that George's security procedures are some of the best."

They sit round the table drinking when Tim realises that Diane is still wearing her holster,

"Why are you wearing that in here; expecting trouble?"

Diane smiles,

"You just never know, no, I'm just trying to get used to wearing it, so that it feels more natural."

Tim asks Mike,

"What's the plan for tomorrow?"

"I've booked three adjoining rooms in our new names at the Grand Hyatt downtown we leave in the morning making our way there by Taxi. When we arrive I should have all the information for our trip."

The rest of the evening is spent emptying the whisky bottle whilst studying as much as possible about the HAARP facilities and their research. Diane and Tim have logged onto the internet and are discussing the HAARP website. Tim is on Google Earth trying to find out exactly where they're going,

"You know what's strange, the site is supposed to welcome visitors, there's no address, they provide their location as being at 62 degrees 23.5 min North Latitude by 145 degrees 8.8 min West Longitude and 8 miles North of Gakona just West of the Wrangell-Saint Elias National Park. I've just looked on Google maps and Google Earth and the area is blanked out very odd for a scientific research observatory."

Mike points to their sat phones,

"Don't worry I know how to get there, it's programmed into our GPS, after all, it's a government facility."

Diane says,

"That's another thing that bothers me. The only available publicity about HAARP's activities is based on their ionospheric research and gives the appearance that they are not involved in any other type of research. We know that they're funded by the military strikes me they could be hiding an awful lot."

Chapter - 15

Arrival in Alaska

The next morning they prepare their growing amount of luggage, under their jackets they're wearing their weapons holsters with the sat phones clipped to their belts. Mike calls his agent in reception to organise a 'special' taxi, it looks normal but is driven by the same agent that drove the Range Rover. They leave the suite together looking like tourists with their bags, head down to reception then to the waiting vehicle. It's a short drive downtown to the Hyatt, within 20 minutes they are in the Hyatt reception with its spectacular lobby and atrium. The lobby floor is covered by a beautiful blue carpet with a large, colourful old compass rose in the centre. Mike has pre booked three King rooms which are together at the end of the corridor on the top floor with interconnecting doors. Ten minutes later they're in their rooms with the interconnecting doors open. Mike warns them,

"We're here for one night, tomorrow we leave for Alaska."

Diane asks,

"What time are we leaving, and how long will it take?"

Mike has been pondering over the most time efficient and secure method of getting to Alaska,

"Well there's good news and bad news, when I checked the Continental flights from Washington to Fairbanks it took two stops for connecting flights at Houston and Seattle, this would have made a journey time of 16 hours with connections and our return journey would've meant three stops Anchorage, Seattle and Newark which would take 17 hours. That's the bad news."

Diane is impatient, "What's the good news Mike?"

"Have a little patience, the good news is I called George, we have at our disposal for five days, a Pentagon 'civilian marked' corporate jet which will take us direct to Fairbanks and return us to Washington taking approximately 7 hours each way."

Tim is relieved,

"That saves having to worry about airport police and carrying firearms on scheduled flights."

Diane asks,

"Any more good news, like where're we staying. I draw the line at igloos."

"Not quite an igloo but we'll be sharing a log cabin at the historic Gakona Lodge & Trading Post which was built in 1904, it's the last original roadhouse left in Alaska.

The scenic beauty in that area is awesome, the fishing and outdoor activities are fantastic so you should feel at home. It's on the edge of The Eagle Trail and only a few miles from our destination."

Tim asks,

"Transport from Fairbanks?"

"We've an SUV waiting at the airport, a Chevy Trailblazer."

Diane chips in,

"No doubt it's black?"

"Not this time, it'll probably be the colour of snow, there's a lot of it in Alaska; we leave the hotel at 10:00 tomorrow, departing from Andrews at midday so I recommend an early night."

They agree, taking the HAARP research printouts to their rooms to study. Tim has been reading for half an hour then places the documents beside his bed, he closes his eyes as he mulls over what he's read, when his concentration is disturbed by the voice of Aacaarya,

"Sam, we've some information that may help you in your search for the owners of the stealth aircraft. It was built to order and owned by a Russian Chinese consortium but the attack was commissioned by an organisation in your country; be very attentive on your trip to Alaska, others may be aware of your presence there."

Tim asks him,

"What do you know of the decision to decommission the HAARP installation?"

"All I can tell you is that there's more to this decision than our intervention, if you use your new skills you'll be able to find out more when you're in Alaska, warn Jo and Rick to be on constant alert, there's a threat against you but sadly we don't know yet who from, now get some sleep, good night."

Tim opens his eyes and taps on the adjoining door Mike opens it,

"Not asleep then?"

Tim explains what he has just heard, Mike listens intently,

"It's strange I've had an odd feeling about this trip too, we'll have to be careful, we don't know what games are being played or by whom, other than that they're very powerful enemies, let's get some sleep. I'll relay the information about the stealth to George tomorrow, good night."

The next morning they're up early, Mike checks them out of the hotel and before long, they're in the morning rush hour traffic heading towards Andrews Air Force Base.

After an hour and forty minutes they arrive at the security gates, the driver stops and hands a document to the guard, who after reading it calls a waiting Humvee which pulls alongside, they transfer their baggage to the Humvee which then takes them to the western apron beside the runway. There they find a new 8 passenger Citation XLS twin engine jet waiting for them. They quickly embark into the luxurious leather bound cabin settling into the front four comfortable seats as the ground crew places their luggage in the hold. At 12.00 precisely the aircraft is lining up, after its engine checks it takes off and rapidly climbs away from the air base. The Citation XLS is smaller than the Gulfstream but its twin Pratt & Witney PW545C engines provide more power, before long they are well above the clouds at their cruise altitude of 31,000 feet heading directly for Alaska. The flight is comfortable and uneventful with time passing pleasantly and quickly. As they settle into the flight Mike explains,

"We've a four hour drive when we arrive, I recommend we try and get some rest."

Seven hours later, the pilot's intercom disturbs them announcing that they are commencing their descent into Fairbanks International where the temperature on the ground is two degrees centigrade.

Diane half awake asks,

"Mike did he say two degrees centigrade?"

"Yes, it gets very cold up here when the sun sets, in a few months time it can get as low as minus nineteen. The coldest temperature ever recorded was in February 1947 when it dropped to minus twenty seven degrees."

Diane gets up stretching,

"So that's why Uncle George got us winter clothing."

She reaches up taking down her hand baggage from the overhead locker, pulling out her jacket, socks and boots,

"Time to change clothes,"

She takes off her light jacket under which she has a tight fitting cashmere turtle neck top which added to the straps of the shoulder holster emphasises her fine and perfectly formed figure. Mike is mesmerised,

Diane asks him,

"Mike, have you been to Alaska before?"

Relieved to change the vision he had in his mind,

"Yes, we used to come up here annually for our survival training, it's a very beautiful, unforgiving and very tough place; a bit like you; you should fit in well."

"Thank you kind sir, that's a compliment. What's Fairbanks like?"

She sits down as Mike continues,

"Tim, you been to Alaska before?"

Tim is now awake and alert,

"Once, a long time ago"

Mike explains to Diane,

"Fairbanks is just east of the centre of Alaska, not far from the border with Yukon, it's now a modern city thanks to the discovery of gold in the early 1900's and the gold rush that followed, after that Fairbanks grew into the largest city in Alaska, although today Anchorage is bigger. Between 1975 and 1977 Fairbanks was the construction hub for the Trans Alaskan Pipeline which fuelled a construction boom and runs alongside most of the Richardson Highway which we'll be driving along, the locals call it the Alyeska Pipeline."

Diane is curious,

"Is the Pipeline for oil?"

"Yes. It's the major US oil pipeline starting at the oil fields in Prudhoe Bay on the northern tip of Alaska running almost due south across the country to the Gulf of Alaska at Valdez a distance of 800 miles. It was an amazing construction achievement when you consider the very remote terrain and extremely harsh environment that it passes through, which include three mountain ranges, fault lines and unstable boggy ground on top of ice and frost."

Diane tries to catch him out,

"I bet you don't know what the population of Fairbanks is?"

"Actually I do, there's about 32,000 in the city with another 52,000'ish in the urban areas making it the largest city in the Interior region of Alaska and second largest in the state. It's always been the commercial centre for the Alaskan interior and is at the centre of intersections of all the major transport links, highways, rail and air. In addition to the International Airport there are two military airbases, Ladd Field and Eielson Air Force Base with numerous small airfields including a sea plane base. Ladd Field and Eielson were constructed in 1938 as bases for sending aircraft and supplies to the USSR and the Russian controlled Far East, as part of the governments Lend-Lease program."

The intercom interrupts them,

"Please fasten seat belts, secure any loose items for landing."

The Jet banks to the left then levels out. Shortly after lining up on finals there's the familiar squeal as the wheels touch the tarmac, then they gently taxi to the private arrivals part of the terminal. Diane has been watching their final approach from her window,

"It certainly looks grey and cold out there."

The aircraft comes to a halt and the engines are shut down. They get their gear together as the front cabin door is opened, gusts of cold crisp air stab into the cabin.

They make their way to the private arrivals area to be welcomed by a rough looking, well built man in a heavy khaki parka. He recognises Mike they exchange greetings as he hands over a packet and a set of keys. He leads them out to the car park with their bags then takes them over to an olive green, four-wheel drive SUV Chevy Trailblazer. It has heavily tinted windows and has obviously been adapted for the hard terrain in Alaska; its suspension had been increased in height with heavy duty snow/cross country tyres on larger than standard wheels. Tim and Diane are standing at the front looking at the large electric winch fitted into the front bumper.

Tim comments,

"This is a serious set of wheels, not the standard SUV hire car I was expecting."

"This is one of our special equipment vehicles, lots of extras, the engine is a modified very thirsty V8, let's stow our gear."

They go round to the back and open the tailgate, inside there are three five gallon fuel cans, several black bags and a long flat black case tucked behind the rear seat. Mike helps them load up their bags,

"We've got emergency rations, water, and a few other things in case we run into bad conditions. Alaska is not a forgiving place for the unprepared and it's a place where it's good to remember the old SAS adage, the seven P's; 'Proper Planning and Preparation, Prevents Piss Poor Performance'."

Diane says,

"That's reassuring providing we have."

Tim and Mike get into the front seats, with Diane climbing into the rear amongst several hi tech blankets and a black plastic box, which being curious she opens.

"Oh guys; I've found lots of energy snacks with three flasks, I'm very happy."

She makes herself comfortable. Mike jokingly says,

"They're for emergencies, not now. We'll be stopping for dinner."

He starts the engine which immediately bursts into life with a powerful roar, at the same time he switches on the extra large screen GPS mounted in the centre of the dash board then enters their destination. The GPS immediately plots their route.

Diane asks from the back,

"Where are we going first?"

Mike point to the GPS screen,

"We've a short drive through the city onto our first leg of the main Richardson Highway which we stay on travelling south to Delta Junction about 93.7 miles away where the Alaskan Highway starts, there we take the right fork. We continue on the Richardson Highway which, as a matter of interest, is the oldest road in

Alaska connecting Fairbanks to Valdez 364 miles away on the south coast."

They leave Fairbanks Airport taking the Airport Way, at the first junction they take a right onto Parks Avenue which takes them round the south of the city then directly onto the Richardson Highway where they settle down for the first leg of their journey. After 40 minutes driving the traffic has thinned considerably, they are almost alone on the long bleak cold highway. Diane is half asleep but Tim has been deep in thought and breaks the silence in the vehicle,

"Mike, I've been thinking a lot about HAARP and the other ionospheric research stations around the world. We know that HAARP in Gakona has just increased the number of radio transmitters at its facility to three hundred and sixty, providing a combined power of three point six megawatts and that its five new generators can produce sixteen megawatts of power. In addition the EISCAT heater in Norway is capable of transmitting over one billion watts of effective radiated power (ERF)."

Tim is interrupted by a yawn from the back of the vehicle as Diane drowsily adds,

"And the Russian SURA heater can transmit one hundred and ninety megawatts of ERF added to HIPAS the other HAARP installation and the ARECIBO facility in Puerto Rico, who knows what the Japanese and Chinese are doing."

Mike asks,

"OK, OK what's the point?"

Tim continues,

"The point is that each individual site meets its own countries regulatory controls where they exist' but there's no independent scientific organisation coordinating all of the sites globally. For example, what if there is a limit to how much power and artificial heating the Ionosphere can take before it ignites. What happens if all the world's heaters happen to go on line at the same time and exceed this limit; the scientists all admit that they don't know what'll happen until after they press the button, which when it happens will be too late."

Diane is now fully awake,

"Tim, are you suggesting that we try to set up an international group to monitor and control these experiments?"

"You read my mind."

Mike responds,

"It's an interesting idea but where would you find enough independent physicists and scientists plus the money to pay them?"

"One step at a time, first we identify the problem then work on the solution, I've already considered those points and potentially how to convince various governments to contribute."

Chapter - 16

Ambush

Mike is distracted by his rear view mirror,

"Diane there's a pair of binoculars in the pocket behind my seat, take them out and have a look at the car that's behind us it's been in the distance since we left Fairbanks."

She does as he asks, turning to examine the large dark saloon some way behind them.

"It's a big American saloon with an Alaskan number plate; there's three, no, four hefty looking men in greenish parkers nothing too suspicious for Alaska."

Mike is not convinced,

"Every time I speed up, they speed up; every time I slow down, they do the same, they are definitely following us, watch."

Mike gently increases their speed, the car in the distance does the same, after five minutes he gently slows down the car behind does the same keeping its distance, Mike turns to Tim,

"See what I mean, a normal driver would pass us on this highway."

Mike turns his attention to the GPS scanning the route ahead,

"Tim, take a look at this track 5 miles ahead, it goes off to the right, up into the woods, then turns and loops back. The saloon will have a problem following us up the hill and hopefully will get stuck."

Diane asks,

"And what happens to us?"

"That's why I wanted this vehicle, it's equipped for all terrain, don't worry about us."

Mike slows down as they get closer to the track, the car behind keeps its distance. As they get to the small track Mike swings the Chevy off the highway onto the uneven surface. The four wheel drive and big tyres grip into the gravel and lose stones as the Chevy accelerates up the hill into the forest, Mike shouts,

"Are they still following us?"

Diane is facing backwards,

"Yeah, they've pulled off the highway."

Mike looks ahead,

"In a few yards we can take the left turn that winds up through the forest then loops back on to the track."

The track is now only one car wide, like a fire break between the tall pine trees, as they are getting higher up the mountain the surface is now lightly covered in snow.

"This'll sort them out."

Says Mike to himself as he concentrates on keeping the Chevy straight.

The track swings to the right then they arrive back at the gravel track but higher up. Mike stops the Chevy reversing it between the trees,

"Bring the binoculars we'll see where they are."

Diane asks,

"Won't they be behind us?"

Mike grins,

"There's no way that saloon would make it up through the wood."

They creep to the edge of the track staying hidden amongst the trees so they can see the car below them. The car has slid off the track into a tree at the first bend its rear end is sticking across the track, further below them is the highway. The four men are standing outside looking at the car and up the track, all are carrying weapons. They seem to be discussing what to do as one of them unfolds a map. Tim touches Mike's arm,

"You're right they were following us, it will be nice to find out who they are working for and what they want?"

"Yeah I agree but they don't look like professionals, there's no way any of our people would come out on a mission like this in Alaska; in a saloon."
Diane whispers,

"Well that's good to know, now what?"
Mike is watching the men through the binoculars,

"Let's get back to the Chevy."
They carefully stalk back to the Chevy. Mike asks Diane to get the long black case from the back which she does, snapping open both catches she opens it, issuing a delighted,

"Wow a Heckler and Koch PSG-1 Snipers Rifle."
Mike is surprised,

"How come you know so much about weapons?"
Diane smiles,

"It's a woman thing, I'm curious that's all."
Mike takes the rifle with ammunition from the case clipping on the Hendsoldt '6 x 42' riflescope as Diane continues,

"In skilled hands that's the most accurate semi automatic in the world up to 600 metres."
Mike snaps on the 5 round magazine and puts two spare clips of the 7.62 mm ammunition into his jacket pocket.

"Diane, you stay in the back of the Chevy, Tim and I'll work our way down to find out what this is all about."
Diane protests,

"Why have I got to stay here?"
Mike grins,

"It's a man thing, do as you're told and stay alert."
Diane grumbles quietly and gets into the back of the Chevy. Tim and Mike carefully make their way down the track they keep just inside the tree line to avoid being seen. Whilst Mike and Tim are expertly moving through the trees, one of the men has left the car and is

following their vehicle tracks up into the forest. A second man has left the car he is working his way up through the woods on the opposite side of the track to Mike and Tim, unseen by each other. The two other men remain in ambush near their vehicle in case the Chevy comes back down the track. Diane makes herself comfortable in the back of the Chevy hidden by the tinted glass, as she watches Mike and Tim disappear into the tree line. She pulls a blanket over her for warmth. After 20 minutes she hears a movement, thinking Mike and Tim are returning she reaches for the door handle, at that moment an unshaven 6ft 3" brute of a man in a military green parka steps out of the trees with an automatic pistol in his hand.

Taking out her Beretta she checks the safety, crouching down further behind the rear seat, she keeps her eyes on the man. He cautiously approaches the vehicle, as he does she eases the blanket completely over her, leaving only a small gap so that she can see from between the rear seats. He walks round the vehicle slowly, then approaches weapon at the ready. He looks through the driver's window then she hears the crunch of his boots on the snow as he walks around the front stopping to look into the passenger window, he then moves to the rear door putting his left hand on the handle leaving his pistol ready for use in his right hand.

Diane takes a deep breath as the door mechanism slowly clicks open. She is snugged down between the seats with her Beretta aimed at the door. A crack of light appears as it opens, she readies herself. The man's right arm comes into view, his body hidden mostly behind the door she waits a second longer, hardly daring to breath remaining as still as possible, she seizes her moment as the man's right arm and now right leg are both visible.

She fires two shots in succession, the sound of the shots is deafening in the enclosed vehicle, before the man can react a bullet has passed through his right bicep followed by another smashing into his right kneecap. The man drops his weapon as he crumples to the ground groaning in agony.

Keeping her eye on his weapon Diane pushes the door fully open then steps out, her ears are ringing and her eyes smarting from the cordite inside the vehicle. She covers the man who is completely disabled and screaming in pain. She picks up his pistol then pushes the door shut whilst the man writhes on the ground in front of her. She points her pistol at his head.

"I want your jacket NOW."

She roughly pulls the good arm out then pulls the bloody sleeve of his right arm as he winces in pain, beneath him a red stain is spreading in the snow from his blood. He sits there in great pain trying to stem the flow of blood from his leg.

Diane takes off his trouser belt and uses it to make a tourniquet, so that he can control the blood flow with his left hand. Pointing her pistol again at his head she asks,

"Who are you working for?"

The man grimaces at her in silence; she asks again,

"Who are you working for?"

He spits,

"Fuck you."

She kicks him in the chest knocking him on his back, he cries out with the increased pain from the sudden movement. Diane lowers her pistol to his crotch prodding hard at his private parts,

"Fuck you too, I'm going to give you the count of three to answer my question or say goodbye to your dick forever."

"I'll ask you a final time; who are you working for...ONE...TWO...THREE."

The man screams,

"Wait, wait, I'll tell you, first help prop me up against a tree, I'll tell you everything."

Diane cautiously drags him over to the nearest tree propping him up against it,

"Well?"

The man starts,

"We're hired guns, a guy in New York contacted my brother our boss, offered a million bucks to eliminate you".

Diane is angry prodding her Beretta hard back into his crotch,

"What's his name, who was he?"

The man groans in pain,

"I need medical help."

Diane gives a cold look,

"You'll need an undertaker if you don't answer my questions."

The man gives up,

"OK, OK, we never met him, it was all done by telephone only my brother spoke to him, he told us he sounded foreign, that's all I know."

Diane backs off a distance going through the man's Jacket pockets,

"What's this?"

She pushes the satellite phone into the man's face, he answers,

"It's my brothers jacket, he's down by the car, the phone's to let his client know when the jobs done."

Diane glares at him,

"How was he going to pay you"?

The man is losing strength,

"The boss had 250,000 bucks as a deposit to cover our costs, the rest we get after it's done; the money was paid direct into my boss's bank account."

Diane continues,

"How did you know where to find us?"

The man continues,

"The client told my boss how and when you were arriving then sent us a tracker all we had to do was follow you."

Diane finishes going through the pockets and was about to throw the jacket over to the man when she feels a lump, she traces it to a hidden zipped pocket, opening it she finds a wallet with a wad of hundred dollar bills. She opens the wallet finding an ID card which looks unusual so she puts the lot in her pocket. She drapes the bloody jacket over the man and smiling says,

"It's your lucky day, stay here until we decide what to do with you."

The man groans in pain,

"You bitch."

In the meantime Tim and Mike have worked their way down towards the car, Mike carefully takes a look down the track towards the car. He whispers to Tim,

"There's only two down there, where's the other two? Stay alert."

They continue towards the damaged car which is wedged between two trees with the men crouched down behind it. They stay in the cover of the trees looking round for the other two men.

Carefully they creep round below the men who are armed with powerful hunting rifles and are busy concentrating on the track above them. Mike and Tim quietly get behind them to within twenty feet without being seen. Mike aims his H&K PSG-1 at one of the men as Tim points his Smith & Wesson at the other,

Mike orders,

"Put your weapons on the ground, any sudden movement, it'll be your last."

The men slowly turn their heads, upon seeing Mike and Tim they carefully place their weapons on the ground beside them.

"Now step forward one pace putting your hands on your heads."

They do as he says. Tim searches them both, removing their automatic pistols.

Mike asks,

"Where're the other two?"

The first man nods up the track,

"They went up to find you."

Tim flashes a concerned glance to Mike. Mike pulls some plastic cable ties from his pocket throwing them towards Tim,

"Tie their hands behind their back and their feet together."

Tim does as instructed then moves their weapons away from them.

Mike orders them,

"Sit down with your backs against the car."

They slump down beside the vehicle. Tim steps closer to the first man,

"Who are you and who're you working for?"

The man looks at the ground. Tim grabs him roughly searching his pockets he looks at Mike.

"Nothing"

Tim turns suddenly, swiping his pistol across the man's nose banging his head back against the car,

"NOW who are you working for?"

Both men look towards the ground in silence.

Back up the hill, Diane leaves the injured man by the tree. She jumps into the Chevy starting it she turns it round, then with her Beretta on her lap slowly drives it back the way they came. She drives down the hill and is approaching the track, above where the car is. She stops and backs the Chevy into the trees out of sight. Taking the keys out she silently creeps through the pine trees towards the area where the damaged car is. She makes her way to the edge of the wood where she can see the car without being seen.

Moving slowly to the edge of the tree line she smiles with relief as she sees fifty yards below her the two men tied up in front of Tim and Mike. She is about to break cover when she spots a movement in the trees on her side of the track behind Mike and Tim. It's the fourth man and he's carrying a UZI machine pistol, she watches as he slowly moves out of the tree line then onto the track behind Mike and Tim, levelling his weapon as he closes on them, they're unaware of his presence as they are intent on trying to get their prisoners to talk.

"Put your weapons down very slowly." the man calls,

Tim turns his head in the direction of the voice then seeing the UZI in the man's hand nods to Mike, they slowly do as instructed,

"Now step away from the weapons with your hands where I can see them."

They move forward towards the man one pace, the two men remain sitting on the ground beside the car. Mike still has his pistol in his holster but knows that the UZI is a formidable weapon at such short range, they wouldn't have a chance. The man shouts,

"Where's the girl?"

Mike answers,

"She's at the top of the forest in our car."

The man grins,

"Not any more, didn't you hear the shots? My brother took care of her."

Mike and Tim hadn't heard the shots and look at each other in dismay.

Mike asks,

"Who are you and what do you want from us?"

The man sneers,

"It's none of your fucking business who we are, we just get paid to do our job and you're it."

Diane is focused and thinking on her feet, something she's always been good at, the adrenalin has kicked in, she calculates the distance between her and the man who is now standing sideways to her facing Mike and Tim,

"Around fifty yards in bad light." she whispers.

Taking out her Beretta she carefully moves to a position where she has a clear view,

"It's now or never." she mutters,

Taking up a shooting stance she steadies herself and her nerves,

"Steady girl it's one hell of a distance." she mutters again under her breath,

She's fully aware that she's only got one chance, if she misses Tim and Mike would be dead. Taking a few deep breaths she carefully aims, then whistles, the man turns to face the sound thinking it's his brother returning, giving Diane a clearer shot at the white of his face. She squeezes off three shots in quick succession hoping one will hit him. Mike and Tim watch the man turn, they hear the three shots then the man's head explodes as the bullets hit he drops to the ground. Mike and Tim pick up their weapons rushing over to the man who is clearly dead. The three shots have obliterated his forehead. Diane steps clear of the wood holstering her Beretta, she runs down to her friends throwing herself into Mike's arms. She turns to look at the man as Mike blocks her view.

"Don't he's a bit of a mess he's no longer a threat."

Mike tries to comfort her,

"Diane that was the most remarkable piece of shooting I've ever seen, best part of fifty yards in low light and all three shots hit their target."

Diane is shaking but keeps her poise as Tim gives her a hug,

"Thank you, we owe you our lives, they were paid assassins."

Diane hides her feelings about what she has just done then smiles,

"You should see the other one."

Tim and Mike look shocked,

"What happened to him he's not."

Diane interrupts explaining what happened after they left, finishing with,

"I left him propped up against a tree, he won't be going anywhere."

Mike and Tim are impressed Mike kisses her on the cheek,

"Diane you're one special woman."

She gives a false laugh trying to hide her shock,

"You haven't seen anything yet."

Mike knows that she's suffering inside,

"Diane don't keep it inside it's best to let it out."

She smiles affectionately at him,

"Perhaps later"

Mike and Tim turn their attention to the two men still sitting on the ground who are obviously shocked at what they had just witnessed. Mike takes hold of the first man,

"If you don't tell me exactly who you are working for I'll turn you over to her and she'll shoot little pieces off you until you talk."

The men had overheard what she'd done to their associate and witnessed firsthand her remarkable shooting skills. The man nods,

"I'll tell you. We were hired by the boss he was offered a million dollars to take you three out."

Diane nods at Mike,

"He's telling the truth so far."

Mike asks,

"Which one of you is the boss?"

The man nods in the direction of the corpse,

"He's the brother of the man you shot up on the hill."

Diane utters,

"Oh shit, he was the boss."

She reaches in her pocket giving Mike the satellite phone she had taken from the boss's jacket,

"They were supposed to use this to call their employer once the job was done, he would transfer the rest of the money to their bank."

Mike thinks for a moment then speaks to the two men,

"I've got a proposal for you to consider, you call the number, tell him that the jobs done, that we're dead and buried where no one can find us. That there was some action, your boss is dead, tell him to transfer the money to your account, you split it three ways; we let you go, you disappear and live happily thereafter and we go back under cover."

The men exchange glances, the first one says arrogantly,

"And if we don't?"

Mike smiles,

"Simple you'll end up poor, buried on this mountain and we still go undercover."

The men exchange words,

"We'll do it."

Mike smiles again,

"That's good thinking, a win, win situation all round."

Mike hands the phone to the man as Tim cuts his hands free, the man glances at Diane who is pointing her pistol at his crotch.

"How do we know you won't kill us after we make the call?"

Mike grins,

"You have my word, if I break my word she'll shoot me OK."

The man looks at Diane who nods. The man takes the phone but before he presses the button Diane wants to know,

"What's the name of the person you are about to call?"

"We never knew, he only spoke to Mick, he was the boss."

"OK, make the call, ask him for his name."

Tim has his head close to the phone as the man presses the key then waits as the phone autodials, it's immediately answered by a male voice,

"Hi, it's Chas, Mick asked me to call you immediately the job was done."

The voice at the other end responds,

"Where's Mick? Put him on."

Chas looks at Diane then continues.

"He's no longer with us he took one in the head."

The voice asks,

"Where did you put them?"

Chas continues,

"Halfway up a mountain, buried deep off the beaten track along with Mick. They'll never be found."

The voice sounds pleased,

"Good, good job boys."

Chas interrupts,

"What about the money?"

The voice goes quiet for a moment,

"Text me your bank details from this phone, payment will be in your account tomorrow."

Chas says,

"Thank you, I'll do it immediately, what do I call you?"

The voice replies,

"Sir will do, well done. After you've sent the text destroy the phone completely, understand."

Chas replies,

"Yes Sir."

The phone goes dead, the conversation ended. Tim takes the phone,

"Got your bank details?"

Chas nods touching his head "Here." He gives Tim the account details Tim enters the data and sends the text,

"Job done, now you're rich men but we keep the phone."

Diane asks,

"Where's the receiver unit you were using to track us?"

Chas answers,

"It's in the car."

Diane climbs in and takes out the receiver handing it to Mike,

"They were tracking us with this. We must have a bug on us somewhere."
Mike tells Chas,
"We'll pull your car out you can then recover your associate, then take him to some medical help."
Chas sneers,
"And if I don't?"
Mike is serious,
"That's not our problem as long as you bury him."
Chas nods,
"That's fair enough."
Mike turns and speaks to the other man,
"If he doesn't help your partner, you'd better watch your back because you'll be next." Chas asks,
"One question who the fuck are you?"
Mike leans close to Chas's face,
"We're the US government and your worst nightmare, if we hear that you've not honoured our deal, you can look forward to a great deal of pain before the relief of death arrives."
Mike sends Tim back up the hill to collect the Chevy, whilst Diane keeps her Beretta covering the two men,
Chas asks Mike,
"Is that necessary, she's making me nervous."
Mike retorts,
"You tell her to put it away if it bothers you that much."
Mike looks over the car which has bodywork damage but looks serviceable.
"Chas, once we pull your car back onto the track we'll make sure it starts then leave you to collect your mate you can then make your way back to Fairbanks; OK?"
Chas nods,
"Yeah, thanks."
A few minutes later Tim arrives with the Chevy, Mike positions him behind the damaged car and attaches the

Chevy's electric winch. As soon as it's secure he gives Tim a wave who starts the powerful electric motor, the steel cable tightens as slowly the car creaks free from between the pine trees and is pulled back onto the track. Mike disconnects the winch cable winding it back securely. Mike then gets into the car and turns the key, it starts immediately, he drives it a short distance up the track. He stops, switches off the engine then walks back down to the Chevy,

"Chas the cars OK, it should get you to Fairbanks and one more thing to remember, your employer must have been very powerful to pay you a million dollars, then have the resources at his disposal to have found us. He won't be pleased if he ever finds out you've double crossed him, so make sure you and your partners make a better job of disappearing than you did of trying to take us out."

Chas mutters under his breath,

"Yeah, I'd already thought of that."

Mike, Diane and Tim get back into the Chevy, manoeuvring it down the track to the highway and leaving the two men trudging up the hill towards their associate. After 10 minutes on the highway Mike pulls over to the side onto the rough and stops the engine. Tim asks,

"What's the matter?"

"Nothing serious, we have to find Diane's bug and disable it otherwise they'll know where we are."

Mike takes the tracker and asks both of them to get out of the vehicle they walk in different directions away from the Chevy. After they had covered seventy five yards he calls them back as the tracking signal had moved towards Diane.

"Diane, I think the bug is on you, empty your pockets."

The first thing she takes out is her Satellite phone,

Mike stops her,

"Wait a moment."

He takes her phone, placing it on ground behind the vehicle then jumps in and drives one hundred yards down the highway checking the receiver.

He reverses back to Tim and Diane,

"Give me the phone."

Mike opens the boot taking out a comprehensive tool kit, he quickly dismantles the phone. Carefully concealed behind the circuit board he finds a miniature circuit disc wired into the phones aerial. He shows it to the others,

"This is the transmitter, now watch the receiver."

He pulls the disc breaking the connections, immediately the receiver shows an error message 'signal lost'. Tim asks,

"Are you certain there's not another one?"

Mike walks away from the Chevy with the receiver,

"No, there's nothing else."

He returns and speaks to Diane and Tim,

"You know what this means?"

Diane frowns,

"What?"

"It means that someone at the Pentagon who prepared or handled the Sat Phone is working against us and that could be anyone from Tony down."

Diane queries,

"But why put it in my phone?"

"That's easy they knew that we'd always be sure to look after you."

"Because I'm a woman, that's a joke it's me that's been looking after you two."

"That's true they just didn't know what sort of woman you are."

Tim buts in,

"No, neither did I"

Mike breaks the discussion,

"We now don't trust anyone, let's get going, it's getting late and I want to get to Gakona before nightfall."

They get back into the Chevy, Mike puts his foot down, there's hardly any traffic and the driving conditions are good. The rest of their trip to Delta Junction continues without incident they're making good time as they leave Delta Junction, staying on the Richardson Highway towards Gakona. Tim asks,

"Mike, do you think they'll know where we're staying in Gakona?"

"Very unlikely, I booked the cabin myself with one of my other credit cards in another name, we should be safe there."

Tim turns towards Diane as he hears the sound of her Beretta Magazine being reloaded,

"What're you doing?"

Diane smiles sweetly,

"Reloading, just in case you two are wrong again."

Mike laughs "Touché."

"How far is Gakona?"

Mike points to the GPS,

"Gakona is another hundred miles we're averaging eighty five miles per hour, so we should be there in about an hour and twenty minutes."

Diane grumbles from the back,

"I can't last that long, I'm going to open the food chest, I'm suddenly very hungry."

She rummages in the back opening the plastic box she passes a coffee flask to Tim with three energy bars, she opens her flask, the smell of coffee fills the Chevy,

"Drive steady." she yells at Mike.

It's getting dark as they arrive at the Gakona Lodge and Trading Post on the Tok Cut-Off Road. The lodge is located beside the Wrangell St.Elias National Park and the Copper River Valley one of the most famous salmon fishing spots in the world and surrounded by natural beauty. Pulling up at the Lodge House Mike tells them to stay in the vehicle while he checks in and collects the keys to their log cabin which is nearby. He returns smiling, placing a cardboard box in the back of the Chevy, Diane asks,

"What are you grinning about?"

"Wait and see."

He drives across a small open space to a beautiful, very substantial log cabin parking in front of it, the lights are on inside with smoke rising from the chimney, it looks inviting as it's now dark and getting very cold. Tim and Diane get their bags as Mike opens the door, inside the cabin is very cosy, warmed by a large log fire that completes the romantic atmosphere, Mike takes Diane's bag leading her into the large and comfortable lounge,

"Oh, this is really wonderful; log cabins have always been one of my fantasies."

Diane sighs with pleasure as she slumps down on a large leather sofa. Mike smiles,

"Relax, Tim and I will get the rest of the things."

Diane jumps up,

"No way, I'm going to explore."

She heads to one of the doors off the lounge.

Whilst Tim is unloading Mike takes out a small flat plastic case and screwdriver he goes round to the front number plate. Tim asks,

"Mike, what are you doing?"

Mike takes a new front number plate out of the box,

"I'm changing our plates in case whoever's trying to stop us has access to our military satellites, these are genuine plates and cannot be traced, I chose this vehicle and colour because it's one of the most common in Alaska."

Mike then does the same to the rear plate putting the old ones back in the box. They unload the rest of their things including the rifle case and cardboard box, their breath creating clouds of mist in the freezing night air. Closing the cabin door they dump their gear on the floor and both sit down on the comfortable divan in front of the open fire.

"Mike, it's been one hell of a long day it's nice to slow down for moment."

Tim leans back and closes his eyes but only for a second as Diane bounces in from the kitchen with renewed energy,

"Guys everything we need is here, the kitchen is fully stocked with food and wine, and I'll be cooking dinner tonight." Tim sits up,

"Diane, where do you get your energy from, slow down, I need a bath and bed for an hour to create some space from what we've just been through."

Mike laughs,

"Wimp, I've got just the thing to help us relax."

He opens the cardboard box and hands two bottles of malt whisky to Diane,

"These are for you, with our very grateful thanks, providing we can open one now."

Diane immediately produces three glasses then sits on the floor on the bearskin rug in front of them, the flickering flames crackling from the log fire causing shadows to dance around the room. Tim raises his glass,

"A toast to Diane, our guardian angel"

Mike raises his glass,

"To our guardian angel"

Diane smiles,

"This is one of life's magical moments."

The whisky warms them and helps wind them down as each one of them had subconsciously been thinking about the action in the forest. Diane excitedly tells Mike,

"This cabin is absolutely perfect, there are three double bedrooms all with bathrooms and the kitchen is so well equipped, not what I was expecting at all, how did you find it?"

Mike grins,

"It was very easy it's the only decent place in the area and by coincidence, only fifteen minutes from the HAARP access road which we'll be visiting tomorrow morning."

Tim groans,

"Not early I hope."

Diane gets up,

"Tim it's time to prepare food."

"What are we having?"

"There're fresh Salmon in the fridge and I intend frying them with herbs and serving with boiled potatoes, I hope that's OK."

After dinner they help clear up as Tim yawns, complimenting the chef,

"Diane that was delicious. Now for me, it's time for that long soak in the bath followed by a long sleep, goodnight to you both. Diane thanks again."

Tim retires to his bedroom.

Mike looks at Diane,

"What about you?"

Diane softly,

"I'd like to curl up with you and a bottle of whisky in front of the fire."

Mike pretends to look shocked,

"Well that suits me fine."

He takes her hand, picking up their glasses and the bottle he leads her to the fireplace where she sits down on the rug. After placing another couple of logs on the fire, he sits down beside her.

Diane snuggles up to Mike as he puts his arm round her shoulder she looks into his eyes,

"I wanted to thank you for supporting me today I was so close to breaking down when you saved me with your understanding words."

She leans into him kissing him fully on the lips Mike reciprocates stroking her hair,

"It's getting hot in here."

He takes off his fleece she does the same revealing the tight cashmere pullover hugging her figure. She slowly undoes his shirt buttons. Then, suddenly as if she has had an electric shock, Diane pushes him away, her eyes filling with tears she turns away from him.

"I can't do it, I can't,"

Mike is confused,

"Hey, what's happened, what did I do?"

He moves forward to comfort her, she turns quickly,

"Don't touch me, leave me alone,"

Mike backs away concerned and now even more confused,

"Look Diane, just tell me whats happened, I'm sorry if I've done something that's upset you,"

She slowly turns to look at him, her face wet with tears,

"Mike it's nothing you've done, it's me and something that happened a long time ago,"

Mike passes her a glass of whisky and gently speaks,

"Let's have another drink. We can at least sit together then maybe you can tell me what happened, it looks as if you need to confront whatever is bothering you. Anything you tell me will remain between us"

Diane takes a sip from her glass. The flickering flames from the fire reflecting in her wet face, she takes a deep breath,

"Mike I really like you, you're the first man that I have been attracted to since…"

She stops mid sentence then after a moments silence Mike finishes it,

"Cairo,"

Diane continues,

"Yes, what happened in Cairo was terrible and truthfully I've not been able to deal with it,"

Mike guessed it had something to do with events in Cairo,

"Why not start at the beginning tell me what happened, I'd like to help you if I can, it would help a lot just to share the problem"

Diane takes another large sip of whisky,

"OK, you're the first and only person I've told."
Mike nods,

"Relax I'm a man of my word,"
Diane continues,

"I was working for two years on a large excavation near Cairo. When the excavation came to an end I was preparing to leave when the head of the team of diggers that had been working with me, told me they'd discovered another find at an unexplored site in the desert. He showed me a small figure he said came from the site. It was a fascinating and important piece so I asked them to show me where they found it. They agreed to take me the next morning."

Mike takes a sip of his whisky listening intently as Diane speaks,

"We drove for about two hours into the desert to an area where a large tent had been set up. As we entered the tent I immediately became suspicious, there were three camp beds, a large rug and cushions on the floor, no sign of any excavation. I asked them what was going on then tried to get back to the vehicle, the three of them grabbed me and dragged me into the tent. I struggled to break free when one of them hit me on the head and I lost consciousness. Sometime later I came to, nude and trussed up like a chicken. The bastards abused me violently for three days between me passing out, the last day they knocked me about so badly I became unconscious. When I regained consciousness I discovered I had been left in the desert presumably to die, the tent and the vehicle had gone fortunately they left my clothes. After walking for a day without water I collapsed and passed out. When I came round I discovered I had been rescued by a young goat herd that spotted me in the desert and called his mother, his family looked after me saving my life. I'll always be grateful to them."

Mike is shocked by this revelation and moves to comfort Diane,

"Diane I am so sorry I had no idea that you had suffered so much, what happened when you got back to Cairo, did you report it to the Police?"

Diane seems relieved, having got this terrible trauma into the open,

"No the local police would protect their own in a case as brutal as this. It took several weeks to recover physically although mentally I was completely screwed up I vowed this would never happen to me or anyone else I knew again. I was determined to learn to protect myself. I went back to England for a year and became a qualified Close Protection Officer which included arms training in Slovenia and close physical combat skills. I then spent a year working as a Close Protection Officer for an Arab princess in Dubai then trained for another year to hone my skills. The desire for revenge became so intense that I returned to Cairo to hunt down the three men that hurt me."

Mike asks,

"Did you find them?"

Diane takes another drink, in silence as if uncertain whether to go on, wiping the tears from her face she catches her breath with a sob and continues,

"I read that all three were mysteriously found dead in the desert. The report said that each had first suffered with a shot to their genitals and finally killed with a bullet to the head,"

Diane breaks down in tears. Mike cautiously puts his arm round her as she buries her head in his shoulder sobbing. Mike comforts her, the best he can.

"That's real justice Diane you did the right thing, I would have done the same if it had happened to me. You must let this suffering go it's a painful door in the past that you should leave closed. We have to move on and now have each other, whether you like it or not I have very strong feelings for you."

Diane looks Mike in the eyes,

"But Mike, I killed three men in cold blood"

Mike smiles gently,

"Those animals deserved to die. You probably saved many other women from suffering the same fate. This changes nothing for me other than making me more determined to try and help you forget what happened and to look after you."

Diane smiles lightening up,

"You mean like you did in the forest?"

Mike smiles too,

"That's not fair I was too busy being saved by a remarkable women."

Diane empties her glass,

"Mike thank you, I feel as if a weight has been lifted off my shoulders,"

She kisses him on the lips and pushes his shirt off his shoulders admiring his muscular physique, almost afraid to touch him, she lightly kisses his chest, his excitement roused he very gently lifts her pullover over her head. She shakes her long blonde hair free it falls onto her shoulders Mike is mesmerised,

"You're an extremely beautiful woman."

"And Mike, you are an extremely beautiful man."

He leans forward and kisses her neck working down to her shoulder, her breathing changes into deep gasps as he releases her bra and kisses her porcelain breasts. She whispers in his ear,

"I haven't done this for a long time."

Mike kisses her ear and whispers,

"Neither have I."

Gently between kisses they slowly strip off their clothing, their bodies glistening in the firelight Mike whispers,

"What about Tim?" nodding to the door,

Diane gives a cheeky smile and wipes away the last of the tears from her face,

"I've locked his door."

Their bodies intertwine as they make endless love which seems to release years of pent up frustrations. Two hours later they lay exhausted in each others arms on the bearskin rug, with a blanket pulled over them, the flickering flames the only witness to their passionate lovemaking. The empty whisky bottle lies beside them. At four o'clock with their arms around each other they make their way to the bedroom, quietly unlocking Tim's door as they pass it.

At 9.30 am they're woken by knocking on their door and Tim's voice,

"Breakfast is served."

They get up slipping into the Lodge bath robes then open the door to the wonderful smell of coffee and bacon,

Diane speaks first,

"Good morning Tim, what a lovely surprise."

Mike arrives behind her,

"Morning Tim, you have a good night?"

Tim gives a knowing look,

"It looks as if you two did."

Mike is embarrassed,

"What do you mean?"

"Along with many other gay men, I seem to be more sensitive and perceptive regarding people around me and their feelings. When I met Diane again at the Pyramid in Iraq, she had changed from the women I previously knew there was a certain coldness about her. I sensed that she carried an enormous burden, which from the look in her eyes this morning seems to have been lifted."

Diane responds,

"That's one of the reasons I loved working with you, you were never a threat I could be natural and concentrate on my work without always having to be on my defence against approaches from the men I was working with, who only had one thing on their minds."

Diane places a kiss on Sam's cheek,

Tim sets a plate of bacon, sausages and eggs in front of them with a large coffee,

"Anyway it didn't take a great detective to work out you had a good night, the blanket and the empty whisky bottle were a dead giveaway, strangely during the night my door managed to lock and unlock itself. I'm very pleased for both of you, you'd make a great couple if you let it happen, by the look in each of your eyes you did."

They have a relaxed laugh and attack their breakfasts,

Diane asks,

"What time do we leave?"

Mike wants them ready to leave at eleven as their appointment at HAARP is at twelve. At eleven sharp they open the cabin door stepping out into the cold fresh air. It's a crisp bright day. The panoramic view is breathtaking. The pine trees surrounding the lodge complex have a backdrop of snow covered mountains rising behind them. Diane gasps,

"Mike, it's beautiful."

"Yes, it's a shame it was dark when we travelled down as the scenery would have been spectacular in daylight, let's load up."

They have the cabin for as many days as they need therefore only take the bare essentials needed for their trip including Mike's flat black rifle case. Tim asks,

"Expecting more trouble?"

"After yesterday's experience it's going everywhere with me."

The Chevy starts easily they wait a minute or two while it warms up then Mike drives out of the complex turning left. North West, onto the Glenn Highway Tok Cut Off.

Diane asks,

"How far is it?"

Mike looks at the GPS,

"Ten miles to the HAARP access road say about fifteen minutes. The large river that we're following is the Copper River it runs into the Copper River Valley where our cabin is located."

They cruise along the empty highway. Tim turns to Mike,

"Do you reckon the people behind yesterdays attempt will try again?"

Mike nods,

"It depends on two factors, one if they believed we were eliminated then they may call off their hounds. The other is that once we have visited HAARP I'm sure they'll have a contact there that will let them know we're still around. It's my intention for us to disappear immediately afterwards, we return to the Lodge put the vehicle immediately out of site in the Cabins garage. I have another set of plates which will make it more difficult for satellites to single us out, particularly if we travel at night. I've also arranged another secure transport option at a little airfield in Tok further along on the Alaskan Highway, which is not far from here if we need it."

Tim is impressed,

"Just what I wanted to hear"

From the back of the vehicle,

"Me too"

As they drive along the Glenn Highway Mike points out the fast flowing river running parallel to the road,

"That's the Copper River it's about 287 miles long, it drops 12 feet per mile draining 24,000 square miles of land. It has thirteen major tributaries flowing at an average speed of seven miles per hour. By the time it reaches the Copper Delta at Cordova it's a mile wide."

Diane feints a yawn,

"You really are one of the best informed tour guides I've ever been with."

Tim asks,

"You, been with many then?"

"Tim, I didn't mean it that way."

They arrive at a tiny uneven track as Mike swings the Chevy off the highway,

"Mike you sure this is it? All I can see are woods and the mountain."

"Just wait a moment."

After a half mile he turns left at the end of the track, then onto another unmade up road heading deeper into the pine forest, parallel to the Glenn Highway. They're surrounded by tall pine trees,

Diane pipes up from the back,

"For some reason Pine forests are beginning to make me nervous."

They continue into the forest along the bumpy road for a short distance until the track gets narrower. In front of them there's a very large area that's been cleared of trees, in the centre is a three storey, white, L shaped building with each of the floors smaller than the previous creating a tower like appearance. There's a bank of high power generators attached to the north side.

Chapter - 17

High Frequency Active Aural Research – Alaska

Mike announces,

"Welcome to the HAARP control centre, if we continue up this track we'll end up at the antenna arrays."

Tim suggests,

"I'm curious why not take a look up there first?"

Mike drives past the building which looks deserted, the only signs of life being a few parked cars and two large trucks. The road takes them along the foot of the mountain then on their left they see another massive area cleared from the forest covering thirty five acres with an array of one hundred and eighty, seventy five foot high antenna towers. Each tower is topped with a pair of crossed beams pointing north south and east west with a maze of wires from each cross beam. Mike explains,

"These wire connections allow the people at HAARP to hook the antennas together so that they can act in unison as one gigantic transmitter. The invisible radio waves being transmitted cork screw upwards causing the ions in the upper atmosphere to race round in gigantic circles directly above the antenna array. They can change the direction of rotation of the circles by switching the transmission cycle between the north-south and east-west bars of the antennas."

The area around the antenna array is fenced off to prevent access. Mike turns the Chevy round then heads back down to the building. He parks near the main entrance, after locking the Chevy they enter a small unmanned reception area. Diane presses a bell on the desk, after a few minutes a man with grey hair about fifty five years old appears, introducing himself as Doctor Peter Philips,

"How do you do, I've been expecting you."
He holds out his hand to Diane,

"Doctor Diane Pemberton, it's always a pleasure to meet people of your calibre that have an interest in our work."
Mike shakes his hand,

"Dr Michael Stevenson, Peter it's good to meet you, we've heard so much about your fascinating project I felt that it was time we met the people involved personally."
Mike introduces Tim,

"This is Dr Timothy Knights."
Peter invites them to follow him for coffee,

"This is our meeting and rest room, I'll give you an overview of HAARP then answer your questions prior to our tour, please take a seat."
The room is fairly basic with a large round table surrounded by worn chairs as Peter makes the coffee he notices their surprise,

"We prefer to spend our money on antennas, systems and power generators we have no time for glitzy offices."
Mike asks,

"How many employees are there here?"

"We only have ten full time staff although this is usually augmented by visiting scientists that carry out research, normally university physicists, government scientists and commercial firms involved in communications or radio science, we don't have a visitors centre, your visit is something of an exception. However we're currently winding down some of our activities so I'll have time to show you round, which will be my pleasure, sugar and milk?"

"Yes, in all three thank you."
The four of them sit round the table with their coffee as Peter tells them about his work,

"The objective of our research has always been to expand our knowledge of the physical and electrical

properties of the ionosphere, to gain a comprehensive understanding of the natural phenomena occurring in the Earth's ionosphere and near space environment. These properties can affect our military or civilian communications and navigation systems, which is why it's very important to understand their interaction."
Diane prompts him,

"And have the ability to manipulate them?"

"Well that too is part of our work. You could say we have the ability to manipulate sections of the ionosphere."
Mike is curious about their financiers,

"Peter, how are you funded? It must cost a small fortune to maintain and operate a site like this?"

"Well that's a bit of a sore point; we've just been informed our funding is being cut considerably which could mean our potential closure or merger with another facility."
Tim also wants to know more about their sources of finance,

"But I thought your funding was jointly from the Air Force Research Laboratory and the Office of Naval Research."

"Yes that's true and common knowledge but it's still an embarrassing question to answer."
Diane probes further,

"Peter why?"

"Well, because we do a lot of genuine scientific work here, yet our financial masters are the government and military, this creates large conflicts of interest."
Tim asks,

"How do you mean?"
Peter looks flustered. Diane gently puts her hand on his arm,

"We don't mean to cause you any embarrassment we're only interested in understanding the extent of work HAARP undertakes. In fact we may be able to help you we've many high level contacts in the government."

"Thank you, I'm really only a scientist, dedicated to my work, we never wanted those financial people in their ivory towers disrupting the remarkable progress we're making. We've created a world class research facility at the leading edge of exploration in our field; if you really think there's anything you can do to help."

He stops as the desperation in his voice begins to show through. Mike senses Peter's delusion and decides to exploit it,

"The more you can tell us the more we may be able to help. All we know at present is what's in the public domain, which isn't a lot. We understand the basic principles of ionospheric heating and the principles behind your original research but we'd like to learn more about some of the fringe activities that your financiers have forced upon you, for example we already know about their work with low frequency deep sea communications with submarines."

Peter seems to relax a little,

"I don't suppose it matters any more, I'll try to explain. Originally our research was purely scientific, as our knowledge of the functions of the ionosphere became clearer we could see the potential in tapping into the enormous electrical energy that exists in the magnetosphere and Electrojet, which if safely accomplished could potentially provide the world with endless supplies of environmentally clean energy. This brought our programme into conflict with the Petroleum companies and the major power suppliers. Their only motivation was increasing profits from their consumers not providing them with clean, low cost energy. At this time the military became interested in our work as they saw the Electrojet as a means by which they could listen in to worldwide communications and potentially blocking those of their enemies.

Once they became interested our existing scientific funding mysteriously dried up and the Military stepped in to replace it providing us with more powerful equipment and hardware, hence their control over us.

We had managed to successfully manipulate our Extremely Low Frequency transmissions to provide Radio Tomography of Geologic Strata which allows us to map resources and minerals below the Earth's crust. The military redirected this research towards finding underground military and nuclear facilities around the world. They are currently working on developing this technology further for mind manipulation using ELF transmissions."

Diane interrupts,

"As you know one of my passions is archaeology. This would be an incredible tool for archaeologists."

"Exactly, but the military had another motive, through our research they discovered there was a connection between Low Frequency transmissions, earthquakes and the ionosphere which they wanted to exploit. Since our inception we have understood the important relationship between the Ionosphere and the weather, part of our research was to learn if it was possible to manipulate the weather patterns so that we could bring an end to droughts and floods by balancing the weather across the globe. The military quickly realised that this concept could be used as a potential weapon, pushing forward their experiments without a proper understanding of the consequences if they made mistakes."

Tim asks,

"Do you believe that the current unusual weather patterns with growing numbers of natural disasters around the world could be a result of this programme?"

Peter looks across at Tim,

"Without doubt, they've been carrying out weather manipulation experiments that I would not have believed sensible or possible and certainly without any regard for the consequences, which sadly we are now witnessing all over the world."

Mike asks,

"As the Senior Director of HAARP why didn't you try to stop them?"

"Oh, I tried to I sent numerous messages warning them of possible consequences, recommending that they slow down the pace of their experiments until we knew more about the ionosphere's reaction to ever increasing unnatural voltages. Yes, I am the director here but the ionospheric research sites in the US are now managed by the Tactical Technology Office of DARPA, the Defense Advanced Research Projects Agency, my authority is basically to do as I'm told and keep my mouth shut, to put it bluntly."

Mike is somewhat surprised,

"They told you that?"

"Not in those exact words, they were more subtle. If I didn't do as they demanded, I would never work in this field again."

Peter looks at Diane and adds,

"You must understand this has been my life's work, my passion."

Mike continues his questioning,

"Peter, can you tell us if the Russian concerns about the USA's experiments using Extremely Low Frequencies and magnetic fields to change people's emotions were genuine or propaganda?"

Peter looks drained almost relieved by his confessions,

"There is a secret research facility near New York that has gone far beyond what the Russians suspected."

Diane asks,

"Is that on Long Island?"

"Yes, they took our Radio Tomography research data and developed it themselves into a project that would enable them to manipulate people's state of mind in the receiving area."

Diane looks surprised,

"You mean mind control?"

"Sadly yes, you could call it that and more."

There's a knock on the door another man in his late fifties enters,

"Dr Philips the trucks have arrived, we've started loading, are you ready?"

"Yes, I'll be along in a moment."

The man leaves, Peter looks down at the table,

"This is the beginning of the end for me, I'm sorry it will not possible to take you to lunch as I'm having to supervise the loading of very specialised equipment; would it be possible for you to return this afternoon, I'll show you round then."

Diane is concerned for Peter,

"What do you mean beginning of the end?"

"They've started transferring our most important equipment to another location."

Mike asks the question that they're all thinking,

"Transferring it to where?"

"I'm afraid I'm not party to that information, I'm sorry I have to go."

Mike shakes his hand,

"Peter we're very grateful for your frankness, I know it must've been very difficult, we'll look forward to seeing you at three o'clock. One more thing, if anyone calls asking if we've been here, would you mind telling them that we didn't arrive and you've heard nothing from us, I'll tell you why later."

"No problem, see you later." he leads them out.

They're silent as they get into the Chevy, Mike starts the engine.

Tim exclaims,

"Christ Mike it's all true."

Diane is upset she has great sympathy for Peter, but is cautious,

"Tim do you trust him?"

Tim had been trying to probe Peter's thoughts nods,

"Diane, I'm certain he was telling the truth, he was a completely disillusioned man desperate for someone he could talk to."

Mike adjusts the GPS coldly commenting,

"Then the timing of our visit was perfect."

Mike is about to pull away when Peter rushes out of the door with a small square flat package, Mike opens the window, Peter pushes it into his hand,

"I'm glad I caught you, when you get to a secure computer take a look at this, it may help you understand. All the information you're seeking is there. I've been saving it for years perhaps this is the right moment or rather the right people to see it, see you later."

He dashes back into the building.

"Mike, what was that all about?"

"No idea Diane, we'll find out later."

Mike drives back the way they came, Diane asks,

"Where are we going now?"

Mike is about to answer her as Tim cuts in,

"Back to the Gakona Lodge, they've a fantastic restaurant there called The Carriage House, perfect for lunch."

Mike nudges him in the ribs,

"Enough of that, that's exactly what I was about to say, you're getting as bad as Aacaarya."

"Mike, I'm sorry I was tuned in throughout the meeting and hadn't quite switched off. We don't have a computer with us."

"Yes we do, I've a secure laptop at TOK, just up the highway about seventy five miles, we'll collect it after we've seen Peter this afternoon."

Mike drives them back to the Lodge where they have lunch. Two hours later they are heading back to the HAARP facility. Diane says wistfully,

"Mike that was a wonderful meal, Thank you."

"Yeah, quite exceptional, shame Peter couldn't have been with us."

Arriving at HAARP they park outside the building, immediately noticing that the trucks have gone. On entering reception Diane presses the bell, after a few moments the scientist that interrupted their meeting arrives looking very upset, he asks if he can help them, they explain that they have a meeting with Dr Peter Philips at three. This seems to upset him even more.

Chapter - 18

Death on the highway

The scientist is silent for a moment as if not knowing what to say,

"I'm sorry, I didn't know, are you friends of his?"

"No, we only met him this morning we're from the University, why?"

The scientist continues with a saddened look on his face,

"I'm afraid there's been a terrible accident, I'm sorry to tell you that he."

The man blows his nose looking close to tears,

"He was killed when his car went off the road."

They look at each other in shocked silence,

Tim recovers then asks,

"What happened?"

The man continues,

"It was just after the trucks left he told me he had to go to TOK and left in a hurry, we only heard an hour ago, when the police called to tell us."

Mike asks,

"Where did it happen?"

The man is distraught,

"We worked together for 10 years. I'm so sorry; it was about twenty miles up the highway his car was found in the Copper River."

Tim is deep in thought and asks,

"He was going to show us round."

"I'm afraid that won't be possible now, we're technically shut down."

"Where were the trucks going?"

The man seems uncomfortable,

"They were taking the equipment to an underground storage site, that's all I know, sorry I can't help you."

Mike presses him,

"That's important and expensive equipment surely you know where it's being taken?"

The man is adamant almost angry,

"Look, I told you I don't know."

He quickly shows them to the door. They step out into the fresh air walking slowly towards the Chevy.

Diane has taken the news badly,

"I didn't know Peter but I liked what I saw of him, he was old school, a victim of his work, what do you think Mike?"

"That man was afraid of something, this whole thing stinks. It was no accident. If they were able to get to him to stop him talking then they must know we're still around, let's get away from here we've got work to do."

Once they are moving Tim tells them,

"He was lying, he knew where those trucks were going, I can't be certain but he thought about New York when I asked him the question."

Diane is impressed with Tim's growing ability,

"Long Island perhaps, Tim, I like having you along you are silent and dangerous."

"Not like you then, loud and dangerous."

Diane grins behind him,

"Where are we going next?"

Mike has been thinking about their next move,

"We go back to the Lodge collect our things then we'll relocate to TOK, I want to see the accident site, it's on our way."

They leave the cabin after loading their things. Mike checks out, as he does the girl in reception asks him.

"Where are you off to now? We thought you were staying longer."

"So did we but we've had to cut our trip short, business problems, we're heading down to Anchorage getting a flight back, why?"

The girl looks at her desk,

"No reason just general interest."

Mike wonders 'whose general interest' and leaves the Lodge. As they drive out Mike heads south towards the Glenn Highway, in the direction of Anchorage, after he's certain the Chevy can't be seen from the Lodge he makes a sharp U turn and heads back on the Glenn Tok Highway for TOK. Tim is looking at the GPS,

"What was all that about, forget your way?"

"The girl in reception was new and asked too many questions so I told her we were going to Anchorage to get a plane, she could see which direction we took from the office."

Diane says,

"My dear you do think on your feet."

"I'd have been dead years ago if I didn't, then I wouldn't have met you."

After a short distance they come to the accident site with Police cars, a crane and flat bed truck blocking one side of the Highway, Mike pulls in behind the Police car. They get out; Mike walks over to the first Police officer,

"What's happened here?"

The crane is in the process of pulling a green Jeep Cherokee out of the river,

"A guy from the research place up the road ran off the Highway and killed himself."

Mike asks,

"How could that happen, it's a clear road, no snow or ice."

The officer replies,

"That's what we're trying to find out he was badly smashed up."

"Was there another vehicle involved?"

"Not as far as we know, he just seems to have gone off the road which is unusual for this time of year, unless he'd been drinking or on something."

Mike asks,

"Do you mind if we take a look?"

"Why, did you know him?"

Mike takes out his wallet and flashes a false FBI ID card at the policeman,

"No, just professional curiosity we're on holiday just passing through."

The policeman looks impressed inviting them to have a look round but tells them to be quick as they will have the car out in a few minutes.

Mike waves the others over,

"Thanks we won't be long, will there be an autopsy?"

"Definitely he's on his way to the morgue we'll find out if he had drink or drugs in him." Mike walks over to the others,

"Mike, what was all that about and what did you show him?"

Mike gives his sly grin,

"Showed him my fake FBI ID, said it was professional curiosity that we're on holiday just wanted to have a quick look round."

"Great, let's just get it over with."

Diane wants to be away from here.

They walk over to examine the skid marks leading to the edge of the highway Mike bends down for a closer look,

"He was braking before he went off the road."

Diane asks,

"What does that mean?"

"It looks as if he was trying to avoid something on the road."

"You think it was another vehicle?"

"Exactly from what we know already, this was no accident. That's all we needed to confirm let's get going."

Diane points out,

"What's also strange is that the Police Officer said he was badly smashed up, but just look at his car."

It was slowly being raised from the river,

"It's hardly damaged."

Tim agrees,

"He was more likely beaten up than smashed up."

Mike thanks the Police officer, taking his phone number so he can get the results of the autopsy. They leave the scene, continuing their drive towards TOK. They are silent for the first few miles then Mike who has been deep in thought says out loud,

"Tim, I can't wait to take a look at the CD he gave us, it may provide the key to finding out who was behind Peter's assassination."

"Yeah, whoever it is certainly didn't want him talking to us, the sooner we know who we're up against the better."

Mike drives steadily towards TOK, none of them being in the frame of mind to take in the spectacular scenery they're passing through. An hour later they are close to the outskirts of TOK a few outlying buildings dot the countryside.

Diane asks,

"What's at TOK?"

Mike smiles as he welcomes the distraction by slipping easily into tourist guide mode,

"TOK or TOK Junction is pronounced with a long 'O' 'Toke rhyming with Poke' and is an Athabascan Indian name meaning 'peaceful crossing'. It's located at the junction of the Glenn Tok Highway where it joins the Alaskan Highway which is the main overland point of entry into Alaska from the Yukon Territory. Which I'm sure you'll remember is Canada."

Mike continues, clearly pleased to be able to demonstrate his considerable geographical knowledge of the area,

"TOK boasts one of the harshest climates in the world its winters can be very severe, it's also a major trade centre for the nearby Athabascan Native villages and the Sledge Dog Capital of Alaska. Apparently one in three of its 1200 population are involved in dog breeding and training. The oldest and largest dog sledge race in Alaska is the 'Tok Race of Champions' it takes place here in March of each year."

Tim and Diane look at each other sharing a smile, Diane leans forward teasingly,

"Mike, that's truly very interesting but what I meant was what's at TOK for us, why are we going there?"

Mike is just about to explain, when he sees on the left hand side of the road an inconspicuous log built Motel, The Golden Bear. He brakes, swinging off the highway and parks outside its entrance. He turns to Diane,

"This is why we're here, we're staying for two days to consolidate what we've found out and to implement my back-up plan."

"Which is?"

"Diane, not now, after we're settled and got rid of this car."

They unload their things and enter the motel, Tim and Diane sit in the reception area warming in front of a log fire, watched over by a 10ft tall stuffed Kodiak Bear, Mike checks them in and hands a room key to Tim,

"Our rooms are adjoining they're not 5 star but very clean and comfortable with King size beds."

Diane asks,

"Where's my key?"

"They only had one other double room left, you're with me, hope you don't mind."

Diane laughs,

"It's a tough country alright, no problem I can rough it with you for another night."

"You'll pay for that."

They take their gear up to their rooms. Mike gives Diane a lingering kiss,

"I've got a friend to call if I can find a pay phone, see you in a minute."

"You'd better, a few minutes is all you've got."

Diane starts to organise their things. Mike goes to reception, finding a pay phone he dials a local number, the call is answered immediately,

"Julian we've arrived we're ready for the exchange, see you outside in half an hour."

Mike returns to his room. The Motel consists of two timber constructed buildings. The taller, two storey building is where the rooms are located, whilst the single storey reception building houses a coffee shop, bar and restaurant with an adjoining meeting room. Half an hour later Mike excuses himself from the others who're drinking coffee in the little bar.

"I'm going to exchange our Chevy for another vehicle I'll tell you more when I get back." Mike leaves them and goes outside as a Silver Jeep Grand Cherokee drives into the Motel with a woman and three men inside. They park to the side of the reception building, the driver a tall extremely fit looking man gets out hugging Mike, obviously an old friend. Mike is pleased,

"Julian, it's so good to see you again, you haven't changed a bit."

"Oh yes I have, I'm a little wiser, older and deeper in debt, but you don't look too bad yourself, considering your age and life style. Now to business I haven't a lot of time, I've brought the things you asked for."

He hands Mike a computer bag and keys to the Jeep, Mike gives the Chevy keys to Julian,

"Julian, the three of them will drive the Chevy to Anchorage Airport and take a flight to Los Angeles, make sure they stay alert these people are serious players."

"Don't worry my people are specialists they can look after themselves, we'll get going, if you need anything else call me at the number, I'm staying in TOK until you leave."

Mike gives him a hug and shakes hands with the other three,

"Thanks all of you, hopefully it'll take the heat off us."

Mike watches them leave in the Chevy then returns to the others who were watching from the bar window. They sit down at their table, the bar is deserted apart from the bar girl who cannot hear their conversation. Diane asks suspiciously,

"Who was that woman?"

"She is you and the other two are Tim and me."

Diane frowns for a moment then the penny drops,

"They've taken our car and anyone following us will follow them."

"That's the general idea if it works. They're driving to Anchorage Airport and flying to Los Angeles in our names then they'll return to Alaska under different ID's."

Tim is impressed,

"Mike, that's crafty, who was the other guy?"

"He's a very old friend, we were in the Seal Teams together many lives ago, he has a private security company with extensive contacts throughout the agencies, he's got a temporary office in TOK as our back up facility with a private jet and helicopter at our disposal based at the Tanacross Airport, a small WWII airfield near the Tanacross Indian Village just outside TOK." Tim looks curiously at the bag,

"What's in the bag?"

"It's a rather special laptop, for a start we can examine the CD that Peter gave his life for, and can make secure email contact with Tony at the Pentagon."

Diane looks concerned,

"But can't they trace emails back to their source we don't know who we can trust."

"That's partly what makes this laptop special, its communication software sends the email contemporaneously from 10 different countries, excluding the one we are in, so poor old Tony will receive 10 emails and will respond to each country not knowing where we are."

Tim can't wait to look at the CD,

"Drink up lets get back upstairs."

They finish their coffee and return to Mike and Diane's room, he sets up the Dell laptop on the small table then switches on, after a few seconds its ready Mike inserts the CD which self copies onto the computers' hard disk. A few seconds later they see a video clip of Peter making his introduction,

"This is a true statement and testimonial of the history of my work with the HAARP project. It's with a heavy heart that I have found it necessary to record the events of the past decade in the hope that this information will be preserved after my death and used to bring the people and organisations responsible for transforming HAARP from a peaceful research project for the benefit of mankind, to a potentially disastrous weapon of war, to accountability. I have included my personal concerns regarding other HAARP projects including the global experiments which are taking place to manipulate the earth's magnetic fields and frequencies that if combined could well have a negative impact on the Earth's outer core causing a catastrophic breakdown of the Earth's natural magnetic field, the implications could be terminal for the human race. This CD is the only copy of this testimonial in existence if you are watching it, then it means that my life will have come to a close and I hope for the sake of our planet that you can use this information more successfully than I have been able to do."

The screen fades to black and then an index of the contents appears. Diane is distressed by the statement,

"Poor Peter he must have known his life was in danger."

Tim agrees,

"We've seen firsthand what they're capable of, but who are they?"

Mike scrolls through the index,

"It's all here, experiments, dates, names organisations, emails, reports, his concerns the whole damn shooting match, all we have to do is work through it until we find what we're looking for"

Diane prompts,

"In that case we'll need a printer and paper, there's too much information to look at on screen."

Mike opens the computer bag taking out an encrypted mobile phone given to him by Julian he calls him,

"Hi, Julian we need a fast printer with lots of paper."

"No problem it will be dropped off at reception in an hour."

Diane is impressed,

"Mike your friend is really on the ball."

"He needs to be, or he wouldn't be my friend and he knows it."

Diane points to one of the items on the index 'My personal Radio Tomography Research'

"What's that?"

Mike opens the file it lists four sites:

Montauk Air Force Station (Camp Hero) Long Island

Brookhaven National Laboratory Long Island

Pine Gap, Alice Springs Australia

CERN Geneva

Mike selects the first item 'Montauk Air Force Base' opening an overview of the base with an option to select 'Radio Tomography Analysis' which he selects, a full screen underground view of the site from the surface down shows an enormous underground structure of seven floors built deep into the bedrock. The first four floors are coloured red, the deeper three floors coloured green and dated 1990. Diane is shocked,

"Tim, the US government denies that this underground site exists."

"We ought to read the overview before jumping to conclusions."

Mike agrees returning to the overview. The three of them gather more closely round the laptop's small screen as the first page of Peter's Montauk Air Force Station introduction scrolls up.

"Over the past few years I became curious about other controversial experimental research establishments and started seeking information about the disused, purportedly abandoned Montauk Air Force Station (Camp Hero) on Long Island, New York. I was aware that someone in Long Island was closely monitoring my work. However no conclusions could be drawn from the conflicting information available to me, most of which existed in the public domain. This frustration culminated in me using HAARP's Radio Tomography capability to discover what was really below ground. The following pages are an analysis of what I found and now believe is being carried out at Long Island but first some history as to why this site was chosen as a potential military base in 1910.

In the 1600's when European settlers reached Long Islands' shores they discovered that the Montauks a major Algonquin Indian Tribe had long been established at Turtle Cove which is adjacent to Camp Hero, subsequent archaeological evidence supports the fact that they inhabited this region continuously for over 8000 years, they constructed pyramids the remains of which existed to this century. It's of note that the Chiefs of the Montauk Indians used the name 'Pharaoh's' at a time when the word was unknown to anyone else in the known world apart from the

Egyptians. The eastern part of Long Island at Montauk is geologically different from the rest of the island, as Montauk is the top of a mountain which is why the military were able to create a secure deep and covert underground structure in the bedrock of the old mountain. Another important reason that the Montauks were attracted to Turtle Cove was they believed it had magical properties and emitted special powers therefore they built their pyramids there.

We now know that Turtle Cove is one of the several geomagnetic spots that exist around the world where there are anomalies in the earth's magnetic, gravitational and electromagnetic fields. This was potentially why the sites in the desert where chosen for the Giza pyramids and why HAARP was located in Gakona.

It's my belief that the experiments we were undertaking at HAARP were being replicated below ground on Long Island at Camp Hero or at the Brookhaven National Laboratory and no longer needed external antenna. This was the real reason why the HAARP facility at Gakona was being closed down. As can be observed from the underground images, Camp Hero appears to have a particle accelerator in its lowest level. This would only be needed if they were involved in quantum and particle physics, working with powerful electromagnetic fields for developing particle beam weapon technology, and/or seeking to bend time and space for potential time travel.

If this is true then it would be logical to assume that they must be working closely with their close neighbours at Brookhaven as they too are involved in this field of research. The facility at Montauk Air Base has been shrouded in mystery and secrecy for years. However the numerous sinister stories from researchers that allegedly worked there, local people and journalists that have tried to investigate the facility are hard to dismiss. The government are in denial over its existence. The following radio images provide indisputable proof of a large active research facility beneath the disused radar station at Camp Hero."

The phone rings disturbing them, Mike answers,

"Great, thank you, I'll be down right away."

He tells them the printer's arrived in reception and goes to collect it. After he leaves the room Diane looks at Tim,

"Can you believe what we've just seen?"

"Afraid so Diane, the images leave no doubt that the facility below ground exists, but is it still active?"

"How can they possibly locate such potentially dangerous research on the outskirts of New York?"

Tim smiles,

"That's America for you, no one knows or has any right to know what the military and the administration is involved in or where, until it goes wrong. Peter explained they chose the location because of its geophysical properties."

Diane is thoughtful,

"Actually it's not only America, it's probably happening all over the world controlled by a small number of powerful people with very few knowing the truth about their ambitions. That's a frightening thought."

There's a bump on the door, Tim opens it as Mike struggles in carrying a heavy HP LaserJet Printer with several reams of paper. Diane clears a space beside the laptop as Mike places the printer on the desk,

"Phew! That was a lot heavier than I expected but it'll get the job done."

Within minutes he starts printing out the contents of the CD.

"I'll work through the CD, as the sections are printed I want you to start going through them, we all know what we're looking for. Once we've printed them I want to make a copy of the CD for security."

Tim and Diane start working on the first sections Tim's analytical skills come into their own as the information consists of numerous emails, reports and notes that Peter has compiled some of which are not always clear, Tim is making copious notes. Diane quietly reads.

Chapter - 19

The Organisation

Several hours later they take a break, Mike has ordered coffees to be delivered to their room and gently asks,

"Diane, how are you feeling?"

Rubbing her eyes,

"Tired"

She puts her hand on the pile of papers in front of her,

"This is like something from a science fiction film but worse because we know it's real."

Tim picks up his notepad,

"I've been trying to piece together who is behind these projects by following the money trail. There're a lot of Chinese boxes with each one covering the back of the other."

There's a knock on the door coffee is brought in, once the door closes Mike asks,

"Tim, what exactly have you discovered?"

Tim opens his pad to a clean page and starting at the top commences to explain what he has found, drawing boxes as he does.

"This is an international organisation but if we start with how it works in the USA. In the first box we have the President, administration, pentagon, military and agencies who are secretly funding covert research projects and between them bypassing congress approvals, these activities are hidden under a veil of secrecy.

In the second box and next in the chain, are the consortiums of manufacturers of military hardware, aircraft, missiles, weapons and suppliers of scientific services to the Department of Defence, these are very powerful and wealthy businesses that fund and lobby the government through their financial backing of the right sort of politicians to get them into positions of power and influence to ensure their schemes do not meet resistance."

"Diane, are you with me so far?"

"Yes I think so. The first box funds the projects with money from the second box which controls the first box."

Tim smiles,

"Exactly, now in the third box we have people that provide the money to the different military hardware manufacturers in the second box, thereby controlling them.

These are the major shareholders which are powerful financial institutions. Each major manufacturer seems to have a different financial backer OK?"

Diane is fascinated,

"The third box finances the second box, OK."

"Now we get to the interesting part, the fourth box consists of a globally powerful, independent, very exclusive and secretive organisation which these notes call 'Global Asset Management Trust'. This is a group of around two hundred of the most powerful men and women on earth, all top experts in their various fields ex Presidents, royalty, politicians, government, medical and health, pharmaceuticals, science, physics, biology, religion, media, agriculture, natural resources, geophysics, oil, petroleum, management, geology, astronomy, computer science, genetics, psychology, economics, technology, banking and finance. They have allegiance only to themselves, their agenda and mission which according to Peter's research is to create a new World Order, with one dominant World Government, Them. The controlling shareholders and financial entities funding the companies in box three by chance are all owned by guess who? The Global Asset Management Trust who thereby exercises control of all three boxes."

Mike stops him,

"Do you mean that they are repeating this in every country in the world?"

"Yes, they have autonomous offices in every country in the world making them truly 'Global' and more powerful than any one single country in the world. The principles of the operation and business model in these boxes will be the same for all countries including Russia, China and Europe it's just the names that are different." Diane is taken aback,

"How could they possibly take over the world?" Mike answers,

"If an organisation is powerful enough to control the flows and prices of money and oil they could cause the economy of a target country to collapse."

"Mike, do you mean similar to what's been happening to the USA in the last year with the crisis in the financial markets and the rocketing price of oil, causing the dollar to drop against all world currencies?" Mike nods,

"Yes, added to the massive cost of the various wars we are waging including Iraq and Afghanistan, if they're as globally powerful as this indicates they could manipulate one country against another for their own ends. Interestingly they could easily afford to own and operate a stealth fighter out of their petty cash." Diane queries,

"But what about the voting population wouldn't they stop it?" Tim cuts in,

"No, the population are manipulated by the media they are only given information that the powers that be, want them to have. If this organisation is determined to dominate the world then they would certainly control the media, technology and communications to manipulate the population or worse, to eliminate the countries that resist them." Diane picks up a wad of papers that she had been studying she finds the section on CERN,

"This facility in Geneva is extraordinary listen to this. It's the world's largest Hadron Collider, a machine that's been built in a circular tunnel 27 kilometres in circumference, 100 metres below Switzerland and France its due to be finished early in 2010. It will be seven times more powerful than any other particle accelerator on earth. During its operation it uses 1624 superconducting magnets in a ring around the inside of the tunnel to achieve the high electro magnetic fields needed to bend the paths of the particle beam around the tunnel, they cool the magnets to minus 271 degrees centigrade making it the coldest place in the known universe. These magnets are not small. The largest is the Atlas Barrel Toroid magnet 5 metres wide by 25 metres long and weighing 100 tonnes. My question is, what if the combined magnetic fields from CERN were able to manipulate and control the Earth's magnetic field by making minute changes to the direction of flow of the earth's outer liquid core wouldn't this disturb the biorhythm of people and creatures living on the surface?"

Mike agrees,

"That's probably what Peter was afraid HAARP was going to do. If it was possible to alter the Earth's magnetic field and the electromagnetic frequencies within a certain country you could theoretically change the population's state of mind, create extreme weather patterns and movement in the tectonic plates leading to earthquakes."

Tim goes to the laptop and logs into the internet, after a few minutes he returns to the table,

"Guess who just happens to be one of the biggest financial sponsors of CERN?"

Diane frowns impatiently,

"Tell us?"

Tim shows them the print out,

"A Scientific Research Consultancy, 100% owned by Global Asset Management Trust"

Mike says,

"That doesn't prove that they want to rule the world. We need access to the Pentagon's computers if we really want to dig deeper into this organisation, it's probably time to think about returning to Washington."

Diane is concerned,

"But we don't know who we can trust at the Pentagon."

"Diane, I would only need a few hours, half a day at the most."

Diane responds firmly,

"You mean 'We' not I, we're in this together."

Mike thinks for a moment,

"I want to email Tony there's a possibility he could get us safe access to their system."

Diane doesn't like this idea,

"Like we trusted him to give us secure satellite phones and look what happened."

Tim has a suggestion,

"What if we could find someone that could hack into the Pentagon's system, it's been done before then we wouldn't be putting ourselves at risk."

"Tim, that's not such a bad idea, let me speak to Julian he's the only person I know who might have that sort of contact."

Mike calls Julian again explaining what they need. The voice on the other end of the phone sounds a little excited,

"Mike, you want me to help you do WHAT. When and from Where."

"Here, as soon as possible."

There's silence for a moment then Julian continues,

"Mike, I really wish I wasn't so in debt to you. Leave it with me I'll make some enquiries."

Diane overheard the conversation,

"He didn't like that, did he?"

"No but it's just his way, he'll be fine we go back a long time, in fact we're blood brothers; literally."

"What do you mean?"

"We were on a covert mission together in Vietnam, he took a bad hit and was close to death, so I gave him a few pints of the red stuff, luckily we were the same blood group and he survived."

Tim asks,

"Did you know you were the same blood group?"

"Nope, not at the time, that's why he was lucky."

Mike wants to let Tony know that there's a high level leak in his department,

"I'd like to update Tony by email explaining what happened to us and to Peter so he can start searching for the leak, at least he'll know we're OK but out of circulation. I'll keep it short and he won't be able to trace us from it."

"Mike it'll be interesting to find out how what progress he's made in convincing the other countries to drop their research."

"I've already thought of that, I'll ask him."

Mike prepares the email which explains how they were attacked and how someone knew exactly where to find them, confirming a security leak in his department. He then describes the events during their visit to HAARP, the killing of Peter which forced them further undercover. He ends the message by asking for an update.

Diane is not convinced that the email is safe and asks again,

"You're absolutely certain we can't be traced through this email?"

Mike looks at her,

"Nothing is 100% certain, even if they can find us it will take at least four or five days maybe longer, if we're lucky. They have to check each country the emails have been sent from, by which time we'll be long gone."

Mike presses 'Send'

"It's done."

Tim nods in agreement,

"It'll be interesting to see his reaction."

They break for dinner, making their way down to the Hotel's restaurant. As they sit down Mike's mobile rings, he gets up then walks over to the privacy of the window, after the call is finished he returns to the table, glancing round he quietly tells them,

"Julian's come up trumps we have a computer specialist arriving here tomorrow morning at ten he'll come directly to the room."

The next morning they are up early, after coffee Mike turns on the laptop to find an email from Tony, Diane asks immediately,

"What's it say?"

Mike grunts,

"Give me a chance it'll take a moment to decrypt.

Both Diane and Tim are standing by his shoulder when the message appears on the screen.

Thank you for bringing your complaint regarding the travel arrangement to my notice, I was sorry to hear about your eventful journey, I will speak to the staff responsible for organising the flight to ensure that it cannot happen again. In the interim it may be better for you to make your travel arrangements. Things have become complicated here, you may not have heard that the Russians, Norwegian, Chinese and Japanese have lost certain communication facilities and are considering repercussions against us for taking them. The leased aircraft that you had trouble with was operated by an International Company, we seem to have lost track of it. Once I have resolved your travel problems perhaps we can make contact again. We take all complaints most seriously and rest assured they will be fully investigated.

Sincerely

Pentagon Administration Office

Tim can't believe his eyes,
"You know what this means?"
Diane hasn't quite worked it out yet,
"What, tell me?"
Mike explains,
"He's trying to tell us what's happened without making it obvious, Tony's started an investigation into the leak but what's most worrying is it looks as if Aacaarya's people have run out of patience, they have removed the ionospheric heaters in Russia, Norway, China and Japan who are all blaming America, which is logical as they will know the American facilities have not been touched. And surprise, surprise the stealth fighter that attacked us was operated by the Global Asset Management Trust and it would appear that Aacaarya has moved it. Tim, I think you should have a word with Aacaarya, find out what's going on."
Diane is angry,
"I've a strong dislike for what this Global Asset group is up to, the sooner we know exactly who they are and where we can find them the better." she pats her shoulder holster.
Tim suggests he leaves them for a moment as he needs to contact Aacaarya,
"It's not a good sign, that he did not give us any warning about what they were preparing to do."
There's a knock on the door, Mike takes out his pistol and slowly opens the door.

Chapter - 20

The Hacker

"Hi, I'm James, you're expecting me?"

Mike waves him in, obviously surprised at the new arrivals appearance. He closes the door, keeping his pistol behind his back

"Who sent you?"

The young man is about 27 years old, tall and thin with dark unkempt hair hanging down to his shoulders topped by a black woollen ski hat. His face is very pale emphasised by large glasses. He is wearing a dark blue three quarter length Reefer Jacket over worn blue jeans with old white tennis trainers, he answers,

"Your friend Julian sent me."

"And what did he ask you to help us with?"

The young man has no patience for this,

"Look, I'm here to help you break into the Pentagon's computer system, so can we now get on with it, I presume you're Mike from your description."

He holds out his hand which Mike shakes as he tucks his pistol into the back of his belt. Diane is looking at him in some doubt, shakes his hand,

"Are you really sure you can do it?"

James smiles,

"Diane baby, it's no problem I've done it several times before. I've degrees in computer science from the top universities in the world including MIT with vast experience in breaking into supposedly secure systems."

Mike queries.

"Your accent's Russian isn't it?"

James is very impressed,

"Yeah, I was born in Moscow, my family name is James Vivuenko, Russian father and American mother, but we had to leave in a hurry when I was thirteen, had a 'hacking' cough and was sent to the USA for some fresh air, not many pick up on my accent, well done."

Diane relaxes,

"Would you like coffee?"

"Now you're talking that would be great, I've just driven down from Fairbanks. I've been working there for six months."

For his age James is noticeably very confident in his ability and obviously knows what he has to do,

"Now if you'll tell me exactly what you're looking for I'll get started, Mike if you want, I can show you how to revisit the Pentagon after I've set up the links and connections."

Mike explains what they're looking for; James goes quiet for a moment,

"I've come across Global Asset Management Trust somewhere before, it'll come back to me. Now please leave me to get on with it, could I have the mobile that Julian gave you, I'll use that to connect with, it's about as secure as we can get."

James makes himself comfortable at the keyboard, his fingers skate rapidly over the keyboard.

"I set this computer up for you now all I'll need is a constant supply of coffee, with no one disturbing me for half an hour."

They leave him to it as the screen flashes with information driven by his fingers that dance over the keys. Mike steps back glancing at Diane,

"He's good."

Without turning his head James says,

"Not just good, the best." then silence.

Mike and Diane go into the next room to speak to Tim who is sitting on the side of his bed. "Aacaarya said that the Elders made the decision against his advice, they just went ahead and implemented their demonstration. Apparently no one was hurt only the hardware was removed. They were also responsible for removing the Stealth Fighter, they felt our people had

had enough time to work on it, they didn't want it getting back into the wrong hands, that's all he was able to say, he's going to speak to me later he's with the Elders at present."

They return to where James is working, in the centre of the laptop screen is the logo of the Pentagon, James looks up,

"Nearly done coffee please, Hi Tim."

He gets back to his work as Diane gets him a coffee.

"Bingo"

James has logged into the Pentagon system,

"Now let's see what we have on the 'Global Asset Management' mob."

They bunch round him Mike grips his shoulder,

"Well done, let's download and print everything they have, including the list of members of this organisation."

James starts the printer,

"There's no list of members, we'll have to take break into Global's network to get that."

Tim asks,

"James, once we have this data do you really think it would be possible to us into Global Assets computer network?"

"Tim my man, I can take you wherever you want to go, just give me a little more time. This for me is better than sex and I can go on forever."

Diane glances at Mike,

"You hear that, my new hero, he goes on forever."

Ten minutes later James has downloaded and printed the Pentagon's data on Global Assets. He starts trying to gain access to Global's computer network which is based in Luxembourg. James explains to them,

"This might take a little longer; I've not visited them before."

Tim asks,

"How certain are you that no one will know you have accessed their system?"

"Tim, I really am the best of the best, to stay that way I have to be certain I can't be traced. Don't worry about it."

They leave him to his work and examine the information from the Pentagon. It's several hours later James has been silently working, Mike goes over to him and is mesmerised; watching James rapidly entering vast amounts of code followed by the screen reacting with display after display of seemingly meaningless unreadable numbers and data.

"How's it going James?"

James turns round pointing to the screen,

"This is a completely different ball, much more sophisticated with system defences and protection written by people that really know what they're doing. I've at last got in, I'm searching the system for the list of members which is exceptionally well protected, access is very difficult I have to battle through each level of their very clever defences, this indicates to me that this data is very sensitive and valuable. I've never seen protection this advanced before."

"James you'll be able to get it?"

"Give me a little more time, another coffee and you'll have what you want."

He turns back to the laptop,

"Oh, this might amuse you, because their defences are so sophisticated they're constantly looking for intruders and scanning for the origin of the breach in their security. So I've laid a very subtle trail back to the Pentagon's computer. That should get them a little excited, particularly when they find out that their most valuable and precious treasure has been accessed by such an important visitor."

The three of them laugh.

Diane gives him a peck on the cheek,

"James that's ironic. Who better to blame than the Pentagon."

She hands James another well earned coffee, he gets back to work. After half an hour James sits back in his chair and cracks his knuckles,

Mike looks at him,

"Finished?"

James looks at him,

"No famished, any chance of something to eat its three o'clock I've been working five hours nonstop."

"Sorry, I should've thought about that, I'll get room service to bring up a pile of steak sandwiches."

James smiles,

"Perfect, and don't apologise, I'm having the time of my life, its rare these days to find such a challenging adversary."

Half an hour later there's a knock on the door as the waiter arrives with a very large tray stacked with toasted sandwiches. Mike takes them without opening the door far enough to let the waiter see James, he hands him a hefty tip, the waiter is delighted.

"Mike, bring mine over here, I can eat and work at the same time it's a force of habit."

James has been silent for an hour when suddenly he mutters to himself "That's very strange."

Mike asks,

"What's very strange?"

James is distracted,

"This computer system is something out of science fiction it's acting as if it were biological, similar to the human immune system once it finds an intruder it sends out bugs to surround it and destroy it, that's why I've got to keep moving."

James shouts,

"I've got it."

The printer starts printing, after 5 minutes it stops during which time James has been battling more intensively with the system, his face is covered with sweat from the effort.

Suddenly there's a bang from the computer, James flies backwards tipping his chair onto the floor he lays there still. Smoke is rising from the laptop. Mike pulls its plug out of the wall bending down to look at James he touches his neck checking for a pulse,

Diane looks at him,

> "He's not."

> "No, he's still got a pulse."

A groan passes from James' lips he slowly opens his eyes,

> "What happened?"

Mike helps him back onto the chair,

> "You were at the computer there was a bang, you fell backwards the laptop belched smoke."

James comes to quickly reaching into his computer bag for a small black tool roll which he opens taking out a small screwdriver,

> "I need to look inside."

He opens the computer keyboard removes the hard disk so that he can see the main circuit board, he calls Mike over,

> "Come take a look at this."

Pointing with his screwdriver,

> "Every circuit has been fried."

James sits back in his chair,

> "Mike, this is not possible."

"What's happened?"

"Have you heard of EMP?"

Mike nods,

> "Yes an Electro Magnetic Pulse."

James continues,

> "Yes exactly, somehow their defence system found us, targeted and hit our computer with what I suspect is a Vircator Microwave EMP which destroyed all the high density metal oxide semiconductor components and printed circuit tracks without affecting

the power supply in the building. If I hadn't just seen it, I would not have believed it possible. This is a very serious technological development."

Mike picks up the mobile phone still connected to the computer James takes it from him,

"This will be fried as well it received the pulse first."

James explains,

"The miniature transistors and diodes used in communications devices are particularly sensitive to voltage surges and very easily damaged."

Diane has checked the printer and picks up the 30 page list,

"Well at least we've achieved our objective, thanks to you."

James is concerned,

"Do you realise the implications of this, they can send an electromagnetic pulse over the internet that will only attack the computer they are targeting, that's unbelievable and technically should be impossible."

"I wonder if they hit the Pentagon's computer."

James says,

"That's a thought but I doubt it, they wouldn't want to attract that kind of attention to what they have accomplished, what's more important, they must be close to knowing where we are, so I recommend that we gather up our stuff and clear out immediately."

Mike is curious,

"If you left a trail back to the Pentagon wouldn't they follow that and presumably they transmitted the EMP signal to our computer through the connection, and may not know where we are."

"Mike, that's true but we have no idea how technically capable these people are, we've just witnessed a demonstration of technology that is decade's or more ahead of where we are today. It is better to be safe than sorry."

He takes out another mobile handing it to Mike,

"This is another of Julian's mobiles I always carry a spare."

Diane jokes,

"Just in case you get zapped by an EPM"

James grins,

"I've got to go now I need to work out how to protect myself as I'm definitely going to visit these people again, but this time prepared and armed."

Tim hurries them along,

"Let's pack, we're moving out."

Mike calls down and asks reception to prepare the bill. By the time they start packing James has packed their laptop and is ready to go, he wraps up the last of the cold steak sandwiches in a serviette,

"Don't mind if I take these do you, shame to waste them."

Mike asks,

"Can I contact you on the mobile?"

"No, better to do it through Julian, I'll let him know when I've managed to solve our little problem."

James goes to the door,

"Well guys it's been a great pleasure and lots, and lots of fun, let me know if you need anything else."

Diane gives him a hug as Tim and Mike shake his hand,

"Take care of yourself James. Many thanks."

As James closes the door he says,

"Until the next time,"

Mike calls Julian explaining what's happened and they need a safe location for a couple of days, then a fast ride back to Washington.

"Mike, you can use my friends safe house they're away, we've used it before, it's near the PA TOK Junction airfield, basic but comfortable, it has everything you'll need for two or three days and it's secure."

"Sounds perfect, where shall we meet up?"

Julian is passing the Motel in half an hour and suggests that they follow him, Mike is relieved,

"Great, thanks for your help as always, see you in half an hour we'll be outside in the car."
They move their things into the back of the Jeep. Mike then pays the bill with untraceable cash. He joins Tim and Diane whilst they wait for Julian to appear. A few minutes later Julian's car pulls up in front of them, he pulls slowly away again letting them follow him north up the Glen Tok Highway deeper into the small town of TOK. After five minutes they turn right onto the main Alaskan Highway after a further five minutes they turn left into a thickly wooded area, following a track that leads to a small house set on its own, in the centre of a square cut from the pine forest. Julian parks in front of the large double garage Mike pulls up alongside him. Julian opens the front door handing him the keys and a computer bag

"There's another computer in here, try not to get it fried, I'll quickly show you round then leave you to it. James is staying with me as he wants to start work on his defence system immediately."
Julian shows them round the four bedroom house; it has a large lounge and kitchen. On the worktops are three large cardboard boxes,

"This should keep you going for at least three days. If you need anything else give me a call."
Diane gives Julian a hug,

"Julian, I don't know what we'd do without you, thanks for everything."
She kisses him on the cheek. Slightly embarrassed he says goodbye leaving them to get their things into the house. Tim and Diane unload the Jeep, Mike wanders round the outside of the house, as he returns Diane asks,

"What were you doing outside?"

"Just checking around, in case we have to leave suddenly or have visitors."
Diane looks concerned,

"Visitors, you don't think they know where we are?"

Mike puts his arm round her shoulder,

"No, I don't expect anyone to disturb us here, it's just a habit of mine, now we've a lot of work to do, let's get inside."

Mike unpacks the numerous printouts taking out the last few pages which are the list of members of the Global Asset Management Trust. Diane is preparing coffee in the kitchen. Tim is working through some of the other documents. Mike is silent as he studies the list but as Diane arrives with their coffees he looks up,

"This is inconceivable."

Diane sits down,

"What is?"

"This group has its headquarters in Washington DC, between the White House, Capital Hill and the Pentagon. It's just down the road from the FBI headquarters and amongst its senior executive staff are a former US President; the father of our current President; an ex director of the CIA; a former Secretary of Defense; an ex deputy director of the CIA; an ex US Secretary of State; a White house budget advisor; former foreign Presidents including one of your ex UK Prime Ministers. They've a vast investment portfolio with resources around the world. Amongst their largest investment clients is one of the wealthiest families in Saudi Arabia."

Diane asks,

"What do they do?"

"They invest in industries such as banking, oil, defence, laboratories; media, communication's and is one of the US government's biggest contractors. One of their senior management was appointed envoy in charge of restructuring Iraq's debt and reconstruction."

Diane is shocked,

"It's common knowledge about the corruption and mismanagement of Iraq's funds, it was billions of dollars."

"Diane, they're personally making billions of dollars from the wars in Iraq, Afghanistan and the global war on terrorism."

Tim interrupts them,

"I'm afraid I have some very bad news."

Mike and Diane, look at him as he hands a page over to them,

"Look at the fourth name down."

They cannot believe their eyes, amongst the 'active members' is the name 'General Anthony Mitchell – Pentagon – Director of the Defense Intelligence Agency, along with his secure personal contact data.

Mike is almost speechless with anger,

"He's been their link all along, he knew we were on the Gulfstream and he knew we were coming to Alaska, that man's days are numbered."

Diane is frightened,

"What can we do, these are such powerful people?"

Tim reassures her,

"Don't forget we too have powerful allies, we must be very careful, it's to our advantage that they don't know we've managed to access this list."

Diane suddenly remembers something,

"I've read about this organisation under a different name, I'm sure that they were part of the conspiracy theory allegedly involving the President and his closest advisors in the destruction of the Trade Centre in order to justify their attack on Iraq which created the opportunity for them to profit from billions of dollars of reconstruction spend."

"Yes I remember that too, there was a fair amount of tangible evidence to support that theory."

Mike has scanned the rest of the list,

"One good thing has come out of this. It means we've eliminated George as the leak which leaves us with a high level contact in the pentagon we can trust."

Tim sees another opportunity,

"Mike, we could use the fact that Tony does not know we have the list, meaning we could feed him false information which he would pass on to his masters at Global."

"We have to wade through the rest of this to see if we can discover what their real mission is. I can't believe that this is only about money, I hope James is successful in finding a way to protect himself so we can get into their system again to access their email files."
Tim asks,

"Do you think you should tell George what we know?"

"No, not yet, I'd like to do that once we have more information and tangible evidence, he's known Tony for years and may be difficult to convince. You could contact Aacaarya to see what he recommends as they may be able to find out more about Global. The better informed we are the stronger we'll be."

"Aacaarya and I are making contact this evening I'll tell him about Global Assets EMP capability in case it could be of threat to his people."
Diane seems a little more relaxed,

"We've made some good progress we now know who our enemy is and their man at the Pentagon."

"Diane, I would guarantee that they have more than one person working for them at the Pentagon, we must be very careful not to assume anything and only make our moves based on hard data."
Several hours later they're still working through the computer prints when the telephone rings, it's Julian,

"Mike, since I left you I've been with James, he's been working non-stop, he's just made a breakthrough, he's a genius that lad. He believes he's worked out how to get back into the Global system without their security system identifying he's a threat, he'll have limited time but will target their email files first. If he's successful he wants to come over with the information as soon as he has it, probably later this evening, it's going to be slow progress."

Mike is delighted,

"That's good news, tell him well done and to take great care, we'd be delighted to see him whenever he's ready." and hangs up.

Diane as always is first to ask,

"What's happened?"

Mike tells them what Julian has said,

Diane is excited by this news,

"If James can get hold of their email files we could find the evidence we need to stop them."

Tim is less optimistic,

"Let's wish him luck we'll wait to see if he's successful, these people are unpredictable, as we've already experienced."

Diane is impatient,

"I hate waiting it's not in my character, let's get back to work."

It's now one o'clock in the morning when the phone rings again, Mike responds,

"Julian hi, how's it going?"

"He's on his way over, be with you in fifteen minutes, I'll let him tell you what he's done, he asked if Diane could put the coffee on."

Mike relays the news to Diane who immediately goes into the kitchen starts the coffee machine and makes a pile of sandwiches. By the time she's finished there's a quiet knock on the door, Mike carefully opens it to reveal an exhausted but excited James who rushes into the room with his computer bag over his shoulder. Mike gives him a hug,

"Well done man, make yourself comfortable."

James slumps down in a chair,

"I'm absolutely shattered."

At that moment Diane brings the tray in, to James's delight. She gives him a kiss,

"Here's your reward."

Placing the tray in front of James who immediately tucks in,

"I haven't eaten since I left you, this is most welcome."

After a few minutes of gorging himself and drinking his second coffee he's refreshed,

"Thank's for that, now to business."

James explains that he managed to successfully get into their system again. He found a way inside their defence module then disguised himself as part of it. Their weakness was that they thought they were invincible and were only expecting an intrusion from outside,

"I managed to get into their encrypted email file and copied it, here it is."

He opens his bag and hands a CD to Mike,

"I've decoded their encryption, compiled it so that when you place it in your computer it will open their list of emails in date order, you can scroll through them or search on key words and print whatever you need, each person on the list has a code name which they obviously use for communications, I've kept a security copy."

Mike is amazed,

"That's astonishing."

James continues,

"And for Diane, I left them a present. I buried deep within their security system a very nasty and unique virus bomb, all my own dirty handiwork, it cannot be detected, but within an hour will start destroying their network files from within their own security programmes, this will keep their system busy whilst another of my little masterstrokes convinces their defence system that the attack is from one of the computers attached to their network servers which will immediately trigger their EMP defence mechanism, before they know what hit them, their own EMP counter insurgence measures would have attacked their entire world network, including all communications devices connected to their network, which will be completely self destroyed, along with all their worldwide financial programmes. As I told you, after they fried my laptop they made a big mistake in messing with the cyber world's best or his friends."

Diane is delighted giving James an enormous hug,

"You are my superhero."

Tim shakes James hand,

"If that happens, it'll stop them dead in the water."

James looks hurt,

"What do you mean if?"

He looks at his watch,

"It just has, it's done, if you want proof just try and log onto their web site, the whole lots finished it will take them months to rebuild and colossal amounts of dollars, can you imagine how many computers they must have around the world and the damage to their communications."

Mike is delighted and highly respectful of James ability and achievements,

"James, here we were trying to find a weakness in their defences and hoping to find it amongst their emails, when you present us with the most superb news we could ever have hoped for. There're no words enough to thank you for what you've done. You've hit them where it will hurt most, their communications, making them blind, which will help us a lot. Remember if ever there's anything you need, we'll always be there."

James grins,

"Mike thank you, it's been a lot of fun for me and it just gets better, as far as thanks go, just keep me on your team, I enjoy stimulation like this."

Diane returns with a bottle of champagne she found in the fridge with four glasses,

"Let's drink to James's wonderful achievement, to James."

They raise their glasses.

"James the new addition to our team"

They take a sip as James says,

"There's one more thing, whilst I was immersed in their system I managed to steal the technical specification and overview of their EMP defence system, it's on the CD for your interest because very shortly I'll be able to replicate it with improvements and integrate it into my own armoury for future use."

Mike laughs,

"James what can we say, you are beyond the best."

They finish the champagne. James tells them he has to get back as he wants to start work on his new project. They say goodbye as James leaves for his office.

Located on the top floor of a luxurious office block in Pennsylvania Avenue, Washington DC the Chief Executive of Global Assets Management has called an emergency meeting of his senior directors. The seven directors are seated around the grand boardroom table which is large enough for twenty people with a throne-like chair at one end, they're in heated discussion. The Chief Executive storms in, without a word taking the throne like seat. He looks across at the Security Director and demands,

"Well, what the hell is going on"

The head of security, usually a fairly arrogant, confident character, answers meekly,

"Sir, we don't know yet, we're trying to establish what's happened."

The Chief executive cuts in with a raised voice,

"We have the most expensive, advanced computer system on the Planet which is currently a pile of scrap and you tell me you don't know what's happened to it."

The security director looks at the Director of Systems for support,

"Sir, we have a worldwide network, our defence system thought it was being attacked by our own network and counterattacked it."

The Chief Executive is furious,

"We HAD a worldwide network, our communication networks and computer systems have been destroyed."

He raises his voice higher,

"DO YOU REALISE THAT THIS HAS PUT ALL OUR GLOBAL ACTIVITIES AND COMPANY AT RISK; WE'RE COMPLETELY BLIND."

The Director of Systems steps in,

"Sir, with respect we're working round the clock on this problem, I've called in every member of our programming team, hopefully within 24 hours we'll know how it happened, then we have to replace the damaged equipment at our sites."

The Chief Executive is furious,

"What do you mean 'HOPEFULLY you have 24 hours to find out exactly what has happened, once we know how and by whom, AND you can guarantee with your life that it'll not happen again, ONLY THEN can we reorder the equipment you need. Have you any idea how many hundreds of millions of dollars that will cost! I want an hourly update from you with a detailed report on my desk within 24 hours with all the answers and no excuses. When we find the people responsible for this I want them here, alive, for questioning before we deal with them."

The meeting ends as the Chief Executive stands,

"Now get on with it."

In Alaska, Mike's phone rings, James voice sounds alarmed,

"I'm being followed by two men, their car pulled out as I left the track from your place."

Mike thinks for a moment,

"Don't panic, I remember passing a garage nearby, drive into the forecourt make a U turn then come back to the house, drive steadily so they don't suspect you know they're following. When you get to our track drive down slowly, park where you did before but stay in the car, with luck they'll follow, we'll find out who they are."

Tim and Diane already have their jackets on with weapons checked. Mike explains what's happened,

"We need to find out who they are so no corpses please. We'll hide in the trees Tim and I will take positions each side of the track, Diane you remain near the garage covering James."

They go outside taking up their positions, leaving the outside lights on. Tim and Mike are each side of the track about half way up. They see the lights of James's car entering the track, he does exactly as he was told, slowly making his way down towards the house. He parks turning off his lights. The other vehicle enters the track, switching off its lights it slowly edges down until it has a view of the house, stopping just between Mike and Tim. Mike thinks to himself 'perfect'. The men sit in the car for a minute as if discussing what to do, then get out quietly closing the doors they start creeping towards the house.

Mike places the cross hairs of his rifle scope on the back of the first man's head. He has his hand in his coat pocket. Mike quietly steps out behind them,

"Stay where you are, no sudden movements."

The first man's arm moves, the older man puts his hand on his arm,

"No, leave it."

He's seen Mike's rifle,

Tim steps out of the trees covering the men with his pistol then tells them,

"Place your hands on the roof of the car feet apart, you probably know the drill."

The men do as he orders. Tim moves closer, professionally frisking each of the men for weapons he removes their two revolvers and wallets. Diane arrives with the cable ties Mike had given her and secures each man's hands behind his back. Mike orders them,

"Don't turn round stay looking at the trees."
Mike opens the wallets; both men are CIA agents,

"What are you doing here?"
The men are silent, Mike takes out a NSA ID Card using his torch he quickly flashes the card in front of the men. Mike explains,

"You are intruding on a major NSA operation, what are you doing here and on whose authorisation?"
The elder of the two agents replies,

"We're from the Fairbanks office we were asked to follow him,"
Nodding towards James's car,

"And report his movements."
Mike asks,

"When did you commence surveillance?"
The agent answers,

"24 hours ago, we picked him up as he left Fairbanks, followed him to a Motel down the road, then to an office in TOK and finally here."
Mike presses him,

"Who did he meet in TOK and at the Motel?"
The agent seems embarrassed,

"We were only told to report his movements we've no idea what he was doing there."

"Who authorised you to carry out this task, have you made your report yet?"

"The authorisation came from the DIA, Washington and no we haven't made a report yet we were waiting to follow him back to Fairbanks, that's where he lives."
Mike thinks for a moment,

"Look you two, if you make any report you could jeopardise several years work of a worldwide National Security Agency undercover operation, I'm sure you wouldn't like to find yourselves unemployable, particularly if your bosses at the CIA found out how incompetent you've been on such a simple task. The point is we can't let you do that, so either we send you on a short holiday or you agree to go back to Fairbanks and report that your target evaded you on the way out of Fairbanks and you believe he's left the country."

The two agents speak to each other and the elder agrees,

"We apologise, we weren't told what we were getting into."

Mike laughs,

"That's the DIA for you, never tell anyone anything."

The agent says,

"If we can leave we'll head back and do as you suggested."

Mike is firm,

"Exactly, as I suggested, do not discuss this with anyone, not that you would want to."

The agent responds,

"OK and thanks."

Mike adds

"I'm going to hold your ID cards for five days, once I've confirmation from Washington that you've done as we have agreed I'll have them returned to you, OK."

The agent agrees as Mike nods at Diane who cuts them free, Tim hands them their weapons and says,

"Don't worry it's not your fault, have a good trip back"

They get into their vehicle turn in the track then vanish into the darkness much faster than they arrived. Tim, Mike and Diane walk over to the car escorting James who is a little shaken, into the house. James is the first to speak,

"Thank you guys, that was unbelievable, how did you do it?"

Mike grins,

"I flashed a false NSA identity card in front of their eyes and told them that they were jeopardising a

major NSA operation. I promised I wouldn't tell their bosses how incompetent they've been if they report that you lost them as you were leaving Fairbanks."
James laughs
"Do you trust them?"
"Nope, which is why I've kept their CIA badges, said that I'll send them back in five day's once I've confirmation from Washington that they've done as we agreed."
James is impressed,
"I just love working with you people."
"James, its three o'clock in the morning you'd better sleep here tonight, we'll plan our departure tomorrow morning."
James asks,
"Where are we going?"
"Washington my friend, to the lion's den, you got everything you need?"
James nods,
"I've got my Passport, documents, laptop everything except clothes."
Diane interrupts,
"That's no problem we'll get you whatever you need in Washington."
Tim wants to go through the email files on the CD but Mike overrules him,
"Look it's late, turn in we'll start fresh tomorrow morning, Tim remember you have to speak to Aacaarya."
Tim agrees and then disappears into his room as James settles down with a blanket on the sofa in the lounge. Mike and Diane close their bedroom door.
The next morning at ten o'clock Mike opens the door to find Tim already busy at the computer printing out a selection of emails as James sleeps on, Mike suggests they go into the kitchen.
"Tim didn't you get any sleep last night?"

"Not really, I dozed a bit but woke at eight, decided to search through the email files so we can review them whilst we're travelling."

As Mike is preparing coffee he asks,

"How was Aacaarya?"

"We had a long conversation about what we'd been doing, some of which he was aware of he's convinced that we'll find the evidence we're looking for amongst Global Management's emails which is why I started early. I discussed with him at length my idea about trying to form an independent body to protect the Earth's environment. He believes that this could be a way forward that's supportable, providing we can convince most countries to participate in it. I suggested that the only way of doing this, would be if we could offer their government's something more valuable and important than their perceptions and value of their research programmes."

"What do you have in mind?"

Tim continues,

"I asked Aacaarya if they would consider providing access to their technology for clean electrical energy to the countries that commit to the 'Earth's Environmental Protection Agency' for want of another name."

"That would be great leverage if it was possible, what did he say?"

"He's going to discuss it with the Elders, although he feels it's an idea with merit, he also thinks that the Elders would attach conditions other than giving up dangerous research projects, he'll let me know their reaction later."

Diane joins them having checked on James,

"He's out for the count, but still breathing which must be a good sign, what've you two been up to, apart from making coffee?"

Mike explains what Tim has told him, Diane is impressed,

"That's a great idea, if we could bring all the heads of government together, offer them free energy who wouldn't commit."

Mike smiles,

"The energy companies, who're in love with oil and petroleum they would lose their monopolies and vast profits, like for example the Global Assets Management Trust who would have to be neutralised first."

Tim continues,

"There's a possibility we may have the means to do that from what James has done."

James's voice comes through from the lounge,

"Are you guys talking about me?"

Diane turns as he slowly walks into the kitchen handing him a mug of coffee,

"Welcome back to the land of the living, you were out for the count."

James grins,

"Yeah I was more than exhausted after last night's events, but I'm OK now up and running on all cylinders."

At the Pentagon George enters Tony's office,

"You called me?"

"Yes George, I've been trying to get in touch with Mike, Tim and Diane to see how they are, there's been no response from any of their sat phones since they left. I've been getting a little concerned, you heard anything?"

"No, I've not heard anything other than that they were making their way to Alaska for a few days. I wouldn't be too concerned they're well able to look after themselves."

"I was just a little surprised they hadn't made contact, something's come up it's essential that we find them, can you run checks to find out where they are?"

"Will do, sir"

George leaves the office he's unsettled that Tony's not telling him everything. He knows Tony received and responded to Mike's encrypted email, as his own routine surveillance team picked the message up and passed it on to him, he's also seen other strange encrypted messages to Tony from unknown sources. George is frustrated that the Pentagons cryptology department have so far failed to break the encryption codes used.

Chapter - 21

Washington DC

Back in Alaska Mike is speaking to Julian, he's setting up transport for the four of them from TOK Junction Airport to Washington they leave at 14:00 hours. James asks Julian to bring another computer case that he's left in his office. They prepare their bags to load into the Jeep. Mike tells James to leave his car at the house as Julian has arranged to pick it up after they've left. They leave the house, ten minutes later they arrive at the small TOK Junction airport, as instructed Mike drives to a small hanger and parks beside it. In front of the hanger is an aircraft similar to the one that flew them from Washington, it's an eight passenger Citation XLS with twin Pratt & Witney PW545C engines. Julian greets them, hands James his computer bag and introduces the pilots who are both ex military associates of Julian's. The pilot opens the main door lowering the steps, as there are only four of them they take their bags up into the cabin, immediately making themselves' comfortable in the plush seats, James is in heaven, he loves flying and holds a private pilot's licence, he asks if he can visit the cockpit later.

"James, after we've reviewed the documents."

"Come on then Mike, let's get started."

The pilot closes the door. The aircraft taxis onto runway 25 and is quickly climbing away from the airport, the Citation makes a final turn onto its heading towards Washington levelling out at their 31,000 ft cruising altitude. Mike and Diane are seated opposite Tim and James, the small table between them is covered in piles of paper. They are scanning thousands of Emails which have been split between them, each searching for something that might be useful, when, half an hour later Tim breaks the silence,

"I've found one, just look at this. It's the authorisation to 'eliminate the threat using the F-XX asset'."

James asks,

"What's an F-XX asset?"

Diane surprises him by answering,

"It's the Chinese built stealth fighter they used to attack our aircraft."

"Diane, then this is pretty much tangible evidence."

Tim agrees,

"But strangely the authorisation was from 101010 to 505050."

He checks the code numbers against the names,

"This is from Tony Mitchell to their Vice President and copied to 909090, James who is 909090?"

James looks down his list,

"You're not going to believe this, it's the President."

"What the President of Global Management?"

James moves his head from side to side,

"No man, it's the President of the United States."

Mike asks,

"James how do you know that?"

"There're not too many Presidents at the White House which is where this copy was sent." Diane is shocked,

"Are you are telling me the President approved the attack on our aircraft."

Mike is less surprised,

"It looks that way, but what I find difficulty in accepting is that Tony was not only involved but actually sent the authorisation. We need to find out where the instruction went after it was authorised."

They continue wading through the lists of emails when Mike stops them,

"Maybe this is it. It's a forwarded email from 505050, their Vice President, to 252525 the President of their Russian subsidiary with 'instructions to proceed as discussed' it's dated 24 hours before the attack."
Diane asks,

"What are we going to do with this information, who do we tell that we can trust?"
Mike replies,

"Once we've gone through extracting as much indisputable evidence as we can, I'll set up a secure private meeting with George on neutral ground. This potentially goes right through the administration to the top we have to tread very carefully.
James wants to stretch his legs, he goes forward to the cockpit, closing the door he sits chatting with the pilots. After a few minutes there's a slight lurch as the Citation drops a wing then rocks to the other side Tim concerned asks,

"What's going on?"
Mike goes forward, opening the cockpit door he's surprised to see James sitting in the Captains left hand seat with his hands on the control column,

"What are you doing?"
The second pilot smiles at Mike,

"He's doing pretty well, a slight overreaction when he took over, that's all."
The Citation is now smooth and level again, James turns,

"I've never flown a jet before, guys that was outstanding."
The captain's smiling,

"I think your short lesson just ended James, perhaps another time."
James frowns, passing control back to the pilot, he reluctantly follows Mike back to the others, Diane asks,

"Is anything wrong?"
Mike smiles,

"Depends what you mean by wrong, it was only James flying the damned plane."

James sits down,

"Back to work then, fun over, sorry folks I couldn't resist it, you just never know when a little familiarisation might come in useful."

Mike takes the emails they have selected,

"I'm going to see if I can get hold of George on his private number."

He takes out Julian's secure mobile phone and dials. He waits whilst it answers then asks,

"Are you secure"

George responds,

"That's affirmative."

"George, we're on our way home we need to meet with you urgently at a secure location, only you to know, particularly not 'T'."

"OK, call me when you arrive, I'll let you know where.   I need to speak to you about 'T' too, something's not right there."

"George, we know that. See you this evening."

"Look forward to it."

Mike explains to the others,

"When we're an hour from Reagan National International Airport I'll call again, he'll let us know when we can meet."

It's late in the day, having gone through most of the data on Global Management they decide to call it a day. The second pilot shouts through,

"If you fancy anything from the galley just help yourselves, there's a coffee machine and various sandwiches but don't forget us."

Diane and James immediately go through to the galley pulling out pre-packed sandwiches from the fridge, the pilot shouts through again,

"Sorry about the limited selection it's all we had time to get before we left."

During their snacks round the table James and Tim are discussing James flying experiences which up till today had been limited to his own aircraft, a four seat Beechcraft Bonanza. Mike has been silent and deep in thought, Diane asks,

"Mike you OK?" she disturbs his thoughts,

"I'm sorry, yes, I was thinking about how serious this whole affair is for the United States and the consequences when it goes public."

Diane is intrigued to know more,

"What would happen?"

Mike takes a sip of his coffee, Tim and James stop talking, focusing on Mike who continues, "There's no doubt in my mind that the information in our possession confirms the President's involvement in matters contrary to the security of the USA. This should be brought to the attention of the House of Representatives they in turn would invoke the House Judiciary Committee to investigate the allegations, as they alone have the power to impeach the President. Once this starts the allegations and evidence would be in the public domain, and as always other things will come out of the woodwork such as his involvement in the decision to invade Iraq on questionable intelligence information which is already a hot topic.

This would lead to an investigation into all those involved including Tony, his associates and Global Asset Management's activities. We may all be required to give evidence including Aacaarya if that was possible. It's just as well his people recovered the Stealth as that is prime evidence which would vanish if Global could get their hands on it."

Tim asks,

"Who would we approach first and how do we determine who we could trust?"

"Following the meeting with George and depending on his reaction, I believe we should arrange a meeting with the Chairman of the House Judiciary

Committee. George is certain to know him personally and if he's trustworthy."

James asks,

"Mike, won't this be dangerous for us?"

"Yes, initially but once it's in the hand of the Judiciary Committee and in the public domain we would be protected by the fact that everything is out in the open, it's between now and then we need to be very careful as they'll certainly be looking for us."

Diane asks,

"If the President is impeached and proven guilty what happens to him?"

"The President would have to resign, immediately he loses the immunity of his position it leaves him open to the possibility of being prosecuted for Crimes against Humanity by the International criminal Court of The Hague. If charges are then brought against him and his associates in connection with their roles in profiteering from their manipulation of the invasion of Iraq with Global Management and they're found guilty, they'll face a lifetime in prison."

James is astounded,

"You mean this whole affair could bring down the President."

"Yes, he and his associates in the administration, providing of course the allegations can be proved which won't be easy."

Diane asks,

"But won't the administration protect him?"

"No, as soon as anything this serious becomes public the President's aides and supporters will rapidly distance themselves from him, leaving him exposed."

James asks,

"Would that mean that the administration would be able to carry out a proper investigation into the 9/11 twin towers attack?"

"James, what do you mean?"

"Well there was going to be an independent investigation into 9/11 but that got watered down into an enquiry headed by friends of the President that didn't address the many unanswered questions surrounding the attack, which is one reason why there's still this controversy about whether he and members of his team were involved in it. By the way, it wasn't the first time that an aircraft crashed into a skyscraper in New York. Did you know that on July 28th 1945 a Mitchell B25 twin engine bomber laden with fuel became disorientated in thick fog and although the pilot was not supposed to fly below 2000ft he decided to descend to 1000ft to get his bearings and found himself in the centre of Manhattan, with the tops of skyscrapers all round him.

After miraculously avoiding several large buildings and trying desperately to climb, the pilot made a wrong turn crashing into the 79th floor of The Empire State Building at 300 mph. The major wreckage penetrated the building at the point of impact creating a hole in the building eighteen feet wide by twenty feet tall. One engine hurled itself down the elevator shaft and was found in the basement, the high octane fuel exploded causing severe fires down to the 75th floor.

Parts of the other engine and landing gear actually passed right through the building and ended up on the top of a 12 storey building across the street behind, causing another fire. Fourteen people perished in that disaster although the building was in no danger of collapse and was repaired."

Diane is fascinated,

"I didn't know that, but what's strange is that the Empire State Building's construction was completed in 1931. The World Trade Centre towers construction commenced in 1966 and both towers were completed by 1972, forty years after the Empire State Building. The towers were purposely designed to withstand an aircraft crashing into them, yet collapsed like a pack of cards."

Tim looks at Mike,

"I didn't know that the Empire State Building was hit by an aircraft, did you?"

"No first I ever heard of it. James you are an oracle of interesting facts."

James grins,

"I told you my flying knowledge would come in handy."

The pilot informs them that they're an hour from Reagan National Airport. Mike briefs them,

"When we arrive we'll leave via the private VIP exit then take a taxi with our bags, we'll be staying at the Holiday Inn Central Washington Hotel, its only 15 minutes from the airport just half a mile from the White House. Its time I let George know."

Mike calls George, who answers immediately,

"How about meeting for breakfast, where will you be?"

Mike hesitates for a moment but realises George has to know,

"Holiday Inn Central, I'll leave a note for you in reception with the room location."

George acknowledges,

"Perfect, good choice, see you at 07.30."

Mike then calls the Hotel confirming their reservation.

Diane asks,

"Why choose the Holiday Inn?"

"It's a very popular business hotel right in the centre of Washington, close to everything we'll need, plus it's one of the best Holiday Inn's in the country, George is coming over at 07:30."

"Do you think that's safe?"

"Yeah definitely, George is too much of 'the old school' intelligence professional to be followed we both think the venue is as secure as anywhere in Washington."

An hour later at 22:30 the Citation lands at Reagan National Airport and taxis to the VIP parking area. A few minutes later they have said their goodbyes to the aircrew. They walk across the tarmac to the nearby VIP entrance their breath is visible in the crisp night air then they are immediately ushered straight through VIP arrivals. They join the small taxi queue as their special taxi arrives they squeeze into the cab which whisks them straight to the Hotel reception. They wait in the large reception lounge as Mike collects the room keys.

As Mike returns he says,

"We're on the top floor."

He points to the lift.

Now they've finished travelling, tiredness is beginning to set in as the events of the past few days are catching up with them. Mike takes them up to the top floor, he opens the door to their suite they enter a sumptuous suite with three double bedrooms off the living area. In the large lounge there's a computer with high speed printer, set up beside it is a large photocopier. Tim looks at the copier,

"This will be handy."

"I asked to have it for the duration of our stay as we needed to print conference documentation."

The double rooms are identical, luxuriously equipped with King Size beds. After dumping their bags, their next priority is food. Diane takes control of ordering, after a brief discussion she calls room service for, four T Bone steaks, chips and side dishes, with half a case of Chateau Neuf de Pap wine.

Tim reorganises the lounge tables spreading out the various piles of papers they collated during the flight, after he has finished he informs Mike,

"I'm going to see if I can get hold of Aacaarya whilst I've some energy left, don't let anyone disturb me"

He goes into his room.

Tim lies down using the last of his energy to drift into a state of absolute mental concentration. He visualises Aacaarya then quickly making contact, he quietly speaks to the image he can see in his mind's eye, as if Aacaarya is in the room with him. Tim explains the events that have occurred, their discoveries since their last conversation, their intended strategy tomorrow with George as the first step in disclosing the information they have compiled. Aacaarya listens in silence then responds,

"The Elders have asked me to thank you all, you've done well. They initially had doubts as to whether you and your associates would have the commitment to see this matter through to its completion. The personal risks to you were and not insignificant. You've earned their complete support and where possible protection."

"What was their reaction to the concept of founding the Earth's Environmental Protection Agency (EEPA)?"

"We believe this agency if structured properly with appropriate support and transparency will provide an acceptable mechanism for controlling the types of research experiments that could have detrimental impact on the health of our planet. The Elders have authorised me to work with you to establish the constitution for this Agency and to personally attend the inaugural meetings then to monitor the Agencies ongoing activities."

"What will be the conditions for doing this?"
Aacaarya continues,

"I'll provide you with a draft of our requirements which will become an ultimatum for the participating countries. I would like you to discuss this with your associates and with George when you see him, then let me have you combined reactions."
Tim picks up a pen and pad from beside his bed,

"Ok, go ahead."
Aacaarya smiles,

"Tim, you don't have to write this down"

Six copies of the document appear on the bedside table. Tim picks up the first one then starts reading.

"Our commitment to EEPA:

We will provide free, limitless clean energy to all countries that sign the irrevocable treaty. They must act in accordance with the constitution of the EEPA, a non-profit organisation. There will be no cost for the implementation or technology as physically this will be accomplished by the Elders placing at strategic positions in each country, pyramid energy transceivers similar to the one you are familiar with. These will be managed remotely by the Elders, the technology used will remain their property and under their protection. We will assist with the integration of our energy sources into the various national grids and supply networks where they currently exist. Where third world countries participate that have no established grid network, we will additionally assist them in setting up their energy infrastructures.

After each country has demonstrated a working application of the constitution for a period of 12 months we will consider providing other advanced knowledge and technology to assist further developments for peaceful purposes in the fields of transport, health and food production. The governments that make a full commitment to the principals of EEPA may call upon us to consult on other general matters. Once our energy sources are in place it will make obsolete the need for nuclear and fossil fuels breaking your dependence on these antiquated and polluting sources of energy.

The thirteen conditions demanded by the Elders are:

Participation will require unanimous acceptance and implementation by all countries of the following requirements:

An annual management fee will be paid by each country to EEPA this will be calculated and based upon the wealth of the participating nation this will be used to fund EEPA's actual costs each year.

Participating nations will immediately terminate all experimental research, civilian and military that does not have the prior approval of EEPA. Permission will only be granted to research or experimental projects that are proven by EEPA to have no negative impact on the Earth's magnetic fields, its surface, subterranean levels, atmosphere, ionosphere, its magnetosphere and near space. Any research approvals granted will be monitored and controlled by EEPA.

The governments of participating nations will denounce war, agreeing an immediate reassessment of their foreign policies to ensure diplomatic resolution of international disputes focussing on peaceful, non-aggressive solutions to problems, through integration and support. To facilitate this they will phase in major reductions in military expenditure including terminating the international sale of weaponry to prevent the escalation of armed conflict throughout the world, bringing to an end the profiteering from wars.

Governments will work together to strengthen the powers of their legal systems. This will expedite a global eradication of corruption by implementing transparency and efficiency in all their political parties, administrative departments and commercial organisations. Leaders, politicians and government officials will take full responsibility and be accountable to us for their actions and decisions.
Individuals and government officials guilty of colluding with those that wish to pursue military action against other nations for profit and with those that commit crimes against humanity will be sought out then punished for these crimes in the appropriate International courts.

Governments will work together with us to create a new international intelligence task force to eradicate the power of organised criminal organisations that are endemic throughout the world. This international force will act to eliminate the production of drugs, where necessary they will replace drug production facilities with alternative industries where the economies of these production countries have been dependent on drugs for their survival.

Governments will take full responsibility for implementing and enforcing legislation to protect the world's diminishing resources by restricting and managing the growth of their populations through education, incentives and legislation. Each nation will be required to strengthen its borders to control and manage immigration until such time as they have developed workable strategies for integration. These tight border controls will make the cross border flow of illegal immigrants, drugs and arms more difficult.

Governments will co-operate to create a global medical organisation tasked with the eradication of disease and famine throughout the world. This organisation will be funded from the military budgets previously used for war related expenditure. The existing World Health Organisation would be incorporated into this new task force.

At all levels, governments will re-balance the wealth distribution to close the gap between the very rich and very poor through tax systems that allow investment and appropriate opportunities for the poor to improve their living conditions and status.

All governments will work towards the goal of providing the populations of their countries with access to the highest level of medical care regardless of their status, age or wealth.

Each government will undertake to make education a higher priority, encouraging intellectual and cultural studies as an essential right of their population with increased spending with incentives to encourage access to improved universities and educational facilities.

We will work with the leaders of the elected governments to found a new One World Government or 'think- tank' this will be made up of three elected leaders from each country including three of our Elders with the objective of sharing problems and finding solutions, to establish lasting global stability and peace. This World Government would act as a forum for world leaders and the unanimous decision of the World Government would have priority over any individual countries governments who would be required to act in accordance with the decrees of the One World Government.

Religious leaders will be prohibited from participating in or influencing government decisions. The overall leader of each religion will be allowed a voice at the One World Government but will not have voting powers.

As the new energy becomes available it will make nuclear and fossil based fuels obsolete we would expect all nations to phase out their nuclear programmes and dismantle their existing fossil fuelled power generation sources. The oil companies must cease drilling and extraction of oil from the earth's crust and particularly under the oceans, undertaking to clean up and repair the environments that they have damaged.
Tim is now exhausted by the effort,

"Aacaarya I'm sorry but I have reached my limit of endurance."

"Tim you have done well, take a deserved break, your meal has arrived. Discuss this draft together we'll speak tomorrow after your meeting with George. We realise that these demands will mean major changes in the way your world functions, but when implemented with our help, will not only provide a clean source of energy but will generate massive financial savings which can be used to stabilise your civilisations and create an equilibrium between all countries providing a safer world for us all to live in. Your task is simple sell it first to the seat of power in Washington, good luck."

Tim lies still for a few minutes, there's a gentle knock on his door, its Diane. She slowly opens the door and enters the room,

"Sorry to disturb you, but dinner's served if you're ready."

Tim slowly sits up looking drained and pale,

"Tim, are you OK?"

Tim manages a smile as he slowly swings his legs off the bed,

"I've felt better I'll be through in a minute, I'm just going to stick my head in a sink of cold water."

After a few minutes he joins the others at the dining table, Mike and James notice Tim is rather unsteady on his feet. Mike asks,

"What happened?"

Tim moves his head from one side to the other,

"Not now, let's eat first there's a lot to discuss."

Tim is silent as they finish dinner, not his normal outward going self. After dinner they move into the lounge where Diane recharges their wine glasses.

Mike asks,

"Tim, do you feel up to talking about it?"

"I'm sorry guys that hour I spent with Aacaarya was the most difficult yet, I told him he'd drained my energy resources, wait a minute."

Tim returns to his room to fetches the pile of documents. Handing a copy to each of them he says,

"Take a read, it's a list of the thirteen demands the Elders intend making to all nations in return for an extraordinary incentive."

They each take time to read through the notes, James is first to comment,

"There's no way they'll sign up to this, this is an ideal not a reality."

Tim answers him firmly,

"James, this is a reality they have the capability to enforce these demands, it's for the good of the planet that they live on too."

Mike's reaction is surprise,

"How can America accept this, they're not ready for a New World Order."

"Mike, this is not a New World Order but sensible rules to make America and the World a better place to live in, more secure with a balanced stronger economy. At the moment the economy of America is sliding downhill into a black hole with oil now costing over $100 per barrel and rising added to the tremendous risks the banks have been taking, the USA cannot continue using oil at their current rate, they need change. The predicament facing the world Aacaarya has identified is correct and these issues need to be addressed we are to survive, what do you think Diane?"

"It's rather taken my breath away. If this was possible it would put us back on track for a positive future."

James asks,

"What if the other nations don't play ball?"

"They don't really have a choice these demands are ultimatums from another world that is far more advanced than we are, if we'd not threatened the survival of their planet we would probably not have known that they existed."

Diane asks Mike,

"How do you think George will react to this?"

"He's an intelligent educated man, as far as I know a man of principle that spends his working life surrounded by some of the most powerful, corrupt people in the world, so he may regard this as something to be positively considered. We'll find out in the morning."

Tim suggests they need another early night as they have to be ready for George at 7:30 in the morning. Mike agrees,

"Let's sleep on it we'll review everything tomorrow morning at 6.00."

James asks,

"Where're we meeting George?" Mike points to the table,

"Here, I've left him a note in reception with our room number; he'll be here sharp at 07:30."

Next morning they are up early, refreshed by several cups of Diane's coffee. At exactly 07:30 there's a knock on the door. Mike uses the peephole in the door to confirm that it's George then lets him in. George is dressed casually in jeans with a leather flying jacket, not what they expected but certainly less conspicuous than his uniform. As he steps into the room he smiles,

"It's great to see you safe I've been very worried about you."

Mike introduces James,

"James is a new key member of our team."

After the introductions they sit down to fresh coffee, Mike sits in front of the pile of emails they have accumulated. Before George sits down he takes a small electronic device out of his pocket sweeping it round the room. Diane asks,

"What are you doing?"

George puts his finger to his lips and continues his work, when he's satisfied he sits down smiling at Diane,

"Sorry about that, I was sweeping for surveillance devices."

Diane is shocked,

"You don't mean?"

George cuts in,

"This is Washington, better safe than sorry its standard practice."

Mike asks George,

"How long have you got?" George grins,

"I've taken a day off so it's all yours."

"George, before we start, you mentioned that you thought something was not right with Tony, what was it?"

George explains,

"We knew that he had contact with you by email but when he called me in, to tell me that he was desperate to find you, I asked him if he'd heard anything and he answered no, this made me uncomfortable particularly as we'd been monitoring encrypted emails to and from his computer from unknown sources for some time."

James interrupts,

"Did you manage to decode them?"

"No, not yet it's got our people baffled."

"If it's what I think it is, I've broken their code and can decrypt those messages if you let me have them."

George is stunned and turns to Mike,

"Who is he?"

Mike grins,

"James is full of surprises a real Cyber King what's more he did it in just a few hours." George congratulates James,

"Perhaps you'd consider working for me?"

"No thank you, I am part of a very special squad on an important mission to save the world, but I can certainly make a little time to help you."

They share the joke as Mike becomes more serious,

"Diane could we have a fresh round of coffees I think George is going to need one."

Diane places five mugs on the table as Mike explains in detail the series of events since they left Washington, the ambush on the way from the airport, the incident at HAARP with Peter and the information they were given, how James became involved, how he managed to hack into the Global Asset Management computer system, how they burnt him and his retaliation by bringing down their worldwide system. Then finally Mike explains how they extracted of the list of Global members which included Tony Mitchell, the coded information about their activities and defences, and the CIA agents that followed James. George who is normally unflappable and never silent sits in shocked silence for an hour until Mike is finished then presents him the summary of evidence that they have collated on a CD. George breaks his silence,

"This is far more serious than I could have imagined."
Mike then says,

"There's more, Tim last night spent an hour speaking to Aacaarya."
Mike gestures to Tim,

"Over to you."
Tim describes his discussion with Aacaarya then hands George the draft conditions. George reads through it slowly and carefully,

"Do you think they're serious in expecting our people to sign up to this?"

"Absolutely, the Elders believe that if they commit to this, we'll have a future with the possibility of creating a world that has a chance of growing in peace and equality. As we all know, if the nations of our world don't change course, it'll only be a matter of time before one of them causes our destruction. If you know anything about the ancient prophecies you'll be aware that all the religions in the world are in accordance with the Maya who's calendar ends on 21st December 2012 when they prophesise that the world as we know it, will suffer a cataclysm as it moves into a new cycle with a new order. When I heard the Elders demands my first reaction was the same as James's that they were impossible ideals, but the more I thought about it the more I realised that the benefits far outweigh any downside. The only people that would contest this are those driven by greed, power, crime and environmental destruction."

George nods in agreement as he searches his soul for an answer,

"Tim, what happens if half the Nations agree and half don't?"

"In view of the fact that the world is using more oil than it has available, production has peaked and we're facing a major crisis. China and India's rapid growth in consumption is outpacing the global production capability so I reckon that most nations given time to consider the alternative of a global economic collapse will accept the offer. If not, you've witnessed several small demonstrations of the power of Aacaarya's people, I believe they'll help us, co-operating with the nations that sign up to convince those that do not, by whatever means are necessary."

George asks,

"Tim, what's their real motivation for doing this?"

"They want to stabilise and protect their planet, so that both our worlds can live side by side in peace without disturbing the Earth's delicate equilibrium or each other. The point is they've been here for 20,000 years and have only just decided to intervene making themselves known to us because through our technological progress we are threatening the survival of their planet.

They have no desire or motivation to control our civilisations or to occupy our world despite the fact that over many years they have watched us destroying ourselves and our environment. It's only since we started experimenting with the Earth's electromagnetic fields in the Ionosphere that we became a serious threat to the Earth, this has forced their intervention. We've seen the world they live in, it's paradise compared to ours. They are a very intelligent, cultured and intellectual race. We could learn an enormous amount from them, providing we obey their rules."

Mike asks George,

"What do you think about this, do we have enough to approach the House Judiciary Committee?"

"Mike, before I answer that question I'd like you to swear absolute secrecy to what I'm about to tell you?"

They all agree.

"For the past few years, I and several other close and influential associates have been concerned that some of the events that have taken place around the world seem to be stage managed by our government and its agencies on a vast global scale. We started exploring a theory that the government and administration were being manipulated by a more powerful and shadowy organisation, manipulating events to prepare the world for them to take control of."

Chapter - 22

New World Order

It's been almost impossible to take our research beyond a hypothesis because the suspect organisations are so well protected and impossible to penetrate."
James interrupts,

"George do you mean organisations like Global Asset Management?"

"No, we believe that they are pawns in a bigger game, we've studied several long established groups that have the influence, philosophy and finance to make this possible."
Diane asks,

"Who are they?"

"One such society has its foundations in the early 1700's when certain very powerful leaders, passed on their beliefs and goals to their successors, each generation thereafter became more powerful, building on the strengths of their forefathers."
George then explains,

"To give you an example, what do you know about the history of Washington?"
None of them know too much about the capital except Diane who believed it was originally built in the 1700's.
George sighs,

"I'm about to give you a rather strange alternative history lesson. It's believed by certain parties that the Masonic Brotherhood have been implementing a plan originally conceived between Sir Francis Bacon a Rosicrucian and Masonic Master and Queen Elizabeth I, in the early 1590's to create in North America a nation that would become; and I use the wording of one of these groups 'The new occult Atlantis' which would lead all nations into their New World Order. Keeping that thought in mind, I want to explain how they believe

Washington was planned and designed as there are a large number of very visible coincidences that are difficult to ignore.

When the site was initially designated to become the home of the nation's capital it was mostly swamp area beside the Potomac River, this was chosen because it was believed to be one of the places where there was an intersection of energy lines, creating a vortex of energy over the area. Throughout history, churches temples and important spiritual structures have been strategically located at points where unusual forces where perceived to exist in the Earth's natural energy grid.

The original plans of the Washington street layouts were set out in 1792 by an Architect named Pierre Charles L'Enfant, who by coincidence was a member of the Masonic Brotherhood.

The street layout he planned could be interpreted as forming the evil Goats Head of Mendes Five Point Pentagram, this encompassed the White House, this layout includes large images of the most important and powerful symbols, the Masonic Compass, Square and Rule. These streets exist today and all radiate out from the capital and the White House, in a manner last seen in Babylon.

The most important buildings in the capital are linked together along these lines and can be interpreted as being constructed in specific shapes to focus energy. Many buildings contain symbols that occultists believe reverberate with inherent power from the moment they are created. Similar to the way a witch would lay out symbols on the ground to focus power during rituals and ceremonies. Washington could have been laid out to accomplish the same goal. All the key government buildings constructed since the late 1700's through the middle of Franklin Roosevelt's administration period were consecrated in a Masonic cornerstone laying ceremony. Interestingly most of the Presidents of America since George Washington have all been Masons.

When you examine the design of The Capital Building and Government Centre with this in mind, the Mall resembles the shape of the Sephiroth Tree of Life which encompasses the Lincoln Memorial, Jefferson Memorial, White House and Washington Memorial."

James is fascinated,

"What's the Sephiroth Tree of Life?"

"According to a well known Masonic Encyclopaedia it's described as depicting the occult concept of the creation of the world and the other worlds they believe exist. It's a representation of how the God, En Soph, the Infinite One, created this world and others through ten emanations, each of which is represented in the Government Centre; it's rather complicated but there's masses of information about these theories on the internet if you're interested. Another powerful satanic symbol is the seat of power of our military, the Pentagon another five pointed star regarded by occultists as a symbol of Satan's power.

The Washington Monument is the tallest Obelisk in the world at five hundred feet, Obelisks are understood to represent a very important conductive energy marker, shaped in the form of Atlantean Fire Stone crystals which some believe are life force accumulators and amplifiers. Historically obelisks are supposed to arc the energies that exist between heaven and earth. The Egyptians believed that the spirit of their sun-god Rah resided in the Obelisk which represented the presence of the sun-god who was referred to in the Bible as Satan. The Monument was built to honour the first Masonic President George Washington and was allegedly constructed by Masons in Masonic tradition incorporating many of their secretive symbols and numbers.

In 1915 the House of the Temple was completed, this is the headquarters of the Scottish Rite of Freemasonry, it was built to house the Rite's governing body, the Supreme Council 33°. The architect took his inspiration for this magnificent building from classic architecture he based his design on one of the Seven Wonders of the World, the tomb of King Mausolus which was discovered in what we now call Turkey. This edifice is constructed only thirteen blocks from the White House, the significance of that number will be clear in a moment. It stands at the head of the Goathead Pentagram as the illuminating light of the candle. The inside of this Temple has been reported as being in the shape of a Masonic Coffin which by coincidence is the same shape as The Sephiroth Tree of Life. Another strange fact is that General Granger following a meeting with President Andrew Johnson a mason and Albert Pike who was one of the most famous of all masons, Granger stated that he was surprised that President Johnson considered himself to be subordinate to Albert Pike. This was an interesting comment, because under the oath's taken by masons they promise to obey all summonses given by the hand of a Brother Master Mason, this oath would by its nature include brothers who are Presidents."

Mike, Diane and James are completely absorbed remaining silent whilst George continues.

"In the United States the number thirteen has great significance in its history. The United States was founded once it had thirteen colonies. It then became the United States of America. Number thirteen, is also a mystical number which has been attributed to the number assigned to Satan. The number seven is also considered to be the perfect number by occultists."

George asks Mike,

"Do you have a dollar bill handy?"

Mike takes out his wallet laying a dollar bill on the table in front of him.

"Take a close look at the green treasury badge to the right of Washington's picture and you'll see it contains three important Masonic symbols, the balance, the angle and the key. If you turn the note over you can see on the left hand side The Great Seal, showing the unfinished pyramid topped by the 'all-seeing eye' which represents the ancient symbol of the brotherhood of the snake, in the form of wisdom. For a long time conspiracy theorists have alleged that this symbol has connections with the Illuminati Secret Society, if you look closely you can see that the pyramid has 13 steps to it, the words above it are 'ANNUIT CEOPTIS, each has 7 letters they mean in Latin 'HE FAVOURS THE THINGS HAVING BEEN BEGUN'; Below the seal are the words 'NOVUS ORDO SECLORUM which mean 'A NEW ORDER OF THE AGES', at the base of the pyramid there are the numbers MDCCLXXVI or 1776 the year that the US declaration was signed, this makes up a total of 13 characters including 1776.

On the right hand side of the bill is the Eagle and above it a crown of 13 stars and 13 vertical and 13 horizontal bars in the shield. The Eagle holds a ribbon in its beak with the words 'E PLURIBUS UNUM' 13 letters which means 'FROM MANY, ONE' in its claws it holds 13 arrows and an olive branch with 13 leaves and 13 berries, the olive branch symbolises a desire for peace whilst the arrows symbolise a readiness to fight."

Mike is becoming more and more amazed by these revelations,

"George, surely you can't believe this is true, it's logical that the number 13 has significance because of the 13 colonies that founded the United States."

"Mike, wait a minute, another coincidence is that the well known Astrologer, David Ovason published a book 'The Secret Architecture of our Nation's Capital: The Masons and the Building of Washington' apart from confirming much of what I have just outlined he suggested that the Masons may have been responsible for starting the Revolutionary War. As historians know the first battle of Lexington-

Concord started the war on April 19th 1775, but what's a coincidence is the date, as it falls on an important satanic festival, every year April 19th is the first day of the 13 day satanic high holy period known as the Bloody Sacrifice to the Beast."

Tim is stunned,

"George, I'm surprised that you believe what you're telling us, I didn't rate you as a conspiracy theorist."

"Tim, you miss the point, my long military career in Intelligence has been spent looking for conspiracies and coincidences and then connecting the dots to find the full picture. I started doing the same in this case, because I, along with others could not accept that our great government could make so many grave errors of judgement that were so obvious to intelligent people. The coincidences started to build up pointing to the possible existence of an organisation manipulating our government's decisions, possibly to suit their alternative agenda. From what we see around us this is not in the best interests of America or its population, but only to suit their plans and designs for the future whatever they may be."

Mike is astounded,

"George, do you really think that it's possible that the Masons are controlling our government?"

"It's one possibility but they're not the only secretive organisation, there are others such as the order of the Skull and Bones or the Illuminati."

Diane now very curious asks,

"Who are they?"

George smiles at her,

"Wait a moment we'll come back to them later. In the meantime when we consider your recent experiences with the information you've managed to obtain, I want you to realise that what you've discovered is extremely dangerous material, more so, because you've wounded the heart of an organisation which is part of something more sinister that controls the government of the United States, they will be present at all levels looking for you."

James asks,

"Are you suggesting that the House Judiciary Committee could be part of this too?"

"Well done James, that's exactly what I was getting to, who could be trusted to deliver your message?"

Diane is despondent and asks,

"George, that's why we came to you"

"I know that, I've been thinking about how we can create some insurance that would protect us, my original thought is that we prepare copies of everything we have along with a report of our suspicions then place them in packages addressed to all the International Press and Television Stations, we could then make it known to the Judiciary Committee that we have a protection plan in place that will be released worldwide if anything happens to us."

James interrupts,

"That's primitive and difficult to manage. I suggest we do it electronically, package everything, attach it to an email that we can send round the world in an instant, this email I can place on several selected and secure computers around the world on a 'fail safe' basis, I write a simple program that would require a code to be entered say every twenty four hours, if we failed to do this at the appointed time then the system would automatically transmit the emails to everyone at once."

Mike's impressed,

"James, that's a brilliant idea."

George agrees,

"One problem though, we need to consider the minute we hand this over we would immediately incriminate Tony, who at present doesn't know we have this evidence. I realise he authorised your elimination but he's certainly doing this on behalf of his masters, who we have yet to identify. In the meantime, Tim may need him to bring all the heads of state together for Aacaarya's conference, he's well placed to accomplish this and timing is of the essence."

Tim says,

"You mean we use him in the meantime?"

"He could be useful, more so, if we could read his encrypted private emails we would be pre-warned of any further attempts to stop you. I will also increase the surveillance on him, plus we could feed him false information."

"George, once we present our case to the Judiciary Committee won't they inform Tony anyway?"

"Yes but they'll also tell him we have insurance in place, which he would certainly relay to his masters, so it could work all round. All we have to do is to keep Tony's identity hidden until we're ready to release it."

Diane asks,

"What's the next step then?"

George thinks for a moment,

"If you're in agreement, my suggested strategy would be for me to arrange an unofficial meeting with my friend Alexander Austin, the Chairman of the House Judiciary Committee, on neutral territory. We would brief him on what we've discovered, give him a copy of the CD with all the information along with the condition that as a senior and very high level operative at one of the defence agencies at the Pentagon is involved we cannot name him at this time. This will give him an opportunity to assess the situation then decide what should be done. In parallel with this we arrange a meeting with Tony, again at a neutral venue where we'll update him on the situation with Aacaarya, as if nothing has changed and he's still in our confidence. Tim will ask him to set up the International conference at a suitable venue, probably the White House or the United Nations building for Aacaarya to make his announcement to the representatives of the heads of state. I think Tony would do this because he would have an opportunity to have direct contact with Aacaarya. As soon as the conference is over, we release the identity and evidence incriminating Tony."

"George, how do you know Alexander Austin is not part of one of these organisations and trustworthy?" George thinks a moment then answers,

"We go back a long way, then so did Tony, I trust Alexander but even if he's involved, he'll know that we have insurance if he steps out of line." George looks at his watch,

"It's getting late I'll have to be going shortly, if you're OK with this plan I'll get on with it. Mike, call my private number from a public phone, say tomorrow at ten, I'll let you know where and when we can meet Tony, any questions?" Diane always has a question,

"Yes one, you gave us an example of another secret society the Skull and Bones who are they?" James smiles,

"George, I was just going to ask the same thing."

"I'll keep it short as I have to be leaving in 15 minutes. The Skull and Bones is a secret society founded in 1832 it is one of the oldest secret student societies in the United States based at Yale University and still maintains its Masonic inspired rituals. Its members are selected very carefully from the cream of elite students that are destined for greater things and in some cases from generations of wealthy families such as our President who is a bonesman, as was his father the ex President and his grandfather, who allegedly was responsible for robbing the tomb of the Indian chief Geronimo and removing Geronimo's skull as part of his initiation into the society. Many students went on to the senate all bonesmen. They select only 15 new recruits per year which means that at any one time there are potentially 800 living members. There have been many notable and influential members throughout history including captains of industry, spies and senior figures in the intelligence community. In 1945 the Secretary of War, Robert Patterson was responsible for setting up the Lovett Committee headed by Robert Lovett a bonesman with the objective of creating a new US intelligence system which ultimately became the CIA. The CIA has employed many bonesman in senior positions since it was founded, you may remember that George Bush senior was the Director of the CIA through 1976 and 1977. Interestingly the Skull and Bones Society were instrumental in the founding of the Carnegie Institution, the American Psychological Association and the Economic Association amongst other things. Over time Bonesman have infiltrated many positions of power including the Chief Justices of the Supreme Court. As we have discovered during our discussion there are organisations in existence that certainly have the power, capability and position to manipulate government decisions."

Mike reminds George of the time,

"George it's time you were leaving"

George checks his watch,

"Thanks Mike."

George says goodbye,

"I apologise for talking so much, but we've covered a lot of important ground today, as a result, tomorrow we can begin to implement our strategy."

Diane shakes his hand and asks,

"Can we continue the secret society discussion when we next meet I am intrigued to know more."

"Diane, certainly there's masses of information on the internet in the meantime, providing you can keep it in perspective."

As George is about to leaves Mike tells him,

"We'll be moving shortly from the hotel to a safe apartment we'll speak tomorrow."

The door closes behind George as Mike returns to the others,

"What a day, I really need a drink what about you?"

Diane gets beers from the fridge, sits down and smiles at Mike,

"I'm a little overloaded with the information George has given us, did you know about these societies?"

Mike leans over and kisses her on the cheek,

"I've heard rumours about them but that's all they seemed, I had no reason to pay too much attention to them, I was too busy fighting other battles."

Tim is deep in thought as James asks him a question,

"About the Maya Calendar, I know a little about the Maya civilisation they were very advanced astronomers who measured the time in days and years according to constellations and the path of the sun. They were able to project ahead great cycles of time and events based on their Long Count, but what's the significance of the 21st December 2012?"

Tim explains,

"The Mayan Scholars have been trying for many years to correlate the Maya calendar with our Gregorian calendar, in 1905 one of them, a man named Goodman, established what he thought was a correct correlation which is only 3 days different from the latest correlations today, accordingly this established the start of the Maya Great Cycle as being 11th August 3114BC and the end date of this Great Cycle as being 21st December 2012.

The Maya believed that each Great Cycle commences with a cataclysmic event such as a Polar shift of the Earth's North and South Poles. This is interesting from a purely scientific point of view, NASA physicists have been studying and monitoring the cycle of the Sun, in particular when sunspots are formed as they have a major impact on space and the earth. Solar activity takes place generally in 11 year cycles ranging from quiet to stormy. On July 31st 2006 a tiny sunspot popped up from the suns interior and vanished a few hours later."

Diane is fascinated,

"What actually is a sunspot?"

"A sunspot is the size of a planet and is a giant magnet created from the sun's inner magnetic dynamo and like all magnets have a north and south magnetic pole. What was different and concerned NASA about the one in July 2006 is that its poles were reversed south to north. The significance of this is that the first sunspot of a new sun cycle is always reversed which indicates that we are at the beginning of a new sun cycle of activity which will build up over 11 years. It's predicted by scientists that the next cycle may have commenced in 2006 and could create the highest level of solar activity in 50 years. If this next solar activity is violent it could manifest itself over the next few years bringing us to around 2012 when the Maya Calendar predicted the next cycle would begin following a cataclysm."

James remarks,

"If we don't destroy the world then the sun might."

"Possibly not completely destroy, but if for example it caused a Polar Shift, this would disturb the balance of the earth's magnetic field, potentially moving the continents again, causing floods, extremes of weather and earthquakes, this was why Aacaarya's people were so concerned about our experiments in the ionosphere weakening the layers that protect the earth from solar flares. The changing electromagnetic fields would affect our brains natural resonance causing problems for all life on the planet but man would undoubtedly survive to start again wherever somewhere existed that was still habitable. The main point is that none of these scientific calculations and prophesies have been proven, they are all hypotheses that could be wrong, history is full of 'the end of the world' prophesies that have not happened, so in the meantime I suggest we just keep going and moving forward. In any case if we become involved with Aacaarya and the Elders, they will certainly want to prevent the Mayan prophesies from coming to fruition for the sake of their population"

James gets back to work on his computer,

"Tim I'm really glad I asked that question, I'm going back to work."

"James, what're you doing?"

"I'm writing our 'fail safe' programme so I'll have my head down for a bit, no disturbances please."

Mike has been on the telephone almost continually since George left as he closes his mobile Diane looks at him,

"You said we were moving to an apartment, when and why?"

"I don't trust anyone too much at the moment, however I think we can trust George, but to be on the safe side I've spoken to Julian and he's arranging a safe apartment for us in Washington, all we'll have to do is make sure that we're not followed back to it after we've seen Tony and Alexander, he's calling me back shortly. We move out after the meetings tomorrow, that way no one should know where we are."

Mike's mobile rings, he picks up a pen making quick notes,

"Julian that's great. Many thanks and take care."

Mike turns to the others,

"The keys to our new home are being delivered tomorrow morning to reception."

Tim asks,

"Where is it?"

"Not far from here it's a short walking distance from the Logan Circle, I'm told we'll like it, it's on the tenth floor of The Jefferson on M Street Northwest."

Mike, Diane and Tim retire leaving James working on his computer.

The next morning at 09.45 Mike leaves the hotel, finds a street payphone then calls George who answers immediately, the call is kept short under 30 seconds to avoid any tracking attempt if George is being monitored.

Mike confirms,

"13:00 same location, I'll prepare a meeting room, number in reception, see you later."

Mike returns to the hotel, instinctively checking around him for anyone suspicious.

In the room Tim and Diane are waiting, James is quietly working. Mike taps on the door as Tim carefully opens it, his hand on the butt of his Smith & Wesson. As he closes the door, Diane hands Mike a mug of coffee and asks,

"How did it go?"

James looks up from his computer as Mike replies,

"We have an hour with George and Alexander downstairs at 13:00, I've booked a private meeting room and we've time to move our things over to the apartment first. Our meeting with Tony this afternoon is at 16:00. James, I've discussed this with George and we both agree that it would be better if you remained in the apartment during these meetings, as the fewer people that know who you are, the safer you'll be."

"I'm happy with that I've got a lot to do anyway."

"George has offered to source everything you need for your EMP project all you have to do is let him have a list, you could then build it in the apartment."

James grins,

"Accepted, that would make me very happy, the list will be ready for your 13:00 meeting."

"Mike will George do the same for me?"

"Diane what do you need?"

Diane smiles sweetly,

"Darling, I've lived in the same jeans and old clothes since I met you. I need to go shopping now that we are back in civilisation."

Mike laughs,

"You're right, it's time we all went shopping, let's get packed up and over to the apartment, it's in the centre of the shopping district."

Tim asks,

"How are we getting there?"

"Julian's given me a number of one of his agents in DC he'll be outside with a car at 11:00 so get moving."

At 11:30 the car drops them off with their bags at Logan Circle. After the car departs they walk for a few minutes Diane humps her bag onto her other shoulder and groans,

"Mike, why didn't he drop us off outside the apartment?"

"The less people that know where we're going the better and anyway we're there."

Facing them on the next corner is a magnificent ten story building 'The Jefferson'. They cross the road then enter the sophisticated main entrance where the concierge stops them to confirm Mike's identity.

"Welcome to the Jefferson, you're on the 10th Floor, apartment 1001 the lifts are over there, do you need a hand?"

Mike thanks him,

"No, we'll be OK thanks."

Mike slips him a $100 bill the concierge is pleasantly surprised,

"Thank you sir, anything you need, just call me, my name's Patrick, I'm always around."

They walk through the impressive lobby with its high vaulted ceiling then take the lift to the top floor. Mike finds the apartment door, opening it they step into the height of luxury. Diane is surprised,

"Mike this is beautiful."

James excitedly cuts in,

"Look we've got a pool."

The apartment overlooks the rooftop pool which is near the community bar and terrace. James has picked up a glossy brochure,

"It's got a fitness centre, conference room and most important of all high speed internet."

He immediately searches the lounge for the internet points while the others sort out which bedrooms they're having, they return to the lounge to find James with his laptop open and connected.

Mike tells him,

"James that's your bedroom, there's the kitchen all we have to do now is the shopping." Diane cuts in,

"I've found some boxes of goodies for the fridge with a note from Julian saying 'enjoy' bless him."

James looks up from his improvised work station. He's commandeered one of the lounge tables and placed it with his computer table by the French windows that open onto their large terrace.

"Don't worry about me I'm going to like it here, a lot."

Mike checks his watch,

"We need to leave now for our meeting."

He gives them each a key card to the apartment and main doors,

"James we'll see you in a couple of hours."

James with his head in his laptop says,

"Fine, don't worry about me I've got masses to do, any coffee around?"

Diane says,

"Yeah in the boxes see you later."

As Mike leaves James shouts,

"Don't forget to give George my shopping list."

"I'll remember."

Mike, Diane and Tim take a cab back to the Holiday Inn Hotel. Twenty minutes later they're in the small meeting room on the ground floor getting coffee. At precisely 13:00 the door opens George comes in with a slightly overweight, grey haired man in his early 60's. He's wearing gold rimmed glasses behind which are bright intelligent eyes. George introduces him,

"Alexander Austin"

Alexander shakes hands with them,

"Just call me Alex, everyone else does, I'm sorry I only have an hour today, there's a Judiciary Committee meeting at three o'clock."

They take seats around the table as Alex takes a thick folder with a yellow legal note pad out of his briefcase, he opens the folder.

"George has told me everything about your remarkable adventure and the attempts on your lives. I've studied the information you kindly provided. Needless to say the contents of which came as a great shock as I'm familiar with the organisation, that from the evidence you've provided, is responsible for the attack on a government aircraft. I'm also very concerned that government funds are being misappropriated and directed into underground clandestine research facilities without congress's approval or knowledge. These accusations are extremely serious, as they not only involve the operational management of the company but implicate powerful individuals at the highest levels of our administration. Before I present these matters to the Judiciary Committee I intend carrying out a covert investigation into the corporate affairs of this company, its board of directors, their connections within government and the research activities that you have highlighted. Thanks to the information you have provided, it should take me about 10 days to complete this first task."

Diane asks Alex,

"Will we be called personally to give evidence?"
Alex smiles,

"That may not be necessary, once we're satisfied the evidence is credible we commence questioning the accused parties, depending on the outcome of their responses we will bring appropriate charges against them."

Tim asks,

"Would that include the President?"

Alex looks very serious, there's a slight hesitation before he speaks,

"In this case, yes, if the evidence implicates him personally. You realise you've taken great personal risk in bringing this to my attention?"

Mike smiles,

"It seems we've been at risk since leaving the Pyramid in Iraq. Yes Alex, we're aware of the risk and have taken precautions to protect ourselves."

"Mike, I'm also aware of George's opinion that our government appears to be potentially manipulated by others, over time I have been inclined to agree with him, now having read your documents I'm convinced that George's suspicions will be proven correct, which is why we must search out and destroy this organisation. You have my sincerest thanks for having the courage to confront this enemy on behalf of our country."

Tim asks,

"Have you have read the demands from the Elders with their instructions to present these to the world's heads of state?"

Alex looks intently at them,

"For the second time in the history of our civilisation, we have been given a set of commandments to live by, the first were ten and now thirteen. The Ten Commandments were only ideals as they were unable to be enforced and depended on the population's strength of belief or fear in their god to implement them. Sadly over time they were ignored and forgotten. If the Elders are prepared to assist us in enforcing these new commandments then there is hope for the future, making the world we live in a better and safer place for all. As lawyers we fight everyday to keep the dream of justice and equality alive, but we have to live with the delusion that the laws we create and enforce cannot keep pace with the spread of corruption around us.

You have my wholehearted support in what you're doing. I personally look forward to the day that these commandments will be presented, which I hope will be soon."

George glances at his watch,

"Alex we have to be going, any other questions, we'll stay in daily contact."

Mike hands George a CD,

"No questions, this is from James it's the shopping list he needs for his project."

"Tell him 24 hours they should be ready, I'll call you."

George and Alex get up to leave, George says,

"See you later, I'll be at security, same Pentagon entrance we used before, see you there at 16:00."

They wait until George and Alex have gone, then leave the hotel picking up a cab outside. They arrive near Logan Circle then walk round to their apartment block. As they get to the entrance Patrick opens the door for them,

"You folks find everything you wanted?"

"Patrick, where's the nearest Food Mall?"

Patrick points Diane to the left,

"100 yards you can't miss it."

Once in the apartment James is keen to know what happened,

"How did it go?"

Mike explains what was discussed with Alex, James listens in silence,

"I never thought I'd be involved in anything this big. It's like something you see on television or film, not in real life."

"James, this is the reality of the world we live in. It rarely touches the majority of the population. The trouble is, when a scandal of this magnitude gains momentum we have to see it through, there is no half measure."

James smiles,

"Don't worry I'm with you to the end whatever that'll be."

Tim asks James,

"Did you manage to get done what you wanted?"

James crosses his fingers,

"Yes, it's nearly there, be finished tomorrow. I've brought together all the information we have gathered into an electronic press pack, I want to run some programme checks before I'm completely satisfied."

Mike tells him that George will have all the items he requested within 24 hours and he'll call when they are ready, James is very impressed,

"That's brilliant, but how come, there's a load of specialist equipment on my list I wonder how he could lay his hands on it so fast."

"I think he's trying to impress you, so you'll help him."

"Mike, what's important is that I can start work on our ultimate weapon as soon as I've finished our insurance programme tomorrow."

A short distance from their apartment, in the boardroom at Global Assets Management on Pennsylvania Avenue the Chief Executive has summoned his senior directors again, including the Director of Systems and his senior programmers with the Director of Security for an update from their previous meeting. The executives are sitting round the large table. All are dressed in business suits with the exception of one person, a bearded young man in jeans and sweater. The Chief Executive storms in standing at the head of the table looking down on his management.

"I've read your reports, they tell me nothing. All I know is that we've been without our systems for nearly four days. Now give me some good news."

The Director of Systems stands up,

"Sit down."

Steams the Chief Executive,

"Get on with it."

The director meekly does as he is told,

"Sir, I explained in the reports we've managed to get the internal system repaired and operational using the hardware around the building, the programming department needed to be functional we..."

He's cut off by the Chief Executive,

"Our business is external not internal, I want to know how this happened, who was responsible and when you can fix it."

The young man in Jeans asks the Director of Systems,

"Can I answer that?"

The Chief Executive interrupts,

"If you've got something constructive to say, say it to me."

The young man is a little flustered by this abruptness,

"Sir, my team of programmers is the best that money could buy they've been working every hour for four days, with limited equipment trying to discover how this attack occurred. So far we believe that the programme that caused this entered our system through one of our international offices possibly hidden in an email. The difficulty we are facing is that everything has been destroyed throughout our network, hardware, software, records and audit trails so we have to hypothesise as to what happened. We believe that they introduced a particularly complex virus that was really a decoy, our defence system was kept busy dealing with this, whilst the enemies main programme managed to tag onto our defence system convincing it that we were being infiltrated by our own system, this triggered our EMP Defence system to attack the enemy that it perceived was attacking it, which in fact was our own network. I am around 90% certain that this is what happened. The person that created this programme and infiltrated our system is nothing short of a genius as our network was designed to be impenetrable.

The problem you have to face Sir, is, that, nothing was left as evidence of the intrusion for us to examine, other than to work from what was recorded at the time of the attack, we have a print out of the alarm, a virus warning that stated that the system was dealing with it, which is quite normal and happens frequently these days, we had a print confirmation that our EMP system had activated and prevented an attempted intrusion into our system a few days before and dealt with it." The Chief Executive sits down,

"I see, thank you, do you have any idea where that attempted intrusion came from?"

"No Sir, it was cleverly routed around the world it could have come from anywhere."

The Chief Executive asks,

"Do you have a recommendation as to what we should do?"

The young man responds,

"Yes sir, I believe we should do as The System Director suggested, re equip all our offices to get our communications systems up and running as quickly as possible, we obviously have backups of all our software and the defence programme which is being modifying to prevent it ever attacking our system again."

"What's the time scale?"

The young man responds with a question,

"How quickly can we have the budget approval?"

The Chief Executive thinks for a moment.

"You'll have it today, when can you tell me how long it will take?"

The young man smiles,

"You'll have it today Sir, we've already been working on it, there was really no other option."

The Chief Executive softens a little and asks the young man,

"What's your name?"

The young man closes his pad,

"Albert, Albert Einstein Sir, it's my parents fault they were Einstein's but no connection to the great man. My friends call me Al."

The Chief Executive smiles for the first time,

"Then Al, don't let me down."

He gets up leaving the office without a further word.

Mike, Diane and Tim are dropped off by taxi at the entrance to the Pentagon. They pass through the heavy sliding doors to find George waiting for them by the security booth. He leads them through the security check giving them their passes. They take the lift to the 5th Floor then follow George into Tony's suite number 5E500, Tony seems genuinely pleased to see them greeting them warmly,

"Thanks for coming over, please take a seat, you can update me on your eventful trip."

Mike explains the events from their arrival in Alaska, the ambush attempt and their experience at HAARP with the assassination of the scientist, but taking care not to mention James. He explains that Tim has a very specific message with further instructions from Aacaarya. Tony listens intently then responds,

"I'm surprised that these people were able to find you, you must be more careful, do you know who they were?"

"No, they were hired guns, didn't know who they were working for."

"You said that the scientist was assassinated, what makes you certain of that?"

"I called the local police after the autopsy, he'd been injected with a massive dose of insulin and his car pushed into a river."

Tony is surprised,

"I see. I'll look into that, it's strange because they were decommissioning the site."

Mike is careful with his response,

"Yes, we saw the trucks moving equipment out."

"Did you speak to the scientist?"

"Not really, we arrived as he was supervising the loading. He asked us to come back a few hours later, when we returned we were told by his assistant that he'd just been killed in an accident on the highway. As it was on our way back we visited the scene and were able to speak with the highway police who also thought the accident seemed strange, as there were no other vehicles involved."

"Tim, your friends have been busy, they've caused an international crisis with Russia, China, Norway and Japan, all of whom blame us for removing their ionospheric heaters, Russia has resumed its cold war nuclear bomber flights along our borders over the North Pole they're discussing appropriate retaliation against the USA. Already one of our major financial institutions in Washington has been the victim of a terrorist attack on their computer systems, their whole international network was destroyed. We have been instructed to investigate and find out who was behind it. I suppose your friends were responsible for that too. On top of that they managed to remove the Stealth Aircraft from under our noses to where, we have no idea, have you spoken to them?"

"Tony I don't believe that they had any reason to attack a computer system, they are well above that. They did tell me about the aircraft, they removed the Stealth as they felt we had long enough to discover its origins, they didn't want it falling back into the wrong hands."

"They had no right to do that without telling me first."

"Tony, I disagree, I think they did, unless it was your aircraft."

Tony takes a deep breath for self control,

"What else have they said?"

Tim tells Tony about his conversation, the offer of free energy in return for certain conditions and hands Tony a copy of their demands.

Tony reads in silence his face showing no emotion. After he's read the document he places it in front of him on the table as Tim continues,

"If we did as they have requested it could defuse your diplomatic problem. The other countries would know that this is not a stunt of the USA as they would be able to speak to Aacaarya directly."

Tony glares at them,

"You don't believe the world will buy into this?"

"Tony, when I first heard their demands that was my first reaction. However after I had time to think it through they are 100% correct in their assessment of the problems facing our civilisation these problems will cause our destruction if not addressed. We're also using energy faster than it can be produced the oil fields are running dry. Their offer of free clean electrical energy would help the Earth's environment and our global economies recover. Please understand that these conditions are ultimatums, not options. They have the capability to enforce their acceptance if necessary to protect their planet."

Tony arrogantly responds,

"We could attack them first."

Tim interrupts,

"Tony with respect, that's not an option. Your weapons are primitive compared to their technology and capability. I'm not aware that we have the ability to move between time dimensions. Don't forget if you attacked them you'd be attacking yourself, we share the same planet. My recommendation is that you speak with the President present him with this document, if he's wise he should immediately convene a meeting with the heads of state. I can advise Aacaarya where it will be and when. The heads of state will be more than curious enough to attend. I'm sure that you too would be interested in meeting Aacaarya personally."

Tony is not happy,

"I'll be seeing the President tomorrow morning to discuss this matter with him, how can I get in touch with you?"

George answers,

"Through me, I have their number."

Tony asks,

"Mike, one more thing who else knows about what you've told me?"

"Only us, but we've taken security precautions to protect ourselves, if anything happens to us, the whole story is automatically released to the worlds press."

"What makes you feel that was necessary?"

Diane speaks for the first time,

"The assassination attempts, on the Gulfstream and in Alaska for starters."

"I see. Leave this with me I'll go over it in detail this evening and will let you know the President's decision tomorrow. As you rightly pointed out it would certainly defuse the international situation we currently face."

They shake hands leaving the office in silence. George takes them down to the ground floor and back out through security,

"I've organised a taxi, it's outside he'll take you to wherever you wish. I'll call you tomorrow. You did well. Good night."

Mike gets the taxi to drop them off near Logan Square, they wait until it has gone, since leaving the Pentagon Mike has been checking the taxi was not being followed. They walk round the block to the entrance of their apartment, Patrick opens the door with a friendly greeting Mike whispers something in his ear,

"If anyone enquires after us, you've never seen us OK?"

"Mike don't worry I know the drill well, we're on the same side, I'm on Julian's payroll." Mike slaps him on the back,

"Nice to know we're amongst friends. Good night."

As they get into the lift Diane asks,

"What was all that about?"

Mike tells her what Patrick has said, Diane is relieved,

"Your friend Julian really is remarkable." Mike grins,

"Yeah, so are you."

They open the door to the apartment to be greeted with the strong smell of spices and garlic, Diane asks,

"James what's that lovely smell?"

He smiles,

"I hope you all like Chilli Con Carne, it's my only speciality. I thought you would be shattered, it's been another long day, now we can all relax with a bottle of wine."

James has already set the dining table which is decorated with candles,

"Please take your seats, the wine is aired, help yourselves."

He disappears into the kitchen returning with a large deep casserole, he places it in the centre of the table followed by a basket of hot garlic bread with a large bowl of Basmati rice.

James sits down pouring himself a large glass of Chateau Neuf De Pap, Diane takes the lid off the large steaming casserole, serving Mike, Tim, James and then herself,

"James this looks and smells delicious."

James grins,

"It's the only dish I know how to cook. Now tell me about Tony and the Pentagon."

Between mouthfuls Mike brings James up to date on what was and wasn't said and Tony's reaction. James laughs,

"So now I'm a terrorist, he's a fine one to call me a terrorist, shame you couldn't tell him it was self defence, so tomorrow we'll know the President's reaction."

"James, how have you got on with your programming?"

James finishes his glass of wine,

"This is a celebration feast because I've finished, it's now fully functional, we have 24 hours to enter our code so that it remains dormant, if we don't, all hell will break loose, I'll run through it with each of you tomorrow morning so that any one of us will be able to reset it, all we need is to have access to an internet point anywhere in the world. What's more, I've made a good start on my next project, the ultimate internet weapon."

They congratulate him on his progress. The wine begins to take effect as they start to relax after their very long day.

Diane is most impressed with dinner,

"James that was the best Chilli I've had anywhere in the world."

Mike agrees,

"Yep that was really great, thank you."

They decide to turn in as the wine has made them realise how tired they are. The stress of the past week is catching up with them.

The next day at midday after a slow start, Mike's mobile rings its George,

"I've just seen Tony, he's had his meeting with the President and his advisors, it was a difficult discussion because the President wanted to meet Aacaarya before making any decision, Tony told him that could be arranged prior to the meeting. As a result they've already commenced contacting the embassies to invite the appropriate parties to the emergency session with Aacaarya they expect to have the first confirmations by the end of the day. He's recommended that it should be held at the United Nations General Assembly Building in New York. They are suggesting this should take place in three days to allow time for the security and travel arrangements."
Mike is surprised,

"I didn't think the administration could move that fast."

"They can when they think it's in their best interests, tell James that everything he's asked for is ready, I'll have it delivered to the Holiday Inn reception for your collection after 15:00. One other thing, Alexander called me he's been doing some research into the topographic images of Camp Hero, he admits it definitely shows a large underground facility, but there's no evidence to prove that it's still in use, it could be abandoned like the surface facility, he needs more information, ideally, confirmation that it's still operational before he can use the images."

"George, we'll see what we can find out about Camp Hero, that's brilliant news about James's gear, many thanks. He's already made a start on the software."
George signs off,

"I'll call you tomorrow with an update, stay alert when you visit the Hotel, just in case." Mike calls Julian's taxi explaining that they'll be needing transport at 14:30.

As soon as he puts his mobile down, there are three expectant faces waiting to know the outcome of his conversation. Mike smiles at them,

"Is nothing private in this place?"

Mike explains what George has said, James is delighted,

"That's fantastic news all round, particularly for me, I can't wait to see if he's got everything. Can you guys imagine the power we could wield when we have an operational EMP capability?"

Tim is cautious about how quickly the President has reacted,

"Why so fast?"

"Tim in my opinion they want to use this to get themselves off the hook to prove they'd nothing to do with the disappearance of the other Ionospheric heating sites."

"Mike, I'll let Aacaarya know, he's been told that two of the Elders will also be coming with him."

Chapter - 23

Secret research facility near New York

Diane is curious to know more about what was said about Camp Hero,

"Alexander needs proof that Hero is actually a functioning facility. I can see his point, all the reports I've read of strange things happening that were investigated by various journalists have always confirmed the fact that the facility above ground is abandoned. Another valid point is that such a large underground facility would be manned by many hundreds of staff who would be clearly visible when they arrived for work. So what do we do?"

Mike has been thinking about this since George mentioned it,

"The other facility at Long Island, the Brookhaven National Laboratory is nearby it has something close to 3000 staff and hosts 4000 guest researchers each year, perhaps there's a connection between the two places. I'd like to visit Brookhaven to take a look round."

Diane and Tim respond in unison,

"You mean WE'D like to visit."

"I thought it might be less risky on my own."

"And who would look after you, Mike. Don't forget Alaska."

Mike reluctantly agreed,

"As if you'd let me forget. OK we go together, but under my rules."

James is immersed in work,

"Exclude me from your little jaunt I've got work to complete."

Diane prompts,

"Mike, that's agreed then, speak to George he can arrange our invitations, we could leave for New

York tomorrow. I could do my shopping there too, if we have time."

Mike looks at her,

"Tim, do you remember who was supposed to be in charge, when we started this caper I was led to believe it was me."

Diane smiles sweetly,

"Of course you are my dear. Now call George."

Mike calls George, who will organise their visit to Brookhaven,

"That's no problem, they have a continuous stream of visitors, when?"

"Tomorrow, if that's possible."

George wishes them well then sets up the visit. He calls them back five minutes later,

"It's all's arranged, reception are expecting three VIP visitors for a tour at 11.30 tomorrow, have a safe trip, call me when you get back."

Later that afternoon Mike and Tim leave James and Diane in the apartment, Diane is researching the Brookhaven National Laboratory whilst James is focused on his software development. Mike and Tim arrive at the Holiday Inn reception with Julian's taxi driver, after speaking to the porter he leads them to the luggage storage area,

"I hope you've brought a van."

Mike is surprised and watches as the porter opens the door. In the centre of the room are four 18" cube boxes stacked one on the other, Mike reaches up for the top one as the porter warns him,

"Be careful a couple are very heavy."

They load all four onto the luggage trolley taking them out to the taxi, they put three in the boot and the last on the rear seat.

"Mike, what on earth has James asked for?"

"I thought it was a few computer bits and pieces, we'll find out later."

When they get back to the accommodation Patrick helps them take the boxes up to the apartment, once inside James can't wait to open them, he starts on the heaviest, opening it carefully he takes out a bubble wrapped instrument with a display screen,

Diane smiles,

"What's that, more toys?"

James replies with a large grin on his face,

"An oscilloscope, not just an oscilloscope but one of the best you can get."

He pulls out coils of wire and other heavy smaller boxes littering the lounge as he unpacks the assorted items which include specialist electrician's tools with all types of screwdrivers, pliers, wire cutters, various connectors, a high tech soldering iron and high voltage voltmeters. Mike offers to help unpack, James dismisses his assistance,

"No thanks I can manage, I'll clear up once I've organised my workshop. There is one thing you and Tim could do, bring the table out of the kitchen and set it up beside my desk over there near the window."

They clear a space and bring the table through. Mike asks Diane,

"It looks as if we can't do anything to help him so how about you and I doing a little shopping."

"Great idea I need a few things for New York."

Tim grins,

"You two go out and have a good time, I'll stay and babysit. I want to follow up on Diane's Brookhaven research."

James is too engrossed in his boxes to respond.

A few hours later Mike and Diane return laden with shopping bags. They find that James has turned the lounge into a very professional laboratory with various instruments, cables and circuit boards. He's engrossed in soldering which is filling the room with fumes,

"James, open the damn French window it's lethal in here."

James looks up,

"Sorry, guess I'm used to the smell of burning plastic."

He opens the door to the balcony.

"Where's Tim?"

James points to his bedroom door,

"He escaped to his room."

Tim, hearing their voices, opens his door,

"Hi you two, sorry about James, I've discovered that he's a bit of a pyromaniac. Mike this arrived for you, Patrick brought it up from Julian's driver."

Mike takes the envelope and opens it,

"Great, it's our travel arrangements for tomorrow's flight from Reagan National to JFK New York. We need to be at the airport for a 0900 departure."

Tim asks,

"Scheduled?"

"No, it's the same private aircraft and crew that flew us down from Alaska. We can carry our weapons on board. I suggest we leave at 0800 Julian's driver will be picking us up."

Mike asks James if he'll be OK tomorrow, James nods,

"Yeah no problem I've got lots to do, it'll be great not having people around complaining about the smell."

The next morning Mike, Tim and Diane are ready to leave, as Diane asks,

"How long's the flight to New York?"

"An hour and a half airtime plus an hour drive to Brookhaven. Brookhaven is roughly 60 miles east of New York. Julian's arranged a car and driver for us, if all goes well we should be back tonight."

Mike puts a small digital camera into his pocket.

As they leave the apartment block Mike asks Patrick to keep an eye on James,

"He's working upstairs and shouldn't be disturbed."

Half an hour later they're at the airport passing into the now familiar VIP lounge where their pilot is waiting, they exchange greetings. The pilot has cleared them direct to the aircraft which is waiting on the apron. They board and within five minutes are airborne, climbing away from Washington.

"Mike, Brookhaven Laboratory is enormous its spread over at least 5000 acres, how can we possibly look round it in a day?"

"The standard tour will certainly cover their main research facilities such as their Relativistic Heavy Ion Collider and the Synchrotron Light Source. Between visits I hope to explore another theory I have." Tim asks,

"And that is."

Mike continues,

"Brookhaven was built in 1947 on the site of what was then known as Camp Upton, which was a former US Army Base. A short distance away is the disused radar station and ex-military base Camp Hero, I want to find out if there's a connection between the two places."

Diane who has an insatiable curiosity asks,

"How are you going to do that?"

"I've no idea, that's why we're going today just to nose around."

They arrive at JFK airport and are met outside the VIP exit by Julian's driver. The drive East takes them 40 minutes they arrive at the imposing reception entrance to Brookhaven National Laboratory, the driver gives Mike his number,

"Call me about an hour before you need to leave, I'll pick you up here."

They enter the building checking in at the reception desk, a very efficient young lady welcomes them, Mike explains who they are as she checks the computer in front of her,

"Yes, found you, you're booked in for a tour with Dr Peterson at 11:30."

She hands them each a pass,

"Please take a seat over there, I'll tell him you're here."

She points to a comfortable lounge area,

"You're very lucky Dr Peterson has been here for over 10 years he's one of our leading physicists. After your tour our guests are welcome to use the restaurant for lunch, you'll find it down the corridor on the right, you can't miss it."

Mike thanks her and they sit down nearby, Diane comments,

"She was efficient."

A few minutes later Dr Peterson arrives, tall and good looking in a white research coat he introduces himself,

"Welcome to Brookhaven, I've been asked to give you an overview of our work here at Brookhaven it's always a great pleasure introducing newcomers to our facility. It's one of the best research centres of its kind in the world, please call me Graham."

He shakes hands with each of them with a firm handshake he is obviously passionate about his work. He seems particularly taken by Diane who revels in the extra attention despite Mike's discrete elbow in her side. Graham asks them to follow him as he strides along the corridor describing the various offices they pass,

"First I'll take you to our Relativistic Heavy Ion Collider, the RHIC."

Diane asks having researched the subject,

"Is this similar to the one in CERN Geneva?"

"No Diane, ours is smaller but we're partners with CERN in a new project that's under construction, the completion of a Large Hadron Collider or LHC. The project's name is Atlas and it's due to become operational in early 2009, it will be the largest and most powerful in the world."

They step outside the main building Graham leads them to a nine seat people carrier,

"It's a fair walk so to save time we drive."

Graham parks in the centre of a collection of offices and laboratories that are collectively the RHIC facility. He explains,

"Because of the limited time you have, we'll go directly into the RHIC tunnel where I can explain the principles of this facility."

They follow him down a long slope, through a pair of doors into a massive tunnel which is 12 feet underground, around the side of the tunnel are two large tubes similar to oil pipelines in appearance but polished metal which run round the perimeter of the circular tunnel disappearing into the distance,

Tim asks,

"How long is this tunnel?"

"It's a 2.4 mile circular tunnel, each of the pipes around the perimeter runs in an opposite direction it'll make more sense in a moment."

Graham takes them into a control room where there's an aerial view of the whole inter-connected facility,

"First let me tell you a little about why this facility exists. Every day, each of us uses modern technology, that's only possible because we have a basic understanding of the microscopic structure and properties of matter and their relationships with each other. The RHIC was designed to extend this frontier to provide access to the most fundamental building blocks of nature, quarks and gluons. By colliding the nuclei of gold atoms together at nearly the speed of light RHIC will, for a fleeting moment, heat the matter in the collision to more than a billion times the temperature of the sun. This enables our scientists to study the fundamental properties of the basic building blocks of matter learning how they may have behaved collectively some 15 to 20 billion years ago, a fraction of a second after the universe was created."

Graham leads them over to the wall chart,

"All of the buildings you see are connected, each one is an integral part of the RHIC which is the large circle at the top, I'll explain the various phases, it all starts here at the Tandem Van de Graf which uses static electricity to accelerate atoms, at the same time removing some of their electrons which are a cloud around the atom's nucleus, what remains is a positively charged atom called an Ion. The partial lack of electrons provides each Ion with a strong positive charge the Tandem provides billions of these Ions with a boost of energy which fires them on their way to the next phase from the Tandem, to the Booster Beam Line. This transports them through a vacuum, controlled by a magnetic field. During this part of their journey they're travelling at around 5% of the speed of light; which you may remember is 186,000 miles per second.

In some experiments where we need to collide beams of protons they would then pass through the LINAC or Linear Accelerator where energetic protons are exposed to 200 million electron volts, these protons then travel to the next phase, The Booster Synchrotron, this is the smallest of the three rings and is a compact circular accelerator that provides the Ions with even more energy by making them surf on the downhill slope of radio frequency electromagnetic waves. The Ions are propelled forward at an ever increasing velocity and are now getting closer to the speed of light. Then the Booster feeds the beam into the Alternating Gradient Synchrotron the AGS as we call it."

Graham points,

"Here, this is the next circle which, as you can see, is around an eighth of the size of the RHIC. When the Ions arrive in the AGS they are travelling at about 37% the speed of light which is the natural speed limit in the universe, interestingly Einstein created his special relativity theory to describe the strange behaviour of objects travelling through space at that speed, hence the

Relativistic element of the RHIC name. Once the Ion beam is travelling at its maximum velocity in the AGS, it's taken down another beam line to transfer it finally to the RHIC.

At the end of the beam line there's a Y junction where the direction can be changed using a magnetic switch, one stream of Ions goes clockwise round the ring and the other anticlockwise. The counter rotating beams of Ions are accelerated using intense radio waves to 99.7% the speed of light. Whilst they are circulating there are six interaction points where we can make the two beams collide creating a shower of subsonic sparks that can be observed. The temperature at the point of collision is over a trillion degrees which is hotter than the centre of the sun."

Diane asks,

"But how do you keep the Ions within the beam then bend them round the tunnel?"

"We use powerful electromagnetic fields to bend the beam around the circle. The two concentric rings have within them 1,740 superconducting magnets which are wrapped in 1600 miles of superconducting niobium titanium wire. This enables the magnets to carry electricity without resistance they are also cooled in liquid helium to a temperature of minus 451.6 degrees Fahrenheit, pretty cold eh."

Diane does a mock shiver,

"You mentioned that you use atoms of gold, how much, do you use?"

"In 20 years of running RHIC we've only used one gram of gold, don't forget we work at the atomic sub particle level."

Graham's pager buzzes he goes over to the phone,

"Excuse me a moment." he takes the call then returns, "Unfortunately we have an urgent technical problem needing my presence, sadly I'll have to cut short our discussion do you have any other questions?"

Mike nods,

"Yes, do you have other underground facilities on this site?"

"No, I suppose this what you could call underground, although we have a few storage basements but that's all, why?"

"Just curious, it's spread over such a large area I wondered if it was all on the surface. It must generate considerable electromagnetic fields which might be better below ground."

"That's why the RHIC is 12 feet below ground that's all it needs to be. If you don't mind I'll drive you round to the main reception building where you can have lunch in the restaurant."

Diane invites him to join them,

"Will you be able to join us for lunch later?"

"I would love to, but we've just had a breakdown in the LINAC which means staying until it's fixed, thanks anyway."

They return to the vehicle, Graham drops them off at one of the rear entrances to the reception building.

"Hope to see you again sometime any other questions call me, reception has my numbers."

Graham drives off in a hurry in the direction of the LINAC building.

They enter the main building slowly heading towards the restaurant when Mike stops them,

"Look at this, I wonder what's kept in here?"

Mike is standing near a pair of doors marked Restricted Access – No Entry, looking round he gently pushes against them, they're locked. Tim points to a card reader mounted on the other door. There's a reinforced glass pane in the centre of each door, they peer through the window and can see a very short corridor with no visible doors off it.

Mike's curiosity is aroused,

"Very strange, let's hang around over there for a bit we can discuss the RHIC."

They stand opposite the doors so that Mike can see down the corridor, after a few minutes a group of 10 men in white coats appear at the end of the corridor, Mike notices that the lead man puts a card in his left coat pocket, the group are heading towards the doors. Mike grabs Diane's arm,

"Stay beside me look as if you are concentrating on what I am saying, I want you to bump into the lead man then apologise."

Diane looks indignant,

"You want me to what?"

"Trust me, just do as I say. Here they come, get ready."

Tim stays to one side of the doors. The men reach the doors the first of the men opens one of the doors with his security card. As soon as the group are half way through Mike orders Diane,

"Move now."

He and Diane casually walk over to the group as if in deep conversation, they are about to pass the man, Diane turns slightly bumping innocently into him,

"Oh I'm so sorry I wasn't looking where I was going."

The man recovers his posture apologising too. Mike in the meantime had brushed against the man's side. The group passes them heading towards the restaurant, the first man turns smiling at Diane as he enters the restaurant. Diane turns to Mike,

"What was all that about?"

Mike slowly opens his left hand revealing a plastic card security key,

"I used to work for Fagin."

Tim congratulates him,

"Nice piece of handiwork Mike."

"Let's go to the restaurant I need a coffee, if we can find a quiet corner we can discuss our next move."

They enter the busy café area taking a table in the corner. Mike explains,

"There's something odd about this place, they employ thousands of people, with as you probably noticed on our little drive to the RHIC, lots of full car parks, but where are the workers? Looking around there're not that many people about, the offices are scattered about and seem quite small."
Diane asks,

"What have you got in mind?"

"When we arrived Graham took us down this corridor, I noticed another group coming out of the Restricted Area. I have a suspicion that the facility here acts as a cover for the people that work at the Camp Hero underground facility at Montauk Point."
Tim is intrigued,

"That's an interesting theory, if you're right it would account for why no one has ever seen people going to and from Camp Hero but that's sixty miles East of here, how could they get there, unless there's an underground link."
Mike smiles,

"Exactly the Restricted Area corridor seems to go nowhere. I reckon there's a lift in there which is why I needed the door security key. Those people came from somewhere and needed a security card to get in and out."
Diane asks,

"What do you suggest we do, call George?"

"No, we need to find some tangible proof I propose that I investigate what's behind the Restricted Area. It would be too obvious if all three of us went together. You could wait here and if anything goes wrong I can call you on the mobile."
Diane is not at all happy,

"If you're below ground you won't have a signal."
Mike puts his hand on her arm and speaks quietly,

"This is my work I've been doing it for many years, I promise I won't take any risks, if for any reason

I don't return, you'll be able to call George for back up."

Tim agrees,

"Diane, he's right, he'll be OK."

Then turning to Mike,

"If you're theory's correct and there is a link, it could take a few hours to prove."

"Yes I know that, that's why I suggest you stay here till six o'clock that gives me nearly four hours, the facility here functions 24 hours a day. The restaurant stays open 24 hours to service the staff so I'm sure you'd be able to have a leisurely lunch. Here's the driver's number, if you call him at five, it will take him at least an hour to arrive then when I get back we could leave immediately."

They finally convince Diane to agree to the plan then leave the restaurant. Diane and Tim watch from a distance as Mike reaches the Restricted Area doors, he tries the card in the electronic door lock, it opens he disappears into the corridor, they watch as he reaches the end, he turns and gives a 'thumbs up' sign, then reaches forward with the card and disappears. Tim and Diane return to their corner table at the restaurant.

Mike has entered a large lift which has two buttons one 'up' and the other 'down' as there's no floor above him he presses 'down' the door closes with a hiss, the lift descends rapidly, Mike feels a rising sensation in his stomach, he tries to work out how far the lift has travelled downward but there are no indicators, after what seems a long time the lift stops and the door opens. Carefully he looks round before stepping into what seems to be a deserted underground transit railway station with a low platform and a peculiar double track heading into a tunnel, each track has a 2 feet wall running along each side of it, instead of railway lines there are two narrow wheel support tracks. It reminds him of something similar he had seen in Japan then recalls to himself,

"These are Maglev Trains (Magnetic Levitation) they hover over the track, and are powered by Electromagnetic Propulsion." pleased he remembered, he walks over to his right where parked beside the platform are a row of streamlined futuristic vehicles similar to miniature versions of the TGV high speed trains, he walks over to the first carriage, it's sliding doors are open, there are ten seats with a VDU screen mounted in the centre of the front seats, there does not seem to be any controls, he whispers to himself,

"So that's why they always arrive in tens."

He takes out his camera filming the station, the strange track and carriages. He carefully gets into the first carriage, as he takes the centre seat in front of the screen there's a buzzing alarm the door immediately closes, the word MONTAUK glows on the display screen. He's finished filming from the carriage, wondering what to do next when the carriage silently shoots forward rapidly gathering speed as it enters the two track tunnel. He starts the timer on his wristwatch.

The lights in the tunnel roof flicker past, the intense lights from the carriage probe into the tunnel for some distance ahead, he notices that the display screen has changed, various numbers have appeared in front of him, one of which is showing a speed of 135 mph the other is ETA (Estimated Time of Arrival) and is showing 28 minutes and counting down. Mike smiles and mutters.

"Well at least I know where I'm going and how long it's going to take."

After 25 minutes the carriage starts to slow down, ahead there are bright lights in the distance.

The carriage leaves the dark tunnel entering another brightly lit station then slowly following the track round in semi circle until it faces the direction he arrived from, but on the other side of the track, the vehicle gently stops behind a row of 10 empty carriages in front of him. The door hisses open, he is about to get out, when a large group of people arrive getting into the first two carriages, he watches filming until they move off quickly disappearing into the tunnel leaving the station deserted again.

The station is an exact replica of the one he left at Brookhaven, after taking more film he cautiously steps out of the carriage heading towards the entrance where the men came from. He finds the familiar lift and hoping it will still work, uses his stolen card placing it in the door lock, the lift door slides open. He steps inside noticing there are five floor numbers against five buttons, he takes a photograph then presses the first button. The lift stops after a few minutes as a light appears beside the number five.

Back at Brookhaven Tim and Diane are in the restaurant as the group of men from the Restricted Area finish their lunch and prepare to leave. As they reach the door the man she bumped into earlier smiles at Diane again, the group head down the corridor.

Tim grins,

"I think he likes you."

Diane is thoughtful,

"He won't when he finds out he's lost his key, what then?"

"It's nothing to do with us, we don't have it, Mike said he had to cut short his trip, we'll see, cross your bridges when you get to them."

"I'd rather cross my fingers and hope that one of the others uses their key, that's if they all have one."

Tim gets two espresso coffees from the bar they begin to relax as the next five minutes passes without incident. Then there's a commotion outside the restaurant door, the man that had his key stolen comes in escorted by two heavy built, suited security men,

"That's her." the man says pointing to Diane,

The larger of the two security men comes over to the table quietly asking Tim and Diane

"Would you mind coming with us we've some questions to ask you?"

Tim looks indignant,

"Why, what's happened?" the man leans over him,

"Nothing's happened we only want to ask you a couple of questions about your associate." They have no choice but to follow the men into a security office.

They're seated at a small table, as Tim asks,

"Well?"

The head of security comes in pleasantly introducing himself, he takes a seat with the others then explains,

"The doctor here has lost an important security key."

Diane cuts in,

"That's careless of him, what's it got to do with us."

The security chief continues,

"He had it when he left the Restricted Area and believes he put it in his pocket, I understand that you bumped into him in the corridor."

Diane is quick,

"Yes, that's true, I was distracted by a comment of my associate and didn't see him, we bumped into each other, I apologised and that was it. I can't help you any more you're welcome to search my bag."

She throws it on the table the second security man picks up a small scanner moving it over the bag,

"It's clear. Would you have any objection if we scan your person?"

Tim says

"No problem, but expect a surprise."

The security man carefully runs the scanner around Diane, it immediately beeps she opens her jacket to reveal her shoulder holster and Berretta. Tim opens his jacket showing his holster as the head of security nervously asks,

"What are you doing with those?"

Tim answers,

"As you should know by now, the Pentagon arranged our visit, we're working for the NSA, these, he puts his hand on the holster, are the tools of our trade, that's all we can tell you."

The head of security now a little more respectful asks,

"What about your friend?"

Diane responds,

"He's a genuine scientist, a guest of the Pentagon but sadly had to leave early."

The security man asks,

"Why are you hanging around the restaurant?"

Tim replies,

"We were having a leisurely lunch as our transport does not arrive till six. Our visit was cut short by Dr Peterson who had an emergency to deal with. He recommended we wait in the restaurant, so if it's OK with you we would like to return to the restaurant, as we cannot help you further."

At that moment another security guard comes in and speaks to the head of security in almost a whisper,

"We've tracked the card it's been used at Montauk."

The head of security orders him,

"Alert them and contain him, he's got to be picked up immediately."

Tim asks,

"What's happened?"

The Head of Security turns and smiles,

"The intruder whoever he is has been using the stolen card, as he's still on site we'll soon find him."

Diane cuts in,

"Or her, it could be a woman."

The Head of Security gives a sarcastic grin,

"I don't think so. You are free to return to the restaurant, one of my men will remain with you until your transport arrives."

As they leave Tim notices a small red light on a tiny camera that had been filming them it was part hidden on top of a filing cabinet,

"Excuse me, because of our type of work I have to ask you to delete the film you have just taken to protect our identities."

The Head of Security nods to the other man who takes down the camera passing it to Tim,

"You do it."

Tim deletes the digital file and hands the camera back, knowing full well that they would have been filmed from one of the many CCTV cameras around the building. They return to their table whilst the security man sits at a table near the door.

Diane whispers,

"They know where Mike is, can we warn him?"

Tim leans forward,

"He knew as soon as they discovered the card was missing they'd be able to trace where it was used, just like the police do with credit cards. Don't worry, if he's got as far as Montauk before the alarm was raised he's done well and probably got the proof we need."

Below Camp Hero, Mike leaves the lift finding himself in a brightly lit corridor which down one side is made from glass panels running from the ceiling to the floor, he moves to the edge of the first glass panel then peers through, 50 feet below him there's a massive semi circular laboratory with numerous engineers in white coats. Around the outside of the wall he recognises what seems to be a section of a Particle Accelerator disappearing into a tunnel similar to Brookhaven but much larger. In the centre of the laboratory there's a large electrical machine that has a pyramid shaped barrel tapering out of its top with a large coiled spring pulsing with red light. The machine has heavy duty power lines running into it, Mike has no idea what it is but engineers are working all round it. On the far wall of the laboratory there's a large metal staircase that goes up, via two landings to the floor he's standing on, the door is at the end of the corridor. Mike takes out his camera carefully filming what's below, zooming onto the large machine, he puts his camera away, realising that without a white coat he will stand out like a sore thumb.

He looks along the corridor, midway he sees a door marked 'Changing Room', slowly making his way to the door he uses the card to open it. Once inside he finds the room lined with rows of lockers, it's a changing area, he tries the nearest lockers they're all locked. Looking round he finds a wash room lined with basins and mirrors, as he goes in he notices a large skip shaped laundry bin, opening it, he finds it's full of used white coats, he takes one out that looks the cleanest slipping it on over his clothes, he glances in the mirror and smiles "Perfect." As he turns to leave, he spots a notice board on the far wall and hanging from it a clip board, he pulls the clip board off its chain holding it as if using it "That's all we need." suddenly the door into the locker room opens, voices can be heard as several men come in, chatting as they open their lockers.

Mike casually steps out from the wash room towards the main door, he's about to open it when another man comes in, Mike smiles "Good afternoon." The man nods in acknowledgement Mike is back in the corridor.

He makes his way back to the lift noticing nearby an old military style metal door with a very small dirty wire-reinforced window in its centre. The door is recessed into the wall beside the lift, after glancing round he presses his face against the glass, he can just see inside a flight of concrete stairs.

He tries the door it's locked, examining the keyhole whilst checking around him he takes out his electric lock pick, after a few attempts and a whir the lock levers click. He gently turns the large circular handle then with effort pushes the heavy blast door which slowly opens, its hinges squeaking loudly, he steps onto the dim landing, pushes the door closed behind him. He turns the inner circular handle which moves four heavy steel plates on each side of the door into the metal frame, similar to a bank vault.

He looks around through the musty darkness, discovering he's in a dusty concrete service staircase, the narrow stairs go up and down with a single rusty tubular metal hand rail on one side it's obvious from the amount of dust it's not been used for many years. Mike carefully relocks the door and takes a look down the stairwell, it disappears into darkness,

"Probably down to the underground." he whispers to himself.

The stairway is completely dark, the only light coming in through the small window in the door which makes the landing area glow against its dark surroundings.

In the corridor the lift door opens a squad of four armed, heavily built, black uniformed security men start to search the corridor, one checks that the stair door is locked, Mike hears them trying to turn the door handle and their voices, as the leader tells them,

"He's on this floor somewhere. Find him."

He hands each of them a photograph then pointing to one of the men,

"You, stay by the lift to block this exit."

Mike presses himself back against the wall,

"So now they know I'm here, let's see what's upstairs."

Mike takes a small but powerful halogen torch out of his jacket pocket shining it down the stairwell, the stairs disappear into the deep black pit beyond the range of his torch, slowly he makes his way up the stairs leaving an unavoidable trail of footprints in the thick dust on each stair, it's a long climb and several landings later, he sees a very slight glow on the next landing which has a door similar to the one on the fifth level. He cautiously looks through the small glass window, outside the door is a corridor lined with windows exactly the same as the level below, he can just see to his left the lift. It's clear.

Mike unlocks the door using his electric lock pick, he turns the handle wheel pulling the heavy door towards him, very cautiously, he steps into the corridor closing the door behind him but leaving it unlocked. It takes a moment before his eyes adjust to the bright lights in the corridor. Realising that his white coat and shoes are covered in dust from the stairs he does his best to shake himself clean then moves over to the nearest section of the glass wall.

Below him there's a massive open plan area divided into smaller laboratories with assembly plants, the walls are lined with large VDU screens with large items of unrecognisable electrical equipment fed by massive electricity cables, the floor is teeming with scientists and engineers, male and female, at the far end are offices with meeting rooms all have half glass walls.

In the centre of the room is a large round silver object like a bathysphere around which are four portacabin type structures with large power lines leading from them to the sphere, each portacabin has the name 'General Electric Army Model Gravity Distortion Time Displacement Unit', the men working around the sphere are in blue uniforms with the General Electric logo on their backs.

Mike estimates that the area must be a minimum of 20,000 square feet. He starts filming slowly working his way along the corridor towards the stairway to get a better view of the sphere and heavy equipment. He's concentrating so much on the view through the camera that he fails to notice that one of the engineers is looking up watching him, the engineer is about to glance away when he spots the camera. The engineer quickly walks over to another engineer pointing to Mike, who has already started backtracking away from the window towards the lift. The second engineer picks up a telephone within seconds the alarm sounds throughout the building, an electronic voice broadcasts through the 'Tannoy'

"INTRUDER ALERT - INTRUDER ALERT"

Mike quickens his pace as a group of engineers start running up the metal stairs towards the corridor. He gets back to the lift area recess where he cannot be seen then enters the stair doorway, he closes and locks the door just as he hears the lift arriving. After quickly looking round for something to jamb the lock, he forces his pen into the door lock as far as it will go. He stumbles his way up the dark stairs as quickly as he can without using his torch.

As the lift doors open another four armed security men rush out into the corridor meeting the engineers half way round the bend in the corridor, the leading engineer speaks to the first armed guard,

"There was a man up here in a white coat using a camera."

"Which way did he go?"

The engineer points down the corridor past the lift.

The guards retrace their steps back down the corridor which bends round to the right, whilst the other checks the Changing Room. One of them stays by the lift, the other two, weapons at the ready head off round the long corridor, within a few moments the lift doors open and another four Security men arrive, running the opposite way round the corridor which forms a very large circle around the laboratory facility.

Mike is now able to use his torch and races up the stairs, after several flights of stairs he arrives panting at another landing with a similar door, after looking through the small glass window he decides to pass this landing continuing quickly up more flights of stairs until he gets to the next landing which has a similar door. He sits down near the door to get his breath back and letting his racing heart recover, he thinks to himself,

"I must be getting old and disorientated this must be the fourth level up from the underground, strange as this should be the surface level yet the stairs continue upwards."

Two floors below the eight security guards meet outside the lift having combed the whole of the second floor the man in charge is confused,

"He has to be on this floor, there's no way out other than the lift,"

He then spots the recessed door and asks the nearest engineer,

"What's in there?"

The engineer explains its part of the old WW2 building it's never been used, the security guard asks impatiently,

"Where's it go?"

The engineer responds,

"No idea it's never been open."

The guard strides across and tries the door,

"It's locked."

He squints through the dirty glass panel then unclips a powerful torch from his black coverall shining it into the dark space,

"He's been in here, there's footprints in the dust, get the door open."

The engineer asks the others where the key is, none of them know. The guard tells two of his men to break the door open, they crash against it in unison without success, the engineers tell him,

"It's a World War 2 anti blast door you'll never break it open."

The guard uses his radio and calls control,

"Where do these blast doors lead and where's the key?"

Control checks their plans,

"It's an old internal service stairway, not been used since the last war, wait a moment, we may have a key, no guarantee it's the right one, stay where you are, we'll send it down."

The guard replies,

"Good, get a fucking move on."

The leader orders his men,

"I want two men stationed at every door on each floor starting from the top down to the underground station. We'll trap him on the stairs."

The men immediately take the lift to their various stations as the lead guard calls up reinforcements.

Mike continues to explore up the stairs past the fourth storey door, he goes up two flights where the stairs stop at a solid wall it doesn't make sense. He flashes his torch around then finds some rusty metal steps set into the wall, the same as they fit in man holes. He shines his torch on the steps they ascend into a three feet diameter circular chamber in the ceiling, he slowly makes his way up the vertical steps, praying that they'll hold his weight, he continues for about thirty feet then discovers a rusty hatch cover blocking his way.

He pushes against it the best he can, it moves slightly and stops, the dust blows in around him. Holding onto the steps with one hand he moves his torch round the cover finding that it has an old padlock fastening it from the inside.

He hangs on the steps thinking for a moment, then with difficulty loops an arm round the step and taking out his Smith & Wesson screws on the silencer, he moves down three rungs and aims carefully, he knows that there is a good chance he could be hit by the ricochet in such a small place, he squeezes the trigger, the sound is louder than he expected the old lock crumbles apart dropping down below him. He slides his pistol into his jacket pocket then using both hands climbs back up to the cover, pushing against it with all his strength the heavy lid slowly creaks open enabling him to climb higher getting better leverage. In a second he's out into the cold night air.

Looking round he realises that he's on the roof of a large square windowless building about thirty feet tall, similar to an old military air traffic control tower, high above him is the disused radar antenna, its massive rusty steel legs are fixed into the roof of the building,

"So this is Camp Hero."

He searches around avoiding blocks of concrete lying on the roof, finding there's no way down,

"Shit, from the frying pan to the fire." he mutters.

He returns to the hatch making his way back down to the stairwell to find another way out.

"Better try the last door." he tells himself.

On the third floor the security guard reinforcements have arrived, one of them has brought the key, handing it to the team leader who gives them a direct order,

"Wound him if you have to but we need him alive, understood."

They acknowledge with a nod,

The team leader tries putting the key into the lock finding it obstructed, after a few minutes of manipulation he manages to push the key in and turns, he spins the handle pulling the door open, then leads the squad onto the dark stairway, their powerful torches cut through the darkness. Mike's footprints are easy to follow,

"Come on this way."

They run up the flights of stairs their boots clattering on the hard surface.

Mike has descended to the door on the fourth floor, he carefully slides along the wall to the window and looks through the glass straight into the squinting face of a security guard, the man shouts into his intercom,

"He's at the fourth floor door, get up here quick."

Mike hears the running footsteps coming up from below he turns to head back up the stairs, just as he leaves the glow of the light from the window, a shot rings out from below hitting the wall a foot behind his head, one of the small fragments from the wall cuts his forehead. He takes out his pistol moving further into the darkness up the stairs. Now he can see torches below him, he takes aim at just below the first torch aiming where he would expect the legs to be then squeezes off two rounds the silencer hides his muzzle flash. A man cries out in pain as a torch clatters down the stairs, the three other torches are immediately extinguished as the footsteps stop. He turns quickly then silently makes his way up the last two flights to the ladder, after checking behind him he climbs the rusty steps to the top.

Once outside he closes the hatch dragging several large heavy concrete blocks over the hatch cover

"That'll hold them." he mutters under his breath, Exhausted by the effort he sits for a moment on the roof gathering his thoughts. He gets up walking round the roof again surveying the perimeter for a way down, half way down on one side he sees some old metal girders sticking out of the side of the building, the remains of an adjoining structure.

He fastens his jacket securing his camera and pistol, putting on his leather gloves he walks over to the small parapet that surrounds the top, stopping at a point directly over one of the girders which are about fifteen feet below him. Behind him he can now hear banging on the hatch cover.

Decision made, he lowers himself over the parapet as far as he can then releases his grip dropping fifteen feet. He grabs at the girder which holds his weight stopping his fall, nearly dragging his arms out of their sockets in the process. Having stopped his momentum, he drops the remaining fifteen feet to the ground, breaking his fall as he used to do during his parachute training, but landing heavily on the uneven ground he twists his right ankle badly. He rests for a moment then hearing the banging continuing from the hatch realises he has to get to the cover of the trees surrounding the radar station tower, which is in the centre of a big open space. He stands up, the pain from his ankle is excruciating, he hobbles slowly and painfully across the space, it seems to take forever. On reaching the safety of the trees he finds a spot for concealment. Mike takes out his mobile and calls Tim, who is still in the restaurant with Diane and their security chaperone, Tim answers quietly,

"Mike you OK, they know."

Mike quickly explains where he is and where to pick him up. Tim turns to Diane,

"He's OK."

Then calls their driver to hurry him up,

"He'll be here in about 15 minutes. We can wait and talk outside."

Diane and Tim say goodbye to the security guard who follows them to the front entrance checking them out of reception,

"We'll wait over here for our driver."

Tim points to an outside seat, the guard nods OK then returns to the building watching them from a window, Diane is concerned,

"Mike's really alright?"

"Yes, he's OK he just couldn't talk, he's in the woods beside Camp Hero Radar station sixty miles East of here."

"That man of mine has an obsession with trees, how did he end up there?"

"That's a story he'll tell us shortly."

Twenty minutes later Julian's driver has picked them up, they're in the car speeding east along the highway towards Montauk Point, Tim tells the driver to make sure they're not being followed, the driver laughs,

"I've been doing this for too many years to be caught that easily."

Tim explains,

"We have to extract Mike from the Radar Tower at Camp Hero, you know where it is?"

The driver says,

"Yeah no problem, just got to watch the security guards up there, they're like a small army and armed."

Diane asks,

"Why armed?"

The driver smiles,

"Guess they have something they want to keep hidden or so I hear."

Tim asks,

"How long will it take to get there?"

"Maximum of an hour hopefully less"

Tim calls Mike, who responds immediately,

"We should be with you in forty five minutes."

Mike gives Tim his position.

At Camp Hero, Mike is well concealed in the tree's, nursing his ankle which is already swollen badly but fortunately not broken. From his position he has a good view of the Radar Tower so taking out his camera he films what he can see of the roof and surrounding area, the digital camera has no problem with the current level of darkness. Suddenly he hears the sound of engines. He keeps the camera filming as three black unmarked Humvee's speed from the approach track racing across the space and stopping near the tower.

They illuminate the tower with their vehicle searchlights as an armed security team leaps out of the vehicles surrounding the building. Mike watches as two of the guard's take up positions on opposite sides of the tower then fire grappling irons up on to the roof, they tension them professionally climbing to the top, whilst being covered from the ground by the other guards. Mike recognises these skills and whispers into the camera,

"These are not normal security guards, they're military."

The two climbers get to the top with weapons at the ready thoroughly searching the roof area. They drag the heavy concrete blocks off the hatch which bursts open as three men in black climb out. The guard that has just climbed out shouts at the two men on the roof,

"Where is the bastard, have you got him?"

The two men move their heads from side to side,

"He's not here."

Even from his distance from the tower Mike can see that the lead guard is furious,

"That's fucking impossible."

The guard screams, stomping around the roof checking over each side.

He shouts down to the squad below,

"Search the area."

The men on the ground start to spread out moving away from the tower their torches flicking backwards and forwards as the darkness engulfs them. The Humvee's drive round the area their powerful searchlights scanning the trees, Mike has already moved deeper into the wood finding a defendable spot where he is reasonably camouflaged, he settles down to wait in silence, he switches his mobile to silent and sends a text to Tim warning him that they must be very careful, he suggests they meet him at a small car park further down the approach road.

Mike watches the frenzy of activity in the distance, the lights from the torches flashing back and forth, fortunately heading away from him. He makes his way slowly and deliberately towards the rendezvous point, stopping frequently because of the intense pain from his ankle. The approach road sweeps round a long bend before it enters the radar tower open space, the wood he is in fortunately follows the approach road. The pain from his ankle slows him down added to having to be constantly alert for the searchers. It takes him over half an hour to cover the short distance through the woods. At last he reaches the road opposite the car park. He cannot see the car but stands still listening, and hearing the Humvee's some distance behind him decides to cross the road.

The car with Tim and Diane arrived five minutes ago the driver backed it out of sight into a fire break between the trees, at the rear of the car park.

As Mike breaks cover the driver gives a short flash of his torch. Mike spots the light then hobbles slowly across the road towards it, Diane sees him struggling,

"He's hurt."

She opens the door and runs to meet him as the driver starts the engine driving the car towards them without lights, he faces the car downhill. They quickly help Mike into the rear seat. The driver lets the car roll down the hill gathering speed. Once they are well down the hill the car increases speed until well clear of the area and safely back on the highway.

Diane realises that Mike has blood on his forehead and wipes it clean, Mike smiles,

"It's only a scratch from a piece of the wall the bullet missed me by a foot."

Diane is not pleased,

"They were shooting at you after you promised me that you wouldn't take any risks."

Mike gives her a kiss,

"It's an occupational hazard I got some fantastic pictures though. You would never believe what's down there."

Tim impatiently asks,

"What happened, what did you find?"

Mike goes through in great detail his adventure since he left them, after he finishes, Tim explains what happened to them, Diane adds in a fake hurt voice,

"They wanted to search me."

Mike grins,

"I'm not surprised, so would I."

Diane retorts,

"It was not a funny experience."

Mike winces in pain as he moves, trying to make his ankle more comfortable.

"Serves you right, I suppose we ought to get it x-rayed."

Mike doesn't think its necessary,

"I've broken ankles before, this is only a bad sprain the sooner I can get an ice pack on it the better hopefully it'll be OK in a few days."

Tim has been trying to remember something then asks Mike about the sphere he saw,

"You said that the sphere had General Electric people working on it?"

"Yes, what's significant in that?"

"Mike the name you mentioned seeing on the portacabin's rang a bell, you said it was a Gravity Distortion Time Displacement Unit."

Mike is curious,

"Yes. So what does that mean?"

"It may be a long shot but a man named John Titor started a web site in 2001, he claimed to be an American soldier that travelled back in time from 2036. John Titor was supposedly sent back from the future to obtain an obscure IBM 5100 computer which was made in 1975. The time machine that he published details of, including an operation manual, was described as a Stationary Mass, Temporal Displacement Unit manufactured by, guess who, General Electric. He published on his web site prophesies and scientific discoveries relating to time travel and how it could be accomplished, he explained that he was here for one year during which time he continued to update his website, after a year he vanished."

Mike laughs,

"That was ridiculed as a hoax."

"Yes it was, but it's a strange coincidence that you have stumbled across General Electric working on what could be a time machine and in one of his prophesies he suggested that CERN in Geneva would accidentally discover how time travel could be achieved."

Diane muses,

"That's an interesting link; Brookhaven, CERN and CAMP HERO all working with large magnetic fields and particle accelerators."

Mike is sceptical about this but remains silent, he believes without doubt what he saw in the laboratory was a time machine. Their car arrives outside the VIP entrance at JFK airport, the driver has already alerted the pilots to be ready to depart and that they've a minor casualty. They enter the VIP lounge supporting Mike, to find one of the pilots waiting for them with a wheel chair.

"In you get Mike we've got ice packs ready in the aircraft, all part of the service."

Mike reluctantly sits down in the wheel chair, silently pleased to have the weight off his foot.

They wheel him across the tarmac to the aircraft, helping him up the stairs as the lightweight wheel chair is folded and stowed aboard the Citation Jet. Five minutes later they are airborne heading for Washington. Mike has his foot up with ice packs being changed regularly by Diane.

In the security offices below Camp Hero, the Security Director from Global Asset management is pacing up and down the office, sitting at the table are the four senior security officers who were managing the operation to contain the intruder. The Security Director is raging,

"With all the resources at your disposal you managed to allow an unknown intruder access to our most secret laboratory then to take pictures, and, if I have it right, you brought in reinforcements trapping him in the disused staircase, you then followed him trapping him again on the roof of the radar installation which is thirty feet above ground, from where he vanished after shooting one of your foot soldiers. WHAT THE HELL DO WE PAY YOU FOR; YOU'RE SUPPOSED TO BE PROFESSIONALS."

The most senior of the Security Team speaks,

"Our CCTV cameras will have filmed him."

"Right, at least we'll their faces, take me to the monitor room."

They go into the monitoring station next door. The room is full of panicking engineers who are checking the equipment and computers, the director asks,

"What's going on?" the senior engineer turns to face him,

"We've just had the last 48 hours of CCTV records erased including the backups."

The director grabs him by the front of his overalls pulling his face close, in a raised voice that silences the room,

"HOW THE FUCK DID THAT HAPPEN?" The engineer's face is white,

"Sir it was impossible for this to happen, but it has and we don't know how."

The director throws him backwards onto another engineer,

"FIND OUT AND QUICKLY."

The director storms out of the office with the security team leader and slams the door,

"I'm going back to Washington, if you don't have some good news before my meeting tomorrow you can all pack your bags, because I'm transferring the whole lot of you to Nigeria to guard pipelines."

The Citation is on the approach to Washington Reagan National Airport, Diane and Tim couldn't relax on the flight but Mike drifted into restless sleep from the painkillers he had been given. They hear the intercom announcing their imminent arrival, it's now well past midnight. The aircraft parks close to the VIP lounge, the second pilot helps Mike into the building,

"Your taxi's waiting outside, we've another flight tonight so a quick goodbye, till next time."

They shake hands and thank him, he returns to the aircraft. Mike is supported between Diane and Tim, the ice packs have reduced the swelling but he's still suffering from his injury, they take a slow walk to Julian's taxi and 20 minutes later enter the apartment to find James still working at his computer.

James is pleased to see them, he rushes to help Mike when he sees that he's been hurt,

Mike tells him,

"James I'm OK it's only a sprained ankle."

They sit down together in the lounge which now looks like a science lab with James's equipment humming away in the background with a large flat screen next to his laptop. Mike immediately takes the camera out of his pocket,

"James I want you to download everything, make some security copies, let's see what we've got."

James takes the camera, goes over to his work station two minutes later he turns to them,

"Are you ready to watch some interesting television?"

He hits a key, the large screen starts showing Mike's adventure, from the moment he entered the lift through to the laboratory where James pauses the film at the sphere,

"You know what this is, don't you?"

Diane nods,

"Yes a time machine."

James is surprised,

"How did you know that?"

Tim responds,

"James how did you know that?"

"Time travel has always been a hobby of mine, I read all of the postings of John Titor and his science stacked up against loads of criticism, let's discuss the details later."

He presses play and the video continues to Mike's final filming at Camp Hero,

"Wow, that's fantastic stuff, so you jumped off that building?"

James is obviously very impressed by what he has seen,

"It's all great and Mike I've a surprise for you. You've not been alone on your trip."

The others look at him in anticipation Mike says,

"Go on surprise us."

"Well I finished my EMP project which works perfectly, so wondering what to do next I'd see if it was possible to join you, I explored the computer systems at Brookhaven tapping into their CCTV system so I could track you. I then found a well hidden link to another site and made my way to Camp Hero via the underground CCTV following Mike all the way, right up till the time he went into the staircase, then I thought, 'Oh shit' if I can see this so can they, so I copied all their CCTV footage over the past 48 hours then erased it completely off their system. I would imagine by now they're tearing their hair out trying to find out how it happened."

Mike is incredulous,

"You did that from here and I nearly got shot getting that film." James laughs,

"No, I didn't expect to be able to break in so easy, Brookhaven's system security was elementary stuff, anyway your pictures are much better quality and more specific. We can put both videos on a CD for the Judge that way no one can say we faked the pictures, its brilliant."

"James you are a formidable member of our team."

Tim asks James,

"Can you do that anywhere, get into CCTV records?" James grins,

"Oh yes, and I can edit them if I want."

"You're more dangerous than Diane." James laughs,

"Yeah I like that, but I'm no good face to face, I'm only a virtual hero."

Diane gets Mike some more anti-inflammatory painkillers,

"You, young man are going to have a hot bath and then to bed."

They say goodnight as James shuts down his system.

Early the next morning George calls Mike who is wrapping his ankle in a support bandage telling him that Tony has requested an urgent meeting with them at the Pentagon at 12.00 to discuss the conference arrangements. Mike suggests that they meet him privately to update him first, George agrees,

"See you at 10:00 same place as before, I'll see if Alexander is free."

Mike tells Tim and Diane to prepare for the meeting as James produces two copies of the CD with their combined photographs for George and Alexander.

James asks,

"When can I visit the Pentagon with you?"

"It'll be safer for you and the Pentagon if it's after the conference."

James looks disgruntled,

"I've broken that coded stuff for George and need to explain it to him."

Mike agrees,

"OK that's a good idea, then you come with us to the first meeting we'll drop you back here on our way to the Pentagon."

They arrive at the Hotel and are sitting around the table drinking coffee, which these days they seem to be living on, five minutes later there's a knock on the door, George and Alexander arrive. Mike hobbles to the door and greets them, Alexander apologises,

"I was passing when George called me I only have 15 minutes so if we could deal with the business that involves me first I would be grateful."

"No problem, let's get started."

They sit down together as Mike outlines all that happened at Brookhaven then his visit to Camp Hero by which time James has his laptop open showing Alexander the video and CCTV footage. George asks,

"James, how did you manage to get the CCTV data?"

James smiles explaining how he managed to break into their security system,

"It was a surprise, relatively easily done."

George is very impressed,

"If ever you want a job, your country needs you."

"George, many thanks for the offer but my friends still need my help and we are serving our country."

George and Alexander watch in disbelief as James shows them the final video and CCTV footage. The silence is broken by Alexander with an anger and determination in his voice that they had not heard before,

Alexander almost demands,

"Can I take a copy of this material?"

James hands him a CD, Alexander turns to George,

"You've suspected that something was going on for some time but this is beyond what I imagined was possible. A covert base carrying out potentially dangerous experiments sixty miles from the centre of New York, without our knowledge or senate approvals is unbelievable. How something that big with hundreds of staff can remain secret for so long indicates the potency of those behind it. Gentlemen, and lady, you've put yourselves at great risk to obtain this startling and compelling evidence which I'll integrate into what we already know, we have discovered financial links between Global Assets and Brookhaven but these videos change everything we need to move fast."

He gets up, says good bye and almost rushes out. George is also in a state of surprise,

"I've not seen Alexander act like that before. You've really got his attention."

James gives George his CD with several pages of notes,

"This tells your people how to decrypt the encoded emails you're intercepting and explains how to use the program I created. I think you'll find the content of Tony's emails of special interest."

George takes the files,

"James, thank you, if ever you need anything just let me know, was the equipment OK?"

"Fantastic thanks, it was the best I could have wished for. Thanks to you my project is complete and fully operational ready for when we need it. Once we have a little more time I'll arrange a demonstration of its awesome capabilities."

George tells them,

"By the way we've had a tail on the Security Director of Global, guess where he was yesterday? He visited Brookhaven."

James interrupts,

"Do you know what he looks like?

"Yes I'm sure I'd recognise him, I've seen his photograph, why?"

James turns his laptop towards George,

"The CCTV tapes show everything that happened over 48 hours, take a look."

They watch as James sets the file to cover the 24 hour period, after fast forwarding they study the Brookhaven reception area CCTV camera's images watching the large numbers of people arriving when George says,

"That's him." pointing to the man as he walks in through the entrance doors,

James say's,

"Watch this."

He puts the curser over the man's face makes an adjustment to one of the settings on his programme,

"I've just tagged him, now we can now see exactly where he goes."

They follow him as he goes into the building then as he uses a card to open the Restricted Area door. They track him into the lift then getting out of the hover train at Camp Hero then taking the lift. He then goes into an office. George is amazed,

"That's absolutely remarkable I've never seen software that could tag someone like that before."

"You won't have done, it's all my own work you haven't seen anything yet."

"I can't wait." and then to Mike,

"You have a phenomenal asset in this young man."

"Thanks George. You're pretty good yourself. I couldn't have done this without the gear you got me."

It's time for their meeting at the Pentagon James says goodbye then takes Julian's taxi back to the apartment. George has his car parked outside to run them back after the Pentagon meeting.

A little distance away on Pennsylvania Avenue in Global Assets penthouse boardroom the Security Director is speaking on the secure telephone to the Head of Security at Camp Hero.

"What news do you have for me?"

"We have our CCTV system functioning again but don't know how the files were deleted it's a mystery, maybe a computer fault."

The Director raises his voice,

"Solve it. What else?"

The voice continues,

"I've made some enquiries about those three people. We discovered that the CCTV system at the RHIC building is stand alone it's not connected to the main system. I've scanned the file we have clear photographs of all three of them. You should have them in about ten minutes. One of our couriers is delivering them to you personally."

"Well that's something, did you find out who they were?"

"No, we believe their ID's were false I've confirmed that the Pentagon did arrange their visit."

"That's serious I'll check the photographs as soon as they arrive, if you find out anything else call me I'll be with the Chairman."

The courier arrives handing the director the CD package and leaves, he immediately takes it to the Head of Systems,

"I want to take a look at this immediately. Make some prints I'm seeing the Chairman in five minutes."

They place the CD into a computer, opening the files there are six clear photographs of Mike Tim and Diane, the Security Director exclaims,

"Damn, these guys were supposed to have been taken care of in Alaska."

He grabs the photographs and storms into the boardroom. The Chairman is sitting waiting for him a large cigar in his hand,

"Give me some good news."

The director lays the photographs in front of the Chairman,

"Sir, do you recognise these people?"

"Yes, we had them taken care of by our man in New York."

The director continues,

"Yesterday they were at Brookhaven, one of these two men got into Camp Hero filming the place before the local security team could stop him."

The Chairman blows cigar smoke into the Directors face,

"You were responsible for their elimination?"

The director sits down,

"No sir, it was done by our associate at the Pentagon, I was told by him that he had confirmation that it was done, that's all."

The chairman takes a deep breath,

"Do you know how much that operation cost us?"

"Yes sir."

"Where are these people now?"

"I only received this information five minutes ago I'll work on it immediately I want to speak to Tony at the Pentagon. He's screwed this one up badly but has the resources to find them for us we need that film back before they do anything with it."

The chairman is thinking,

"If these three were able to get into Camp Hero they were probably behind the attack on our computer systems that makes them very dangerous indeed, we need them found immediately. I'm now making that your personal responsibility to find and secure them where I can have access to them.

I understand from Tony that there's going to be a presentation to the world's leaders in two days time at the United Nations General Assembly Building by those people from the other dimension. They're offering free energy, there's a good possibility that those three will be there too. Maybe we can get the lot together, think about it. You have contacts at the United Nations?"

"Yes sir, we've two of the UN's security teams on our books."

"Good get Tony to call me immediately."

Mike, Tim, Diane and George arrive at the Pentagon and quickly pass through security to Tony's office. Tony is waiting for them to arrive he's sitting at his desk when a telephone buzzes in his drawer. He takes out a satellite phone and answers it. It's the security director.

"Tony you have a big problem, the three targets that you arranged to be eliminated are still active. Yesterday they managed to infiltrate our restricted facility on Long Island with a camera. We need to find them immediately. The Chairman wants them delivered to him personally. You were responsible for this operation and screwed it up, so now fix it. Find them fast and let me know if they'll be at the UN tomorrow as it may present an opportunity to put things right. If not the boss wants your head on a plate."

"I've heard that they intend going public releasing everything they have, if anything happens to them."

"I'll cross that bridge at the time. Goodbye."

Tony closes the phone then after slowly replacing it in the drawer he leans forward, putting his head in his hands. His thoughts are broken by a knock at the door, His assistant says,

"Sir, they're here shall I show them in."

Tony looks at her and nods,

George leads them in, they sit around the large table. Tony greets them,

"Thanks for coming over, I'm sorry it's at such short notice but I've important news for you and your friends."

Tony explains that the President and his advisors have arranged for the presentation to take place in two days at 14:00 hours, they decided the most appropriate venue would be the General Assembly Building of the United Nations where the whole UN membership of 190 odd countries have agreed to attend, so we're expecting something over 350 people to be present. We have the security in place already the President has asked if he could meet the three ambassadors from Atlantis at 13:00 prior to the presentation. In view of their height we've had three large seats made that will be on the podium.

The Vice President will introduce your people and has asked for you to be with them the whole time, for continuity and communication. Tim is distracted by something that is bothering him, Mike asks,

"Tim do you think that the venue will be acceptable?"

Tim seems not to hear him. Mike touches his arm repeating the question Tim recovers his composure,

"Yes I think it's perfect, a familiar environment for the member countries. I'll speak with Aacaarya as soon as I get back to confirm that everything is in order."

Diane is quietly concerned as she has not seen Tim act like that before. Tony makes his apologies,

"I'm afraid I have other urgent business with the President so I must leave you now. By the way where are you staying?"

Mike quickly tells him,

"In a local hotel we keep moving every few days for our own security."

"Good, just as well, do you have a number I can get you on?"

"No we use pay phones when we call George."

Tony agrees,

"Good idea can't be too careful, I'm sorry I have to leave, George can you see them out please."

They leave, George drives them back into the centre of Washington, once in the car Mike asks Tim,

"What's wrong?"

"Tony was distracted and not telling us everything, he's had some bad news about us, I think his masters have just discovered that we've not been eliminated." Diane asks,

"What does that mean?"

"They'll try again."

George is concerned for their safety,

"Mike, you sure you don't want me to provide security?"

"No thanks, we're better on our own, if you drop us near Logan Circle we'll check there's no one following."

George pulls the vehicle into the kerb. They get out helping Mike who is still having difficulty with his ankle. They make a small but slow detour back to the apartment.

James is pleased to see them,

"How was the meeting with Tony?"

Tim explains what happened and that Tony was acting very strangely not his normal self,

"I had a very strong instinct that someone had put pressure on him to find us, he was in conflict as if he didn't know what to do, I think he's having doubts about carrying out the orders he's been given."

James nods knowingly,

"I know."

Tim and Mike look at him in surprise,

"James what do you mean?"

"When you left for the Pentagon I decided to spend my time seeing if I could get back into their system and surprise, surprise, it took some time but I managed to discover that they have visual and audio scanning cameras throughout the building, I remembered you mentioned Tony's office number so used that to gain access to his office. Although you couldn't take me with you I decided to come along virtually. I arrived before you did, saw him take a call on his satellite phone and after making some adjustments I managed to enhance the reception so that I could hear both sides of the conversation and here it is."

They are shocked at this further revelation from James, Mike is stunned,

"Is nothing secure anymore?"

"Not when it's a large arrogant organisation that thinks they are completely secure, there's always a way in, it's the small outfits that are more difficult because they are not so well organised."

On the large screen is a clear view of Tony's office with him sitting at his desk, his satellite phone buzzes in his drawer, he takes it out. James adjusts the settings in his system,

"You can just about hear what the caller is saying and you won't like it."

They listen intently to the recording in silence. Mike is first to speak,

"James, burn this video onto a CD, we need to get it to Alexander immediately; I'll call George".

Diane looks at Tim,

"They won't stop until."

Tim cuts her off,

"Until they're all behind bars, which, with the evidence we have provided will be very soon, we just have to be extra careful till then."

Mike asks James,

"How did Global find out it was us at Brookhaven, you deleted their CCTV images?"

James sighs,

"Good question, I've thought about that, the only way was if there was a stand alone CCTV system, I've had another look at their CCTV coverage and the only area that's not linked is the HRIC building, where you went first. They could have an old system that's not tied into their main CCTV security system, if so; they would have images and could have identified you from them. I can't see any other possibility."

Diane is worried,

"Mike what do we do?"

Mike is hiding his anger at this new development he is concerned for Diane's safety,

"First we get this new CD to George and Alexander, they'll know what can be done and how fast, Tim must speak with Aacaarya to organise their arrival. Once the meeting is over at the UN the whole thing will be in the open then we can stop hiding."

Diane is not convinced,

"It's as easy as that?"

"No, we still have to be on our guard for a little while longer."

Tim gets up to leave,

"I'm going to contact Aacaarya."

Mike asks Diane,

"Would you like some fresh air, I'm going to hobble out to a payphone to call George, fancy coming?"

Diane smiles,

"I suppose so you'll need someone to look after you."

In the lush boardroom of Global's office's the Chairman is waiting for the Director of Security, there's a knock on the heavy polished door, the Chairman looks up from his papers,

"Enter."

The Security Director walks in,

"Good afternoon Sir."

The Chairman nods in acknowledgement and points to a seat next to him,

"What news do you have for me?"

The director answers,

"I've spoken to Tony about the trio, he says he doesn't know where they are but is certain they'll be at the UN meeting."

The Chairman smiles,

"Then that's good news we can rid ourselves of all the birds with one stone."

The Director is surprised,

"What do you mean Sir?"

The Chairman lights his cigar,

"We've prepared for this moment for many years our New World Order is ready, all we are doing is bringing forward its implementation a little. The device is in place and we'll start causing world chaos by eliminating their leaders and our enemies in one flash."

He laughs,

"And what's more these Ambassadors from the Parallel World will be blamed, it's perfect timing. We control most of the world's major banks, financial institutions and oil supplies, with our ESP system can bring down the world's economies and communications."

The Director asks,

"But surely our computer systems are not fully operational."

The Chairman gives a crooked smile,

"I've had the whole computer team working on an alternative plan, they're ready to transmit our message to our commercial and military targets, our masters will be the only ones remaining with a communication network controlling the media to the populations of the world."

The Director is impressed with his superior,

"Sir, that's brilliant news, I thought our computer problems would cause delays to our plans. The device has been ready for six months all we have to do is to activate its systems."

The Chairman leans close to the Director,

"That's your responsibility, the General Assembly starts at 14:00 I suggest we set it for 15:30 they will have settled in by then and will be concentrating on their visitor's message. You're absolutely certain that it will do what's needed?"

The director nods,

"Sir, without any doubt, no one will survive."

The Chairman goes over to a spectacular drinks cabinet,

"Would you like a Whisky?"

The Director is honoured he has never been offered a drink from the Chairman before,

"Yes sir, neat."

The Chairman brings over two crystal whisky glasses that are a third full with a very special Scottish single malt,

"You'll like this."

He hands the glass to the Director as he raises his glass to make a toast,

The Director has one more concern,

"What do we do about our man at the Pentagon; he's become a liability I think he's weakening."

The Chairman asks,

"He will be there?"

The Director smiles,

"Yes he'll be there with the President and the Ambassadors."

The Chairman sits back,

"Then that's another problem solved. When do you intend to activate the device?"

The Director continues,

"This evening, I'm taking the man that designed it to check it over thoroughly before setting the timer we're the only ones who know where it is. The security squad on duty this evening are all on our payroll, we have easy access."

The Chairman gets up and slaps The Director on the back,

"That's perfect, just perfect. Sean, we've worked together for many years, you've been my most trusted and reliable director, don't let us down now in this final moment, we will fulfil our destinies and those of the new world, where we'll reap the rewards from our efforts."

Mike and Diane reach the payphone in Logan Square; Mike calls George and tells him that they have important news,

"I'm just leaving the Pentagon and can be in the Square in 10 minutes, where?"

Mike suggests a coffee bar which is nearby,

"OK, I know where you mean, see you in ten."

Mike takes Diane's arm,

"We've time for a coffee. George is on his way."

They go into the coffee bar ordering two Espresso coffees,

Diane smiles,

"It's nice to have a moment alone together."

"Yes it is, I can't wait to take you away for a honeymoon, oops, I meant holiday." Diane asks,

"Was that nearly, an, oops proposal?"

Mike puts his hand on Diane's,

"And if it was, what would you say?"

She squeezes his hand,

"I only deal in certainties. When an offer's made I'd consider it probably favourably in this instance, particularly once this business is over."

Mike is embarrassed,

"Yeah, you're right, let's get the work out of the way. We can discuss my offer seriously during our holiday."

George arrives in civilian clothes sitting down with them,

"What a day, I've been chasing round like a headless chicken, double checking the security arrangements for tomorrow. How are you two?"

Mike grins,

"We were discussing our future, once this thing's over."

George smiles,

"I thought you two were becoming close."

Then returning to the reason for their meeting asks,

"What have you got for me?"

"James wanted to join us at the Pentagon meeting with you and Tony. I told him it was better for the moment if he stays out of sight, perhaps next time. Anyway when we got back we discovered that James had decided to see if he could make a virtual visit and managed to get into the Pentagons' internal CCTV system and tracked us down, filming us in Tony's office."

George is astounded,

"What. He did what. That's impossible."

Mike smiles, proud of James achievement,

"It surprised me too, but there's more, he arrived in the office before we did and filmed Tony taking a call on a satellite phone, I don't know how he did it but he was able to enhance the audio signal so that we could hear the caller's voice."

George is dumfounded,

"My God that's impossible."

Mike then describes the content of the conversation,

"It's all here on the DVD in glorious Technicolor, now we know why Tony was distracted during our meeting. This needs to be seen by Alexander immediately, as I think that if he called Tony in for questioning he would break, he has an internal conflict at the moment the evidence is undeniable."

George agrees,

"I can't get over James, many people have tried to crack the Pentagon system but he just strolls in and goes where ever he wants. He's a genius who I will say again, should definitely be working for me."

Diane agrees,

"Once this is over I think he might."

George asks,

"Do you have copies of this?"

Mike grins,

"Oh yes, James has added it to our worldwide broadcast if anything should happen to us." George turns serious,

"We have a difficult few days ahead of us I'd feel happier if you had some protection."

"George, we appreciate the offer but are unanimous in wishing to stay submerged we're not alone, I have professional friends working for me behind the scenes."

George acknowledges,

"I know that, but tomorrow you'll be in the open, it's the next few days I'm concerned about."

Diane explains,

"George we're taking great care, a lot depends on how quickly Alexander can start bringing these people to justice."

"I'm seeing him directly after leaving you I think this new evidence is the link he's been waiting for to start pulling them in, commencing with Tony who I agree is ready to jump ship. I'll call you after my meeting."

Mike asks,

"What security does Alexander have?"

"I was waiting for you to ask that, he has one of my top teams covering him 24 hours a day plus a specialist unit working with him in his offices, he's more secure than the President and well knows the risks involved in his type of work."

George gets up, kisses Diane and shaking Mike's hand leaves the coffee bar.

At midnight a car arrives at the UN General Assembly Building, it's waved through the security cordon to a small side service entrance where it parks. Sean and another man carrying a silver metal briefcase go to the door where a security guard greets Sean, unlocking the door as Sean asks him,

"How are the Security Cameras?"

The guard whispers,

"Sir, this zone has been switched off for one hour as you instructed, the tapes will be edited accordingly."

Sean thanks him,

"Well done."

Sean and the man enter the building, the guard locks the door behind them, they are walking down a small corridor and stop at a locked door marked "NO ENTRY SERVICE PERSONELL ONLY." Sean looks round keying a number into the security lock pad they open the door which locks behind them, heading down a flight of stairs into the low lit service basement. They walk along passages lined with heating pipes and wiring cables until they reach a point under the centre of the building where there is a locked cage the size of a small room, housing a mass of electrical control system boxes. Unlocking the door they work their way to the back of the cage stopping at one of the control boxes, which looks the same as the others, with panels of flickering lights on the front. The man with Sean gets down on his knees opening his briefcase, half of which is a diagnostic panel with a keypad the other half is lined with sophisticated tools. Taking out a special key he opens the whole of the front of the box which is fake, inside there is a large stainless steel cylinder on top of which is an electrical control unit. The man unlocks the lid of the control unit connecting the diagnostic unit to the electrical panel, an array of lights flicker on, then stabilise. The man carries out various diagnostics taking the readings from his meter,

"It's all in order, we're ready to program, what time?" Sean says,

"15:30."

The man enters the data and asks again "15:30 confirm."

Sean says,

"That's confirmed."

The man hits a key, a digital clock starts counting down, The man looks up at Sean,

"It's done. There's no way of stopping it now."

Sean nods,

"Good, let's clear up and get out of here."

The man closes the front panel relocking the control box which blends in with the others around it. Sean and the man leave the cage locking it behind them, Sean checks his watch,

"Perfect it's only taken half an hour."

They retrace their steps to the entrance door to the building Sean taps on the door it's opened by the same security guard, who asks,

"You all done?"

Sean replies,

"Yes. We only wanted a quick look round. Good night."

The car leaves the area and once again is waved through the security barrier.

Diane and Mike arrive back at the apartment to find James trying on a new Italian designed suit,

"I've been shopping I could hardly turn up at the United Nations in my Jeans and old leather jacket what do you think?"

Diane wolf whistles,

"Very elegant, where's Tim?"

James nods towards Tim's room,

"He's been in there ever since you left; I didn't like to disturb him as he was going to speak to Aacaarya."

Mike knocks gently on the door, there's a movement, Tim comes out looking as if he had just woken up, Mike asks,

"How are you?"

"OK, just shattered, I've had an hour's conversation with Aacaarya."

Diane offers him sustenance,

"Come and sit down I'll make you a very strong coffee and you can tell us all about it."

James enquires,

"Have you guys seen the news?"

He switches on the large television, on every channel there is coverage of tomorrow's meeting.

The newscaster is excitedly explaining,

"The world's press are converging on New York for tomorrow's unprecedented UN General Assembly meeting with ambassadors from another world, it's said that these people are ten feet tall and bring with them offers of clean energy, what we want to know is what are they seeking in return. The heads of states from all over the world have started arriving, to be ready for the meeting at 14:00 which this network will be covering. What will these people be like? What do they want from us? Find out tomorrow at 2.00 o'clock, tune in we'll be there live. In the meantime, on the hour, we'll be following the build up to this remarkable event as dignitaries arrive and we interview leading energy experts. Will the world ever be the same again? I don't think so."

Mike turns to Diane,

"Well we're now approaching the grand finale."
Tim finishes his second mug of coffee,

"That's better, now I'll tell you what Aacaarya said, they're very pleased with what we've achieved and confirmed that they will arrive at the UN General Assembly building at 12:30, they said it was the most suitable venue as the heads of state will be on familiar territory. They've requested half an hour with us privately before seeing the President. There's a small meeting room off the main hall where the President will be arriving at 13:00."

Mike interrupts,

"How did they know that?"

"They know everything about what we've been doing including James's activities, of which they were highly complementary. Apparently the President is attending a private meeting with the Elders first then will then hand over to the Vice President."

Diane comments,

"That's a strange thing to do."
Tim continues,

"Not really, the Vice President is more of an environmentalist than the President a lot of this will be over his head. The Elders were encouraged that the whole membership of the United Nations General Assembly will be present and are looking forward to meeting us again."

James is delighted,

"I just can't wait to meet these guys, the security for this session must be colossal with all the world's leaders together in one place, plus all the worlds press, we're going to be famous at last." Diane is not in favour of being famous,

"That's the only thing I'm afraid of."

"Diane, we couldn't remain submerged forever."

"Mike, how are we getting to New York?"

"We leave here at 08:00 sharp, we're meeting George at the Pentagon, flying up with him in a private jet from Reagan National with four of his most trusted security people, he's arranged secure transport to and from the UN we'll return with him tomorrow evening."
Diane asks about weapons,

"Do we carry arms?"

"Not tomorrow, we'd have too much trouble with the security systems there."
James asks Diane,

"What's the United Nations General Assembly building like, it's not the tall building we always see on television is it?"
Diane smiles pointing at Mike,

"Ask the oracle here, he's a great tour guide and knows a lot about America, particularly its forests."

"James, the tall building you referred to is the Secretariat home of the United Nations administration. It was opened in 1950 at that time with a height of 544 feet and 39 stories it was one of the tallest modern buildings in New York and the most stylish with its green glass reflective windows."
Mike continues his little lecture which he always enjoys giving,

"There are four buildings making up the United Nations complex, the Secretariat Tower, a conference and visitor's centre, the General Assembly Building which has five floors with a domed roof and the Conference building that is the home of the Security Council and the Economic and Social Council"
Diane reminds them of the early start tomorrow as James quickly searches the internet for pictures of the General Assembly Building. James finds what he wanted,

"It looks like a gigantic nuclear submarine to me, with that dome."
Mike laughs,

"It's just the angle of the shot, I agree with you it does in that picture."

James closes down his system.

The next morning they are up early and for the first time in their business suits. Diane is dressed in a chic black trouser suit that shows off her figure James is full of admiration,

"Diane you look fantastic."

"James, so do you."

James grins with satisfaction,

"This is the first suit I have ever owned, my life has been spent in Jeans."

They leave the apartment at 07:30 after a short journey Julian's driver drops them off outside the Pentagon entrance at 08:00 where they find George in uniform with four security men, George introduces the team pulling Diane to one side,

"Don't worry these guys are the best, they have to be, they're my personal escort."

They travel to the nearby Reagan National Airport in two standard black GMC vehicles with tinted windows. The are taken directly to the VIP entrance where an Air Force pilot salutes George showing them to the waiting Air Force Jet, Diane nudges Mike,

"Another Citation, I'm beginning to feel at home in these."

By the time they are seated, the aircraft is taxiing to the end of the runway the pilots have immediate clearance to take off. The engine whine increases, after a brief take off run they are airborne and climbing to their cruise altitude.

Chapter - 24

The United Nations General Assembly

The flight to JFK takes one hour and twenty minutes they're met at the airport by a pristine uniformed Marines driver with side arm. He guides them to two GMC vehicles, to Diane's amusement she smiles at the first driver,

"Your vehicles are always black."

The driver stands at attention,

"Yes miss, we have them on loan from the FBI vehicle pool, they only have black."

Once in the vehicles they travel in convoy weaving their way through the heavy traffic from the airport. Heading for Manhattan the driver takes the North Van Wyck Expressway, before long they are in the Midtown Tunnel taking them under the East River, six minutes after leaving the tunnel they're pulling into the security area at the United Nations Plaza. The drive has taken just over an hour at one of the busiest times of day.

The United Nations plaza is a hive of activity, queues of limousines line the plaza as heads of state arrive. Squads of armed marines patrol the area. The area is littered with the world's press vans their parabolic satellite aerials pointing into space. The journalists throng together in a pack attempting to extract comments from the dignitaries before they are whisked into the reception hall. The two black GMCs are waved to a side security check point where their identities are checked by armed marines, then escorted to a secure parking area beside the General Assembly Building. Stepping out of the vehicles James stares up at the enormous five storey building in front of them, this is dwarfed by the thirty nine storey green glassed UN Secretariat block adjoining it. Turning to George, James asks,

"Why so much security, this seems excessive?"

"James, this is almost normal for a General Assembly meeting, the heads of almost every country in the world are in one place. It has to be secure. The press always makes our job more difficult as the crews have to be vetted and given appropriate clearances."

"Will the press be inside?"

"Afraid so, they'll be in the press gallery, this is the most newsworthy meeting in history with our visitors from another world. The press build up has been phenomenal they seem to have interviewed everyone that has an opinion on Extra Terrestrials as they've called our friends."

James laughs,

"I've seen some of the television interviews, mostly from people with vivid imaginations rather than any scientific knowledge. I can't wait to see tomorrow's news."

They are escorted into the building through to the beautifully furnished private lounge area beside the great assembly hall. They hubbub of voices from the reception area is making it difficult to hear conversations. Diane asks,

"George, can we have a quick look inside the hall?"

George nods to the nearest marine, a Sergeant, who asks them to follow him. George opens one of a pair of double doors which opens directly into the assembly hall. The magnificent hall is outstanding. Rising, the full height of the five story building, it is an enormous open space, its walls taper inwards up to the spectacular glass dome above the presentation area. They are alone apart from the security teams with their dogs, doing a last minute check between the rows of seats. In the centre front stands a large marble podium, behind it is a wide golden buttress leading up to the ceiling. Just above the podium is the large gold coloured disc with the emblem of the United Nations. The raised podium is reached by a flight of stairs on either side from where one has a view of the seating arrangement that stretches back to the rear of the building, arranged in tiers so that all delegates have a good view of the speakers.

The rows of seats are in banks of six making 1800 in total, each bank having a green topped table extending their whole width with individual headsets connected to the appropriate interpreters. On each side of the hall, almost to ceiling height, are two modern paintings by the French Artist Fernand Leger. On the main floor which is carpeted in green, there's a gallery to one side of the podium which has four blocks of eighteen seats above these are the first and second floor galleries that look down into the hall.

On each side of the podium there are two massive visual display screens that project clear images of the speakers to the rear of the hall. The tiered beige ceiling is fitted with numerous spotlights that create a unique soft atmosphere, highlighting the gold buttress behind the podium and the UN emblem, almost like stars glowing in a night sky. James is in awe at the sight before them,

"It's fantastic Mike, you been here before?"

"No, it's a first for all of us and the perfect venue for this meeting."

Tim checks his watch,

"We'd better get back to the lounge area Aacaarya and the Elders will be here in a few minutes."

They retrace their steps back to the lounge the marine opens the door for them stopping in amazement as he sees Aacaarya and the Elders standing by the windows. He snaps to attention giving George a crisp salute,

"Sir, your guests have arrived."

The stunned marine, steps sharply to one side to let the others through. Aacaarya smiles as they enter the room, obviously very pleased to see them. Mike introduces George, who even though he knew what to expect is taken aback at the sight of the Elders. James despite being prepared is amazed by the height and charisma of their visitors in their flowing white robes. They all shake hands. George asks Aacaarya,

"How did you get in here?

Aacaarya smiles showing his brilliant white teeth,

"I suppose you would say we materialised, it's a very useful method of travel, saves the hassle of going through your tedious security checks."

James is very taken with Aacaarya and asks him,

"Tim told me you are over 200 years old, but you look."

Aacaarya cuts him off answering,

"Your age"

James smiles,

"Exactly, Tim also told me that you communicate with the mind. I find that fascinating."

"James it's a skill that you are capable of learning to use. A long time ago your people stopped using telepathy but all you have to do is start working that section of your brain. It will take time with persistence and practice to perfect, as Tim has discovered."

James asks,

"Can you help me?"

"It has to start from within you but with your beautifully curious mind, I am certain you would not need any help. Try it sometime, start with Tim."

Mike asks Aacaarya and the Elders to take a seat,

"You asked to meet with us before the President arrived, was there something specific?"

George asks the marine to wait outside, he has to repeat the order as the marine is very distracted and completely focussed on the visitors,

"Sorry Sir, of course."

He snaps another salute at the guests as Aacaarya smiles at the marine,

"Thank you Sergeant, I imagine we must appear very strange to you."

The Sergeant replies,

"To say the very least, yes Sir." he leaves the room closing the door behind him.

Aacaarya continues,

"The Elders and I wanted to thank you personally for being instrumental in bringing us together for this important meeting. It would not have been possible without your initiative and the personal risks that you have taken on behalf of both our civilisations. You've created a unique opportunity for us to meet your world's leaders in a neutral environment befitting such an important and historic occasion. The United Nations goal, albeit currently unsuccessful, is dedicated to World Peace. We wanted to tell you before we announced it, that we believe our suggestions for a World Government could be integrated into the United Nations providing of course they're given the power to implement and enforce their decisions. At present unfortunately they are not able to do so. This is something we need to address and help them with. As you know we value your opinion, what do you think?"

George responds immediately,

"I think upgrading the UN is a great idea, when I first read your proposals I couldn't quite see how you could create a World Government, as most countries are full of suspicion and resistance to new ideas they would regard any superior government as a take-over of their powers. However, piggy backing on the UN would be far more acceptable. It's an existing organisation with goals they've already committed to. If you could provide the teeth that the UN lacks it would be good for all."

Mike agrees,

"That's more or less what I was going to say, it's an idea with great merit without any threat to their existing governments."

Their conversation is interrupted by a knock on the door, which opens immediately. Two of the President's personal security agents come in, without a word they take a brief look round the room, one of them speaks to another two stationed outside the door,

"It's clear."

The President of the United States is ushered into the room by his security squad along with his Vice President. George greets them introducing the Elders and Aacaarya. The President despite his briefing is very surprised by the three men in front of him.

"Ambassadors may I welcome you to the United States, it's a great honour for me and the people of my country."

"Mr President, we have been here for over 20,000 years, perhaps it is we that should be welcoming you."

The President laughs,

"So I understand either way it's an honour to make your acquaintance we look forward to working closely with you to achieve the exciting possibilities that we are here to discuss."

George introduces Mike, Tim, Diane and James as the President continues,

"I'm pleased to meet you at last, I've been following your extraordinary adventures with great interest, your country is forever grateful to you for what you've accomplished in bringing us together on this historic day."

The President turns to Aacaarya,

"Perhaps we may have a private word together?"

Aacaarya is curt,

"Anything you wish to say can be said in front of the people in this room, they are our trusted advisors."

The President looks slightly annoyed,

"OK if you're happy, so am I."

He sits down next to Aacaarya who looks down on the grey haired man. The President hesitates,

"I want to offer you our full and unconditional co-operation in what you're seeking to achieve, we would be pleased to act as your representatives and advisors to the World Government. The United States has long been active in working for peace throughout the world we have strong relationships with every other country. Our scientists and intelligence agencies are some of the best in the world and could assist you in implementing your energy technology installations globally."

"Mr President, thank you for your offer, we are obviously aware of America's power, and how it has been abused. As for working for peace your misguided foreign policies have destabilised your world, for reasons that we are both aware of, these are responsible for wars that have no end. The United States of America must put its own house in order before involving itself in the affairs of others. It would be counterproductive to our concept of an independent World Government if the United States was seen to be driving our initiative. Despite what you have convinced yourself to believe, the sad fact is that the worldwide reputation of the United States is at its lowest point in history, the credit for this lies solely in your hands and that of your administration. Your government has consistently ignored the environmental impacts of its growth.

Your military have funded the very experiments that are close to causing a collapse of the ionosphere and potential destruction of our planet. The combined irresponsible activities of the United States are the very reason that we have been forced to intervene to protect the future survival of both our worlds. I'm sorry to be frank but greed, power and wealth are not part of our agenda."

The President is flabbergasted. He gives an incriminating glance at Mike, Tim and Diane,

"Mr Ambassador, you have been misled this is not true."

Aacaarya looks down into the eyes of the President firmly stating,

"Mr President, we've not been misled, our intelligence organisation knows everything. And I mean everything that takes place in your world. Our sources are first hand, we rely on no one for information but our own intelligence. However we still sincerely welcome the United States as an essential member of the World Government, but its involvement has to be on an equal basis with other member states, however large or small they may be."

One of the Presidents agents leans over and whispers in his ear, the President looks at his watch and nods to the agent,

"Mr Ambassador I'm afraid I have to leave for another meeting. Please be assured that we will do everything necessary to meet your requirements, my Vice President will be standing in for me this afternoon. It has been a pleasure meeting you."

The President shakes their hands and leaves with his security team. Tim smiles at Aacaarya,

"Aacaarya that was probably the first time anyone has spoken to the President like that. Well done, he needs it."

Mike asks,

"George what meeting does he have to go to that's more important than this one?"

The Vice President looks at George,

"He has a hearing with a senate committee that was planned some time ago."

George asks,

"Where's Tony, I understood he was to be here?"

The Vice President, who knows and has great respects for George explains,

"He's been called to a meeting with the House Judiciary Committee. Before you ask, I have no idea why, it's probably routine."

Mike looks at Tim and Diane both have a look of satisfaction on their faces.

The Vice President explains the procedure for the meeting,

"The meeting will be opened by the Secretary General of the United Nations he will hand over to me for a few words of welcome on behalf of the United States. I will then hand the meeting over to you Mr Ambassador. We will go together to the podium after our visitors are seated, with the exception of George who will be sitting nearby."

James interrupts,

"And me, I'm staying with George there's no way I'm going out onto the podium."

"James, no problem"

Turning to Aacaarya he asks,

"Mr Ambassador, are you all ready?"

"Yes, we are ready, please call me Aacaarya."

George nods,

"Thank you I will, my friends call me George."

The heads of state have started entering the Assembly Hall the hubbub of their voices as they go to their designated seats can be heard in the lounge. James is becoming nervous as this the first time he has been to an event of this size and importance,

"Now I know how actors must feel before going on stage and I don't like it."

Diane says,

"At least we've spared you being on the podium."

The door opens and one of the UN organisers comes in,

"Be ready in ten minutes, I'll collect you from here."

He stops staring at the three ambassadors then apologises,

"Sorry sirs, you rather took me by surprise."
He leaves as Tim grins at Aacaarya,
"I think they're all going to be in for a shock in a moment, even if we'd been told about you before we met it would not have lessened the shock of seeing you in the flesh."
Five minutes later the UN organiser arrives with the UN Secretary General after introducing him to the Group, he shakes hands prepares them,
"We're ready, shall we go through, a lot of people are anxious to meet you."
They follow the Vice President and Secretary General into the Great Hall it's exactly 14:00 hours. The organiser leads George and James to their seats at the front of the gallery nearest the podium, a few seconds later the Secretary General leads the three ambassadors with the Vice President, Mike, Tim and Diane behind them. As they enter the hall a silence of disbelief falls over the gathering. The party start to mount the steps to the podium as a barrage of flashes commences from the Press. The Secretary General leads them to their high backed seats in the centre of the podium with Tim sitting beside Aacaarya.
The Secretary General and Vice President sits on one side of the two Elders and Tim, Mike and Diane are on the other side. The display screens show large images of the Elders as they settle down together on the podium, slowly the silence is broken by a growing whispering from the delegates. The Secretary General lean's forward towards the microphone in front of him to formally welcomes the distinguished guests to this extraordinary meeting of the United Nations General Assembly he introduces the Ambassadors from the 'Parallel World'. He then turns to Mike, Tim and Diane and to their embarrassment thanks them for making this historic meeting possible. He introduces the Vice President of the United States who takes the microphone on behalf of the United States of America

welcoming the Ambassadors and heads of the member states to the Assembly. He explains that this is fundamentally the most important gathering ever held in this magnificent building and in the history of our world.

"If we are tolerant and open minded we have an opportunity to achieve the true global peace that we have been seeking since the UN was founded. We hope it will lead to a greater integration and co-operation between our nations bringing an end to the suffering and starvation that exists today throughout our world."

The Vice President then presents the Ambassadors and their spokesman 'Aacaarya'. He hands over to Aacaarya the time is now 14:15. Aacaarya stands up causing frenzy in the press area, the flashes from their cameras reach a crescendo as they jostle each other for the best shots. The numerous international television crews are filming and relaying the images from the meeting live by satellite around the world.

As the activity dies down he introduces himself and the Elders,

"It's a great pleasure for us to have this opportunity to address such an esteemed group of key leaders from your world. For your convenience you will not need to use interpreters or headsets as I am speaking to each of you simultaneously in your own language, I have made a specific study of your languages and felt that this would be a more personal method of communication. The Elders that accompany me are the most senior leaders of my world they only communicate through telepathy. Everything I'll be telling you originated from them and has their counsel. Hopefully you will all have had an opportunity to review the written brief that was sent to you outlining the content of our presentation. I'm sure it will have generated many questions, concerns and doubts that you would like answered. At the end of my presentation there will be ample opportunity for dialogue between us during which your questions will be answered to your satisfaction. I would like to start by telling you a little about my civilisation and the reason this meeting between our Parallel Worlds has become necessary.

Its outcome, if together we implement it successfully, will secure the survival of our great planet, both our civilisations and enhance the future of the populations of your countries."

Aacaarya spends the next half an hour explaining the history of their civilisation, how they have lived on Earth for over 20,000 years in peace then how they helped other races with their technology which was turned against them by a small number of power hungry individuals de-stabilising the planet and destroying their homeland of Atlantis. He explains how the Elders were forced to create another world for the survival of their people, a world in a different time and space.

In Washington, at the offices of Global Asset Management, the Chairman is sitting at his desk lighting a cigar, he glances at his watch, its 15:00 and whispers to himself,

"Half an hour"

The delegates in the General Assembly are mesmerised by Aacaarya's history of his people

"At this point I would like to provide a visual demonstration of how we propose to supply your world with the energy we have promised. As I have previously explained, many thousands of years ago we successfully and safely developed technology to tap into a little of the vast electrical energies that exist in the magnetosphere, these limitless energies have consistently powered our world's needs without causing damage or pollution. If you watch the open area beside the podium I will demonstrate the basic mechanics of how we propose to make this energy source available to you, providing of course you accept our proposals which we will discuss shortly."

A twenty foot high hologram of a Pyramid appears beside the podium high above it a grey mist appears close to the ceiling of the hall, a short distance from the pyramid is a typical power relay station.

"This image is obviously not to scale but if we imagine that the grey area above is the magnetosphere, the master pyramid with its internal technology acts both as a receiver and a transmitter. The Pyramid focuses a beam with a pulsed signal into the magnetosphere this acts as a conduit down which electrical energy flows. This is completely safe it has been proven and functioning for thousands of years, the signals we use do not create adverse electromagnetic fields."

An image of the beam flows up from the Pyramid into the simulated magnetosphere and returns back down to the Pyramid then a different coloured beam passes from the Pyramid to the power station,

"The technology within the pyramid accumulates and concentrates the energy before transmitting it to local receivers which would be connected to your national grids. The quantity of this energy is only limited by your national grid capacities where necessary we can assist you in increasing the levels of energy you can access.

The benefit of this energy is that it is 100% clean, reliable and free, it will allow the nations using it to shut down their existing oil and fossil fuel power stations that are causing much of the pollution responsible for damaging your environment. This will release the considerable budgets you are spending on energy which can be redirected into meeting our requirements for a better world for you all."

The time is now 15:25. Aacaarya stops speaking as if distracted by something, he turns abruptly to the Elders, who both nod in agreement, turning back to the delegates,

"Please excuse me there is a matter of great urgency that has just come to my attention which threatens our security, I must deal with it immediately."

This announcement causes a murmur of concerned voices from the delegates.

"Please remain seated, don't be afraid. This will conclusively demonstrate to you that we're here on a peaceful mission."

Aacaarya and the Elders close their eyes, after a few moments of combined concentration an object materialises in front of the podium it's the electronic control box that was installed in the basement. George leaves his seat crossing the room to examine the box, as he does the four special screws holding the front in place drop out onto the floor allowing the door to swing open revealing the explosive device, George looks at the bomb, glances at the timer, then at his watch and speaks to himself,

"It's some sort of nuclear device. The timer stopped with sixty seconds to go."

Unfortunately a nearby microphone picks up his voice transmitting it round the room causing mayhem as many frightened delegates stand up and start moving to the exits. Aacaarya recovers his composure,

"Gentlemen, gentlemen please sit down, the device has been made safe and deactivated. It was placed in the basement of this building with the intention of destroying us all. The culprits are an international organisation based in Washington who wanted to impose a New Order on the World, some of you will have had dealings with them. We've just transmitted evidence confirming their involvement to the United States intelligence agencies, the guilty parties are being apprehended as I speak. There is absolutely no need to panic the situation is now under control, this device can never be activated again. For your information, I was only alerted to this threat a few minutes ago, you could call it a sixth sense that we developed for our protection, in this case yours too. I would normally have sensed the threat much earlier but we were distracted by the effort involved in speaking to you in so many languages."

George organises six security men to carefully move the device into the adjoining meeting room, once out of sight the delegates settle down although uneasily.

On Pennsylvania Avenue in the centre of Washington eight large black FBI vehicles supported by numerous police cars screech to a halt outside the offices of Global Assets Management. The police cordon off the building as armed agents rush into the reception area then split into teams heading for the management floors, a specialist unit heads for the computer systems department. The Police and FBI take over the reception area and security office preventing the receptionists alerting the floors above. On the top floor the senior management are sitting round the boardroom table with champagne glasses as the Chairman outlines their next step for world chaos then ultimate world control. They sit waiting for the News flash to arrive on the large television, suddenly the boardroom doors burst open, the first FBI squad arrives, the squad leader tells them,

"The party's over, you're all under arrest."

Without resistance the whole group are handcuffed then led down to waiting vans that have now arrived. Once the key management have been arrested the squads start collecting files and computer records from the whole building assisted by additional police teams. The reception area is a hive of activity, boxes of records, documents and computers are being wheeled out on trolleys then loaded onto a waiting FBI truck. The massive building is closed down as more FBI and Police arrive to start clearing and sealing off the floors with the operational staff being interrogated, all the management and directors are taken to the FBI headquarters building for formal interrogation. The front of the building has now been cordoned off to hold back the press and television cameras which have rapidly arrived to find out what has happened.

In the offices of the House Judiciary Committee, Tony has been called to Alexander Austin's office to answer questions and allegations as to his activities at the Pentagon and his relationship with Global Assets Management. Tony who had already been having second thoughts about the direction of Global Assets ambitions is shocked by the disclosure of evidence and the intimate knowledge of his affairs that Alex has accumulated.

There's no way out, Tony has no defence but to tell Alex everything from the moment he was first contacted and recruited by Global Assets including their last instruction to carry out the previously botched attempts to eliminate Mike, Tim and Diane. This further evidence from Tony added to Global's failed attack on the General Assembly building has given Alex sufficient proof to call the President before him to answer preliminary questions about his direct involvement with Global Asset Management.

Back in the General Assembly the delegates have settled down a little as Aacaarya continues,

"Now that the excitement is over I can concentrate fully on our proposals, I hope that from what I have explained already you have a better understanding of the concepts of how we are able to provide you with a remarkable source of limitless energy. Those of you that make the commitment to a new and better future will be invited in groups to visit our world to see firsthand what you can expect to achieve for your nations through working with us. In our written brief to you I proposed that we create together a One World Government to oversee the governments of your countries, having re-considered this proposal we would recommend that this organisation and the Earth's Environmental Protection Agency should be extensions of the United Nations functioning within its auspices. This would provide the United Nations with the power to take action where necessary to deal with problems that are brought to its attention. Participation will require unanimous acceptance by all Nations and agreement by all countries that they will implement the conditions of our treaty. Implementing our requirements will not be easy it will take time but we'll be with you every step of the way to assist, provide advice and where necessary provide back up to enforce your actions where resistance is encountered. You may feel that our requirements are idealistic however I can assure you that we can help you make these a reality. We have lived in peace for many thousands of years with these realities as the cornerstone of our success. Our treaty will include the following conditions:

Participating nations will immediately terminate all research experiments, civilian and military that does not have the prior approval of EEPA. Permission will only be granted to research and experimental projects that are proven by EEPA to have no negative impact on the Earth's magnetic fields, its surface, subterranean levels, atmosphere, ionosphere, and magnetosphere or near space. Any research approvals granted will be monitored and controlled by EEPA.

The governments of participating nations will denounce war and undertake a major re-assessment of their foreign policies to ensure diplomatic resolution of international disputes using the new United Nations powers focusing on peaceful dialogue, non-aggressive solutions, driven by integration and support. To facilitate this they will immediately phase in a major reduction in military expenditure and cease the international sale and production of weaponry to stop the current escalation of armed conflict throughout the world. This will bring an end to profiteering from wars by governments and private organisations.

We will work closely with your Governments under the new United Nations to strengthen and reform the powers of your legal systems to enable the global eradication of corruption, creating transparency in all political parties, administrative departments and commercial organisations. Leaders, politicians and government officials must accept full responsibility and full accountability for their actions, decisions and failures. Individuals and government officials guilty of corruption and colluding to military action against other nations for profit and those that commit crimes against humanity will answer these crimes in the appropriate International courts.

Governments will work with us to create a new and powerful International Intelligence Task Force to eradicate the power of organised crime organisations that are endemic throughout the world. This international force will act to eliminate the production and marketing of drugs and where necessary we will replace their production facilities with alternative industries where the economies of these production countries have been dependent on drugs for their survival. This new organisation will become an extension of our own Intelligence Service with controlled access to our superior global intelligence networks.

Governments will take full responsibility for implementing and enforcing legislation to protect the environment and educating their populations to understand the urgent need to manage the growth of their populations through incentives and legislation. Each nation will be required to strengthen its borders to control and manage immigration until such time as they have developed workable strategies for successful integration of their existing immigrants. These tight border controls will in time help eliminate the current cross border flow of illegal immigrants, drugs and arms.

Governments working through the new United Nations will co-operate to create a global medical organisation, tasked with the eradication of disease and famine throughout the world. This organisation will be funded from the military budgets previously used for war related activities. The World Health Organisation will be an integral part of this new task force.

At all levels governments will endeavour to rebalance their wealth distribution to close the gap between the very rich and very poor by creating tax systems that encourage investment and appropriate opportunities for the poor to improve their living conditions.

All governments will work with the United Nations to ensure that their populations have access to the highest level of medical care regardless of their status, age or wealth.

Each government will make education a priority, encourage and establish intellectual and cultural studies as an essential right of their population with increased spending and incentives to encourage access to improved universities and educational facilities.

We will work with the leaders of the elected governments to restructure within the United Nations a new One World Government or 'think-tank' made up from three elected leaders from each country including three of our Elders with the objective of overseeing and guiding the United Nations, sharing problems and finding solutions for global stability and peace.

This World Government will act as a forum for world leaders. The unanimous decision of the World Government will have priority over any individual country's governments who would be required to act in accordance with the decrees of the One World Government.

Religious leaders will be prohibited from participating in or influencing government decisions. The overall leader of each religion will have a voice in the One World Government but will not have any voting powers.

As the new energy comes on line it will make nuclear and fossil based fuels obsolete. We would require that all nations immediately phase out their nuclear programmes and commence dismantling their existing fossil fuelled power generation sources."

"We believe that these are the priorities facing your world today. We'll be working with you during their resolution and we'll be constantly available for consultation on all matters that concern you. I'm sure you have many questions that you wish to ask, many of which would be specific to the individual needs of your countries. Therefore I and the Elders will remain here for the rest of the week during which time you can arrange private appointments with us at any time during that period through the General Secretary."
The General Secretary nods in agreement,
"Copies of the full treaty have just materialised on your desk in each of your languages."
In front of each delegate a bound copy of the treaty appears. Aacaarya asks,
"Without making a commitment at this stage and assuming your questions are answered to your satisfaction, could you indicate by raising your right

hands how many of you would seriously consider accepting our proposals."

Slowly one hand after another is raised, gathering momentum until there is almost 100%. Aacaarya smiles,

"Thank you for your show of confidence."

For a moment there is silence in the hall then slowly applause starts, growing to fill the hall as delegates stand in ovation. As the applause dies down the General Secretary thanks Aacaarya and the Elders then facing his microphone speaks to the delegates,

"We must embrace this unique and historic opportunity to rid ourselves of the evils affecting our world, to prepare the foundations for a better future for our children and future generations. I thank our visitors from the bottom of my heart for offering us this salvation. Please use my staff and offices to make your appointments for the 'one to one' discussions, thank you."

They leave the podium as the applause starts again, returning to the nearby lounge. James is already in the room with the large television showing Breaking News, film of the FBI, the Police raid on Global Asset Management's offices with handcuffed executives being led to the vans. As Mike, Tim and Diane walk over James is excited,

"It's on all the channels, they've arrested the entire management plus a bunch of FBI agents including your associate Steve, there's talk of the President being impeached by the House Judiciary Committee, someone has leaked a mass of information incriminating the President and his senior advisors."

Aacaarya walks over smiling,

"James, what you four started, we've just finished, but it could not have happened without your skills and intelligence. We were very fortunate today, there's no doubt that all those involved in the plan to murder the heads of state of every nation, will be severely punished."

"Aacaarya, we were all very lucky you were not distracted by your translations for a minute longer." Aacaarya laughs,

"Mike, yes that was a little too close even for us."
The Secretary General comes in speaking to Aacaarya,

"We've set up appointments for the next few days as you instructed, the first groups are waiting for me to call them in."

"Thank you, we will commence in 15 minutes." Mike asks,

"Will you be working through the night?"

"We'll work nonstop until we have seen everyone."
The Secretary General asks,

"Will you be alright here, what arrangements shall I make for your meals?"

"We can look after ourselves. We need no sleep but perhaps a supply of appropriate coffee or teas for your delegates as they arrive."
George tells them he's arranged for the security coverage to remain in place until the delegates have completed their interviews.
Mike asks,

"Is there anything we can do to help?"
Aacaarya smiles,

"Thank you but that will not be necessary, if we do need to contact you I'll let Tim know, in the meantime we'll keep you up to date through him. I recommend that you return to Washington and get some well earned rest it's been an exciting day. We will see you again before we depart. We're deeply indebted to you for what you've achieved."
George checks with his head of the security team, as he now has urgent business at the Pentagon then offers to drive them back to the Airport where his jet is waiting,

"The world's press are hungry to interview you so I recommend you keep a very low profile for a few days more, otherwise you'll be hounded wherever you go."

They say goodbye to Aacaarya and the Elders. Then follow George out of the building through the rear entrance to where his vehicle is waiting, they are driven through the clamouring mob of the press. Diane looks out of the window at the horde of paparazzi and comments to Mike,

"I'm at last converted to black windows."

The trip to the airport takes longer this time. The news is spreading that something has happened at the United Nations Building increasing the traffic considerably. They arrive at the airport VIP entrance, half an hour later they are in the air heading for Washington.

Chapter - 25

Justice and Wedding

An hour and a half later they're back in Washington, the driver takes them into the centre, George asks him to make a diversion down Pennsylvania Avenue past Global's offices. George points them out. As they approach the building the whole area is sealed off with numerous Police and FBI men going in and out of the building, surrounded by the ring of press vehicles and cameramen pressing against the Police barriers all begging for snippets of information. Diane asks, "Mike is that what would've happened to us?"

"Afraid so, once the press know who and where we are, it will be the same for a few days until the dust settles and the story replaced by something bigger."
Tim comments,

"What could be bigger than this, it's the biggest scandal in the history of this country."
They squeeze through the traffic, George's driver parks outside their apartment. Mike looks at him,

"How long have you known where we were?"

"Since you moved in, Julian and I've worked together for years too, he's an old trusted friend, he asked me to find you a safe house."
As they get out of the vehicle, James turns back to the vehicle he puts his head into the open door and speaks to George,

"I've been thinking about what you said in New York the answer is YES."
George is delighted,

"Fantastic news, we'll have some fun, I'll get the wheels in motion. Good Night."
They enter the reception to find Patrick waiting for them,

"Welcome back. The Famous Four"
Diane asks with panic in her voice,
"What do you mean?"
Patrick goes to a small table picking up a handful of the evening papers on every front page is the headline NUCLEAR ATTACK ON UNITED NATIONS - Thwarted with 60 seconds to go. There are pictures of the building, the Assembly building including photographs of the podium with them all present. Lower down the page there are enlargements of Tim, Mike and Diane and the headline 'Heroes of the day – but who are they?'
Mike smiles,
"Obviously our false identities and cover stories held enough water to fool the press for the time being."
The rest of the front page is covering Aacaarya's speech under the headline FREE ENERGY FROM A PARALLEL WORLD.
Patrick offers them the papers,
"Take the papers up with you the scandals just breaking. You should watch the news it's getting bigger with every report."
They wish him good night then return to their apartment. James switches the large television on, the screen bursts into life the first image is of their three faces Diane groans."
James laughs,
"Now we'll need to submerge completely."
The news anchorman covers the latest breaking story about the potential damage that could have been caused if the device had exploded. Various experts are mapping where the fallout area would have been with figures of how many thousands would have been killed by the initial blast. The debate leads onto the New World Order Conspiracy behind the bomb and outlines what they know of Global Assets Management a company whose directors included the President's father.

There are further allegations that evidence exists proving the President was aware this attack was going to take place, allegedly that was why he left the Assembly Building exactly one hour and a half before the bomb was due to explode. He was safely on board Air Force One Heading for Washington by the time it was due to detonate. The report continues, these allegations implicate many senior senators and members of the security services, if these allegations are proven it will be the end of this government. One of the guest experts is asked,

"If the President is found guilty losing his Presidential immunity will he then be answerable for the potentially illegal invasion of Iraq?"
The expert replies,

"Yes, if guilty he can be charged with war crimes, he would be called to answer these charges at the International Court of the Hague, if proven guilty he would then be imprisoned." James who is glued to the television says,

"Cool."

"James, what was that all about with George?"

"Mike, I forgot to tell you in the excitement, George has offered me an amazing opportunity to head up the Computer Systems Department supporting the new Intelligence Task Force.
I'll be working with him at the Pentagon and on the most fantastic financial package. Whats more important is that I'll have access to the very latest computer equipment and all the toys I want."

"James, my heartiest congratulations, you deserve it, George is a great guy to work with."
Diane gives James a kiss,

"I think that's wonderful news although I'll miss having you around, you make so much mess."
Tim gives James a hug,

"Congratulations, we'll have to work on your telepathic powers"

James grins,

"Thanks all of you, if ever you need anything, just let me know I'll always be there for you."

"James the same goes for us, anything at anytime just call."

Diane asks Mike,

"What do we do now?"

"Diane, we take a few day's holiday and relax, there's nothing more we're needed for at the moment. We just wait until we hear how Aacaarya has got on with convincing the delegates."

Diane asks,

"James when do you start work at the Pentagon?"

James looks up from the television,

"George said I could start immediately if I wanted to, it really depends on you guys. I didn't want to rush away."

"Why not start immediately, obviously we'll miss you, but you could still use the apartment until you find somewhere else, can't he Mike."

"Of course he can, for as long as he likes, the government is paying for it, James now works for the government."

"Mike that would be fantastic if you don't mind I'll call George tomorrow to make a start, it would be important to be in at the beginning of this new Task Force, particularly as I'm supposed to heading it up."

James asks,

"What about you Tim what'll you do next?"

"I've an interesting translation job for a very dear friend in Timbuktu which will mean 10 days in West Africa after that I'd like to work for the Earth's Environmental Protection Agency. It's something I've thought about for some time. I mentioned this to Aacaarya who thinks it's a good idea, but we'll see. Mike what are you planning to do?"

"Well it rather depends on this young lady."

"I am thinking of retiring from the NSA to become a married man."

Diane looks in mock surprise,

"A married man, married to whom, who will have you?"

Mike looks into her eyes,

"I was hoping you might consider taking me on."

Diane looks serious,

"Is that a formal proposal this time?"

"Well yes, there're two witnesses."

Diane looks at James and Tim then back at Mike,

"I had imagined something a little more romantic."

Mike gets down on one knee and asks,

"Diane or should I say Joanne Simons will you marry me?"

Diane sits down for a moment pretending to be thinking, then smiles at Mike still on one knee

"Mike or should I say Rick Taylor, Yes, I would be delighted to become your wife, on one condition."

Mike looks worried,

"And that is?"

"That it's a very small private affair with just a few close friends, I mean like George, Tim and James."

Mike is relieved,

"That's exactly what I wanted. Then let's do it."

Diane asks,

"When shall we do it?"

"Next week after the dust has begun to settle."

Diane throws herself into his arms and kisses him,

"Perfect, that's absolutely perfect."

James pushes Mike to one side,

"Now I get a chance to kiss the bride, "congratulations", planting a large kiss on Diane." Mike grabs him,

"That's enough."

Tim hugs them both,

"I'm so pleased for you. I've always thought you two would make a great couple you've got so much in common, you know, guns and things."
Mike suggests,

"Why don't we go across to the restaurant, have dinner to celebrate our engagement."
Diane agrees,

"Great I don't feel like cooking tonight."
They go across to the restaurant and enjoy a celebration dinner with lots of champagne then make their way back to the apartment, feeling very happy, relaxed and slightly drunk. Early next morning James calls George and makes arrangements to start work.

"George if it's OK with you I'd like to start immediately."
George is delighted,

"I'll send a car over at 11:30 see you later."
James goes to his computer cancelling his 'insurance programme' he puts it on hold, for future use if ever needed. He speaks to himself,

"That's good, now I don't have to remember to log on every 24 hours."
By the time James is ready to leave the others are up Mike's mobile rings, it's George

"Mike I just wanted to congratulate you and Diane on your engagement, its great news."
Mike thanks him,

"And how did you find out?"

"Don't worry, the apartments not bugged, it was James. Would you all like to meet up for lunch say in two days. I'll be able to update you on the latest events. By the way I've just heard that Steve was amongst the FBI agents arrested."

"George that's no surprise, no one trusted him. Just let me know where and when, that would be great, thank you again, we're off to choose a ring today."
George signs off,

"Good luck and don't use your government credit card."

"This is very personal, I'll use mine. See you tomorrow have a good day."

Over the next two days Tim, Mike and Diane hardly see James, he leaves early getting back late. He is thoroughly enjoying the new challenges of working with George at the Pentagon.

They follow the news broadcasts on television watching as the scandal continues and a growing number of the President's closest advisors including senators are called to give evidence before the House Judiciary Committee. Tim has a communication from Aacaarya, when Diane and Mike return from their shopping trip he asks them to sit down,

"I have some fantastic news Aacaarya has told me that 85% of the United Nations member states have already signed the treaty."

Mike is surprised,

"I didn't expect that many to agree first time round, how did he do it?"

Tim laughs,

"You'll never guess. In addition to the Free Energy, he transported one of the Ion hover cars into the lounge and offered to provide the technology to enable a variation to be built in each country that signs the treaty and they're not allowed to sell them outside their country."

"Aacaarya's formidable. You never know, perhaps we'll get one as our personal transport. General Motors will not be happy with that news."

"Mike, there's more, they'll help them with the design adaptation so that we'll be able drive them on our highways without using our minds to control them."

Mike laughs again,

"That's not new our highways are full of cars driven by mindless drivers already."

"Aacaarya has asked if I would consider being the first President of the Earth Environmental Protection Agency, he's cleared it with the delegates. The UN wants me to start setting it up in conjunction with the UN General Secretary."
Diane is pleased,
"Tim, that's wonderful, it was your idea from the very beginning. You are going to accept?"
"I already have, it beats digging around in dusty deserts looking for strange languages. They want me in New York to start when I get back from Africa."
Diane waves her left hand under Tim's nose,
"Now for my news, take a look at this, Mike's really going to do it."
She shows off the magnificent diamond engagement ring on her finger.
Tim is genuinely impressed,
"It's very beautiful you both deserve each other. What do you plan to do after your wedding?"
Diane looks at Mike,
"Well, I've always wanted to write about my work with Pyramids but never had the chance and Mike has often thought about writing about some of his adventures in the NSA. It would be an ideal occupation as we could be anywhere in the world and still be working. All we need are laptops and we'd always be together."
Tim looks at Mike,
"Not, all of your adventures?"
"No only a careful selection, no real names."
"Mike, when will you start?"
"Probably after the wedding ceremony, we want to have a short honeymoon in Alaska which will give me an opportunity to see Julian, he's got a lot of my old files stored away and Diane fell in love with the cabin at Gakona Lodge. We can explore the beautiful country that we didn't have s time to see."

The next morning the World news channels are full of headline news about the visitors from the Parallel World, the new treaty and how this new energy will positively impact on the world, particularly as oil has just gone over $150 per barrel. The world's environmentalists are backing the treaty. The only organisations that are creating arguments against it are the major oil companies. The Energy news is followed by allegations against the President which is now international news with suggestions that he may shortly have to resign.

Diane asks Mike,

"If the President resigns who will take over?"

"Probably the Vice President, he would take over in the interim until the next election which is in six months time, he would also have to reorganise the administration as many of the key players will go down with the President"

The phone rings and Mike answers,

"Hi George, how are you?"

George asks if they have been watching the news. Mike tells him they have and asks,

"What's new?"

George explains,

"The President is going to face some very serious charges, including treason and accessory to the attempted homicide of the delegates at the UN and War Profiteering for starters. He's just made a statement that he will be resigning later today supposedly so that he can concentrate on proving his innocence. Virtually all the directors of Global have been charged their hearings are next week along with some of the President's closest Senators.

The president's father has also been accused of war profiteering as one of the board directors of Global Asset Management. The Vice President is ready to be sworn in as interim President within twenty four hours."

Mike is surprised at how fast things are happening,

George asks,

"Can you three meet me for a working lunch at the Pentagon, my office at 14:00 I'll send a car for you?"

"That's perfect see you later."

Mike relays George's conversation to Tim and Diane who are equally surprised at the speed of the unfolding events.

Arriving at the Pentagon they are escorted to George's office, they enter to find that his office has expanded in size to incorporate what was Tony's office area. They're invited in as George gives them a warm welcome, a buffet is set up on one of the large tables near a small lounge area, there are two bottles of Cristal Champagne on ice, George immediately opens one pouring several glasses, he passes them round,

"First let's drink to Mike and Diane's engagement."

After the toast George continues,

"The reason I have invited you here is because the Vice President, soon to be the President, wants you to meet him at the White House after he's sworn in. He believes that the Nation owes you a great debt and wants to know what he can do for you. He has asked me on behalf of the United Nations to offer you Mike, the position of Director of the new International Intelligence Task Force."

Mike is shocked,

"George that's a fantastic offer but Diane and I are about to get married after which I was going to write my memoirs so to speak, so that I could be with Diane. She wants to write about her experiences with Pyramids so that we would be working together."

George smiles,

"The offer would include Diane if she wished. Why not think it over during your honeymoon, there's no hurry. Where are you going?"

Mike explains that they are going back to Alaska for a week. George is delighted,

"In that case you have the company jet and pilots at your disposal for wherever you want to go with the compliments of the United States President to be, just let me know when you get back about the job. We'll be keeping it open for you."

Mike is moved by the offer,

"George, thank you for your trust in me, please thank the Vice President for the great opportunity, we'll give it some thought, but will immediately accept the offer of the aircraft."

George grins and tells him,

"Aacaarya and the Elders want you to take the job"

Then asks,

"When and where will you get married? James told me it's going to be a small and very private affair."

Mike looks at Diane,

"Is that before or after the honeymoon?"

Diane nudges him,

"I'll either go to Alaska alone or we go together as man and wife."

Mike responds to George's question,

"In that case it takes five days to get the marriage licence which we can apply for, as long as we have passports and a valid blood test. We then have to decide where and locate a Justice of the Peace or Church Minister."

Diane asks,

"Why do we need a blood test?"

Mike smiles,

"In the District of Columbia they have to have a VDRC test for syphilis."

Diane is shocked,

"I don't believe it."

George grins,

"It's true and the same for everyone."

"Diane, where would you like the marriage ceremony to be?"

Diane hesitates, thinking of options when George interrupts,

"If I could make a suggestion, it would be quite unique, what about the Pentagon Chapel at 1E438. We have an Army Chaplain who could marry you and I would be honoured to make the arrangements. It would be quite a special venue as I don't believe anyone has been married there before. The Chapel, although small has a beautiful stained glass window. It's just an idea."

Mike looks at Diane, who smiles,

"That's a fantastic idea George, what do you think Mike?"

"I think it would be brilliant George. Thank you that would be absolutely perfect given our backgrounds."

George smiles,

"Right then it's done I'll call the Chaplain, all you have to do is get the licence and bloods done, any hospital would do that for you. Its time you dropped your false identities I've almost forgotten what your real names were."

George's receptionist comes in,

"There's an important call for you Sir."

George asks to be excused and takes the call in his office, he returns a few minutes later,

"That was Alex. The President has just resigned, the Vice President has just been sworn in as President."

Tim (Sam) is surprised,

"That was quick I thought it was going to be tomorrow."

George is serious,

"His position was untenable, there's no doubt about his guilt the evidence is more than sufficient to back up the charges. He's finished."

Diane (Jo) asks,

"What happens next?"

Mike (Rick) answers,

"It's now down to the courts to charge and sentence him."

George nods,

"The press have condemned him already he was the least popular President in the history of the United States before this scandal started. I'm afraid that I have to cut our meeting short I have to see the new President immediately. He wants to discuss his new administration. I'll call you once I've spoken to the Chaplain."

Sam, Rick and Jo now using their true identities leave the Pentagon and are driven back into Washington. The next week is busy as Sam is spending most of his time at the UN in New York with the Secretary General, planning the structure and personnel for the Earth Environmental Protection Agency. James is hardly seen, he's completely immersed in his new role. Rick and Jo have been busy, between monitoring the news of the rapid changes taking place in the government. They've obtained their marriage licence and blood tests. George has confirmed that the Chaplain can marry them the following Monday at 11:30. Rick has made their booking at the Gakona Lodge in the same cabin they used previously and bought Jo a new Dell XPS laptop as a wedding present.

With all the activity around them they manage to avoid the press.

As Monday morning arrives they are collected from the apartment then driven to the Pentagon along with their bags for the journey to Alaska. They are taken to George's office where Sam, Alexander and James are waiting with glasses of champagne.

James greets them both with a hug,

"Jo you've broken my heart, I thought you'd wait for me."

George asks,

"Are you nervous?"

"I don't think we have had time to be nervous, everything seems so natural."

Jo gives him a kiss,

"I agree."

George looks at his watch,

"It's time to go down to the Chapel."

They walk over to the lift that takes them to the first floor, then walk the short distance to room 1E438. George opens one of the double doors, as Jo and Rick go in they are surprised to see the Elders with Aacaarya sitting tall in the front row of the tiny bench seats, they stand as Rick and Jo walk down the isle between the rows. Jo says,

"Aacaarya, what a wonderful surprise we didn't expect you to be here."

Aacaarya hugs them both as, surprisingly, do the Elders. Aacaarya apologises,

"I hope you didn't mind the surprise visit but we wanted to wish you well in your union." Rick smiles,

"It's our honour you're most welcome to be here."

The very surprised Chaplain arrives. The short but solemn ceremony is quickly over when Aacaarya explains they have to leave as they're about to start implementing the first energy supplies next week. After saying goodbye the Elders and Aacaarya dematerialise before them and the now very shocked Chaplain. After a short celebration drink they say their emotional goodbyes. An hour and a half later they are once again at the VIP entrance of Reagan National Airport. The pilots greet them with 'congratulations' as they board the Citation, the cabin is full of roses with further bottles of Cristal on ice, organised by an air force hostess,

"On George's instructions"

She says as they stop in surprise.

Chapter - 26

Death and Resurrection

Within fifteen minutes the Citation is airborne climbing away from Washington. They start to relax as the champagne takes effect Rick kisses Jo,

"Do you realise Mrs Taylor this is the first time we've been alone together since we were married?"
Jo cuddles up to him,

"Mr Rick Taylor I just love being called Mrs Taylor, I can't wait to get to our log cabin."
They're alone in the cabin as the hostess is forward with the pilots. Before they know it the pilot's voice on the intercom disturbs them with,

"Mr and Mrs Taylor your flight will be landing in half an hour, please get dressed, finish your champagne and fasten your seatbelts."
They both laugh,
The Citation touches down at Fairbanks International Airport in a flurry of light snow. They disembark, their bags are carried by the pilots through the VIP lounge to a waiting Black GMC four wheel drive with blackened windows, it's minus one degree outside and lightly snowing, their chauffer helps them both into the back of the GMC.

"My name's Edward, Ed to my friends I'll be driving you whilst you're here, compliments of the US Government and our friend Julian. The road is clear this snow shower has just started and will blow out shortly."
Watching them from across the car park are two men in dark all weather motorcycle clothing with black helmets and visors standing beside two Indigo Blue BMW HP2 ENDURO 1170 cc 105 BHP high performance off road bikes fitted with snow tyres, the smaller man nudges the larger man,

"Hey, look over there. Recognise them?"
The other man lifts his black visor and limps over to a nearby car for a better look,

"Wait a minute yeah, yeah it's them alright, what a nice surprise, come on let's get going."
The GMC heads slowly out of the airport onto the highway, retracing the route that Rick had taken when they last arrived in Alaska. Unseen in the far distance behind them the two motorcycles have following them out of the Airport. The snow flurries have finished as the GMC moves onto the Richardson Highway, the road is almost empty as they cruise along with Rick and Jo being able to take in the incredible country they are driving through. Half an hour out from Fairbanks the two bikes close the distance between them, Rick notices Ed looking in his mirror,

"What's up?"

"Nothing, just a couple of off road bikers they must be masochists riding in this temperature, it's the latest craze round here, they look like the new BMW Enduro's."
The bikes stay behind for five minutes then pull out and overtake, the first one screams past them followed by the second which slows down a little as it becomes parallel to them, suddenly the man's left hand turns towards the windscreen of the GMC. A hail of bullets pours from the UZI machine pistol in his hand, shattering the windscreen.
The GMC swerves crashing off the road then down a steep embankment, rolling over as it does, onto its roof then rolling again back onto its wheels and continues sliding down the snowy bank. Its momentum is finally stopped with a sudden bang as it slides headlong into a large pine tree. Then there's silence, Rick slowly comes round, he has blood pouring from a large gash on his forehead he slowly undoes his seatbelt, his body wracked with pain. He leans towards Jo, who is slumped against the window,

"Jo you OK?"

She does not respond, he tries to raise his left arm to reach her but a stabbing pain stops him, he realises it's broken. He struggles closer releasing her seatbelt with his right hand then manages to turn towards her, using his right hand he turns her head towards him. In the centre of her forehead is a round hole with blood trickling from it, his eyes fill with tears, he checks the pulse in her neck knowing that he wouldn't find one. The shock wells over him, she's been hit by one of the bullets, he crawls closer to her hugging her lifeless body as tears flow down his cheeks, he can't speak his throat is choked with emotion as he hugs her in the vain hope of bringing her back to him. The noise of bike engines in the distance shakes him back to reality "Bastards." he utters then vengeance takes over from his grief and pain.

Rick realises he has no weapon and slumps back against Jo, then he thinks about the driver. He painfully leans forward to check him, his face and chest are riddled with bullets, Rick leans forward using his right hand checks inside Ed's bloody jacket, finding an automatic pistol he checks that it has a full magazine. The bike engines are now much closer and within a few seconds are stopping above him on the road. He can just hear voices but cannot move to get out of the vehicle he slowly eases himself back, next to Jo.

The professional soldier, overpowering anger and desire for vengeance take over from the pain. The two men are coming down to him, he hears them sliding down the bank, the first one is getting close when the second man calls out,

"If the bitch is alive leave her to me, I'll give her the same chance she gave my brother."

The first man shouts back,

"No one could've survived that crash, I can see the drivers face he's full of holes."

The two men stumble down to the car, Rick stays very still watching them through the black window, he painfully raises the automatic pistol as the men slide down to the side of the vehicle, he seizes his moment, both are close together, making an enormous effort to focus, his eyesight is blurred, he fires two shots through the glass, which shatters, into the head of the first man. Before the second man can react he is also hit with two more shots to the head, they drop down beside the GMC Rick leans his weapon on the edge of the window firing rounds into both bodies until the magazine is almost empty. He then slumps back against Jo kissing her as tears and blood stream down his face. Slowly he brings the automatic up to his bloody temple his finger slowly tightens on the trigger when he imagines he hears Jo's voice in his head.

"Rick no, you must go on, you have work to do."

He stops, relaxing his trigger finger then very slowly lowers the automatic, he sobs telling Jo,

"Yes, yes I do, but how can I, without you?"

He holds her in his arms until her body is cold then painfully searches for his mobile which he locates on the floor, he calls George the phone rings three times, George answers,

"Rick I didn't expect to hear from you."

Rick cuts him off sobbing trying to get the words out,

"She's dead, George, she's dead."

He breaks down again, George is concerned,

"Rick, who's dead are you alright?"

Rick pulls himself together for a moment,

"Jo's dead, we've been hit, the driver too."

George tries to calm him,

"Rick tell me where you are I'll get people to you immediately."

Rick continues,

"It's too late she's dead we're, we're half an hour out of Fairbanks forced off the road, there're two BMW motorbikes parked above us."

Rick breaks into uncontrollable sobbing as George tells him,

"Stay with the vehicle I'll get a helicopter to you in 15 minutes."

Rick throws the mobile onto the floor then still hugging Jo, passes out.

A short time later two helicopters arrive, one medical the other FBI followed by Police vehicles. Rick is carefully moved, still unconscious, by the paramedics into the helicopter with the bodies of the driver and Jo. The helicopter takes off blowing the loose snow around, taking them directly to Fairbanks hospital where Rick is rushed into intensive care, having lost a large amount of blood from his head wound. Twenty four hours later Rick slowly comes round in the private room of the hospital with his left arm in plaster and his head bandaged, he's in considerable pain despite the powerful pain killers he's been given, he calls to a nurse,

"Where's Jo?"

She kindly and quietly tells him,

"She's here, in the hospital mortuary."

"I was hoping it was a bad dream can I see her?"

"Yes, probably tomorrow when you have a little more strength, you've lost a lot of blood you took quite a bashing in the crash. You have visitors shall I ask them to come in, you can only see them for ten minutes?"

Rick gives a weak smile,

"Yes please."

She leaves to get the visitors shortly after George, Sam and James arrive. Sam does not know what to say but smiles,

"Rick, I'm so very sorry, it's such a tragedy?"

Rick looks at him his eyes wet,

"Thanks, it's awful, I keep expecting to wake up from this nightmare but its real she's gone."

George comes over carefully sitting on the edge of the bed takes Rick's right hand in his,

"Can you tell me what happened?"

Rick looks at him explaining what happened and what the men said,

"They were after Jo but who were they?"

George explains,

"We've run some checks it seems they just happened to be at the airport as you arrived, they recognised you. It was the guys that had the contract on the three of you. You may remember one of them was the brother of the man Jo killed. Is there anything I can do for you?"

Ricks looks determined,

"Yes there is, after Jo was killed, I put the pistol to my head she stopped me I heard her voice telling me to go on. I want that job for both of us I have a mission to complete."

George smiles,

"Rest easy it's yours, as soon as you've recovered. Just concentrate on getting back on your feet."

The nurse comes in,

"Your time is up gentlemen."

George is the last to leave as Rick calls him back,

"George I really must have that job."

"Rick you are now the Director of the UN International Intelligence Task Force. See you in Washington, call me as soon as you're ready, we'll pick you up."

The next day Rick is feeling a little stronger although still very emotional from shock he asks his nurse if she will take him to the mortuary to see Jo for one last time. The nurse asks,

"You're sure you're up to this?"

Rick replies quietly,

"Yes, I have to."

The nurse checks with the doctor who nods, she brings over a wheel chair. Rick slowly is helped into the chair. Moving is very painful, the nurse takes him along the corridor to the lift and wheels him in. She presses the button for the basement where the morgue is located. The lift stops, she wheels him into the morgue to be met by one of the pathologists,

"You're looking for Jo Taylor, correct?"

"Yes."

The pathologist invites her to follow him. They go through into a cold room which is lined down each side with large draws that slide into the wall. As they walk down the room the pathologist checks his clip board,

"Number 17, here we are. Sure you're ready?"

Rick nods, the pathologist takes the handle pulling the draw open, Rick tenses for the shock of what he is about to see, the draw is empty. The pathologist apologises,

"Must be a mistake, please wait a moment."

He goes to an office nearby speaking to the Senior Pathologist who comes out with him and also checks draw 17,

"That's very strange she was definitely here last night."

Turning to the nurse and Rick who is now getting upset,

"Please take Mr Taylor back I'm sorry there seems to have been a mix up, if you return to the ward we'll call you as soon as we have found her, she's not far away."

The nurse and Rick leave making their way back to his room where she helps him back into bed. After the effort of moving and the emotional shock, Rick falls into a troubled sleep. An hour later, the nurse gets a call from the pathologist,

"We've searched everywhere, Mrs Taylor's not here, we're checking to see if the night people moved her."

The nurse is also now very upset,

"What do I tell Mr Taylor? He's sleeping at the moment but will be sure to ask me when he wakes."
The pathologist tells her,

"Leave him to sleep, we'll call you immediately we've spoken to the night staff, I'm sure they'll know where she's been taken."
A few hours later Rick wakes, the nurse who has been watching him tells him,

"Mr Taylor you have a very strange visitor who has asked to see you immediately."
Rick is still drowsy not fully awake,
"Yeah OK if he must."
As soon as he sees who it is, he has mixed emotions of pleasure and extreme sadness, Aacaarya walks across the room with the very surprised nurse who cannot take her eyes off him. As he gets to Rick he takes his hand

"Sam spoke to me yesterday and told me what had happened. The Elders and I were greatly distressed by the terrible news we felt responsible, in the past we'd been able to protect you because you were with Sam with whom we had a connection, had he been with you, we would have been alerted to the attack, we're so very sorry that you've had to suffer so much."
Rick's eyes are wet, as a wave of pain and emotion rises within him,

"Aacaarya thank you, but it's my responsibility not yours, I brought her back to Alaska without thinking there could still be a potential threat here."

"That's not true I've brought someone to see you, who may convince you otherwise."
The door opens to Rick's utter shock, surprise and disbelief. Jo walks in and over to his bed, leans forward kissing and hugging him until he speaks. With tears streaming down his face, he reaches out taking Aacaarya's hand,

"Thank you, thank you. Thank you."
Rick slumps back on his pillow with Jo sitting next to him, her arm round his shoulder. Aacaarya smiles,

"We are normally forbidden to interfere in the biological lives of other civilisations, but as the Elders and my people owe you such a debt we could not let this terrible suffering continue. The love that you have for each other is needed in your world. I have to go now, but we'll meet again when you have fully recovered."

He hugs Jo, who whispers,

"Aacaarya thank you and please thank the Elders for what they have done for us."

Aacaarya gives Rick a kiss on the forehead,

"Please forgive us."

Rick drowsily says "Thanks." closing his eyes as the emotional exhaustion pushes him into a shallow sleep, something in the kiss seems to have sedated his mind and soul as he drifts into a healing and tranquil deeper sleep.

Later that afternoon he stirs, slowly waking and feeling a lot more refreshed he immediately looks round for Jo who is sitting reading a newspaper in a chair beside the bed,

"Thank god I wasn't dreaming."

"No, thank Aacaarya."

They sit together, Rick is looking much stronger and more alert, Jo says,

"I've no memory of what happened, only being in the car with you and arriving here this morning with Aacaarya."

"Then best let's leave it at that for the moment."

Jo says,

"Oh and congratulations, I understand you are the Director of the UN Intelligence Task Force."

"That was only accepted when I thought I'd lost you. But now you're back."

"Rick this is something we should do together it'll be a lot more exciting than writing about Pyramids, so if you're happy to have me working with you in some close role, perhaps even as your personal Close

Protection Officer, it'll make me very happy. There's so much that needs doing in the world, we owe it our attention we have work to do."

Rick takes her hand,

"Mrs Taylor, you always make the right decision, we'll discuss this matter once I'm back on my feet and only after our honeymoon."

End

Thank you for reading Parallel Worlds, we hoped you enjoyed the experience and found the story interesting and absorbing. If you would like to contact the author with any feedback or review comments we would be pleased to receive them. Contact details are as follows:

Email: parallelworlds@btconnect.com

Web: www.parallelworldspublishing.com

Scan QR code with Smartphone